The Second Chair

Also by John Lescroart
in Large Print:

The First Law
The Hearing
The Oath
The Mercy Rule

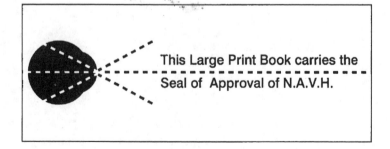

The Second Chair

John Lescroart

Waterville, Maine

Published in 2004 by arrangement with Dutton, a member of Penguin Group (USA) Inc.

The text of this Large Print edition is unabridged. Other aspects of the book may vary from the original edition.

Set in 16 pt. Plantin by Elena Picard.

Printed in the United States on permanent paper.

The Library of Congress has cataloged the Thorndike Press® edition as follows:

Lescroart, John T.
    The second chair / John Lescroart.
        p. cm.
        ISBN 0-7862-6302-4 (lg. print : hc : alk. paper)
        ISBN 1-59413-049-3 (lg. print : sc : alk. paper)
        1. Hardy, Dismas (Fictitious character) — Fiction.
2. San Francisco (Calif.) — Fiction. 3. Trials (Murder)
— Fiction. 4. Serial murders — Fiction. 5. Large type
books. I. Title.
PS3562.E78S43 2004
    813'.54—dc22   2003071187

To Jack Sawyer Lescroart

As the Founder/CEO of NAVH, the only national health agency solely devoted to those who, although not totally blind, have an eye disease which could lead to serious visual impairment, I am pleased to recognize Thorndike Press* as one of the leading publishers in the large print field.

Founded in 1954 in San Francisco to prepare large print textbooks for partially seeing children, NAVH became the pioneer and standard setting agency in the preparation of large type.

Today, those publishers who meet our standards carry the prestigious "Seal of Approval" indicating high quality large print. We are delighted that Thorndike Press is one of the publishers whose titles meet these standards. We are also pleased to recognize the significant contribution Thorndike Press is making in this important and growing field.

Lorraine H. Marchi, L.H.D.
Founder/CEO
NAVH

* Thorndike Press encompasses the following imprints: Thorndike, Wheeler, Walker and Large Print Press.

Almost all our faults
are more pardonable
than the methods
we think up to hide them.

— François de la Rochefoucauld

Part One

Prologue

Only four minutes remained in sixteen-year-old Laura Wright's life as she came out of the bathroom of the small apartment on Beaumont Street in San Francisco. Her eyes glistened with the residue of recent tears. But in the bathroom she'd splashed water over her face and washed away the smeared mascara and makeup, and now her skin glowed. A damp tendril of blond hair hung over a broad, unlined forehead.

She walked through the tiny living room and over to where Mr. Mooney, her drama coach, leaned over the kitchen table, making some notes in his neat hand in the margins of the script they were rehearsing. At her approach, he straightened up. In the brighter light of the kitchen, Laura's eyes picked up some of the turquoise in her blouse.

Mooney wore a kind face, projected an easy manner. Ten years before he'd been leading man material and now, though still trim and good-looking in a conventional way, his hair had thinned and gone slightly gray, a hint of jowl marred his jawline. He smiled down at her.

"Better?" he asked.

She nodded, still too emotional to trust herself with her voice.

The two stood facing each other for a moment, and then Laura reached out her hands and stepped into him. After a minute, her shoulders began to shake and Mooney, holding her, moved his hands over her back, the smooth fabric of the silk. "It's all right," he said. "It's going to be all right."

"I know. I know it will be." Her face was buried into the hollow of his neck.

"It is now," Mooney said.

She nodded again. "I know. Just . . . just thank you." She stepped back, a little away, and looked up at him. "I didn't mean to get this way."

"The way you are is fine. I'm just glad you found the courage to tell somebody. Holding that inside can be so hard."

"I figured I could trust you."

"You figured right."

"I know, but . . . what was that?"

Mooney crossed to the window, looked out to the street. "Nobody. Nothing."

Laura sighed, a deep exhalation. "I didn't think Andrew could be back already. I don't know if I'm ready to face him. He'll be upset if he finds out I told you first. I mean, it's his baby, too. Maybe I can just say I started crying right after he left and you asked what was wrong . . ."

"Which is exactly what happened."

12

She nodded. "I know. But Andrew's been a little funny about you and me."

"You and me? What about you and me?"

"Our relationship. Yours and mine. We actually broke up about it once."

Mooney had to suppress a laugh. "About what, exactly?"

"He thought I had a crush on you. I did, in fact."

"You had a crush on me?"

"When we started the play, yeah, rehearsing here. A little. He was just so jealous, and then I got so mad when he accused me."

"Of what?"

"You know. Having a thing with you."

Now Mooney did allow a small chuckle. "Well, by now I hope he knows that didn't happen. And besides, this is about you. It's your body. You get to decide what to do." A pause. "And you know, it might not be the worst idea in the world to talk to your parents."

"No way," she said, shaking her head. "They'd kill me. They wouldn't want to be bothered. Trust me, this I know." Her eyes began to well up again.

Mooney stepped near to her and brushed a tear where it had fallen onto her cheek. "It's okay," he said. "In a few months this will all be behind you. It's just getting through the tough part."

"I so hope you're right. I feel like such a

fool for letting this happen. I mean, it was just the one time."

"It only takes once." Mooney spoke gently. "You might want to keep that in mind, though, in the future."

"Don't worry," she said. "It's locked in." But again her composure slipped. Tears still threatening, she stood looking helplessly up at him. "Do you think I could get one more hug?"

"As a special request, one short one." He put his arms around her.

She pressed herself against him, squeezed hard, then all but jumped back out of his embrace as a knock came on the door. "Oh God," she said. "There's my great timing again. That's got to be Andrew. What if he saw us?"

Mooney held her at arm's length. "Laura," he said, "Andrew's a great guy. You don't have to worry about him, and even if he saw us, he knows you love him. Really. You just take care of yourself and do what you have to do and everything will be fine. I promise."

Mooney didn't know it, but his last words were a lie. Another knock sounded, and he moved to get the door.

1

"Hello."

"Amy Wu, please."

"This is Amy."

"You sleeping? I wake you up?"

"No. Just lying down for a minute."

"So Friday afternoon, you're not at work?"

"No. Right. I'm not feeling too well. Who is this anyway?"

"Hal North. You remember me."

"Of course, Mr. North. How are you? How'd you get my home number?"

"You gave it to us last time, remember?"

"Right. That's right. I gave it to you. So how can I help you?"

"Andrew's in trouble again."

"I'm sorry to hear that. What kind of trouble?"

"Big trouble. The police just came and arrested him for murder. You still there?"

"Yeah. Did you say murder? Andrew?"

"Yeah, I know. But right. Two of 'em, actually."

"I'm sorry. Two of what?"

"What did I just say? You paying attention? Murders. His teacher and his girlfriend."

"Where is he now?"

"They took him to jail. I mean, to the Youth Guidance Center. He's still not eighteen, or it would have been the jail."

"Is that where you're calling from, the YGC?"

"No. Me and Linda, we got a benefit tonight, so we're still home for another two hours at least. We could probably be late to the thing and make it three if you . . ."

"I could be over in, say, a half hour."

"Good. We'll be looking for you."

Wu checked herself in the bathroom mirror. No amount of makeup was going to camouflage the swollen bags under her eyes. Half-Chinese and half-black, Wu had a complexion that was dark enough as it was, and when exhaustion got the better of her, the hollows around her eyes deepened. Now, between the crying jags, the lack of sleep and the hangover, Wu thought she looked positively haggard, at least a decade older than her thirty years. Why guys would hit on her looking like this, she didn't know, but there didn't seem to be a shortage of them, not since she'd started going out almost every night to find whatever the hell she was seeking in the four

16

months since her father died.

Still, prepping herself to visit Hal North, she did her best to make herself presentable. It wouldn't do to look unprofessional. This was a legal matter, and she knew the potential client had made millions from his chain of multiplex movie theaters. At least he had been worth millions a couple of years ago, when Hal North's corporate attorney — a classmate from law school — had recommended Wu for criminal work and she'd represented his stepson Andrew for a minor joyride beef. She'd gotten him off with a fine and some community service. The fees at her hourly rate had come to a little under two thousand dollars, but when the judge came down with his wrist-slap judgment, North wrote her a check for ten grand. She wasn't sure if she should be flattered or insulted that he assumed he should tip his lawyer.

From now on, North had said in his forceful manner, she was *his* lawyer, that was all there was to it. Andrew, who'd been sullen and distant throughout the entire proceeding, even broke a rare smile and concurred. She'd told them both that though she was flattered that they liked her work, all in all it would be better if the family wouldn't need a criminal lawyer ever again. They both conceded that she probably had a point.

She lay down on the bed for two minutes, timed, with ice wrapped in a dish towel over her eyes. When she got up, she dried her face and started applying eyeshadow, mascara, lipstick. Her hand was steady enough, which was a nice surprise. This morning, brushing her teeth after she'd gotten home from whatever-his-name's place a little after dawn, she'd dropped the toothbrush twice before she'd given up, called work for the fourth time in four months — very bad — to say she was sick, and crashed.

For a moment she considered calling North back and making another appointment for tomorrow. After all, the Norths had a benefit tonight — it came back to her now, they always had something going on — and they'd be in a rush. And she really did feel horrible. She wouldn't be as sharp as she liked. But hell, that was getting to be the norm, wasn't it? No sleep, no focus.

She hated herself for it, but she couldn't seem to stop feeling that it didn't matter anyway. *Of course it mattered,* she told herself. As her old boss David Freeman never tired of saying, the law was a sacred and beautiful thing. And Wu hadn't dreamt of a career in it for five years, then studied it for three, and now have worked in it for five only to lose her faith and become cynical about it. That wasn't who she was, not at her core. But it was who she acted like — and felt like — all too often lately.

The truth was — her bad angels kept telling her — that you didn't really have to be as much on your game as she'd always taken as gospel, since law school. She'd proven that clearly enough in the past four months, when she'd essentially sleepwalked through no fewer than ten court appearances. No one — not even her see-all boss Dismas Hardy — had alluded to any problems with her work. She could mail it in, which was lucky, since that's what she had been doing.

The clients were always guilty anyway. It wasn't as though you were trying to get them off, cleanly acquitted. No, what you did was you squeezed a little here, flirted with a DA there, got a tiny bit of a better deal, and everybody was generally happy. That was the business she was in. It was a business, and she'd come to understand how it worked.

Mr. North had said that his son had been charged with murder, and if this were true, it would be her first. But her experience led her to believe that it probably wouldn't turn out to be a righteous murder, charged as such. If it wasn't simply confusion with another person, at worst an accident, it was probably some kind of manslaughter. And of course the Norths would want to get an attorney on board. If Wu went over now, at least she would get a feel for the case, some of the salient details. It would give her the weekend to get her hands on some discovery, if it was available yet.

And if she could keep herself straight and productive for two whole days in a row.

*

The Norths' home was a beauty near the Embassy Row section of Clay Street in Pacific Heights. Old trees shaded the sidewalks on both sides, and most of the residences hid behind some barrier — a hedge or fence or stucco wall.

At a few minutes past four o'clock, Wu got out of her car to push the button on the green-tinged brass plate built into the faux-adobe post that held the swinging grille gate to the driveway. When she identified herself, she heard a soft click, then a whirr, and the gate swung open.

For all of the security, there was very little actual room between the gate and the house. Wu got inside, then turned left before she came to the garage. The driveway was quite narrow as it passed in front of the house, but widened into a larger circle near the entryway, and this was where she parked, the area deep in shadow. Getting out of her car, she could see blue sky above her through the trees and hear a steady shush of April breeze, but here in this small leafy enclosure, it was still. Brief-case in hand, she drew a breath, closed her eyes for an instant to gather herself, then went around her car, up the steps to the semi-enclosed brick porch, and rang the bell.

Hal North was in his early fifties, a short, wiry man who tended to dress, as he talked, loudly. Today he answered the door in a canary yellow, open-necked shirt that revealed a robust growth of chest hair into which was nestled a thick gold chain; white slacks; penny loafers with no socks. He hadn't aged one week since Wu had seen him last. He wore his thick black hair short and basically uncombed — the tousled look. His face was not-unattractive, slab-sided with a strong nose and piercing green eyes that sized Wu up afresh as he crushed her hand. "Thanks for coming," he said. "You don't look too sick." He backed away a step. "You remember Linda."

"Sure." Wu stepped over the threshhold and extended her hand. "Nice to see you again, Mrs. North."

Linda North was at least three inches taller than Hal and in another age would have been called a bombshell. Blond, buxom, thin and long-legged, she had always struck Wu as one of those freak-of-nature women over whom age and experience seem to pass without leaving a scar, a line, a trace. Though Wu knew that she was somewhere close to either side of forty — she'd delivered Andrew when she was just a year out of high school — in her jeans and tennis shoes and men's T-shirt, with her hair back in a ponytail, she looked about seventeen herself.

"Ellie's got some coffee going." Hal was already moving, shooing the women before him down the short hallway from the foyer into the dining room. "Ellie!" He pushed open the door to the adjoining kitchen. "In here, okay?" He turned around, motioning to the women. "Sit, sit. She'll be right in." He pulled a chair next to his wife and sat in it, threw a last look at the kitchen door where Ellie would presumably soon appear, then came back to Wu. "Really," he said, "we appreciate you coming out."

"We just can't believe this is happening," Linda said. "It's just a total shock. I mean, out of nowhere."

"You didn't expect something like this?"

"Never," Linda said.

"Complete blindside." Hal was shaking his head, his lips tight. "They kept saying Andrew wasn't a suspect."

"They always say that. You know why?

So you might not think you need to have a lawyer with him." She paused. "So I'm assuming you let him talk to the police?"

"Of course," Linda said. "We thought it would help to be as cooperative as we could."

The couple exchanged a glance.

"Why don't we start by you telling me what has happened," Wu said, "starting from the beginning, the crime." She turned to Hal. "You said he's accused of killing his teacher and his girlfriend?"

Linda answered for her husband. "Mike Mooney and Laura Wright. They were in the school play and . . ."

"What school?"

"Sutro."

Wu wasn't surprised to hear this. Among the city's private schools, Sutro was a common choice among people with real money. "Okay, they were in the school play . . ."

"Yes," Linda said. "Andrew and Laura were the leads, and they'd been rehearsing nights at Mr. Mooney's house rather than the school. Then, the night it happened, somebody just came and shot them down. Luckily, Andrew had gone out for a walk to memorize his lines and wasn't there when it happened or he might've been shot, too."

Luckily or too conveniently, Wu thought.

But she moved along. "And Andrew got arrested when?"

"They came by about twelve-thirty, one o'clock. School is out for spring break. And they just took him."

"I was at work," Hal said, "or I would have tried to slow them down, at least."

"Then it's probably better you weren't here." Wu was sitting beyond Linda at the table and could see them both at once. "When did the crimes happen?"

"February," Linda said. "Mid-February."

Wu's face showed her confusion.

"What's the problem?" Hal asked her.

"I guess I don't understand how two months have gone by and all that time, with the police coming by, neither of you thought Andrew was a suspect?"

"He said he didn't do it," Linda said, as though that answered the question. "I know he didn't. He couldn't have."

Ellie came through the door and the conversation stopped while she set out the coffee service. As soon as the door to the kitchen closed back behind her, Wu began again. "Mrs. North, you just said that Andrew couldn't have done these killings. Why not? Do you mean he physically couldn't have done them because, for example, he wasn't there? Does he have an alibi? I mean, beyond the walk he took."

"But he *did* go for that walk," Linda

said. "There's no doubt about that. Besides," she added, "Andrew's just not that kind of person."

Wu's experience was that anyone — if sufficiently motivated — could be driven to kill. And Hal, she'd noticed, had stopped talking, was looking down into his coffee cup. "Mr. North," she said, "why'd they decide just now, after two months, and after they'd talked to Andrew several times? Did something new come up? Do you have any ideas?"

He raised his eyes to her, made a face. "Well, the gun," he whispered.

"That's nothing!" Linda's eyes flared and her voice snapped. "That's not even been definitely connected to Andrew."

Hal, muzzled, shut up and shrugged at Wu, who then spoke gently to Linda. "I don't believe I've heard anything yet about a gun."

She was prepared to answer. "This was early on, in the first week or so. The police asked Hal if we owned any guns, and Hal told them he had an old registered weapon . . ."

"Nine-millimeter Glock semi-auto," Hal said.

Again, Linda snapped. "Whatever. And when Hal went to find it, he couldn't." She turned to her husband. "But you know you're always misplacing things. It didn't mean Andrew took it."

Wu touched Linda's arm. "But the police think he did?"

Linda looked at Hal, who answered for her. "They found a casing in his car."

"So what?" Wu asked "Without the gun, you can't have a ballistics test."

"It was just a random piece of junk under the seat," Linda said. "It might have been there forever. It was nothing."

Wu tried to look sympathetic. "So the police didn't specifically refer to that when they came today?"

"No. They just said he was under arrest. They had enough evidence, they said. Something about a lineup," she added.

"He stood in a lineup? You let him do that? Who was trying to identify him?"

Hal North bristled. "I don't know. Some witness. Someone identifying Andrew, obviously."

"And wrongly," Linda said.

"Although," Wu phrased it gently, "as you say, he was there at Mooney's place. So someone might have seen him. Yes?"

"Yes, but . . ." Linda slapped at the table.

Hal reached out and put a hand over hers. "Look," he said to Wu, "we're not sure why any of this is happening. We don't think Andrew did this."

Linda slapped the table again. "We *know*

he didn't do this."

"Okay, okay, that's what I meant," Hal said. He turned to Wu. "But they must have built a pretty impressive case against him if they got all the way to arresting him, wouldn't you think?"

Wu more than thought it. They had a case, and — since Andrew was the son of a wealthy and prominent man — it was probably a strong one. A gun in the house, a casing in Andrew's car, a positive lineup identification. What she had here, she was beginning to believe, was a young man who'd made an awful mistake.

"What are you thinking?" Hal asked her abruptly.

"Nothing," Wu said. "It's too soon. I don't know anything yet."

"You know he's innocent," Linda said. "We know that."

"Of course," Wu said. "Other than that, though."

By Sunday afternoon, when she met with Hal North again, Wu knew that they had a substantial problem. She also thought she had a solution.

This time it was just she and Hal in the large, bright, and high-ceilinged living room. Hal sat in the middle of a loveseat while Wu perched on a couch.

Linda had gone to visit Andrew and

would be gone for at least two hours.

Wu had been lucky to get a couple of folders of discovery on Andrew's case from the DA's office before close of business on Friday. She had spent all day Saturday going over what the police had assembled. It looked very, very bad.

"What's so bad?" North asked.

Wu sat all the way forward on the couch, hunched over in tension. Her folders rested unopened on the coffee table in front of her. "Where do you want to start? It could be almost anywhere. They've got a good case."

"It looks like he did it?"

"Do you know anything beyond what we talked about on Friday?"

North shrugged. "I figured the gun was a problem, but I didn't know how they'd tied that to him. They didn't find it, did they?"

"No. Still no weapon, but there's plenty in here" — she tapped the folders — "to prove to me that he had the gun with him that night. You want me to go over it piece by piece?"

North waved impatiently. "I don't need it. If you're convinced, it'll be good enough for a jury." He slammed a palm against the side of his seat. "I *knew* he took it, goddamn it. I knew he was lying to me." Smoldering, North sat forward with his shoulders hunched, his elbows resting on his knees, head down. Finally, he looked up at Wu. "What about the lineup?"

"The man upstairs saw him leave just after the shots. Positive ID."

North slumped again, shook his head from side to side wearily, came back up to face her. "So he did it." Not a question.

"Well, maybe he wasn't taking that walk to rehearse his lines, let's say that."

"Jesus. This is going to kill Linda."

"She really believes him?"

"We're talking faith here, not reason. I thought that alibi story was like the ultimate in lame myself, but once Andrew came up with it, he had to stick to it. I just wish he would have invented something else, almost anything else." North shook himself all over, then straightened his back and threw Wu a determined, pugnacious look. "Okay, Counselor, what do we do now?"

Wu was ready for the question, and suddenly glad that Linda wasn't here. Hal would play much more into her plan that she'd reluctantly come to believe was the boy's best hope — albeit a defeatist and cynical one because it was based on the absolute fact of Andrew's guilt.

As a good lawyer with a difficult case before her — hell, as a good *person* — she knew she should have been consumed with getting Andrew off. That was in many ways the definition of what her job was all about. Give her client the best defense the law allowed. And myriad defenses — insanity, psychiatric, diminished capacity, some form of self-defense or manslaughter — were always available, a veritable smorgasbord of reasons that homicide could be if not forgiven entirely, then mitigated. But all of those defenses and strategies involved huge expense for her client's family, a year or more of her life's commitment, and tremendous risk to her client should she fail, or even not completely succeed.

On the other hand, assuming that Andrew was guilty in actual fact (and every other client she'd ever defended had been), Wu knew that she could get him a deal that would give him a life after he turned twenty-five years old, eight years from now. And this when the best result she could reasonably expect under the other various defense scenarios was ten years — and probably many, many more.

And so, though it was a terrible choice, she had convinced herself that, all things considered, it was the best possible strategy in these circumstances. "I think our primary goal," she said, "ought to be to keep Andrew in the juvenile system, not let them try him as an adult."

"Why would they do that? He's not eighteen. It's eighteen, right?"

"Right. At eighteen, it's automatic, he's an adult. But that doesn't mean the DA can't charge younger people. It's a discretionary call."

"Depending on what?"

"The criminal history of the person charged, the seriousness of the crime, some other intangibles." She took a breath, held it a moment, let it out. "I have to tell you, I've already talked to the chief assistant DA — his name's Allan Boscacci — and as of this moment, they're planning to file Andrew as an adult."

"Why? That makes no sense. This is his first real offense. He's a little hard to talk to sometimes, okay, but it's not like he's some kind of hardened criminal or anything."

"Yeah, but two killings, point-blank. Pretty serious. They're even talking special circumstances. Multiple murders, in fact, again, it's automatic."

"Special circumstances? You're not talking the death penalty?"

"No, you can't get that no matter what if you're under eighteen at the time of the offense."

North quickly cast his eyes around the room. "Okay, so what happens when he's an adult? Different, I mean."

Wu knew she had to deliver it straight

and fast. If she was going to get North to agree with her strategy, she had to make it look as bad as she could for Andrew as quickly as possible. "A couple of major issues. First, most importantly, if he's an adult, life without parole is in play. If he's a juvenile, it's not. The worst he can get as a juvenile is up to age twenty-five in a juvie facility."

But North, not too surprisingly, was struck by the worst-case scenario. "Jesus Christ! Life without parole. You've got to be shitting me."

"No, sir. If he's convicted."

"Okay, then, he doesn't get convicted. Last time you got him off clean. It's not even on his record."

"Last time, sir, with all respect, he borrowed a car for half an hour. That's a long way from murder."

"Yeah, but I'm paying you to get him off. You can't do that, I'll find me somebody else who can."

Wu expected this — denial, anger, threats. She held her ground. "You might find somebody who'll say they can." She fixed him with a firm gaze. "They'd be blowing smoke up your ass."

"You're saying you can't do it?"

"No, sir, I'm not saying that. If that's your decision, I'll sure try. I might succeed, like I did before. Get him a reduced sentence, maybe even an acquittal. But no-body — and I mean nobody — can predict how a trial's going to come out. Anybody who says different is a liar. And the risks in this case, given just the evidence we've seen so far, are enormous." She reined her-self in, took a deep breath. "What I can do, maybe, is avoid the adult disposition. If Andrew goes as a juvenile, the worst case is he's in custody at the youth farm — which is way better than state prison, believe me — until he turns twenty-five. Then he's free, with his whole life still in front of him."

"Okay, so how do you do that? Avoid the adult disposition?"

"Well, that's both our problem and our solution. To have any chance of convincing the DA at all, we'd have to tell him An-drew would admit the crime."

North snorted. "That I'd like to see. That's not happening."

Wu shrugged and waited, content to let the concept work on him. North did his quick scan of the room again, sat back in his loveseat, frowned. Finally, he met her eyes, shook his head. "No fucking way," he said.

"Okay."

"Shit."

"Yes, sir."

"I'll never get Linda to go for that. She'll

33

never believe he did it."

"All right. But what do you believe?"

"I don't know what I believe. The kid and I never bonded really well, you know what I mean. I don't know him. He's all right, I guess. I love his mother, I'd kill for her, but the kid's a mystery. But whether he could kill somebody . . ." He shrugged, helpless. "I don't know. I guess I think it's possible. I'd bet he's lying about the walk he took. I *know* he took my gun, and he's lying about that, too. And why'd he take it if he wasn't going to use it?"

"That's a good question." Wu kept her responses low-key, not wanting to push. North, she was sure, would come to his conclusions on his own. As she had. At least that Andrew's situation looked bad enough to make the risks of an adult trial not worth taking. Still, in a matter-of-fact tone, she said, "They don't usually arrest innocent people, sir. No matter what you see in the movies." Then she added, "I'm not saying Andrew is guilty, but last time, if you remember, he started out saying he never took the car. Never drove in it at all. Didn't know what the cops were talking about. He *swore* to it."

"Just like now." North was slumped back in his chair, his palm up against the side of his head. "This is going to kill Linda," he said again.

"Well, if he really isn't guilty . . ." Wu let the words hang.

North shook his head. "Even if he isn't, how's a jury going to like the eyewitness and the gun and the motive? Jealousy, right?"

Wu had read the testimony of one of Andrew's friends, alluding to the jealousy motive — he evidently thought the teacher and his girlfriend were at least on the verge of starting — if not engaged in — an affair. But it was the first time North had mentioned anything about it, and the independent, unsolicited confirmation was a bit chilling.

Still, Wu restrained herself from trying to convince. She believed that forceful men like Hal North stuck far more tenaciously with decisions that they reached on their own. So she changed tack. "Here's the thing, Mr. North. He's up at the YGC now, they haven't filed against him as an adult yet, so practically speaking he's being treated as a juvenile. They have to hold what's called a detention hearing right away — I've already checked and it's tomorrow — to decide if they're going let Andrew go back home under your supervision."

"No reason they shouldn't do that."

Except for the fact that he's killed two people, she thought. But she only let out a breath and said, "In any case, as long as he's considered a juvenile, administratively they've got to have this detention hearing. That might give you some time, not much admittedly, to walk through some of these other issues with Linda, and even with Andrew."

He shook his head. "No, *she'll* talk to him, but maybe I can make her see what's happening."

Wu drew another breath and came out with it. She was going to need her client's approval before she took her next gamble, and this was the moment. "In light of everything we've been talking about here, Mr. North, I'd very much like to try to keep him in the juvenile system and avoid an adult trial if there's any way at all to do it, but that means he admits guilt right now. Immediately. Not maybe. I tell the DA he will admit and clear the case, in return they let him stay in juvenile court."

He sat stone still for a long beat, then nodded once.

Ambiguous enough, but Wu took it as an acceptance. "Do you think you can get your wife to go along with that? I want you to understand clearly that if Andrew admits, there won't be a trial, either in juvie or adult court. He'll just be sentenced. But the worst sentence he could get is the youth farm until he turns twenty-five."

"Eight years," he said. His shoulders slumped around him. "Eight years. Jesus Christ."

"That's the maximum. The actual sentence may be less. With the crowding at the youth work farms and time off for good behavior, he might not be as old when he gets out as when he'd finish college."

North may have been starting to see it, but the pill wasn't getting any less bitter. He rubbed his hand against the slab of his cheek. "Still, we're talking *years*."

Wu nodded soberly. "Yes, sir. But compared to the rest of his life. Even if I could plead him to a lesser charge as an adult — say second degree murder or manslaughter — he'll do at least double that time." She came forward. "And it would be in an adult prison, which is like it appears in the movies. But if we can get him declared a juvenile, which is not certain . . ."

"It seems to me we've got to do that. At least try for it."

"I can do it, but I'll have to move quickly." She consciously repeated herself. "You might want to talk to Linda first."

He gave it another few seconds of thought, then nodded again, spoke as if to himself. "Andrew's stubborn, but he'll come around when he sees the alternative. If he goes adult and gets convicted, Linda

37

couldn't handle it. She really couldn't."
Tortured, he looked across at her. "So
what do we do?"

"I'm afraid that's got to be your decision."

He blew out heavily in frustration. "And
when is this filing decision, adult or juvie?"

"Soon. It might have already happened,
except that Andrew got arrested on a
Friday afternoon and Boscacci is off on the
weekend. But by sometime tomorrow morning, probably."

"Tomorrow morning?" His eyes seemed
to be looking into hers for some reprieve,
but the situation as they both sat there
seemed to keep getting worse. "And once a
decision comes down, then what? I mean,
is it appealable or something?"

"You mean, once he's declared an adult?
No. Then he's an adult."

"God damn." He shook his head, side to
side, side to side. "This isn't possible." At
last, he seemed to gather himself. "So if
they decide he's an adult tomorrow, we're
screwed?"

"Well, we go to trial, yes."

"But you might be able to talk to this
guy Boscacci before then?"

"I'd call him at home today if you want
me to."

"And that gives us a better deal?"

She phrased it carefully. "Less of a potential downside, let's say that."

"And that's definite. I mean, we go juvie, he's out at twenty-five?"

"Yes, sir."

"That's the best deal we can get, don't you think?"

"As a sure thing? Yes, sir, all else being equal, I do. But I don't want to hurry you in any way. This is a huge decision and right now Andrew stands presumed innocent. If he admits, that changes."

North shook his head, dismissing that concern. His stepson, with whom communication was so difficult, who'd screwed up so many times before, had done it again. He was a constant burden and strain, and now he was putting his mother through more and more heartache. But North couldn't yet admit out loud what he might believe, and so he simply said, "He might be innocent, okay, but tell me there's a jury in the world that's going to see it." A sigh. "At least he'll have a life afterwards, when he gets out."

Wu watched the second hand on the mantel clock move through ninety degrees, then spoke in a gentle tone. "So do you want me to see what I can do?"

A last, long, agonizing moment. Then: "Yeah, I think you've got to."

Sitting back on the couch, she let herself sink into the deep cushions. "Okay," she said. "Okay."

2

Deputy Chief of Investigations Abe Glitsky was sitting in his old office in homicide on the fourth floor of San Francisco's Hall of Justice. He was talking to the detail's lieutenant, Marcel Lanier. When another old homicide chief, Frank Batiste, had finally been appointed chief of police the previous summer, he'd rewarded Glitsky, his longtime colleague, with the plum job of deputy chief. Though Glitsky's civil service rank was lieutenant, for the year preceding his appointment he had labored unhappily in a sergeant's position as head of payroll. Now, as deputy chief, and still a civil service lieutenant, Glitsky supervised captains and commanders and, of course, every one of the two hundred and forty police inspectors in the city.

As deputy chief, Glitsky's role was important but nebulous. The Investigations Bureau had taken a very public hit about six months before, when the *Chronicle* had run a weeklong feature exposing the fact that of all the nation's largest cities, San

Francisco came in dead last for its police record in arresting criminals and solving crimes of all types.

The article had revealed that during the previous four years, over 80 percent of all crimes committed in the city had gone unsolved. Many criminal acts, even violent ones such as street muggings, were never investigated at all, and with others — residential burglaries and the like — the investigation would consist of one inspector making one phone call to the victim, asking if anyone would like to come down to the Hall of Justice and file a report on what was missing. Though the scathing report had not yet seen print at the time, Batiste had of course been aware of the dismal numbers, the lackluster performance, and generally low morale of the department as a whole, and he'd brought Glitsky on to galvanize the bureau, to kick ass and take names, and above all to see that more bad guys actually found themselves arrested.

It was true that many inspectors had fallen into bad habits, but this was not always because they didn't care about their jobs. In many cases, budget cuts to the PD had eliminated overtime pay for interviewing witnesses or writing up incidents. More systemically, a culture had arisen in the DA's office — Sharron Pratt's legacy — that placed a premium only on cases where the evidence was so over-whelming that a conviction could be guar-anteed, and that encouraged assistant district attorneys to ask officers not to ar-rest suspects until they had the strongest possible case. If they had a guy cold on one count, for example, they should wait until they could get him for three or four, as that would make conviction more likely. This kept that particular scumbag out on the street, when in most other big cities he would already have been locked up.

Glitsky's first few months on the job had been characterized by his rather forceful presence working over the bureau, collaring inspectors in the Hall and even patrolmen in the precincts or out in the streets on surprise inspections. He'd put a friendly and unbreakable armlock on one of his troops and get right in his face. "I know you've got suspects and you're waiting till they do something more. But I say let's put 'em in jail. And I mean *today!*"

Glitsky also set an example by showing up at work no later than seven-thirty and staying until at least six o'clock, and not putting in for overtime. He believed that the badge was a calling and a public re-sponsibility more than it was a job. He made it clear to the people under him that they would have greater satisfaction in their work if they came to share that view. And ironically, after requests for overtime fell off slightly, Glitsky started getting more of it approved by Batiste. The Investigations Bureau was still far from perfect, but things seemed to be improving.

A fortuitous sidelight that had opened up as a result of Glitsky's flexible schedule was that he found himself free to stroll down the hallway from time to time, as he had this morning, and keep up on the workings of the homicide department. From his earliest days as a patrolman, Glitsky had viewed homicide as Action Central. This was where he wanted to be. These were the crimes that mattered the most. For twelve years he'd been an inspector with that detail, and for another eight the head of it. It wasn't ever going to get out of his blood.

When Batiste had offered him the post of deputy chief, he'd almost countered with the suggestion that he'd be happier back running homicide. Fortunately, before he said those fateful words, he'd recognized the faux pas they would constitute. Any response but an unqualified yes to Batiste's thoughtful and generous offer would justifiably have made him appear to be ungrateful and would have driven a wedge between him and the new chief. If Glitsky had requested the job in homicide, not only would he never have gotten it, he'd never have left payroll. The Chief had picked him out from far down in the ranks and elevated him above many others to a truly exalted position. Glitsky even had his own driver!

So reluctantly he'd accepted the new job, believing this meant that his time in homicide, the work he had always loved the best, was behind him forever. But now here he was, less than a year after his promotion, sitting with his feet up in his old office, discussing a particularly baffling murder case with Lieutenant Lanier. Who woulda thunk? But he'd take it.

A middle-aged, happily married, slightly overweight white housewife named Elizabeth Cary had been shot at her front door about a week before. To date, inspectors had found no clues as to who had killed her, or why. "And you sweated the husband hard?" Glitsky asked. "Wasn't his alibi soft?"

"Robert. Yeah," Lanier said. "He says he was driving home. He's the one called nine one one. But Pat Belou — you know her? She's new, but good. Anyway, she had him in there" — the interrogation room on the other side of the homicide detail — "six hours last Thursday, then we did him again four hours the next day, Russell in with her this time doing good cop/bad cop." He shook his head. "Nothin', Abe. If he did it, he's good. Belou and Russell both say they couldn't break him. Plus, no sign of another girlfriend on the side. The guy's not exactly Casanova. Bald, fat, old."

"How old?"

"Sixty. She was fifty."

Glitsky shrugged. "Bald fat old guys can get girlfriends, Marcel."

"Not as often as you think, Abe. And not Robert, I promise. They were redoing their wedding vows for their twenty-fifth anniversary next month."

"Doesn't mean they couldn't have had a fight."

"About what?"

"I don't know. Maybe they couldn't agree on the guest list and he really wanted this old friend of his to come, but she hated him — the friend — so he had to kill her." Glitsky scratched his cheek. "All right, maybe not. So who else could it have been? One of the kids?"

"I don't think so. They're all wrecked. I've talked to all three of them myself. Nobody's that good an actor, especially the young one, Carlene. I think she's eleven. Besides, they alibi each other — all watching some action video in the back of the house. Never even heard the shot. Must have thought it was part of the movie. Plus, finally," he sighed, "no motive in the whole world. They loved her. I really think they did. You should have seen them. They're all just completely fucked up around this. Excuse me the French."

Glitsky waved off the apology. He disliked profanity, but he'd heard all the words before and at the moment his mind was taken up with the case. "What about her friends?"

"She's got a regular book club and this group of other mothers from the neighborhood that meet every week or so, but we've talked to every one of them. All shocked. Stunned. Nobody had even a small problem with Elizabeth. Everybody came to her for everything and she never said no."

Lanier had reconfigured the office pretty much back to the way it had been when it had been Glitsky's. One desk took up most of the center of the room and he sat behind it, with Glitsky across from him, his feet up, his fingers templed in front of his mouth.

"I went to the funeral on Saturday, Abe," he continued. "Huge crowd. Everybody loved this woman."

"Somebody didn't."

Lanier conceded the point. "Well, whoever it was did it right. Took the gun with him, touched nothing. One shot, point-blank to the heart."

"You checking phone records?" Glitsky

46

asked. "Maybe she had a boyfriend?"

"We're looking."

"Money?"

Lanier spread his hands. "Not a problem. She was frugal. Robert makes enough that they're okay. They went on vacation every year. Houseboat on Shasta."

Glitsky brought his feet to the floor. "So your absolutely typical average American housewife answers the door on a Tuesday evening and somebody shoots her for no reason?"

"Right. That's what we got."

"It's unlikely."

"Agreed." Lanier came forward. "Look, Abe, if you're not so subtly hinting that you'd like to talk to some of the players here yourself, I would invite any and all input. Belou and Russell are stumped and have other cases with better chances of getting solved. So if you want to jump in on this, have at it."

Glitsky was standing. "If I get the time, I might like to have a word with the husband."

"Knock yourself out," Lanier said.

To avoid the gauntlet of Sixth Street south of Mission — perhaps the city's most blighted stretch of asphalt and hopelessness — Dismas Hardy chose to drive the ten blocks or so from his Sutter Street office to the Hall of Justice. Only eighteen months before, his ex-partner David Freeman had been mugged and killed when he chose to walk home from the office one night rather than drive. Freeman's attackers hadn't come from the ranks of miscreants and drug-addled denizens of Sixth Street, true, but the old man's death had brought home to Hardy in a visceral way the literal danger of the streets. You entered certain areas at your own risk, and the greater part of valor was avoiding them if at all possible.

As he crossed Mission today in his flashy new, silver Honda S2000 convertible, on his way to what was sure to be a controversial meeting, his thoughts, as they did with an exhausting regularity, went back to the events surrounding Freeman's death — events that had been the proximate cause of another, far more profound, change in Hardy and several of his closest friends.

For the attack that killed David had been the penultimate escalation in a pattern of violence that had begun with the murder of a pawnshop owner named Sam Silverman, and continued through the deaths of two policemen, then to an attempt on Hardy's own life. When he and his best friend, Glitsky, learned that a man named Wade Panos was behind this vendetta, they had of course taken their suspicions to the proper authorities — the DA, the police, the FBI. But Panos owned a private security force sanctioned by the city, and the lieutenant in charge of homicide turned out to be on Panos's payroll as well. Hardy's and Glitsky's accusations fell on deaf ears, and before they could take it to the next level of legitimate authority, they had both received threats to the lives of their families.

To protect themselves and their loved ones, out of time and frustrated by the law they'd both sworn to uphold, the two of them — along with Hardy's brother-in-law Moses McGuire, his partner Gina Roake, and his client John Holiday — found themselves forced into a shoot-out with Panos's men at a deserted pier near the abandoned waterfront. In a brief but furious gunfight, in pure self-defense, they had killed four of Panos's men, including Lieutenant Barry Gerson, and had lost one of their own, John Holiday.

The four survivors — Hardy, Glitsky, McGuire, and Roake — were physically untouched and made a clean escape. But there was much collateral damage.

If Hardy had considered himself cynical about abusing the letter of the law in his practice before, now he was past entertaining any qualms at all. He still considered himself a "good guy," whatever that meant, but he also recognized that a kind of a scab had grown over the wound his softer instincts had sustained. He'd been doubted, betrayed, lied to, threatened, and abandoned both by those in whom he'd put his trust and in the system he'd believed in intrinsically. Now he wasn't about to squander any more emotional investment in a process that hadn't worked for him when he'd needed it most. He did what he did and if sometimes it was ugly, well, sometimes life was ugly. Get over it. He didn't care if everybody liked him anymore.

Sometimes he didn't like himself very much, either.

As he turned into the All-Day Lot at the end of the alley across from the Hall of Justice, he found that his hands ached from gripping the wheel so firmly. His jaw throbbed from the constant pressure he'd been putting on it.

His appointment was with the district attorney, Clarence Jackman. He was here to cut a deal for a client he despised, whom he wouldn't have gone near a couple of years ago. In those days, he would simply have declined to take the case. In his earlier career, he'd turned down business many times when he didn't personally like a prospective client. But more often than not lately he found himself inclined to choose to profit from his squeamishness, and would take the case at double or even triple his normal rate. It was all a game anyway, and if he didn't profit from it when he could, he was a fool.

So when an ex-cop named Harlan Fisk, now a city supervisor, came to Hardy the fixer to talk about Peter Chase, a big-time property manager/developer who'd been caught fondling his eleven-year-old nephew, Hardy forced himself to listen. Chase was one of Fisk's big donors. Hardy heard the facts and said he'd see what he could do to keep the case from coming to trial, but it would cost Chase fifty thousand dollars. Up front.

Now he had done his homework and perfected his pitch. He delivered it to Jackman in his third-floor office in the Hall of Justice. Also in the room were Supervisor Fisk, Chief of Police Batiste, and Celia Bonham, a representative from the mayor's office.

Winding it up, Hardy said, "Look, Clarence, I don't like this any better than you do, but I'm just the messenger."

Jackman, a physically imposing African-American, was a powerful and charismatic figure. When Sharron Pratt, his predecessor as district attorney, had resigned in disgrace three years before, Mayor Washington had appointed Jackman to fill out the remainder of her term, and Jackman had hired a team of aggressive prosecutors who much preferred putting criminals in jail to understanding them and their problems. He was running for election in his own right next November, and was ahead in all the early polls.

Now sitting behind his desk, his hands clasped in front of him, his voice mild, he said, "I'm of course happy to hear the mayor's position on criminal cases. But there was a victim in this case, an innocent little boy, and this office has his rights to protect. Are you telling me his abuser should go unpunished? You'll pardon me for speaking frankly, Diz, but I'm a little surprised you're taking this tack. This discussion is beneath you."

Hardy controlled a grimace, took a breath. "You should know he's reached a financial settlement with his sister, the boy's mother, Clarence. Will that make up to the boy for what he did to him? Will any amount of money address the human issue? No, it won't. But it will pay for counseling for the victim, and then perhaps help with his schooling and even college. In return, the family has agreed to my proposal. To the mayor's proposal, really."

"He can't want us to drop the charges, Diz. Even if the victim's family agrees, I'm inclined to pursue them. We're a tolerant city, God knows, but not for this kind of stuff. Not on my watch."

Hardy turned to share a glance with Fisk, then came back around to the DA. "I'm not talking about dropping charges, Clarence. He remains charged. The case stays open."

Jackman frowned. "Then what do you want?"

"I want the case to stay open. That's all. My client gives you his word that nothing like this will ever happen again. Ever. He remains in counseling in perpetuity. He goes to meetings every week. His life changes. It has changed. He is always in treatment. And if he ever does cross the line again, Clarence, you've already got him charged. You just pull him in."

"If I may," Ms. Bonham said, "I'm at this meeting because Mayor Washington wanted his feelings known. He has been acquainted both personally and professionally with Mr. Chase for many years, and while he in no way countenances his behavior in this case, he sees it as a one-time failing of an otherwise good man with a real sickness, a disease if you will, who may have let the stresses of his work get the better of him."

Jackman listened with interest to this extraordinary little speech, then nodded and looked at Chief Batiste. "Frank?" he asked.

"What's the police position here?"

"I serve at the mayor's pleasure, Clarence, as you know. If the mayor's okay with holding off on a trial . . ." He let the sentence hang.

Jackman brought his eyes back to Hardy. "This is a nonstarter, Diz, and you know it. What's really going on here?"

This was getting to the meat of it. "As you know, Clarence, Mr. Chase manages several city properties in the blocks surrounding city hall. Beyond those, he also holds the contract for the police department's motor pool. He leases all the city cars. What he's proposing is a yearlong moratorium on rents for all these properties, starting this month."

In a long legal career, Jackman had fielded a host of bizarre settlement offers, but this one rocked him. He blew out a lungful of air, pushed his chair back, got up quickly and walked over to his windows. He was close to losing his temper, something that he had not allowed himself for years.

"So Mr. Chase wants to buy his way out of child molestation charges? Why send you, Diz? Why not a plain envelope stuffed with hundreds delivered by some hoodlum in a dark bar?" He actually spoke more softly. "I won't be bribed, Diz, and I'm disgusted that you think I could be." He looked from eye to eye at the assembled legation. "I think you all had better leave."

Hardy stood up, put out a restraining hand to the others, crossed over to where Jackman stood. "Look, Clarence, I said at the outset that I knew this stinks. The guy hired me because he figures I can pull a personal string here, and I have the right to be as insulted as you do.

"But I think you've got to do this. Listen. Washington says the city will make about three mil on this deal. If you won't do it, he'll just cut the difference out of your budget. You're being extorted, Clarence, plain and simple, squeezed by a child molester and a venal political hack."

Behind him, he heard Ms. Bonham make a kind of gurgling noise. He was talking loud enough for her to hear, and this was getting rather more raw than she'd expected.

"But the bottom line," Hardy concluded, "is I think they've got you."

Hardy knew that three million dollars was about 10 percent of the DA's already lean budget. The office had already made deep cuts, and three million more would be a catastrophe. Jackman would have to lay off 15 percent of his staff. And because most of his nonlabor expenses were fixed, salaries were all he had to work with.

"Clarence," Hardy concluded, lowering

his own voice now, "believe it or not, I'm here as your friend because nobody else would have told you what was really going on. I think you have to do this."

Hardy walked back to the couches. Jackman returned to his desk and sat back down in the heavy, expectant silence. After a moment, he looked up and nodded. "If he so much as spits on the sidewalk, I'll have him hauled in and fast-track him to Superior Court. Is that clear to each and every one of you?"

"Yes, sir," they intoned as with one voice.

"All right. You make sure the paperwork is tight and have it back here by this evening for my signature. Ms. Bonham, while I'm talking about signatures, I wouldn't mind his honor's position in writing. At his and your convenience, of course. Other than that," he pointed toward his door, "I've got a couple of appointments scheduled. I appreciate you all coming to talk to me about this problem."

Bonham, Fisk and Batiste were through the door when Clarence called out for Hardy to stay behind a minute. After the door closed, he sat looking down at his desk. When he spoke, the words came out with a scalpel-like precision. "I accept you came here as a friend, Diz. But, as a friend, never come here with a deal like this again. Not ever. Understood?"

"Understood."

With more than just a bad taste in his mouth, Hardy went into the bathroom in the hallway outside Jackman's office. There he leaned over one of the sinks for a few seconds, his head hanging as though from a thread. Then he turned on the cold water and threw several handfuls into his face. Drying off with a paper towel from the roll, he suddenly stopped and stood studying his face in the mirror for a long moment. The conversation with Jackman had netted him and his firm fifty thousand dollars, and though he told himself that it was a decent deal all around, his body was telling him something else. His head was light, his heart pounded. A wave of nausea made him hang his head again. When the dizziness passed, he ran his palms over his face, trying to recognize the person he was staring at. Would Clarence ever forgive him, he asked himself. Would he forgive himself? Could he continue to live like this?

I have no choice, he told himself. *Don't confuse a job with a vocation. This is a job. You do it. You get paid for it. That's what it's about. It's not about you. It's not personal. Don't lose that focus. If it gets personal, you lose.*

When he got his breathing and the rest of his body under some degree of control, he rode the elevator up one floor. Looking in at the suites of administrative offices that opened onto the lobby, he noticed with some surprise that the reception area was empty. He stood inside the double doors for a moment, making sure no one was guarding the entrance, then reached behind the waist-high wooden door by the reception desk and pressed the button that admitted visitors to the inner sanctum. In a few steps, silently, he'd passed through the outer office, then the conference room. Neither of the deputy chiefs was in their adjacent offices.

The room to his left was Glitsky's office. Far from the norm at the Hall, his office was expansive, nearly as large as Hardy's own, and almost as well furnished. Windows along the Bryant Street wall provided lots of natural light.

The bookshelves behind his desk testified to Glitsky's love of books. A knowledge junkie, he stocked hundreds of paperback novels, a full set of the *Encyclopedia Britannica*, an abridged, although still enormous, *Oxford English Dictionary*. There was a shelf of history, another of forensics, criminology, the *Compendium of Drug Therapy* and other medical references. One whole section was devoted to Patrick O'Brian's seafaring books, Glitsky's ongoing passion now for the past few years, and the other highly esoteric reference books that accompanied these novels — *Lobscouse and Spotted Dog*, *Harbors and High Seas*, *A Sea of Words*, a biography of Thomas Cochrane, who'd been O'Brian's inspiration for Jack Aubrey.

On these shelves, too, were a number of personal artifacts — a football signed by all of his college teammates at San Jose State; pictures of him and his sons on most if not all of the Pop Warner teams he'd coached; his old patrolman's hat; a menorah (Glitsky was half Jewish and half African-American); lots of police-themed bric-a-brac from citations he'd been awarded, classes and conferences he'd attended, decorations and medals he'd acquired. The walls were covered with even more citations, including Police Officer of the Year in 1987, plaques, diplomas, the (premature) obituary that Jeff Elliot had written about him after he'd been shot. There were also two family photos — one about twelve years old featuring his then-young boys and his wife Flo before she'd died; the other taken only last December with Treya and their baby Rachel, Treya's twenty-year-old daughter, Raney, and his three now-grown young men — Isaac, Jacob and Orel.

In Glitsky's new position, he spent a good portion of every day going to meetings, holding press conferences to manage the spin on police issues, representing the Chief at various functions. Hardy assumed he'd been at such a meeting this morning, and saw no reason not to take advantage of his friend's absence to inject a little lightness into his afternoon. He walked behind the desk and opened the top left drawer, which as he knew was filled with peanuts in the shell.

Quickly, looking up lest one of the gatekeepers bust him, he pulled the drawer all the way out and set it on the desk. He then took out the right-hand drawer — pens, Post-it pads, business cards, paper clips — and inserted it into the left-hand slot. When the peanuts were in on the wrong side, he checked his handiwork and saw that lo, it was good.

Glitsky the control freak would go into fits.

Hardy made it out of the administrative offices without running into a human being. When he got back on the elevator going down, his good humor had mostly returned, and he was whistling to himself.

3

Hardy pulled his convertible into the garage of the Freeman Building, underneath the law offices of Freeman, Farrell, Hardy & Roake. When Freeman had died, he had left the building that bore his name to his fiancee, Gina Roake, and the firm's business to Hardy, and they'd formed a new firm, keeping Freeman's name in it, immediately and almost without discussion. The arrangement had somehow seemed foreordained. Now, with the top down, Hardy parked in the primo spot next to the elevator that was reserved for the managing partner. For a moment, he sat listening to the terrific interplay of guitar, bouzouki, mandolin, violin and vocals of Nickel Creek's "Sweet Afton," a song from the CD his daughter Rebecca had recommended.

It did his heart good to know that this old poem by Robert Burns had somehow attained a kind of limited hipness again. It was a mostly acoustic country group, after all, melodic and musical, so it didn't exactly rule the airwaves, but his daughter and her teenage friends loved it for a' that. Here alone was reason to have hope and faith in the next generation, he thought. It wasn't all rap and crap.

He set the brake, took off his sunglasses, and pushed the button that got the roof back up in under six seconds, a little more than the time it took the car to hit sixty on the open road. In another minute, he exited the elevator into the main lobby on the second floor and was gratified to hear the steady thrum of activity. It was nearly ten a.m. and most of the fourteen associates had already been here since at least eight o'clock, on their way to billing at least eight hours of their time, as they did every day at $150 an hour.

From where he stood, Hardy could see three associates meeting with some clients in the Solarium, the firm's large, glass-enclosed conference room. Directly in front of him at the receptionist's workstation, Phyllis seemed to be answering five calls at once. The hallway to his right bustled with mail delivery and some other associates talking with their secretaries or paralegals. The Xerox machines were humming in the background.

Hardy crossed the space in front of him and poked his head into the office of Norma Towne, his office manager, a humorless woman of uncertain vintage who had conceived an affection of sorts for him, in spite of his tendency to crack wise. She pulled her eyes from her computer long enough to give him a little wave, to ask if he needed anything.

"An oil well would be nice," he said, "if you've got a spare. Everything okay here?"

It was, and he proceeded to his own office. In the past year, he'd moved down to the main floor from the one above, bequeathing his old office to his new partner, Wes Farrell. As managing partner, Hardy felt he ought to have more of a presence in the day-to-day workings of the firm, and he'd ensconced himself in a room directly next to David Freeman's old office.

A year ago, Hardy's current work space had enclosed a four-desk paralegal station, the stationery room and the semi-warehouse where the firm had kept the old, physical files. Now, with a couple of interior walls removed and twenty-five thousand dollars' worth of interior decorating, it was a large, airy and imposing executive suite. He had his own wall of law books, several somber original oils suitably framed, a sink and large wet bar, and two seating areas with Persian throw rugs, like the one in front of his custom cherry desk. He did bring the dartboard down from upstairs, but now it hid behind a pair of cherry cabinet doors — the only hint of its presence was the thirty-inch slat of dark teak set into the oak hardwood floor exactly seven feet, nine and one-quarter inches from the face of the dartboard. Similar cabinet doors also hid his entertainment center, audio system and huge television set.

Hardy pushed the button on his espresso machine and crossed to his desk just in time to respond to his buzzer. Phyllis announced that his ten o'clock, Mrs. Oliva, had arrived. He crossed to the door, paused to take a breath and get his smile in place, then walked out to meet his client.

The area over by the bar and the law books was the more formal of the two seating arrangements — the other had a loveseat and upholstered wing chairs — and Mrs. Oliva and Hardy sat kitty-corner to each other on stiff-backed Empire chairs. She had taken a cup of espresso, too, though it rested untouched on the low table in front of her. Not yet thirty years old, she was carefully made up and as well dressed as Wal-Mart could make her. She was explaining why she supported the charges the DA had filed against Hardy's client, her ex-husband James, a San Francisco policeman.

"I completely understand," Hardy said when she'd finished.

"I don't know if you can. I realize it sounds ridiculous. I mean, a box of baby wipes." She smiled almost apologetically at the absurdity of the words. But the reality was too serious to allow that. She'd called police alleging that James had gotten angry during a scheduled visitation with their one-year-old, Amanda. From a distance of less than five feet he had thrown a full box of baby wipes at his estranged wife. The force and surprise of the thing had knocked Mrs. Oliva down, broken her nose, blackened both eyes. Hardy thought he could still detect halos of bluish bruise under her foundation.

"The issue isn't what may or may not have been in the box. The issue is that he threw it in anger at you."

As though curious, she cocked her head to one side. "You're not trying to defend it?"

"Call me old-fashioned," Hardy said, breaking a small grin, "but I'm opposed to guys hitting girls. Throwing things at them, too, if you want to get technical." His voice went dead sober. "I'm acting on behalf of your husband, Mrs. Oliva, but not trying to defend what he did. I've suggested he get himself into an anger management program and he's done that, but what he did to you, he and I both agree, is completely inexcusable. He wants you to

65

know that that's how he feels."

Mrs. Oliva digested this unexpected viewpoint for a short moment. She seemed to remember the demitasse on the table and reached down, picked it up, took a sip. "So, if that's the case, why are we having this meeting?" she asked. "Why are you defending him?"

"Well, as I've indicated, I'm really not there yet. Defending him, I mean, in the legal sense. At this point, he's retained me and I'm representing him. If this case eventually comes to trial, I'll probably advise him to seek other counsel."

She carefully put her coffee cup back down and faced Hardy, her lips now tight. "What do you mean, if this case goes to trial? The DA's charged it and they're planning to go forward."

"I know that. Of course." Hardy sat back, crossed one leg over the other. "But I wanted to talk to you in person and ask you if in your heart you really wanted Jim to go to jail over this. I'm sure you've heard stories about what happens to cops when they go to jail."

Her mouth worked, but she didn't speak.

Hardy pressed her moment of hesitancy. "I'm not suggesting that Jim not be punished, or that if he does go to jail he wouldn't deserve whatever happened to him there. What I am saying is that I'd like you to consider what that type of punishment for him would do to *you*." He uncrossed his legs and came forward. "If Jim gets convicted, Mrs. Oliva, he loses his job, which in the here and now means no income for you and no child support. I understand he's been good about those payments up until now."

She nodded. Her face showed that this was something she hadn't considered. The possibility of losing that precious income clearly struck a nerve.

Hardy continued. "He's not trying to duck his responsibility to you, Mrs. Oliva, or even his punishment, which he knows he deserves." He lowered his voice to near inaudibility. "I doubt if he would want anyone to know about this, but I sat across from him in this very seat two days ago and watched him break down in remorse for what he'd done to you. He'd never harmed you physically before this one incident, had he?"

"No." Suddenly one of Mrs. Oliva's eyes overflowed. She made no effort to wipe the tear away.

Hardy handed her a Kleenex from the box on the table beside him, his voice a caressing whisper. "He lost his temper, Mrs. Oliva. He never meant to hurt you, and certainly not so badly. He says he thinks you know that. Is that true?"

"No. I mean yes. I don't think he meant to do it. But it was so . . . so violent. And in front of Amanda."

"I know. Amanda. She's his main concern, too. What's going to happen to her if Jim's in jail and you've got to be working to support the both of you? What's that going to do to her, living in a succession of daycare places, as opposed to her having her own mother . . ." He stopped.

Her tears flowed over her cheeks and she dabbed at them with the Kleenex. She sat straight-backed, under rigid control.

"Mrs. Oliva," Hardy said, "Jim is more sorry for this than he can express. He plans to write you a formal apology. Beyond that, he doesn't want the baby you had together to be brought up by strangers. He understands that you're not comfortable seeing him for a time, or having him around Amanda. But these anger management classes can work wonders. I've seen it happen many times. In the meanwhile, at my suggestion, Jim has agreed to double his monthly child support payments to you, which will be a burden on him, but one that he accepts, would gladly accept if you'd agree to it and ask the DA to drop these criminal charges."

Hardy knew that it was up to the DA to press or drop the charges. Jackman felt continual pressure from women's groups to go to the max on every case such as this one. Nevertheless, with the victim on board, Hardy thought he had a good shot at getting his client into some kind of program that would result in the charges being dismissed. Jackman might not like these diversion programs, where nothing substantive ever really happened, but he was stuck with them. And sometimes, as in this case, they served a purpose.

"You know your husband," Hardy continued. "Basically, he's a good man. He'll honor his debts, especially to Amanda. You know he will. But he needs to keep his job. He needs to go back to work, for all of your sakes."

Every day, under his dress shirt and tie Wes Farrell wore a T-shirt with a message. He was buttoning up now, having just shown Hardy today's: "Dyslexics of the world, untie!" Now Farrell, religious in his avoidance of good posture, had gotten himself comfortable sideways and slumped in the loveseat, his legs up over the armrest. He said, "For this twenty minutes you made five thousand dollars?"

Hardy had his cabinet open and was throwing darts in an abstracted manner. Now he turned to face his partner. "It was grueling work. But it wasn't any twenty minutes. More like fifteen."

"Fifteen minutes. And what's this, the fifth one this month?"

"The fifth what?"

"Whatever you call it. Facilitation?"

"I love that word." Hardy threw a dart. "But I don't keep track of the numbers. It's bad luck, counting your money at the table." He threw another dart. "More than a couple anyway."

"And this one, she's calling the DA today?"

"That's the deal."

"And her husband doubles the child support and also pays you five grand?"

Hardy felt enough guilt about it himself. He didn't need to get an extra dose from his partner. "Don't look at me like that. He's still better off. It's way cheaper than if he went to trial. I didn't do anything unethical. Everybody wins here."

"If you believe that, I believe you," Farrell said. "I'm just trying to figure out how I can get some of that action."

"Well, I'm not really sure I do believe it, to tell you the truth. But it seems to be what I'm doing lately. Nobody really wants to go to trial anyway. It's too expensive and time-consuming."

"You're kidding. When did that start?" Farrell stood and walked over to the dart board, from which he extracted Hardy's last round, all twenties. "Although if memory serves, those pesky trials are the traditional way we establish guilt or innocence."

Hardy chortled — short, dry, mirthless. "Uh huh. And I've got this bridge . . . I'd think that you, Wes, of all people, might harbor a little skepticism about that issue." A few years before, in a highly-publicized murder trial, Farrell had made his reputation as a defense attorney by getting an acquittal for his best friend who, as it turned out, and unbeknownst to his lawyer, had been guilty as hell. "I should also think," Hardy went on, "that instead of this show of unseemly envy, you would pause to admire the finesse with which your friend and partner has mastered the fine art of fattening the firm's account, and hence your own, without having to resort to the tedium of hourly billing."

Farrell threw a dart. "I'm constantly in a state of high awe."

Hardy nodded. "There you go."

Someone knocked and his door opened. Amy Wu stood for a moment in the doorway, all but gaping. "Partners with darts," she said.

"Now you know why Phyllis guards the door," Hardy said.

"I waited until she took a break."

Farrell threw. "Bull's-eye."

Both Hardy and Wu turned. The dart

was nowhere near the center of the board. "Made you look," Farrell said.

"You guys are weird, you know that?" Wu looked at Hardy. "I don't know if you're still interested in these things, sir, but I've got a question about a case. You know, the law?"

"I've heard of it," Hardy said. "Can Wes stay and listen?"

Wu cast a baleful eye at Farrell. "If he can spare the time."

"Can't," Farrell said. "Duty calls. Well, whispers." He threw his last dart and headed for the door.

Hardy closed up his dart closet and went around behind his desk. He stole a glance at Wu as he passed her. She projected at least the illusion of efficient competence, but he wasn't fooled. Wu's performance had slipped since her father's death. She'd also missed a lot of work, really an unconscionable amount for someone in her position. But he believed she'd make it up by the end of the year. She was having a hard time, and understandably.

All in all, Hardy felt that it was much preferable, and far easier, to pretend that all was well when that's what it looked like. And Wu certainly still looked the part of hotshot young associate — she wore her hair short and cropped around her ears;

her always-crisp business attire couldn't be faulted. Besides, with an IQ of around one fifty, Wu could be firing on only half of her cylinders and still blow away a great deal of the competition. Or so Hardy chose to believe.

Certainly he didn't want to inquire too pointedly about her personal life. That was neither his job nor his inclination. But he was her boss, and at the very least he should be awake to nuances that might affect her performance.

The real problem, he knew, was that he was having some nuances himself. He'd be damned if he was going to think about those much, either, but Wu had missed another day of work on Friday — if she kept her absences at anything like this rate much longer, she would have some difficulty making the firm's annual hourly billing minimum. He really felt he had to say something. He sat back in his chair, hands folded in his lap. "You've got a law question," he said.

"Yes, sir."

"Well, before we get to that, can I ask you a bit of a personal one?"

Her face closed up. "Of course."

"How are you holding up?"

"Fine," she answered automatically.

"I noticed you were out on Friday."

"I saw a client in the afternoon. The

case I wanted to ask you about, in fact."

"Ah." He scratched at his desk. "I just thought that if you wanted some time off, you could ask and get it, you know. Even an extended leave if you felt you needed it. Sometimes that's a better idea than taking a day at a time, piecemeal."

"I'm fine. Really."

"Okay. I'm not meaning to pry. Just making the offer. The firm places a high value on you and your work, and if you feel like you'd be more productive after a bit of a break, we'd be happy to give you one, that's all."

"I don't think I need that. I'm just working through some stuff, sir." She tried a game smile. "Getting used to the new world order."

"Okay, but if it gets tough and you change your mind, you can come in here. Anytime."

"Thank you." Wu half turned her head to the door behind her. "But maybe you could mention that to Phyllis first, just in case."

A ghost of a smile played around Hardy's mouth. "You said you got by her this time?"

"Yes. But I cheated and watched from my office until she left her post and went to the bathroom."

Hardy nodded, his smile genuine now.

"You know," he said, "when David was still with us, sometimes I used to do that, too. I'd be hiding on the stairs just out of sight and wait for Phyllis to get up off her phones, then I'd zip across the lobby and get inside David's lair before she could stop me. She hated it. It was great. But I must say," he went on, "since then I've gotten some appreciation of why he kept her around, in spite of that slightly witch-like quality. The gatekeeping does serve a purpose. Me, I'm trying to emulate how David did things. Keep an open door."

"But he didn't keep an open door."

"Exactly. Except when he did." Hardy came forward and linked his hands in front of him on the desk. "He always said that if it was important enough to make me figure out how to get around Phyllis, it was important enough for him."

It was a challenge and a question, and Wu nodded. "Seventeen-year-old kid up for double murder. How's that?"

"If that's the case you wanted to ask me about, I'd say it's good enough." Hardy sat back, his own face tightening down. "Tell me about it."

Wu settled into her leather chair and gave him the short version.

When she finished, Hardy didn't move for a while; then he brought himself up to his desk, ready for business. "You say the teacher was with this girl? How old was he?"

"Forty."

"Forty," Hardy said. "And Laura?"

"Sixteen."

"What a lovely world. And they picked up your client — Andrew? — when?"

"Last Friday."

Hardy nodded. "So nobody's rushing to judgment. Homicide must have worked the case pretty well."

"Looks like." Wu hesitated. "Also, and you might find this interesting, Andrew Bartlett's stepfather is Hal North."

"Is he now?" Hardy, no stranger to the power players in the city, nodded with approval. "So where are you now?"

"Well, I've talked to Boscacci. They've got a witness who picked Andrew out of a lineup. No question, first try. Beyond that, Andrew's on the record with half a dozen lies, plus he stole his father's gun — a nine-millimeter automatic, which in this case is bad luck. Oh, and they found a casing in the car. Andrew's car."

"Okay, and the boy's story?"

"He didn't do it. He didn't even realize he was being considered a suspect until the police came and put the cuffs on him. He liked Mooney. He loved Laura."

When she mentioned the alibi, Hardy asked immediately, without inflection,

76

"Anybody see him while he was taking this walk?"

"No sign of it."

"What does he say?"

Wu shifted in her chair. "Well, I haven't talked to him yet, gotten his story."

Hardy cocked his head. "You haven't talked to him yet? It's been, what, four days?"

"I've been going over the discovery, sir, talking with the parents, and negotiating with Allan Boscacci. I've met Andrew before. I defended him for a joyride a couple of years ago, and didn't see any immediate need to go and introduce myself again."

"Okay," Hardy said. "Sorry to jump." But the fact remained that, in his opinion, Wu had slipped again. One of the fundamentals was that you went and talked to the client.

But Wu seemed oblivious. "Anyway, the point is that Boscacci wouldn't have arrested Andrew if his alibi held up. And it doesn't. The eyewitness."

"All right. But if they just hired you on Friday, who'd Andrew have with him all the times when he talked to the homicide guys since February?"

"Nobody. No lawyer anyway. His parents saw it the way he did, and really didn't believe he was a suspect. They just let him talk and talk and talk."

Hardy shook his head. "How deep a hole did he dig?"

"He's pretty well hit China."

"Well, then, it looks like you've got your first bona fide murder case. Congratulations, I think. If you've come to me for my imprimatur, you've got it" — as managing partner, Hardy approved all of the firm's new business — "although I'm not sure you'll wind up thanking me for it. Murder trials can kill you."

"I've heard," she said, "but I'm not planning to take him to trial."

"No? How's that going to happen?"

"I think you'll be happy," Amy said. "My idea is to keep him in the juvie system."

"How old is he, did you say?"

"Seventeen."

Hardy sat back. "Last I heard, seventeen-year-olds got filed adult around here. Mr. Jackman's been a little rigid on the topic." Jackman had very publicly adopted a very tough stance on juvenile crime. A seventeen-year-old who'd killed two people did not elicit much sympathy from the new prosecutors in the DA's office. "You're telling me Boscacci has already filed him juvie?"

"Yes, sir." She paused. "After I told him Andrew would admit."

But Hardy's expression grew perplexed.

78

"He's going to admit? How do you know he's going to do that? You said you hadn't talked to him yet."

"I talked to his stepfather."

"Okay, all well and good, but the one who pays the bills isn't necessarily the client." Hardy scratched behind his ear, interrupted Wu as she started to reply. "No, wait," he said. "And what if in fact he didn't actually do it?"

Wu came forward with some enthusiasm, obviously feeling that this question put her on firmer ground. "He did, though," she said. "Look, we know homicide took two months building the case. They played it slow and steady. He did it, sir, and specials as an adult puts him in prison for the rest of his life. He'll admit to avoid that."

"But you just told me he says he's innocent."

Wu shook her head. "They don't arrest innocent people anymore."

"It's happened to clients of mine."

"Yes, sir. All two of them, I believe, right?"

"Actually, three."

"Well, the exceptions that prove the rule. Three is more than an entire century's allotment right there."

Hardy wasn't really amused, but he broke a small smile. "I hate to mention it, but they *were* last century's cases. Now we're working on the new one."

"When Andrew sees the evidence against him, he's going to get religion. You watch. I promise. Really, sir. This is a sweet deal for everybody."

"I can't believe Boscacci's going along."

"To avoid the trial? Why not? He gets two convictions out of this, so he wins. Wouldn't you take the deal?"

Hardy thought if he were Boscacci he might, but depending on the evidence, he might not. Though there was always an incentive among administrators to clear docket time, a high-profile murder case often sought its own level and provided potentially positive intangibles, such as name recognition for the politically ambitious. And even if Wu's strategy worked, it wouldn't be without its drawbacks.

Wu sat back, cocked her head, spoke in a measured tone. "What I'm doing here, sir, is making sure that Andrew gets out of custody in eight years instead of never."

Hardy, unsatisfied, glanced at his watch. "All right," he said. Getting up out of his chair, he pulled some papers on his desk together. "I'm hoping you're right in every respect. Meanwhile, I've got another client coming in, so may I be so crass as to inquire about your retainer? This is still criminal law . . ."

"And you get your money up front."

"Words to live by. How much?"

"Well," she said. "The plea won't take too long to get processed. I figured it was worth about five grand."

At the figure, Hardy stopped his paper gathering, looked up with another question on his face, worry in his eye. Even if everything went exactly according to Wu's plan and she was uncommonly lucky — and Hardy thought neither of these was a lock — then she would certainly spend at least forty hours, and maybe as many as sixty, in the next week or so preparing Andrew, convincing him that it was in his favor to say that he was guilty of murder so that he could avoid being tried as an adult.

Hardy had been doing a lot of math in his head lately, and immediately sensed that five thousand dollars wasn't close to Wu's standard rate of $150 an hour. He punched at the adding machine in front of him. It was worse than he'd thought. "You're only planning on putting in thirty-three hours on this?"

"I figured that was about what it was worth." She fidgeted with her hands opening her purse.

Hardy shook his head. "So you were going to put in the extra time without billing it, which would not only be cheating you, but the client and the firm, and . . ."

She pulled the check from her purse, interrupted his rebuke. "So I told Mr. North I'd take twenty down. Thousand, that is."

She put the check face up on the desk.

Hardy looked down at it, up at her. Nodded. "Okay, Wu," he said, "you're starting to get it."

Into the phone, Hardy said, "I would have bet your office was a veritable fortress of solitude."

"I would have, too, but I guess not," Glitsky said. "I even thought of dusting for prints, except everybody who works in the Hall was here for the open house when I took office."

"You don't have any idea who it was?"

"I can't imagine anybody who'd take the chance. I mean, I'm the deputy chief. They get caught, they're toast. Who'd risk it?"

Hardy was standing behind the desk in his office. The shades were down, cutting some of the afternoon glare, but his eyes were twinkling, his color high. He'd had a martini and most of a bottle of Pinot Grigio at lunch at Sam's, with a plate of sand dabs. He'd reeled in another client from the bottomless pool of troubled police persons. And now for an unexpected bonus, he was getting to console Glitsky on the terrible breach of security in his office, somebody moving his drawers around. The way it was going, Hardy thought there was some small chance he could talk Abe into paying him to put a private investigator on it.

But then Glitsky said, "Well, it was probably some stupid prank anyway."

The opening was just too wide, and Hardy couldn't resist stepping into it. "I don't know, Abe. There are some bona fide crazies in your building. At least I might send a sample of the peanuts to the lab and throw the rest out."

"You think?"

"Better safe than dead."

"How could I get dead around this?"

"I don't know. Was there any powder in the bottom of the drawer?"

Glitsky snorted. "Yeah, but they're salted in the shell peanuts, so the trained inspector in me thinks the white powder is probably salt. And if it was anthrax, it's too late already."

"Did you taste it?"

"No. Just a minute. Yep. Salt."

Hardy clucked. "Your tongue goes numb in five minutes, do me a favor and call nine one one. And I'd still send some of the goobers to the lab. You never know."

"I'll consider it."

"You don't sound sincere. You remember the song 'Found a Peanut'? The guy in that song died if you recall. I'm serious."

"That's what worries me, that you're serious." Glitsky sighed. "Can we leave the peanuts, please? I didn't call about the peanuts anyway."

"All right. It's your funeral. So what do you want?"

"I wondered what time you might be going home. I've got a five o'clock meeting with Batiste that just came up and Treya's got to be home at the regular time because Rita's . . . never mind. The point is if you're staying a little late, maybe I could bum a ride with you."

"Your driver ought to take you to and from work."

"My driver works the day shift. I come in too early and go home too late. I think I've mentioned this to you before."

"I probably didn't pay attention. So what time?"

Glitsky said six-thirty or so and Hardy told him it was his lucky day. He had his own meeting after close of business with Amy Wu about this double homicide she was handling.

"That would be Andrew Bartlett," Glitsky said. It wasn't a question.

"Doesn't it get boring when you already know everything?" Hardy asked. "But I bet you haven't heard that Boscacci's filed him juvie."

"Sure he did. And next year I'm quarterback for the Forty-Niners."

"I'll expect great tickets. But it's true. Boscacci, I mean."

Silence. Then, "How did that happen?"

"Wu is having him cop a guilty plea in exchange for juvenile sentencing."

"And Jackman agreed? Jackman who likes to say if you're old enough to kill somebody, you're an adult? That Jackman?"

"The very same. And I've heard him say the same thing. But Wu says it's a done deal."

"I'd make sure before I go real large telling anybody. Like the newspapers."

"Well, that's what Wu and I are going to be talking about, so I'll let you know."

4

The name Youth Guidance Center, or YGC, had an avuncular ring to it, as though the juvenile detention facility were some kind of a counseling haven for wayward children, a rest stop filled with soft stuffed chairs and couches, pastel colors, New Age music in the background. And in reality, in simpler times when the place was new, it had pretty much been like that. Kids who stole hubcaps, or smoked a joint, or played hooky from school, would wind up at the YGC and receive counseling, maybe a day or so of lockup to impress upon them the serious consequences of breaking the law.

Nowadays these relatively petty crimes never hit the radar of the police department. Juvenile felonies were commonly every bit as serious as crimes committed by adults, so in today's San Francisco, the YGC's primary function was, mostly, to lock up seriously dangerous criminals who happened to be under the age of eighteen. True, the center had a suicide-prevention watch. It also held a few dozen abandoned or abused children while they awaited suitable outplacement to foster homes. But in the main, "the cottages," as the jail facility was called, housed murderers, rapists and a varied assortment of vandals, robbers, muggers and burglars. Most of the inmates were awaiting or in the middle of their respective trials or hearings, which occurred in courtrooms on the premises, just adjacent in the administrative wing.

Wu hated being late. This morning between Boscacci and Hardy, she had also talked to Hal North, told him about her success with Boscacci, and scheduled what she thought might be a relatively lengthy appointment with the North family before the detention hearing — they had a lot they had to go over. She particularly wanted to hear more about the results of Hal's discussions on the admission issue with his wife and stepson, about which he'd been disconcertedly vague, telling her that he and Linda hadn't had as much time as he would have liked to talk because of an event they had to attend at the yacht club. Wu shouldn't worry, though, he told her. He'd have it all worked out with Andrew and Linda by the time they got to court.

This was Wu's first formal court appearance at the YGC, and she had gotten lost on the way up, then caught in traffic. After the uphill half-jog from down the street where she'd managed to find a parking place, through the admin building and up the steep walk to the cottages, she fought to catch her breath for a minute just outside the gate in the razor-wire-topped Cyclone fence. A bailiff appeared in response to her ring and escorted her without a word into the building proper — a one-story structure that reminded her of a cross between a military barracks and an inner-city high school. Drab and institutional and depressing as hell, she thought.

The bailiff led her to a pocked wooden door in the hallway and opened it. Sitting in an old-fashioned school desk in the opposite corner of the tiny room, next to the one outside window, Andrew Bartlett lifted a hand about an inch in a halfhearted greeting.

"Here she is." Hal stood to Wu's right, leaning back against the wall, arms crossed and clearly unhappy. "At last."

"Hal." Linda shot a frustrated look at her husband, then turned and smiled at Wu. "It's all right. You're here."

"I'm sorry. Terrible traffic. I even gave myself an extra half hour," she lied, then showed some more teeth, took a breath, turned to her client. "It's good to see you again, Andrew. How are you holding up?"

The boy dropped his head, lifted it, shrugged. " 'kay."

Confident and prepared, Wu smiled at him. "Good," she said. "Don't worry. We'll get you out of here today."

Linda piped in. "You think we can do that?"

"Oh, I think so."

"Really?" Hal asked.

"Probably," she said. "The hearing today is about whether they keep Andrew here until he's sentenced, and I don't see why they'll need to do that."

"So what happens?" he asked. "What about bail?"

Wu shook her head. "No. I thought I'd explained that. Juveniles don't get bail. The judge either lets Andrew go home with you and Linda, or he orders him kept here — detained."

"Just like that?" Linda shot a hopeful glance at her son. "One way or the other."

"Yes. And in this case, look what we've got. Both parents here showing support and concern. A minor with no previous record who poses no risk of flight — you'll both watch out for him, right?" She turned to Hal. "Then there's your standing in the community, sir. Beyond that, if the judge wanted more assurance, I'm assuming you'd be willing to pay for whatever private security, even a twenty-four-hour-a-day guard, that the court could want to be sure Andrew stayed out of trouble."

"He wouldn't need that," Hal said.

"No, I don't think so either. So I think . . ."

But Andrew finally spoke up, interrupting her. "What do you mean, 'sentencing'? Don't you mean 'trial'?"

Wu's startled glance went from her client to his stepfather, back over to Linda. "That's one of the other issues we're going to have to discuss. I thought you might already have . . ."

Hal cut her off. "I was waiting for you to get here . . ."

"To what?" Andrew asked.

"Just talk about the case."

"What about it?"

"The evidence, your plea, like that."

"What do you mean, his plea?" Linda, her voice suddenly very sharp, backed up a step so she could face both Hal and Wu together. "His plea is not guilty. It has to be not guilty, right?"

Wu drew a quick breath. "Well, as I said, there are a few legal issues . . ."

Three sharp raps sounded on the door to the room and it immediately opened to the bailiff. "Time," he said. "Let's go. Can't keep the judge waiting." Then, perhaps sensing the tension in the room, he asked, "Everything all right in here?"

"Fine," Wu said. She turned to Linda and Andrew. "We'll have all the time in

90

the world to talk about everything after the hearing. It'll all make sense, you'll see."

Linda looked to Hal for support. "I hope so."

But the bailiff had his job to do. "Sorry, but you've all got to move out," he said. "Hearing's in ten minutes." He looked at Andrew. "You're going to want to hit the can first. And quick."

"Can't he walk down with us?" Linda asked.

"No, ma'am. He's in custody. Rules."

Out on the pavement, walking down to the admin building, Wu broke the uncomfortable silence that had been holding since the three of them left the visitors' room. "The main thing," she said, "is that we're all in agreement as to what's best for Andrew."

"Hon," Hal stopped and put a hand on her arm, "we went over all of this yesterday."

"I know, but I thought it was more hypothetical, all this about Andrew admitting something. But in there you both sounded like Andrew is going to confess and then go to prison. How can he do that?"

Wu forced herself to look into Linda's eyes, to feign a confidence she didn't feel. "The fact is, we have to face that as an option. If we plead him out as a juvenile, then there's no life without parole hanging over his head."

"But he's not guilty," Linda repeated. She turned to Hal. "We talked about this every time the inspectors came by with some new thing, didn't we? And then this terrible lineup mistake . . ." The voice wore down. "He just didn't do this, Hal. Don't tell me you don't believe that."

Wu was fairly certain that she knew what Hal believed, and stepped in to save him. "I don't think we have to discuss the actual fact of whether he's innocent or guilty right now, Mrs. North. The issue is that he saves the court the considerable time and expense of a trial if he admits. In return, the DA agrees he's a juvenile and he avoids the LWOP."

"LWOP?" Linda asked. "What's LWOP?"

"Life without parole. That's what he would get as an adult."

North let out a snort. "But it's moot for now, anyway. He's *not* charged as an adult today, right?"

Linda turned to Wu. "He's not?"

"No, ma'am. That's why we're here, having this detention hearing. So we have a chance to let Andrew go home for a few days."

"We can get it all straightened out there," Hal said, "at home. We'll have plenty of time there."

Still unsure, Linda blew out in evident

frustration. She looked back up to the cottages, wrapped in their razor-wire dressing, and her shoulders sank. "Okay," she said with great weariness. "Let's at least first get him out of here."

"That's the plan." Wu offered her a brave smile. "Really."

Wu sat at the defense table awaiting the judge's entrance. In juvenile court proceedings, the district attorney was said to represent not the people, but the petitioner, and the person accused of a crime was not the defendant, but the minor. This nicety functioned to preserve the legal fiction that youthful felons were not lost causes. The district attorney's role was not to prosecute miscreants, but rather to ask, or petition, the state to recommend a treatment for the minor that stood a chance to result in the child's complete rehabilitation back into society. Even if that treatment was six or eight years locked up at the California Youth Authority, or CYA, it technically wasn't the same thing as prison, although its inmates might be hard-pressed to elucidate the precise difference.

To Wu's left, at the petitioner's table, sat her opposite number, Jason Brandt. Not yet thirty, Brandt already had four years as a prosecutor under his belt, all of it here at the YGC. Brandt had a full head of neatly

93

combed dark brown hair and wore a well-cut dark gray suit with a white shirt and muted blue tie. Affable, quick-witted, charming even, he smiled a lot and made it a point to get along well with everyone, including the defense attorneys against whom he was pitted. Wu, herself, had long harbored a bit of a secret crush on him. They'd shared drinks more than once — although his reputation was that as soon as the gavel came down, he was nobody to play with.

Suddenly Brandt lifted his head like an animal catching a scent. He caught Wu in the middle of her surreptitious glance at him and, nodding genially, went back to his papers. Wu made it a point to continue looking about the room, which was smaller than most of the courtrooms downtown at the Hall of Justice, but had the advantage of natural light pouring in from large windows set high in one wall.

Beyond Brandt, a very young-looking uniformed bailiff sat talking to a middle-aged woman whom Wu presumed was the court recorder. There were no jurors — juvenile trials did not have juries — and yet a nice jury box held twelve perennially empty chairs. There was no one in the gallery on the prosecution side — for the protection of the minors involved, the public was not admitted into the courtroom.

Wu turned around farther in her chair and gave a confident nod to Andrew's parents, the sole occupants of Wu's side of the gallery. Hal and Linda sat hip to hip, next to each other on the bench behind the bar rail. They held hands and seemed to be leaning into each other. Wu's eyes went briefly to Hal, and he inclined his head an inch, then raised a finger and pointed to one side of the room, where the door had started to open. Wu turned at the sound and watched as the bailiff from the cottages ushered Andrew ahead of him into the bullpen.

As Andrew shuffled toward her now, handcuffed in his shapeless gray prisoner's clothes, he seemed to her utterly defeated. Stopping in front of her table, he raised his head to look at his mother. His eyes opened in a silent plea, lips tightened down over a frankly quaking jaw. She was afraid that in another moment he might start to cry, and to forestall that, she stood, came around her table and helped him get seated.

"He doesn't need to be handcuffed," she said to the bailiff. "What's your name?"

"Nelson." The bailiff kept his hand on Andrew's shoulder and replied in some surprise. He played no formal role in this proceeding, and it was decidedly unusual for an attorney to speak to him for any reason.

"Well, Officer Nelson, this young man doesn't need to be handcuffed."

It didn't matter to Nelson one way or the other. "That's up to the judge," he said. He did take his hand off Andrew, however, and stepped aside a few paces. He stood leaning against the front of the jury box, facing Wu, sublimely indifferent, which was almost more chilling to her than outright antagonism would have been.

Wu reached over and patted Andrew's arm. "It's all right," she said. "It'll be fine."

He turned his face to her, then farther around, back to his mother again. "Mom," he said, then couldn't continue. Tears threatened to spill, but he blinked them back. Raw vulnerability took years off his age. The idea of this pathetic boy aiming a gun at a person and pulling a trigger not once but twice suddenly struck Wu for the first time as incongruous.

Her heart went out to him, while at the same time she was a bit relieved to see the depth of his despair. He would probably have to hit bottom and see that there was no hope in pleading not guilty. After they got to talk and she showed him the evidence, he'd realize the futility of pretending he hadn't done it. When the truth must be clear to him if he dared to look at it objectively. Andrew wasn't stupid — she glanced over at him one last time, confident that he would come to accept that he had to admit if he wanted to save himself.

Now in his early sixties, Judge W. Arvid Johnson had built a reputation as a reasonable and fair jurist with no particular ax to grind. Irreverently, secretly and universally called "Warvid" by the city's legal community, Johnson took the bench today with little fanfare and no formal announcement by the bailiff or court recorder. Suddenly, it seemed, he had materialized up there, seated behind the slightly raised podium — white-haired and faintly jocular, he projected an amiable solidity.

After a business-like nod to both counsel, he said, "All right" to no one in particular, pulled his glasses down to the end of his patrician nose and asked the probation officer to call the first case. When he'd done this, the officer listed those present in the courtroom, including the gallery, for the record, and then Judge Johnson began. "Mr. Brandt, comments on detention?"

"Yes, your honor."

"Go ahead."

Brandt stood up behind his table. His voice sounded clear and relaxed in the small room. "Your honor, as this is a murder case, the petitioner requests that the minor be detained."

"He's here under juvenile jurisdiction," the judge said sharply. "The district attorney has decided not to file against him directly as an adult. I have to gather that that was done on purpose? Am I wrong?"

"No, your honor, not at all." Brandt took the rebuke calmly, probably because he had a ready answer, and a good one. "We anticipate that Mr. Bartlett will admit this petition and receive the maximum commitment to the YA" — the Youth Authority. "He'll still be confined here at YGC, of course, rather than downtown, for a brief period since he's under eighteen, but we anticipate a quick disposition on two counts of first degree murder. So naturally the petitioner considers this a detention case."

Planted in her seat, Wu was surprised when Brandt thanked the judge and sat down. He'd said what he'd come here to say, short and sweet.

Judge Johnson nodded and turned. "Ms. Wu?"

Wu tried to swallow but her mouth had gone dry. She knew that Brandt liked to keep his opponents off-balance and that one way to do this was to mess with their timing. But he'd still surprised her, catching her in mid-thought with such a bare-bones statement. Detained. End of story.

"Ms. Wu," Johnson repeated. "Would you care to make a reply?"

She got to her feet. "I'm sorry, your honor. I was just . . ." She stopped herself, willed her mind clear and started again. "Your honor, before we go any further, I'd like to request that the handcuffs be removed from my client's wrists."

"Request denied. I don't believe this hearing will take enough time to make the exercise worthwhile. Detention has been requested by petitioner." Johnson pulled his glasses down to the end of his nose and peered over them. "This is a double murder we're talking about. We detain on murder cases."

"Yes, your honor, I understand that," Wu said, "but Mr. Bartlett can by no stretch be considered a danger to the community . . ."

Over at his table, Brandt cracked, "As long as we don't give him back his gun."

Johnson whirled on him. "That's enough of that, Mr. Brandt."

"I'm sorry, your honor," Brandt said. "I was driven to it."

Johnson frowned. "Be that as it may, see that it doesn't happen again."

"Yes, your honor."

But, no doubt as he'd intended, Brandt's interruption had blindsided Wu. Again, she'd lost her focus, and stood waiting for the judge to say something.

"Go on, Ms. Wu," Johnson said.

She threw a fast look over at Brandt, who let his mouth twitch, a pastiche of a smile. Wu glanced at her client, then back to Johnson, and finally found the thread. "Your honor, the fact remains that Andrew is a minor, not an adult. A minor with no previous record."

"Your honor, if I may." Brandt, up again. "I spoke to Mr. Boscacci on this very point not an hour ago, and he informs me, as I've already indicated to the court, that he did not direct file as an adult based on the anticipation of a quick admission."

"Your honor," Wu said, "my client has no criminal history . . ."

"He does now," Brandt said.

Johnson stared hard at the prosecutor, a warning. Coming back to Wu, he pushed his glasses back to the bridge of his nose. "Ms. Wu, this hearing is concerned only with the continued detention of Mr. Bartlett, and I'm not hearing any argument from you on why I should overrule the petitioner's suggestion."

"Your honor." Wu took a breath. "My client has been living a normal life for two months since these murders took place. He has known he's a suspect for most of that time and has caused no civil disturbance of any kind, nor has he tried to flee."

"True," Johnson said, "but surely you are not arguing that knowing you're a possible suspect and actually being an arrested suspect are the same thing, are you?"

"No, your honor, but his parents are here in the courtroom today, waiting to take him home. There is no reason they shouldn't be able to do that. Surely there is no risk of flight. He has another two months in this school year, and he's an excellent student. Surely he poses no worse danger to the community than he has for the past two months while he's gone to school and lived at home."

Johnson showed nothing. Wu supposed he'd heard the same argument a thousand times. He straightened at the bench, turned to the prosecutor. "Counselor."

Brandt stood up slowly, turned to look past Wu squarely at Andrew Bartlett, then shook his head. Suddenly he pointed a finger at Andrew. His voice took on an edge. "That's not somebody's good little boy sitting over there. That's a man who's killed two people already this year, and the district attorney is not going to give him a chance to hurt anyone else."

Andrew started to come to his feet. "But I *didn't*," he cried out.

"Yes, you did," Brandt shot back. "You damn well did."

The judge cracked down his gavel. "Ms.

Wu, no more of that from your client. Mr. Brandt, I'm warning you for the last time. No more outbursts, do you hear me? You address your remarks to the bench."

"Yes, your honor. I'm sorry."

"You've been sorry before, too. Don't let it happen again." Johnson made a notation in front of him and came back, fixing Wu with an impatient and angry glare, as if she'd been the one abusing the court's protocol. "Minor is ordered detained," Johnson said. "Bailiffs, take him back to the cabins."

And with that, Johnson tapped his gavel, stood and made his exit out the back door to the courtroom.

So abrupt was the decision and Johnson's disappearance that for a minute a dead calm settled over the courtroom. Wu's hand went to her stomach, where she felt a deep and sudden hollowness. Behind her, she heard Linda saying, "That's it? That can't be it. They're not letting him out?" Then, as Bailiff Nelson approached the table: "Wait a minute. *Andrew!*"

The boy whirled around in his seat to face his mother.

Wu held out a hand to the bailiff. "Please! Give us one minute, all right?"

In the gallery, Linda North had left her seat and was coming forward. She was nearly to the bullpen's railing and then suddenly Andrew, too, was on his feet. Nelson, though, had reached him. He growled "Uh, uh" and put a restraining hand on his shoulder with enough force to topple the chair and send him sprawling. With his handcuffs on, Andrew couldn't reach out to break his fall. His head hit the linoleum floor and for an instant he lay stunned.

"What are you doing?" Linda was now at the guardrail, and she screamed. *"Leave him alone!"*

"Linda!" Hal North, too, was out of his seat, coming up behind his wife.

The other bailiff, the young-looking one who'd been talking with the court reporter before the judge appeared, came from nowhere and insinuated himself in the space between Wu and Linda, blocking the mother's access to her son. "Take it easy," he said, holding up both his hands. "Easy. That's enough! *Enough!*" Then he turned to Nelson. "You, too, Ray. I'll take him."

"I got him," Nelson said with some heat.

"Go easy, then," the second bailiff retorted.

"It's okay, Mom! I'm okay." Andrew, from the floor. "I got caught off-balance, that's all. I'm fine."

On either side of him, the bailiffs seemed to have worked out their turf differences, and now raised Andrew to his feet.

"Let him go," Wu said. "You don't have to manhandle him."

The second bailiff turned and looked at her. Up close, she saw that the face, youthful and innocent from a distance, was heavily pockmarked and held a pair of gray, old, empty eyes. Wu thought that in spite of his relatively few years, the officer had already worked in the system long enough to become inured to the innate horror of it. He was a jailer, plain and simple. A zookeeper. And yet, he'd almost apologized to her, and still appeared more humane than his partner, for all that. "No one's going to hurt your client," he said.

But Wu checked him. "That's already happened. I want that bump on his head looked at right away. I'll be along to see him in a few minutes, and I want him to have seen somebody by then. Is that clear?" Wu included them both in her sights. "And while we're at it, Officer," she said to the second bailiff, "what's your name?"

"Cottrell," he said. "Ray Cottrell."

She wrote it down on her legal pad, looked up again at both of them with a question. "You just called him . . ." She motioned to Nelson. "You just called *him* Ray."

"That's what his mother called him, too. What about it?"

Nothing, Wu realized, and said, "I'm holding you both responsible." Her threat didn't much instill the fear of God in either of them. The two men, unmoved, shared a glance. But then it was Nelson who touched Andrew's shoulder and said, "Let's go. Easy."

Andrew threw his mother a last look of despair, then turned and started walking with the bailiffs, back toward the lockup.

5

Wu had been an attorney for five years. During that time, she'd mostly done litigation work for Freeman's firm, mixed with a steady if unexceptional flow of criminal cases that she picked up in the usual way, the so-called conflicts cases. She was on the list for court appointments, and once a month she would appear in court while a succession of criminal cases were called and doled out mostly to the Public Defender's Office. Every few cases, though, there would be more than one defendant — accomplices in robberies or drug deals.

In these cases, the Public Defender's Office could not take on more than one of the defendants; it would be a conflict of interest. And so the court would appoint one of the on-hand lawyers sitting in the courtroom on conflicts day to represent the other defendants. In this way, Wu had represented a wide variety of clients and gotten what she had thought (until today) was a well-grounded schooling in the nuts and bolts and even some of the intricacies of criminal law.

But she'd never been assigned to a murder case. Never before had she confronted such a serious charge. In fact, until this weekend no criminal client had ever paid her directly — her fees in the conflicts cases were paid by the court. She was standing on new ground now, and finding that it shook perilously under her feet. She'd blown her first skirmish badly. Ill-prepared and overconfident, she'd foolishly failed to prepare her clients for the worst, in part because she didn't believe that the worst was going to transpire. In her experience thus far, deals were always a possibility.

Now, out in the hallway with the Norths, Wu spoke up right away, a stab at damage control. "I've got those bailiffs' names and badge numbers and I want to assure you both that I'm going to file a complaint before I leave this building."

North spoke up. "I wouldn't waste my time. Andrew admitted he was off-balance. The guy was just doing his job. My question is what the hell just happened? You told us you'd get him out."

"I said I thought it was possible."

"It never seemed to get close to possible in there. There wasn't any real discussion at all." North wore running shoes, jeans, a blue denim shirt, a corduroy sports coat, but the casual dress was nowhere reflected in his posture or attitude. The bulldog face was shut down, expressionless, the ice-blue eyes fathomless. "It doesn't give me a whole hell of a lot of faith in all the rest, I'll tell you that."

"Hal." Linda put a hand on her husband's arm.

He kept his eyes on Wu. "So where does this leave us?"

"I'm going to talk to the DA," Wu said. "Appeal the detention."

"I would hope so," North said. "I don't care what it costs."

"I don't think the money's the point, sir."

"Well, if it isn't, that would be a first. Maybe I'll go have a word with the man myself."

In an odd reversal, Wu looked to the wife for support, but Linda's eyes never left the door to the courtroom. It was almost as though she still expected her son to walk out any minute. Wu came back to North. "That really wouldn't be a good idea, sir. Look," she said, "whatever the judge said in there, the truth is that minors get out on serious charges all the time."

"Not this time," he said.

"No. I know that."

Linda spoke up. "So what do we do now?"

Before the fiasco in the courtroom, Wu had been hoping to get a chance to sit with Andrew and his parents in the relatively comfortable environment of their home. There, she would show all of them the evidence she'd already assembled from the discovery documents she'd received that so clearly — in her opinion — would damn Andrew if he went to trial as an adult. With Hal North in her corner, and Linda presumably already on board, it would be the three of them "against" the son, and Wu would be able to orchestrate the talk that would result in Andrew's understanding that he needed to admit.

Now, with Hal in a slow-boiling fury at her failure to get the detention lifted, with Linda still woefully ignorant of the strategy Wu had already put in motion, and with Andrew back in his cell, Wu realized that she had to change her plan on the wing. If they all sat down together right now — in Andrew's cell or anywhere else — the three-to-one odds in her favor would be closer to three-to-one against, with Hal quite possibly unwilling to argue with his characteristic force for the need to admit, and Linda and Andrew dead set against.

The dynamic had become completely skewed. Her best bet now — as the most committed to her position — was to take on Andrew one on one. Win him over as she'd won his stepfather the day before. Andrew didn't need to hear Linda's arguments why he should consider the feasibility of an adult trial on the really very unlikely chance that he would get acquitted. He didn't need that kind of support. He needed to be frightened, and convinced.

Linda repeated her question. "So what do we do now?"

"Now," Wu said, "I think it's critical that I spend some time alone with Andrew. He needs to understand what he's up against, that he's here for the long haul. He's got to see the evidence they've got. Mostly, he's got to realize that he's in the system, and that he needs his lawyer more than he needs his parents right now."

"You don't think we should see him?" Linda clearly didn't like the decision. "I mean, while we're already here? This is a good time for us."

"You can visit him anytime, Mrs. North, anytime you want. But right now he's going to be pretty upset with me, as I realize that both of you are. I need to try to make that right with Andrew, though, as soon as I can, so we can begin to cooperate and work together." She looked from Hal to Linda. "Look, I don't blame either of you for being frustrated, but in a sense the hearing in there didn't change anything.

Andrew still needs to be clear on what he needs to do." She threw what she hoped was a meaningful glance at Hal. "That hasn't changed. I really think both of you need to talk, so the next time you're with him, you present a united front. So we're all saying the same thing."

She waited, holding her breath. From Linda's perspective, she knew that her words were probably close to indecipherable. But she hoped that Hal would understand her allusion and step in. And he did. "She's right, hon," he said. "You held his hand all weekend. He doesn't need any more of that now. He needs some solid advice, legal advice. And Amy here is right. We need to talk, too, you and me."

"About what?"

"This whole plea business." At the mention of the topic again, Linda's eyes went wide with surprise, perhaps with anger. But Hal cut off her reply. "I just said it needs to be discussed. It's complicated."

"I don't even like the sound of it," Linda said.

Wu stepped in. "That's why I think it's important that both of you talk. Meanwhile, this is when I need to go up and see Andrew."

Linda stood still for a moment, then nodded, turned and, without another word, walked off. Hal hung back another second.

"Don't fuck this one up, too," he told her, then whirled and jogged after his wife.

But before she went up to see Andrew, Wu knocked at the door to Johnson's chambers and was told to enter. He was out of his robes now, standing at the side of the room, a golf club in his hand. "Ah, Ms. Wu. Just one second." A black plastic contraption with a little blue flag in it popped a golf ball back across the rug, right to his feet, and he stopped it with his putter.

What was it, Wu thought, with men and these games in their offices?

She got right to her point. "Your honor, I'm sorry to interrupt you, but you'll want to know what happened in the courtroom just after you left the bench."

When she finished her description of Andrew's mistreatment, Johnson sighed with resignation. "My bailiffs. I call them my two rays of sunshine. It's a very little bit of a joke."

He leaned to pick up his ball. Pocketing it, replacing his putter in the golf bag next to his desk, he turned back to her and was all business. "Ms. Wu," he said, "I realize you must be a bit disappointed at my ruling in there, although I don't know what else you could have possibly expected. But given what you just told me — that Mr.

112

Bartlett himself admitted that he got off-balance and fell — what do you expect me to do? The bailiffs are there to keep order in the courtroom. Sometimes — right after a prosecution verdict, for example, or a ruling like today — that takes some physical restraint. You'd be surprised. I've seen kids turn on their lawyers, even rush the bench. It happens. The bailiffs have to be, if not primed for action, then at least in a perpetually aggressive state of mind. You said your client was getting up, turning to get in physical contact with his mother. That can't be allowed to occur."

"Your honor, did you see Mrs. North? She was coming up to hug her son. She wasn't going to slip him a weapon."

"Maybe not, but you sure can't treat people differently depending on what they look like, can you? It sounded to me like Officer Nelson applied a little force and your client lost his balance. And Cottrell? If anything, it sounds like he took your side."

Wu shrugged. "I don't know if I'd go that far. It wasn't like what had happened bothered him. He just wanted to avoid the hassle getting any bigger."

"Right." Johnson raised a finger. "That's because Officer Cottrell knows how to keep things under control up here. You know why? 'Cause he's been on the other side."

At Wu's questioning look, Johnson nodded. "This isn't a secret. He's been featured in several articles. When he was a kid, he was at that same table as your client, next to a defense attorney very much like you. He's spent time in the cottages, so he knows how it works up there."

"The bailiff's done time?"

He nodded. "Juvenile time. He slid from a bad foster care situation into the juvie system. But he's the success story — why we do this complicated fandango around rehabbing kids as opposed to punishing them. Sometimes it works. Often enough to make the effort worthwhile."

Wu thought back to the courtroom, to the look she'd gotten at Cottrell's eyes, with their strange flat affect. She'd attributed it to a boredom with the bureaucratic routines of his job. But Johnson's remarks struck a deeper chord. The long-term denizens of the legal system had learned, out of a sense of self-preservation, to live below the radar.

Johnson, reading her mind, said, "Most of these guys, they know how to get by here. You'd be surprised how many juvenile veterans of the system get out and then when they grow up want to work in it. It's where they're comfortable. They know how things work. So if somebody like Cottrell goes proactive around a situation like today in the courtroom, my bet is it's because he wants to keep things on an even keel between Nelson and your client. Not because he's some super-aggressive sociopath."

"I didn't say that, your honor. I didn't even imply it. But the one bailiff — the other one, Nelson — it wasn't as innocent as all that. I thought you'd just want to know."

"I do want to know," Johnson said. "Of course I want to know. And I'm grateful that you thought to come and tell me."

This time, Wu got to the attorney visiting room before Andrew and so had a moment to take in some of its admittedly unpleasant flavor. It reminded her of nothing so much as the dean's office at her old high school — linoleum floor, pitted green metal table in the center of the room, cork bulletin boards on both sides, a gray filing cabinet, that one window by the old-fashioned one-piece desk that Andrew had used earlier, a faint smell of disinfectant and sweat.

Andrew came to the door, escorted by a bailiff Wu didn't recognize. He wasn't handcuffed, though, and after he'd taken a step inside the small room, he stopped, his head turning quickly from side to side. "Where's my mom?" he asked.

"Not here." Wu kept the explanation un-adorned.

He let out some sort of disaffected grunt, shook his head, shrugged, and slouched over to his desk, throwing an arm over the back of it. Wu was aware that the bailiff had closed the door, leaving them alone. She looked back down to Andrew, who was busy barely acknowledging her. He tossed the brown hair that hung over his forehead, swiped at it with his hand. When he'd been in the courtroom, he'd appeared to be truly vulnerable and harmless. Here Wu saw him in a different, perhaps a truer, light. He was an angry young adult — tall, well-proportioned, muscular. Traces of acne and a few days' worth of stubble added to the picture.

Wu asked about his head, if it hurt where he'd cracked it against the floor. He told her it was fine. Staring down at his fingers, he scratched at the desk, the noise like a mouse scampering in drywall. She continued to stare down and across at him until eventually he looked up, brushed back his forelock again, crossed his arms over his chest.

They held each other's gaze.

"So?" he said.

Wu wasn't about to put herself through the same discussion she'd just had with his parents. Neither was she inclined to start out on the defensive, so she took a deep breath and came right back at him. "So here's the thing, Andrew. With what just happened down there, you might be starting to get the picture that you're in a world of hurt. This isn't some situation where you pay the fine and do community service like last time and it's all over. This is murder. This is as serious as it gets."

Andrew started to open his mouth, "But I didn't —"

She cut him off. "Do it? Not the point right now. I heard you say it in court. Then I heard it again from your mother just now. Maybe we'll get to it sometime, what you did or didn't do. For the moment, though, we need to talk about the evidence they've got. You know what discovery is?"

"Yeah. It's when somebody finds something for the first time, like Columbus and America, that kind of thing."

The little shithead was being wise with her. She flared, her voice harsh. "Yeah, that's right. Good guess." She stood up, grabbed her briefcase, went to the locked door and knocked on it. "Guard!"

Andrew tipped his desk over getting out of it. "What are you doing?"

She ignored him, knocked again. "Guard!"

"Wait a minute!"

This time the bailiff Cottrell came to the

door, his face in the barred window. Wu said, "Open up," and the sound of the key turning filled the room.

"Where are you going? Wait a minute."

She whirled on him. "I don't have a minute. Not for games. You don't want to help me, fine, I'll do it alone."

The guard stood waiting behind her, the door now ajar.

"No, wait, please . . ."

Wu motioned to the guard. The door closed. She turned around. "Get wise with me again, good-bye," she said. She pulled a chair to the center table, hoisted her briefcase, sat down, stared at her client for a long moment. Eventually, he righted his own desk, squeezed into the seat, waited.

An uneasy truce.

"First," she said, "let's talk about what you've admitted and see where we are after that. You were in fact at Mr. Mooney's the night it happened, practicing for a play. Then, sometime around nine o'clock, you left to walk around the neighborhood and memorize some lines you were having trouble with. You were gone for about a half hour."

"I was."

"Okay. Then when you got back, you saw what had happened and called nine one one."

"Right."

Wu came forward, elbows on the table between them. "But you didn't wait for the police to come? Even though the dispatcher asked you to stay at the scene?"

"I was right down the street." He shifted where he sat, defensively, and Wu felt some gratification. At least Andrew knew that he'd done *something* wrong, that was certain. "I couldn't handle waiting inside with both of them there." His voice rose, more defensiveness. "What was I supposed to do? They were just . . . It didn't matter. They weren't going to move. Nothing changed in there."

Wu sat back with an exaggerated calm, crossed her own arms, leveled her eyes at him. "Okay, then. I think it's time to talk about discovery. Leaving Columbus out of it."

Wu had her documents out on the table and she was popping Andrew pretty hard with some of the facts they contained. "So you say here in this interview that you and Laura were getting along great?"

"Right."

Wu flipped to another page she'd marked. "Then how come, do you think, Laura's mother says you were close to breaking up?"

"I don't know." He squirmed. "Okay, maybe we were having some troubles, but nothing big."

119

"Having some troubles isn't really the same as getting along great, though, is it?" She pressed him. "So you lied about it. Why didn't you want the police to know?"

"That's pretty obvious, isn't it?" Then he added, "But I didn't know they'd talked to Laura's mom."

"That's not why you lied, Andrew," she said. "It's why you thought you could get away with the lie." She paused, then continued almost gently. "They talk to everybody, Andrew. Don't you understand that yet? *Everybody*. Family, friends, friends of friends, neighbors, acquaintances, co-workers, students, teachers — you name it. And everybody's got a story. When it doesn't agree with yours, guess who looks bad?"

But Andrew was shaking his head. "Still, no way they can prove I did this," he said. "I haven't told that many lies. Maybe some small ones."

"You mean like your car? You call that a small one?"

He threw a glance at the ceiling, then leaned onto the back legs of his chair. Lifting then dropping his shoulders, he stared into emptiness.

Wu found her place in the documents, read silently, then raised her eyes to his. "When the police arrived, Andrew, you told them you'd walked to the rehearsal that night. You remember that? You don't call that a lie?"

"I couldn't have them go look at the car right then. I went down to it after I called them."

"You mean after your nine one one call?"

"Yeah. To get away from the scene. I already told you I couldn't stand being in the room with them."

Wu clasped her hands in front of her. "So instead of waiting just outside Mooney's door for the police to arrive, you walked — what, a block or two? — back to your car."

"That's right."

"And why, again, did you do that?"

He moved his hair out of his eyes. "I already told you, I . . ."

Bam! She slapped down hard on the table between them. *"Cut the shit, Andrew! Right now!"* She raised a finger and pointed it at him. "You went to the car to get rid of the gun and you lied to the cops because you didn't want them to look where you'd hidden it. Isn't that it?"

He stared at her, openmouthed. Wu had truly frightened him now. For the truth was that she hadn't read anywhere in discovery that Andrew had ever mentioned the gun that night. She had read nearly all of the eyewitness testimony and had come to the conclusion that he'd just gotten rid of it. And now his terrified visage verified that she'd guessed right.

Andrew's hand again went to his forehead. "How do you know about that?"

"The same way the police do, Andrew. They know there was a gun left in the room after the shooting, and —"

"But how could *they* know it?"

"The upstairs neighbor told them."

"Who's he? How did he know about any gun?"

"His name's Juan Salarco. Another witness the cops managed to talk to. Also, you might like to know, he's the man who picked you out of the lineup."

"I don't even know the guy."

She pulled some copied and stapled pages from one of her folders, held them up for him to see. "You want to read his statement to the police, or should I just give you the highlights?" But it wasn't really a question and she didn't wait for an answer. "He and his wife happened to hear the shots and right after they both saw you leave —"

"They saw *me* leave? Right after the shots?"

She nodded. "Both of 'em."

"Then they're lying. They've got to be lying."

She had him running now, badly scared,

and this served her purpose. Time to hit him again, make him begin to see how really bad it was. "Lying or not, the fact remains that Mr. Salarco did call nine one one from the phone at Mooney's place" — she looked down at the pages — "exactly six minutes and forty seconds *before* you called from the same phone. And he later told Sergeant Taylor that while he was there making the emergency call, he saw a gun on the coffee table, which wasn't there when the first police unit arrived."

Now she leaned forward, her eyes boring into his. "Do the math, Andrew. Only one person could have taken and hidden the gun, and that's you. You took it to your car to get rid of it later, and that's why you had to lie. And that's not a small lie. It's a whopper."

Ray Nelson escorted Andrew back to his cell, while Cottrell led Wu down the corridor in the other direction. At the door to the cabins, he held the door open for her.

"Thank you," she said.

"That turn out all right?"

She stopped in mild surprise.

"You weren't in there too long before you wanted out," he said. "Sometimes that's a bad sign."

"We just had to establish a few ground rules," she said. "After that it went fine."

He was walking next to her on the short path that led down to the razor-wire gate. "He doesn't want to admit, does he?"

They'd come to the gate and she stopped and turned to face him. The walkway wasn't very wide. She looked up into his face. "I can't really discuss that, you know. I'm sorry."

"Sure. I understand." He unlocked the gate, pulled it open for her. "That's the hardest part, realizing you're really in. You're not getting out and going home with Mom and Dad."

"Yes, well . . ."

He held up a hand, perhaps an apology, if one was needed, that he'd made her uncomfortable. "Just making conversation," he said. "Have a nice day, Ms. . . . ?"

Wu realized that she didn't need to be such a hard-ass. She extended a hand, offered a smile. "I'm sorry, my mind's still back in there. Amy Wu."

"Nice to meet you."

"You, too. Well, I'm sure we'll be seeing more of each other."

"I'll watch out for your boy."

She briefly met his eyes. "I'd appreciate that," she said. "He might need it. Thank you."

6

"Am I interrupting?" Wu asked.

Hardy looked up from the billing and utilization numbers report, one of several similar management tools that Norma gave him every week for his review and comments — good enough numbers, but numbers nevertheless. He jumped at the opportunity to leave them, closing the folder, motioning with his hand. "I was hoping you'd make it back today."

"Actually, I've been back awhile, hunkered down in my office." Wu motioned behind her. "I waited until Attila abandoned her post out there."

"Probably a good idea." He pushed his chair back from his desk, stood up and stretched, moved toward the bar counter. "You want some coffee, a beer, water, a rare old Bordeaux?"

"No, thanks. I'm fine."

"Just as well," Hardy said. "I don't have any rare old Bordeaux. David did, though. About this time of day, I'd often come down and he'd be halfway through a bottle of something outrageous."

"You miss him a lot, don't you?"

Hardy opened the refrigerator, then straightened up. He turned to her and nodded. "Yeah, I do." Then, shrugging with some awkwardness, he reached down and grabbed a bottled water, turned back again. "So how'd it go?"

Wu lowered herself onto the couch. "Not perfectly, I'm afraid. The judge — Johnson — detained him."

"No surprise there. It was murder. They always detain."

"I know, but I thought maybe with his age and no previous record, plus Hal North's money if they asked him to pay for a private security guard for Andrew . . . Anyway, it doesn't matter — I never even got the chance to argue that." She paused again. "Jason Brandt — the prosecutor? — he came out swinging and got all histrionic. I guess it worked."

"How'd the clients take it? They fire you?"

She broke a bare smile. "Not yet, but every call I got this afternoon when I got back here, I thought I'd throw up."

"Thanks for sharing." But he grinned, softening it. "So what's the status now?"

"Well," she said, "if there's any silver lining, it's a loud wake-up call for Andrew. The continued detention blew him away.

He thought North would somehow take care of it like he always has. But when Andrew realized that wasn't happening, it gave me the chance to acquaint him with a few hard truths."

"Like?"

"Like the evidence." Suddenly animated, Wu came forward on the couch. "It might have been the first time he actually realized *why* they arrested him. So I went through what little discovery I'd seen, which was a good start, since it placed him at the murder scene with the weapon, for example."

"He didn't already know that?"

She shook her head. "He thought he'd gotten rid of the gun without having mentioned it to anybody. Which in fact he did. But — bad luck — a witness saw it first. I surprised him with what he must have done, and sure enough, he admitted it. And this is to say nothing of five or six other evasions and outright lies, or the ID."

"He didn't know he'd been ID'd?"

"Not the specifics. Though by the time I left him I believe he was getting a clue."

Hardy sat back in his chair. "And how, again, is this a silver lining?"

"Well, it is," she said. "It really is."

"I want to believe you, but traditionally it's not good news for the client when the DA's got you nailed."

"It is this time."

"And why is that?"

"Because Andrew finally sees that they can put him away for life."

"And that's good news? Maybe it's semantics," Hardy said. "The meaning of 'good.'"

"It is good. It means Andrew's on his way to admitting."

"I would hope so, given the fact that you've already made a deal to that effect with Mr. Boscacci, haven't you? I didn't imagine that whole thing, did I? Boscacci filing juvie? All of that?" Hardy chewed on the inside of his cheek, added ruminatively, "Although I still can't imagine why Boscacci went for it."

Wu curled a leg under herself on the couch. "Because it's all about numbers. The public understands convictions. Jackman's gearing up for reelection. If Andrew admits, Jackman gets not one, but two murder convictions on the books, instead of a long messy trial with a sympathetic teenage defendant and a wealthy stepfather with ties to the media. You would have done the same thing."

"Maybe, but that's me. And I'm notoriously softhearted."

"Right. Anyway, I reminded Allan how hard it is to get convictions, San Francisco juries, blah, blah, blah. I told him it was possible North might even be monetarily grateful at some time in the future for saving his son the extra fifty years in the slammer, perhaps a slight exaggeration on my part."

"I hope slight," Hardy said.

Wu shrugged that away. "I don't think Allan bought it anyway. But he did buy the fact that this was a young man's crime of passion. By the time Andrew's twenty-five, he'll be a different person, rehabilitated by the juvenile system instead of hardened by the hard time. And so on."

"In other words, you snowed him."

"Maybe I did pile it on a little. But this is such a classically good move. It's actually got some moral underpinnings."

"Always a plus." Hardy drank from his bottled water. He put the bottle down on his desk, took a deep breath, let it out. A longer silence settled in the space. The plantation shutters over the office windows weren't drawn, and outside the shafts of early evening sun suddenly seemed glaringly bright in contrast to the muted office lighting. Finally Hardy spoke. "I bet you can guess what's going through my mind."

Her face tight with tension, Wu nodded, but answered confidently enough. "I'll be seeing Andrew first thing again tomorrow morning and tie it up tight. Believe me, he definitely got it by the time I left today. He sees it."

"He'll admit?"

"I'm sure he will."

"You're sure he will. But Allan Boscacci thinks he already has? Is that right?"

"No. Not that he already has. Just that he will."

"But Boscacci's acted on that. And he'll expect you to do what you promised in return?"

"And I will. Andrew will. He'll see there's no other real option. He already sees it, I'm sure."

"You're sure." Hardy cast his eyes at his ceiling, brought them down and ran a hand over his cheek. Now he looked over at his young associate. He knew that she was still suffering over the loss of her father, laboring under who knew what other pressures. The last thing Hardy wanted to do was kill her initiative or micromanage her cases to death, but for a moment he was tempted to have her call Boscacci right there from his office. Clear the air with the DA's office, at least. Let the chief assistant know that the deal might not be as solid as he'd been led to believe. Later, privately, Hardy could even plead Wu's pain and suffering to Boscacci, and this might somehow mitigate the consequences if things went wrong, which according to Murphy's Law they must, since they could.

On the other hand, he didn't want to send a no-confidence message to one of his bright young lights. He himself had carved his own niche in San Francisco's legal world by being somewhat of a loose cannon, taking risks beyond those which, he knew, any responsible boss would have approved. He strongly believed in the advice of Admiral Nelson, "Always go right at 'em." Ask permission later. That's what victorious sea captains — and winners in general — always did.

Didn't they?

Hardy gave his associate a last, ambiguous look that mingled worry and hope, and she responded with a quick bob of her head. "Don't worry, sir. It'll happen."

"I tell you what, Wu," he said. "I'm sure hoping you're right."

Hardy parked on Bryant Street across from the Hall of Justice. Traffic was light and curb space, so precious during the workday, was everywhere. Behind him, the sun was going down with a gaudy splash. The usual sunset gale had started up off the Bay and it whistled by the windows of his car, throwing pages of newspapers, candy wrappers, random grit and other debris through the long shadows in front of him.

He checked his watch. Glitsky was ten minutes late.

Hardy had paged him, their signal, before he'd left his office. He wasn't thrilled at having to wait. It gave him too much time to think about what Wu had done. He pushed the knob in his dash, turned up the latest Fleetwood Mac, who'd somehow managed to lift themselves off the oldies heap and get back in the game again.

Wu's situation? It would play the way it played.

"Sorry I'm late." Glitsky opened the door and slid into the seat beside him.

Lost in the music, Hardy hadn't seen him leave the Hall or approach the car. Now he found himself mildly surprised by the sight of his friend in full uniform. In the nearly dozen years during which Glitsky had been the lieutenant in charge of the homicide detail, he hadn't often worn his blues, preferring instead the more informal look of khaki slacks, usually a shirt and tie, and almost invariably a flight jacket, faux fur collar and all.

Now Glitsky was the picture of proper police protocol. He wore the uniform, his shield and decorations, gunbelt and gun. He held his hat in his lap at the moment, and the rest of him and his gear seemed to take up more space than he had when he dressed more like a civilian. Hardy thought it interesting that even the face looked more at home and, ironically, less threatening, with the uniform under it. Law officers were supposed to look authoritative and tough, and Glitsky, with his hatchet nose, cropped graying hair and the distinctive scar that ran through both lips, looked like a working cop, not like a scary citizen.

Now the working cop, fixing his seat belt, shot a look across the seat, saw Hardy's eyes on him and said, "What?"

Hardy turned the key in the ignition, put the car in gear, started rolling. "Just admiring the fancy figure you cut in your uniform. I can't seem to get used to it. You catch the peanut thief?"

"He wasn't a thief. He just changed the drawers."

"Somebody goofing with you."

"Maybe," Glitsky said, "knowing I'm such a big fan of practical jokes."

"You are? And to think that all this while I understood you favored the death penalty for practical jokes."

"I do." Glitsky squirmed in his seat, getting himself arranged. "These seats are too small for normal people, you know that?"

"Wouldn't one have to have a nodding acquaintance with normal to make that statement? And if so, how could you?"

Glitsky sat, not exactly squirming, but shifting in his seat. After a bit, he seemed to be probing with his right hand into the left side of his torso. He took in a big breath and released it, looking ahead, quiet, frowning.

"You okay, Abe?"

Glitsky sucked in a breath again, settled into his seat. In another minute, he sighed heavily. "My guts," he said.

They drove another block or two in silence. "Me, I keep waking up." Hardy spoke without any preamble. "It's not like I don't go to sleep. After I drink myself into oblivion, I do, but then a couple of times every week I have these dreams, always different but always with the same theme, like somebody's closing in on me and I've got to shoot them, but there's no bullets in the gun, or the knife disintegrates in my hand, or the cage they're in, the bars melt, and then they rush me and I wake up."

"I don't dream at all," Glitsky said. "But my guts hurt."

Another block and they hit a light. "You ever think about seeing somebody? Maybe talk about it?"

"Nobody can talk about it." His tone made it clear: this was Glitsky's last word on the subject.

The subject, of course, was the shootout.

Since then, each of the four survivors

were suffering, dealing in their own respective ways with the psychic toll of what they'd had to do. Gina Roake, who'd been engaged to Freeman when he died, spent most of her time exercising in martial arts or shooting at the range. Her earlier and lifelong passion for defense work had all but dissipated and she came into work only sporadically. She had completed a few hundred pages of a legal thriller that, she said, was going to expose the rottenness of the whole system.

Hardy's brother-in-law, Moses McGuire, previously a heavy but controlled social drinker, had descended into a deep fog of alcohol. He wasn't yet drinking in the mornings, but Hardy hadn't seen him close to sober in eight months. He'd gained thirty pounds. He hadn't shaved or trimmed his beard and his hair hung down to his shoulders. He and Susan were having problems in their marriage.

Hardy knew all about his own dreams, his problems with motivation, his feelings about the system he worked in, the cynical machinations he orchestrated nearly daily, the bibulous lunches, then dinners, then late nights. He figured his problems, too, would pass. In some ways the shaken foundations of his life seemed all of a piece with the world in general, the terrorism and war and madness that were now part of the daily fabric and that, for him at least, hadn't existed since he'd been in Vietnam, and that since those long ago days, he'd naively allowed himself to believe would never exist again.

And now Abe and his guts. "Nobody can talk about it," Glitsky repeated.

"I heard you the first time," Hardy said. Then, "You worried somebody's going to find out someday?"

"You're not?"

"It crosses my mind from time to time."

"It's eating me up from inside." As though to prove it, Glitsky pushed again at his side. "Especially since my promotion."

They drove. Hardy said, "What does Treya say?"

"Nothing." Then: "I don't talk about it. Nothing's wrong. She doesn't need to worry about it. I'll get over it." Glitsky stared out the side window while pushing his right hand into his guts, just above his gunbelt. "I don't understand this," he said. "When Bruce Willis shoots somebody, they roll the credits and everybody's fine."

Hardy dropped Glitsky a few blocks beyond his own house, at the corner of Lake and Twenty-first. The deputy chief walked, counting ten houses up to the address. He stopped and noted the location of the garage to the side and a little behind the two-story, stand-alone stucco house. Then he continued on the sidewalk and turned up the polished riverstone path that bisected a neat lawn. Up three steps to an unlit brick and stucco porch, he stood on the landing and waited for a moment, listening. Through the glass at eye level in the door, he saw lights in the back of the house, some shadows dancing on the walls.

He turned back and checked the street. Like Glitsky's own block, it dead-ended at the southern edge of the Presidio. From what he had heard and read about the murder of Elizabeth Cary, it had been just about at this time of day, a week ago tomorrow. Still not exactly full night. Witnesses certainly could have seen something. Especially if they ran to a window, as someone must have after hearing the enormous boom of a .9mm handgun. But no one had reported seeing anyone.

Glitsky pushed at the doorbell. The sound echoed in the house and a dog barked.

A dog? Glitsky hadn't realized there was a dog, and didn't know if it meant anything. Still, he wished he'd read it someplace, in one of the reports. For a moment, apprehension swept over him, the feeling that he wasn't prepared enough for this interview, that he shouldn't be here. His role in the gunfight last year had forfeited his right to be here, to be a cop at all.

It was just like he felt every day, at his regular job — deputy chief of investigations. He didn't deserve to be where he was.

But then a figure was visible through the glass down the hallway. Glitsky put aside his own angst and stood straight, arranging his face to show sympathy. If the man he was about to interview was not a cold-blooded wife killer, then he was himself a victim who'd recently lost his life companion to violence.

The door opened. "Yes?"

Cary came as advertised — he looked at least sixty, was thirty or more pounds over-weight and sported a thinning tonsure around a shiny dome of a head. He wore rimless bifocals, a white shirt and solid dark tie, loosened at the neck. Glitsky knew that the man had worked as the head accountant of a medium-sized engineering firm located in Embarcadero Two for the past seventeen years. From the look of him, he didn't get out of the office much.

"Mr. Cary? I'm Deputy Chief Glitsky. I wonder if you could spare me a few minutes of your time?"

"Of course," he said with a weary resignation. Then added, "Sorry," for no apparent reason. He reached over, flicked a switch, and suddenly there was light in the living room and over the porch. "Come on in."

Glitsky stepped over into the house, followed Cary a few steps over to a couch, where they sat. The dog was a light brown, medium-sized mutt with a lot of Lab in him, and he gave Glitsky's legs the once-over. "If you're not okay with dogs, Ranger can go."

"Dogs are fine." Glitsky gave him a little scratch behind his ears. Satisfied after a second or two, Ranger went over next to Cary and sat against the couch. His master began to pet him absently. Glitsky suddenly became aware of the smell of pizza just as Cary said, "We were having some dinner, but I wasn't hungry anyway. Do you need to see the kids, too? They're back in the kitchen."

"Maybe after a while. We'll see." Glitsky cleared his throat. "First, I wanted to say how sorry I am about your loss. You have my deepest sympathy."

Cary managed to nod.

"Secondly, I know that we, the police, haven't made much progress yet, but I wanted to assure you that we have no intention of letting up on the investigation. He is out there and we still have every hope of finding him."

"You're assuming it was a man, then?"

"No. I didn't mean to give that impression. Is there some reason you think it might have been a woman?"

Cary lifted his head and shook it. "No. I was just reacting to what you said. I have no idea in the world who it could have been." He sighed, scratched at Ranger's head. "I'm so tired of saying that, but it's true. You had to know Elizabeth. She had no enemies. Really. I mean, nobody's perfect, but she was a cheerful, sweet . . ." He stopped, blinked a couple of times, finally completed the thought: "A cheerful, sweet woman."

"We keep hearing that from all reports, sir. And Inspector Belou tells me that the two of you were getting along as well. No conflicts." He didn't phrase it as a question.

Cary shrugged, then sighed. There wasn't a trace of defensiveness about him. "We were a team," he said. "That's how we always talked about one another. I don't know what else I can say. We may have had an argument in the past year or so, but if we did, I don't even remember what it was about. We were a team," he repeated. "We just lived a normal life."

Glitsky's original conception of this interview had been that he would start out slow and gradually grill the husband hard on his movements on the night of the murder, and maybe find a hole in the story he'd given to Inspectors Belou and Russell. But now, in the small room, seeing the man in such obvious, all-inclusive pain, he found himself unable to get warm to the idea that Cary was a killer. "I know the inspectors have gone over this with you, sir, but in the past few days, I wonder if something else might have occurred to you — some disagreement your wife might have had with, I don't know, a neighbor, one of your relatives, somebody from your children's school. Maybe even something from a long time ago that you didn't remember in the first days of shock and grief? That you originally didn't see as having any possible connection."

Cary looked down at his dog, stopped petting him and sat back on the couch. He took off his glasses, rubbed them on his pants leg, put them back on. "No," he said, and shook his head.

"What?"

"Nothing, I'm sure." But he went on. "This really isn't possible, I don't think, but Elizabeth does have . . . I mean she did . . . I mean he's still alive."

"Who's that?"

"One of her brothers. She's got three of them, but one of them, Ted, is crazy. He lives down south at Lake Elsinore. He didn't make the funeral."

"And he's, what? Institutionalized?"

"No. He's not clinically crazy, I don't think. Just not completely right, you know what I mean?"

"Why don't you tell me." Glitsky had a small notepad out. "Ted. Last name?"

"Reed. R-E-E-D."

"Okay. And how is he crazy?"

"I shouldn't say crazy. That's just how we always refer to him. He was born premature and always had lots of learning problems. His IQ's probably about eighty-five. He's sad more than anything, really. I haven't seen him in, I don't know, five years or more. But Elizabeth tried to stay in touch on his birthday and Christmas, like that. That's the way she was, she wasn't going to abandon her brother." He sighed. "Anyway, I know she talked to him at Christmas because she made the kids say hi to their Uncle Ted."

"He yelled at us, too."

Glitsky looked up in surprise. Ranger ran over to the tall, gangly boy of about fourteen, hands in his pockets, who had appeared in the hallway. Cary stood up. "Scott . . ." He turned. "Inspector, this is my oldest, Scott. He's sorry that he was eavesdropping. Scott, Inspector . . . I'm sorry."

"Glitsky." On his feet, shaking the boy's hand.

A good solid grip. The boy even made

eye contact. "Nice to meet you, sir."

Cary raised his voice. "You other kids back there, too?"

In a second, the two younger sisters were in the room. Both of them had been crying. Cary introduced them, too, Patricia and Carlene, then apologized to Glitsky again.

He waved it off and looked at the son. "So you were saying, Scott, that your Uncle Ted yelled at you on this phone call?"

"Yes, sir. I finally had to hang up on him."

"What was he yelling about?"

Scott glanced at his father, got a nod and went ahead. "All the presents I got."

"What about them?"

"Well, he asked what I'd got for Christmas and I started to tell him and go down the list, like, you know, and suddenly he's all 'Your mother's got that kind of money?' Really yelling at me. Like if Mom's got all that money, she could send some to him instead of spoiling us . . ." He turned to his father. "You think it might have been him, Dad?"

"No, I don't know. I can't imagine . . ." Cary to Glitsky now: "That's just the way he is. He thinks because we have a little money, we . . . He just doesn't understand. But he's really harmless, I think. Just a little crazy."

"He's a jerk," the son said. "A total jerk."

Cary's face relaxed into something like a smile for the first time. "I can't really argue with that. Even Elizabeth thought he was a pain in the ass. And she liked everybody."

"And he didn't come to the funeral?" Glitsky asked.

"Thank God," Scott said.

"No," Cary answered. "Nobody could reach him."

"So he might not have been down at Lake Elsinore?"

"I don't know. I don't know if the other brothers have reached him yet."

"I bet he did it, the son of a bitch."

"Scott! That's enough. All right." The rebuke's tone wasn't harsh, but it was firm, and effective. The boy still fumed, but in silence. Cary turned to Glitsky. "I've got an address and a phone number down there I can give you, but I'd be very surprised."

Glitsky shrugged. "You never know. It's worth following up."

"I'll go get it."

As Cary went out to the hallway, Glitsky faced the children. "Do any of you guys have any ideas of who might have wanted to hurt your mother?"

The two young girls started crying again,

144

quietly. Ranger started whimpering around them and Scott, repeating over again that he bet it was Uncle Ted, went over to join in the comforting. Glitsky's own emotions began to roil, and incredibly moved, he had to look away for a moment.

Then Cary was back with Ted's numbers on a yellow Post-it. He absently handed it to Glitsky as he gathered his children around him, telling them to go back into the kitchen and finish dinner, then do the dishes and get going on their homework. He'd be in to help in a minute.

When they'd gone, Glitsky said, "You've done well with them. They're good kids."

"All Elizabeth," he said. "I'm only here for decoration." He sighed. "I notice the girls were crying again. Did something happen?"

"I asked if they had any idea of anyone who might have wanted to hurt their mother."

Cary's shoulders sagged. "That's just it. No one could have wanted to hurt her." He seemed to be searching for a way to express it more compellingly. "I mean, she couldn't abide anything even remotely violent, so what reason could anyone have to do this to her? She refused to be in the same room with me when I watched *Law & Order* because she said it reminded her too much of a murder trial she had to sit

145

on a long time ago before I even knew her. That's how she was. So how could someone hurt a person like her? It makes no sense . . ."

But suddenly, Cary's explanation had sparked a question. "What was this murder trial?" Glitsky asked.

"The one Elizabeth was on? I don't really know anything about it. She didn't like to talk about it. As I said, it was before we were even together. At least twenty-five years ago. They found the man guilty and he went to jail."

"You remember his name?"

"No. I don't know if I ever knew it." Cary pushed at the bridge of his eyeglasses. "She really wouldn't talk about it at all. It bothered her that she'd been a part of putting this guy away forever. She just felt tremendous guilt about the whole thing."

"Why? Didn't she think they reached the right verdict?"

"No. It wasn't that. Mostly it was she didn't feel like she should have been sitting in judgment of another person. Even if he was guilty. She wished she'd never done it." Cary put his hand to his head and closed his eyes. After a moment, he opened them again.

"Was it here in San Francisco?" Glitsky asked.

A shrug. "I don't even know that, for

146

sure. I think it must have been right after she got out of school, college. She went to Santa Clara. She may have still been living down there. Maybe one of her brothers would know." He pointed to the Post-it. "Anyway, I've included them in with Ted's number there. But again," he said, "I can't imagine . . ." His voice petered out. "It doesn't really matter anyway. It won't bring her back, will it?"

Even though it was a Monday night, by a little after nine-thirty the crowd was four deep at the bar of the Balboa Cafe, at the corner of Greenwich and Divisadero. Although the intersection had four corners and not three, it went by the nickname of "the triangle" — after the Bermuda Triangle — where singles went to disappear for the weekend. By ten o'clock every night of the week, the three major bars and the streets in front of them were clogged mostly with young professionals, but also (what gave the place its uniquely privileged character) with the sons and daughters of the older generation of San Francisco's elite society.

These people weren't out slumming — they owned the bars and restaurants, and this was where they played with their friends. But the influence and surface glitter drew a fast, smart, ambitious crowd

— local politicians, music celebrities, movie stars in town for a shoot or a party. And, of course, all the others — lawyers on the make, lovelies of both sexes, suppliers of different kinds of fuel.

And because so much juice flowed to this one spot, a regular contingent of hangers-on was also always on hand, literally out in the street, adding to the color. Two well-connected, extremely personable and relatively hip San Francisco cops — Dan Bascom and Jerry Santangelo — had the best and most lucrative permanent assignment in the city. Eight to two, they kept their squad car parked across from the entrance to the Balboa, a presence that only rarely required any muscle. The two of them, along with Tommy Amici, the Balboa's chief valet, hauled in Cuban cigars, tickets to every artistic, cultural or sports event in the tricounty area, business cards and introductions, as though they ran clearinghouses. The *Bay Guardian* had done a story on Amici a few months before where he claimed he made eight thousand dollars a month to park cars. Bascom and Santangelo, also featured prominently in the piece, refused to comment about their income or the other undocumented perks.

Three and a half months ago, Amy Wu had come here for the first time. Since then she'd become one of the regulars.

Tonight she had somehow claimed a stool before the nighttime mob had begun to appear in strength. Now, two cosmopolitans down, she sat sideways to the bar near the front door with her back held straight. A lot of her crossed legs showed beneath her black leather miniskirt.

The noise wasn't jet-engine level, but between the canned music, the buzz of the hundred or so customers in a space that could comfortably hold eighty, and the televisions, nobody here was sharing intimate secrets. Wu was half watching the Giants game and half stringing along two guys, Wayne somebody and his friend. The two of them couldn't seem to decide which one was going to make a move. Wayne wore a wedding ring and Wu ached to tell him, if he did come on to her, that he might want to think about the ring next time.

But for the moment, that was premature.

So far he'd only bought her a drink, wedged himself up next to her stool, told her she was too pretty to be a lawyer, only the thousandth time she'd heard that one, whatever it was supposed to mean.

So he was moving toward it, but not there yet.

The crowd suddenly cheered and Wu looked up at the TV. One of the Giants was in a home-run trot.

Wu drank off half of her drink, put it back down. Wayne had a fist raised as though he'd hit the home run himself, and under his arm a space opened in the press of bodies and she caught a glimpse of Jason Brandt as he pushed his way through the swinging door.

And he saw her, flashed a genuine enough smile, started moving in her direction. In a minute, really before she could do anything even if she'd known what it was she wanted to do, he'd come up beside Wayne, pointed to Wu and said to him, "Excuse me, that's my girlfriend," and was standing at the bar, calling over the bedlam to his good friend Cecil to give him a double JD rocks. Then he turned to her, still smiling. "Hey."

"Hey yourself." Then, to Wayne: "He's not my boyfriend."

Before Wayne could respond, Brandt turned and looked him up and down. "Are you married, dude?" he asked, and clucked disapprovingly, then came back to Wu. "That is bad form. If he's looking to hook up, the least he could do is lose the ring."

"I wasn't trying to hook up," Wayne said. "I just bought the lady a drink. I'm not looking for any trouble."

Brandt's own drink, delivered in seconds, was in his hand, and he raised it to clink Wayne's beer glass. "Then we, my friend,

150

are on the same page. Can I buy you another beer?" He turned and yelled out over
the noise, "Cecil?" But Wayne had already
put the remainder of his beer on the
counter and was gone.

Brandt turned back to Wu and cracked a
grin. "Predators. Scumbag's got a wife at
home with the kids and he's hitting on
babes in bars. There ought to be a patrol
out for those guys, publish their names and
pictures in the papers. Wanna bet he's
going across the street, checking out the
action at Indigo's?" Suddenly he seemed to
notice that Wu wasn't smiling. "What?"

"That's what I want to ask you. What
are you doing, Jason? Chasing off somebody I'm talking to? What's that bullshit?"

He cocked his head. "You kidding? You
think that guy, like, wants to be your
friend?"

Wu's eyes flashed. "Whatever he wants
to be, whatever I want him to be, it's none
of your business. How about that?"

He drew his mouth into a pout, picked
up his drink and had some. "You're mad
about today, aren't you? This afternoon?"

"No."

He looked surprised. "You're not. I
would be."

She shrugged. "It was always a detention
case. I knew that going in."

"Okay. So what are you mad about? You

151

are a little pissed off."

"Yeah, I am pissed off."

"You mean me chasing off that married dweeb?"

"His name is Wayne."

"Oh, excuse me, Wayne. Maybe you didn't hear me, but I just offered to buy him a beer. That's not chasing him off."

"You chased him off. You ever think about what if I liked him?"

"It never crossed my mind. Did you like him?"

"I didn't not like him. He seemed nice enough."

"Very strong. If he meant that much to you, I really am sorry I ruined your night."

"You didn't ruin my night and that's not the point anyway. The point is it's my life and it's got nothing to do with you."

Brandt put a hand to his chest. "And I would be the last to deny it. But all the books say you don't want to get involved with a married guy."

"Jesus, Jason, he bought me a drink, that's all. That's not exactly involved."

"It's not exactly uninterested either. Did he let his hand, however casually, fall and rest upon any part of your body?"

"My shoulder. One second, leaning over to pay Cecil. That was all."

"I'm sure. But you notice I managed to pay Cecil already without touching anybody. Did he tell you you looked good?"

"Yes, he did." Finally, beginning to be worn down, she broke a small smile. "He said I was too pretty to be a lawyer."

"I love that. Like what, they have an ugly contest to get into law school?"

"I know," she said. "But guys say it all the time. Like it's a compliment. Wow, imagine that, a woman with enough brains to be an attorney and yet not a total scag."

"Not even half a scag, in your case. Not trying to kiss up or anything."

"No. Calling me half a scag is not kissing up."

"Okay, you're way less than even half a scag. You planning to have another drink?"

"You buying?"

"One. If you promise not to touch me."

"You're safe," she said.

7

For eighteen hundred dollars a month, Wu rented a twenty-by-thirty-foot studio apartment on the top floor of a large building on Fillmore Street, north of Lombard. The unit was essentially one large, high-ceilinged room, with a small but functional open kitchen, a tiny toilet and shower-only bathroom in the back corner, a decent clothes closet. The futon she slept on converted into a sofa during the day. She also had an old upholstered reading chair next to an end table where she kept her magazines. The only really nice pieces of furniture, aside from a relatively new, high-tech television set, were a Japanese changing screen and a cherry dining table that her father had bought her when she passed the bar. More often than not this doubled as her work desk.

The best thing about the apartment, and the reason for the ridiculous rent, was the windows — two oversized ones along the Fillmore wall, and another couple over the sink and counter in the kitchen area. From their vantage four stories up, all of these afforded really nice views of Marina Park, with the Golden Gate Bridge off to the left, Marin County just a swan dive and a long swim away.

The built-in bookshelves on the opposite wall were filled to bursting with her CDs and law books and a wide selection of hardbacks, mostly nonfiction — history, biography, political science — but one shelf of novels. A bright multicolored eight-by-ten rug covered most of the hardwood. She kept the place neatly organized and very clean.

Now, wrapped in a heavy turkish nightgown, she sat at her table with her briefcase open and her third cup of morning coffee in front of her. The sun, just up, came in over the sink windows and sprayed the wall to her left. She'd been awake for forty-five minutes, had taken the hottest shower she could stand and gulped down four aspirins. She'd eaten a banana, half a canteloupe, and then three eggs scrambled up with soy and leftover rice. Two cups — not demitasses, but her old cracked mug — of espresso. The throbbing in her head was getting to the manageable state, she thought, but still she hesitated before opening the folder she'd just taken from her briefcase. She had picked it up — newly transcribed interviews, more discovery — from Boscacci.

Last night she'd never gotten to them. Instead, like almost every other night for the past few months, she had gone out to find a party. For a moment there, in the dead of the night with Jason Brandt, it had almost seemed as though it would turn out to be more than that. But by the time the alarm went off, he had gone.

Just as well, she had told herself after the initial stab of realization that he'd left. Probably just as well.

Now that she'd committed her client to admitting the petition against him, she had a long moment of terror imagining that she'd find something among this latest evidence indicating that Andrew had not in fact murdered his teacher and his girlfriend. She didn't believe it was likely, but Dismas Hardy's reaction had brought home to her the seriousness of the situation. She'd leveraged not just herself and her client, but the reputation of the firm.

If she didn't deliver, it would be bad.

Finally, she reached into her briefcase for the folder, pulled it out and set it in front of her, then opened it.

She sat with Hal and Linda at the dining room table again. No sign of the maid this time. The house was almost eerily quiet to Wu after she'd finished acquainting the

Norths with the most recent developments in the case. She needn't have worried about finding exonerating evidence. The new discovery was, if anything, more damning than what they'd seen so far — the testimony of Andrew's best friend, motives, more about the gun. Tension between the couple was thick but transparent, and to break it, Wu had asked if there was anything else about Andrew that she might need to know.

"You already know about the joyride," Linda said.

"No," Wu replied. "I mean before that. Did Andrew have any kind of history of misbehavior or violence? Anything like that?"

"No," Linda said. "Nothing serious."

Hal North cleared his throat. "Well . . ."

"I said nothing *serious*," Linda snapped. "I didn't say nothing at all. Don't give me that look, Hal. I'm not trying to hide anything."

"I'm not giving you a look. We just disagree about what was serious or not."

"Maybe it would be better," Wu interjected, "if you just told me everything and let me decide whether it seems important now or not. I gather there were a few incidents."

"Years ago," Linda said. "Literally, when Hal and I were first together."

"What happened?" Wu asked.

Linda drew a labored sigh. "All right. The one, it was when I told him that Hal and I were getting married. I remember it was a Saturday afternoon, a nice sunny, warm day, and we had the windows open in the kitchen. Andrew was about ten, and still at the age where he liked to sit on my lap, you know?" She sighed again. "Anyway, Alicia — our daughter, Hal's daughter, really — she was there, too, so we could all share the good news." She stopped.

"And what happened?" Wu prompted her.

Linda's lips were pressed tightly together as she fought for control. "He just . . . He just lost his temper."

"Did he hit you?"

When it became obvious that Linda couldn't or wouldn't answer, Hal took over. "He hit her, me, Alicia. He went over to the sink and started throwing the dishes at us. I took a couple of stitches in the face stopping him." He touched a still-visible scar along his jaw, let out a deep breath. "It wasn't pretty."

"But that was seven years ago," Linda said. "And it was my fault anyway. I think I must have just been a terrible mother."

"You are not."

"But I was, before you. You weren't

158

there." Linda turned to Wu. "You should know all this. Andrew's father walked out on us both when he was three, and I needed to work, so I became a waitress, then later a hostess."

"You know Beaulieu?" Hal interrupted with real pride, pointed at his wife. "Hostess at Beaulieu."

This was one of the city's premier dinner destinations, and a magnet for the power elite. Wu wasn't surprised that Linda Bartlett — beautiful, witty, and sophisticated — had wound up with a highly visible job there.

But this was ancient history to Linda, and she waved off her husband's intended flattery. "Anyway, I was young and selfish and liked to have a good time. I admit it, though I'm not proud of it. I had . . . opportunities come my way and I wanted to take advantage of them. Anyway, most of the opportunities came with men attached — it's okay, Hal, she probably needs to know this. It's not like a state secret anyway." Linda sighed and continued. "In any event, the men I saw often weren't so nice to Andrew. And I didn't have the strength or understanding or simple will to do much about it. So he came to hate the idea of my boyfriends." She reached out a hand to her husband. "Including Hal, I'm afraid. At first, at least."

"He still simmers," Hal said. "Maybe not at me, specifically . . ."

But Linda remained defensive. "It's just that he's got this mistrust. He has trouble believing in people in general. And that's me, too, my fault. In the early years, I was so bitter and mad at being dumped, at the unfairness of the way my life had turned out, I just wanted to make up for lost time, and I took it whenever I got a chance. Andrew couldn't count on me. So he's always expecting to be betrayed or abandoned or let down."

"Still?" Wu asked.

"To some degree," Linda admitted.

"Though Kevin has helped," Hal added.

"Kevin?"

"Kevin Brolin," Linda said. "He's a psychologist who's been seeing Andrew."

"For how long?"

"All this time," Hal said. "On and off. He's an anger management specialist."

Fantastic, Wu thought. A jury would love to hear about all these anger issues. But she had to press on. Knowledge was power, and she needed all she could get. "Mrs. North, when you started to tell me about the day you and Hal announced your engagement, you made it sound like Andrew's tantrum was the first of at least a couple of incidents."

Linda looked to Hal, who nodded and

160

said, "Alicia's party?" He went on. "This was maybe three years ago, Alicia's twelfth or thirteenth birthday party. She invited five or six kids, and we made her include Andrew."

"They're only a year apart," Linda said.

"Anyway," Hal went on, "all the girls got into some PlayStation thing and evidently they all decided to gang up to beat Andrew." He shrugged. "I came home to a smashed big-screen, pieces of remote all over the place. Alicia's lip was cut, her eye . . ."

Linda came to her son's defense. "He's really passionate about video games. That's normal enough nowadays. But he also reads, and writes beautifully. He's getting solid B-pluses at Sutro, and you already know he'd gotten the lead in the play."

Hal's whole body seemed to slump. His voice was deep, depressed. Obviously he and Linda's respective spin on Andrew's character traits was a festering wound, and now here in front of the boy's attorney, its binding was unraveling. He looked directly at Wu. "He never laughs. The boy's just not happy in his skin. He hates all team sports. He's changed his haircut and color ten times in two years. He wears torn T-shirts with butt-crack shorts and combat boots." The slab of Hal's face was a monolith of sadness.

161

Persistent, nearly pleading to Wu, Linda started again. "He can play any musical instrument with strings on it."

"But won't ever perform for anyone, or take lessons."

Wu had to call a stop to it. "I think I get the picture," she said. She sat perfectly still with her hands linked on the table in front of her. The Norths were avoiding eye contact with each other, although Hal caught Wu's gaze for a brief instant and rolled his eyes. Finally, choosing her words with great care, Wu started to speak. "This issue we've got to deal with here is the likelihood of what a jury in an adult trial is going to do when confronted with the facts of this case. The negative character issues we can avoid as long as we don't bring up anything positive."

"What?" Linda asked. "What does that mean?"

"It's just a rule," Wu said. "Character can't be used by the prosecution except if we bring it up first. After that it's open season. Do you think we want to go there, Mrs. North?"

It took her a minute, but she finally shook her head. "I don't think that would be a good idea."

It was the first time that Linda had acknowledged the basic problem: that regardless of the facts, the situation *looked* bad for her son. Wu played to that card. "No, I don't think so, either. And that leads me to the really crucial question." A quick glance at Hal, who nodded encouragement. "From what we've seen of the discovery so far — and this means the whole gun question, the pattern of lies to the police, the eyewitness testimony, and so on — do you really think, Mrs. North, we should advise Andrew to run the risk of an adult trial, or try to talk him out of it if he decides to admit?"

Hal reached over and put his hand over his wife's. "It comes down to how it *looks,* hon. What a jury will probably do with the evidence they see."

Linda sat with it for a long time. Finally, she looked first to Hal, then to Wu. "You don't think it's possible that he actually did do this, do you?"

Wu finessed her answer. "I think that eight years is a far, far better sentence than anything he'd be likely to get in an adult trial. There are no other suspects, Mrs. North. Andrew was the only person that we know was there when the murders happened, and he had a gun and a motive."

Another silence.

"Maybe we should let Andrew decide," Hal's voice was a whisper.

This, of course, had been Wu's goal all along. When Andrew got acquainted with the next round of discovery, which she intended to show him today, Wu believed that he would be a fool to deny the hopelessness of his position, and she did not think him a fool. He would opt to admit. With his mother opposed to that idea, though, urging him to fight for his innocence every step of the way, he was much less likely to come to this obviously correct decision. But if Linda could be convinced not to object, Wu would have a clear field, and convincing her client would be that much easier.

"I'm going up to see him right after I leave here," Wu said.

"Maybe I should go up with you," Linda said. "I don't want to him feel like we think he's guilty. That we're abandoning him."

But Linda's company was the last thing Wu wanted when she made her pitch to Andrew. "It might be better just to leave it to me, Mrs. North. This is really something your son is going to have to come to rationally, and if you're there, it's going to be emotional. If it's just me, his lawyer, explaining that it's not about guilt, it's legal strategy that will give him many more years of freedom, he's at least going to look at it clearly. Then, if he's in fact truly innocent and just won't admit no matter what, we'll go to trial. But if he doesn't think it's worth the risk . . ."

Linda hung her head, finally looked back up. "Then that means he probably did it after all, doesn't it?"

Well, yes, Wu thought. That's certainly what the evidence indicates, doesn't it? But she only said, "If he admits, he admits. That's all. It's about strategy, not factual guilt or innocence."

Hal leaned in, his hand still over his wife's on the table. "It's got to be his decision," he repeated. "He's the only one who knows for sure."

Another lengthy silence. Linda said, "But . . ." and stopped, turned to her husband, shook her head again. Finally, she nodded.

Q: Three two one. This is Homicide Inspector Sergeant Glen Taylor, badge fourteen ten. Case number 003-114279. It is three-thirty in the afternoon, Tuesday, March 4th. I am at the residence of Mark and June Ropke, 2619 Irving Street. With me are the Ropkes and their son, Lanny, Caucasian juvenile aged seventeen. Lanny, would you describe your relationship with Andrew Bartlett.

A: He was, is I mean, my best friend.

Q: And how do you know him?

A: He's in my class at school. We're juniors at Sutro.

Q: Did you also know a Mike Mooney and a Laura Wright?

A: Yeah. Mr. Mooney was my English teacher, and Laura was Andrew's girlfriend.

Q: Okay. Did Andrew talk to you about them?

A: Yeah. He was a little jealous.

Q: Andrew was? Of Mooney?

A: Yeah.

Q: You want to tell me about it.

A: All right. Him and Laura, Andrew and Laura, I mean, had been going out for about a year, something like that, a long time anyway. Then they got in a fight just before Christmas break and broke up.

Q: Do you know what the fight was about?

A: I think it was sex.

Q: Did Andrew tell you that?

A: Kind of, yeah. I guess he was coming on pretty strong and she told him she wasn't ready for that yet, so he got all pissed off — sorry, mad, I mean — and said she was just being a tease, leading him on, what was she making out with him for if they weren't getting to that? Anyway, it was a big fight and they broke up, but then a couple of weeks later, maybe a month before she got killed, they got back together.

Q: Did Andrew tell you why?

A: He didn't have to. It was obvious. But he did tell me he couldn't stand not being with her, sex or no sex. He was really in love with her.

Q: So what happened with Mr. Mooney? How'd he get into this?

A: He was directing the play, and Andrew and Laura were both in it. They're . . . I mean she was, both of them were into drama. So they started going over to his place together at night to do their lines and rehearse, you know. Mooney's. Anyway, one night Laura told Andrew that she wasn't driving back with him. She was going to stay on awhile and do some more rehearsing and Mr. Mooney would take her home.

Q: And what was Andrew's reaction to that?

A: At first, you know, not much. But after it happened again a couple of times, pretty bad. Really bad, I guess.

Q: In what way?

Q: (female voice) It's okay, Lanny. There's no hurry.

Q: (male voice) Just tell him what you've told us. It's all right.

A: He brought a gun to school.

Q: Did you see it?

A: Oh yeah, he showed it to me. It was

in his backpack. It was a real gun, and loaded.

Q: Did he tell you what he was planning to do with it?

A: Yeah, but he wasn't sure exactly.

Q: What do you mean?

A: Well, he was carrying it around for a week, maybe two, I think just seeing how it felt, you know. He talked about killing himself mostly at first.

Q: But that changed?

A: It just . . . I don't know. He told me he was going to find out for sure if something was going on with Mooney and Laura. This was while they were broken up. And meanwhile, he sees her and Mooney goofing at school, all these little jokes they had with each other. So basically, it was this jealousy thing. It was eating him up, the thought of her maybe having sex with him, after only teasing with him for so long. I mean, Mooney's a grown-up and Andrew didn't believe they'd only be making out. So he decided he had to find out for sure.

Q: And how would he do that?

A: He was going to hang around after he told them he was leaving, maybe make up some excuse, and come back and catch them at it.

Q: And then what was he going to do?

A: Well, he said he hoped he'd find out Laura wasn't lying, but if he caught them at something, he hoped he could handle it. He said maybe it would be a good idea if he didn't have the gun with him. If he didn't, maybe he wouldn't kill them on the spot. He hoped he wouldn't do that.

Q: He said he hoped he wouldn't kill them?

A: That's what he said.

Although it was clear and sunny outside, it wasn't warm by any stretch. The small visiting room at the YGC felt to Wu like a refrigerator. She was gauging her client's reaction to his friend's testimony, and it seemed to have hit him pretty hard. Andrew was sitting back, slumped in one of the hard wooden chairs at the table this time, one elbow on the chair's arm and his hand over his mouth. Now he wearily dropped the hand, shook his head.

"This is bad."

She nodded. "Correct."

"He told me the cops had come and he'd talked to them, but he never mentioned anything about the gun. You think Lanny would have been smart enough . . . Nobody had to know about the gun. It's makes it look . . ."

Wu knew what it made it look like. She

169

asked, "You want to talk about the gun?"

"What about it?"

"Well, the gun's kind of an issue. You bring it to school and show it around . . ."

"Not around. Just to Lanny."

"Okay, just to Lanny, although he's enough. He'll testify that you said you were thinking about killing Laura and Mooney, and maybe yourself. The gun is what you presumably would have used to do that. So what were you thinking when you took it? It was Hal's gun, is that right?"

His expression grew sharp. "I never said that."

"No, I know you didn't. But another one of the interviews in here" — she patted the folder that held Lanny's transcript — "is a discussion with your stepfather about when Sergeant Taylor asked him if he owned a gun and he said yes, then went to get it and couldn't find it. Didn't Hal ever ask you if you'd taken it?"

"Yeah, he did."

"And what did you tell him?"

Andrew gave her the bad eye.

"Okay, then," she said, "let me tell you. You denied it, maybe even pitched a little fit of indignation that he'd accuse you of anything like that. Am I close?" She leaned in toward him over the table. "Let me ask you this, Andrew. Why didn't you just put it back from where you'd taken it? If you'd done that, and if you in fact hadn't committed these murders, don't you realize that you wouldn't be here right now?"

His eyes weren't quite to panic, but they flicked to the wall behind her, then to the corners of the room before they got back to her. "Why is that?"

She noticed that he didn't bother with the pro forma denial of the crime this time. She let herself begin to believe that her strategy was working — he was getting used to admitting the basic fact of his guilt. "Because if we had the gun, we could test ballistics with the slugs they recovered from the scene and prove that it wasn't the murder weapon." She gave him a minute to digest this critical information, then pressed on. "You told me you got rid of the gun."

"I did."

"Do you think you could find it again?"

"No. I dropped it off the bridge."

"That would be the Golden Gate?"

"Yeah."

Wu checked a laugh. Perfect, she thought. "I don't understand, and I don't think a jury will understand, why you did that if you didn't kill anybody with it."

"I freaked out, is all. I told you. When I got back to Mike's — Mooney's — and saw it there, I figured the cops would be able to trace it back to Hal and I'd be screwed."

"And why is that?"

"I mean, if it was the murder weapon." His miserable look seemed to plead for her to understand. "I had to get rid of it."

"But it wasn't the murder weapon, was it?"

"I don't know. I mean, it might have been."

Wu straightened up in her chair and faced him head-on. "Let me get this straight. Your theory of the crime, and please correct me if I'm wrong, is that while you were out taking a stroll and memorizing your lines, somebody — you don't know who or why — knocked at Mooney's door, saw your father's gun conveniently sitting out on a coffee table, grabbed it and shot anybody who happened to be standing around. That's it?"

"I don't think that."

"Good. That would be a dumb thing to think. But otherwise, why get rid of the gun?"

"I told you!" Andrew again cast his eyes around the walls. Wu could almost feel his panic, searching for escape, any escape. Finally, he exploded, slamming the table between them with the flat of his palm, coming to his feet, turning around, trapped. "I already told you that!" he screamed. Don't you *get* it? Aren't you listening to me? I was freaked out. I knew it was a mistake the minute I let it go."

Suddenly, his voice broke into an uncontrolled and wrenching sob. He was crying, pleading with her. "I mean, there's Mike and Laura shot dead on the floor. They're *dead*. My mind goes blank and I can't think of anything except to call emergency." He gulped now for a breath, tears streaking his face. "After that . . . I don't know what I did, except finally I turn around and there's my gun on the coffee table. I can't leave it there, can I? I didn't think it out, what I was doing. I just did it. Didn't you get that at all?"

Andrew stood across the table from her, hands limp at his side, staring at her. His breath still came in jagged gasps.

It was all she could do to keep from coming around the table and hugging him.

A knock at the door interrupted and Wu crossed to it. The unpleasant bailiff from the detention hearing, Nelson, had heard a noise and was wondering if everything was all right. She noticed he had a grip on his mace, and she held up her hand, palm out. "We're fine."

When the door had closed and she turned around, Andrew was back in his chair, leaning over, his face down by his knees, his fingers laced over the back of his head. She went to his side of the table, boosted herself onto it, folded her own

173

hands in her lap, and waited.

He was still taking deep, labored breaths, but gradually they slowed, and eventually he looked up. Seeing her so close, nearly hovering over him, he pushed the chair back six inches, then hung his head again, perhaps in shame. "I'm sorry," he said. "I'm so sorry." He brought his hands to his face, said "Oh God," and broke again, a sob that seemed to sound the death knell to all the hopes of his childhood.

Someone else witnessing the breakdown, hearing the same words, might have reached a different conclusion, but to Wu it ratified all of her preconceptions — she'd been expecting something like this, Andrew's show of remorse for what he'd done. To her, the apologetic words sounded exactly like an admission of his guilt.

She pushed herself off the table and went up beside him, put a hand on his opposite shoulder and pulled the close one against her hip. "It's all right," she whispered. "It's okay."

Through the wired windows, steep shafts of sunlight mottled the floor, struck the backs of both of them. The tableau held for nearly a minute, an eternity in that setting. Andrew's breath became more regular. Wu herself was nearly afraid to breathe, hyper-aware of the possible impli-

174

cations of the scene. This proximity was unprofessional. Prompted at first by a genuine sympathy, she remained out of an awkward desire to appear natural. Some small despicable part of her was also aware that even such a slight physical gesture, a hand on his shoulder, her hip against him, might work to her advantage in the next phase of their negotiation.

Finally, he raised his head. "So what am I going to do?"

She moved away, a gentle extrication. Leaning back now against the table, she didn't answer right away. "I don't mean to put you through any more agony, Andrew. God knows you've got enough to deal with as it is. But I needed to make you see, and see very clearly, some of the really powerful and convincing evidence that they've got against you."

"But it's still . . ."

"Please. Let me go on." She paused. "Count the ways," she said. "They've got an eyewitness, someone who saw you at Mr. Mooney's that night both before and after. They've got motive and lots of it. Your gun was there. You were there, walk or no walk. They've got the testimony of your best friend, showing premeditation. They've got the gun that you threw away, when if you'd saved it, it could have proved you innocent. All this, and then

175

there's all the rest of their discovery we haven't even seen yet. Laura's mother's testimony, Mr. Mooney's colleagues and associates, forensics and medical reports. Your lies to the police . . ." She stared fixedly at him.

"What if a jury doesn't believe all that?" he asked.

"They don't have to believe *all* of it." She kept her tone soft. "But let me ask you one, Andrew. What part of it isn't true?"

He bit at his lip, ran his hand back through his hair.

Wu drove home another point. "And even if a jury drew a slightly different conclusion from all this evidence, say they came back with some lesser offense, say second degree murder or even some kind of manslaughter, you're still, best case, looking at a minimum of ten and maybe up to thirty years."

"But none, if I got off."

"No," she agreed. "Not then. But think about what we've just been over in the past two days. That's just a part of what the prosecution is going to present. Think of how you'd feel if you were on your own jury and heard what they were going to hear."

"So you're saying it doesn't matter whether I actually did it or not."

"Of course it does. It's critical to who

you are, to the person you'll be when you get out. I'm just asking you to consider your alternatives with great, great care. We've got a hearing tomorrow, and I have set it up so you can be done with all this and out of custody with your whole life ahead of you in no more than eight years. I know that seems like forever right now, but you'll still be a very young man, believe me, with everything to live for."

"But . . . eight years . . ."

She nodded. "No one's pretending this is an easy call. I understand that. Talk to your mom and to Hal, if you want, get their opinions."

"My mom and Hal," he said with withering dismissal. "My mom and Hal. What are they going to tell me? And whatever it is, why should I listen? They live their own lives, if you haven't noticed. They're not interested in mine."

"That's not true, Andrew. Your mother's been in here to visit you every day so far, hasn't she? She loves you. She wants what's best for you. I've just come from seeing them."

"Yeah? And what did she say?"

"She said this was your decision."

Andrew snorted. "See? She'd love it if somebody else took care of me for eight years. It'd leave her and Hal freer to party."

Wu sat back, shook her head. "I don't think that's true," she said, "but it's really neither here nor there. What's important is that you've seen how hard it is to control the way evidence comes out, what it looks like. Your friend Lanny, your own . . . mistakes in talking to the police."

"So you really don't think you can win?"

Wu empathized with his despair, but it would be a disservice to sugarcoat his predicament. "I will try with everything in me, Andrew. You're free to get another lawyer if you want, but I promise you that I will live and breathe this case for as long as it takes if you decide to go as an adult. But I want you to have a clear understanding of what we're looking at. It will be a long haul, with no guarantees."

"How long?"

She drove in yet another nail. "It might go as long as two years before we can get to trial, maybe eighteen months if we're extremely lucky. And all that time you're in custody anyway. There's no bail, so you're right here until you're eighteen and after that probably at the county lockup downtown."

"Two years?" He swallowed, his eyes pleading. "Two more *years?*"

"I'd try to speed it up, of course, but that's about the average wait."

"Even if I didn't do it? Even if they

found me innocent?"

"I'm afraid so. Either way. I'm sorry."

Bailiff Nelson again picked up Andrew at the door to the visitor's room. If Judge Johnson had reprimanded him over his conduct in the courtroom after the detention hearing, or even discussed it, Nelson gave no sign of it. Wu watched the two of them trundle off to wherever Andrew's cell was located back in the confines of the building. She thought that having a goon like Nelson monitor — hell, *shadow* — your every move must be one of the most debilitating things about confinement here.

In the women's room down in the main admin building, she fixed her makeup, then found she had to gather her emotions for several minutes. Andrew's disaffection with his parents had bothered her more than she could allow herself to show — it so closely mirrored her now forever unresolved ambivalence about her own father. How much had he really cared about her? Now she would never know. Maybe, she thought, Andrew's approach was healthier — just go on the accumulated evidence of absenteeism and benign neglect and admit that there is no profound connection. If you really believe that there is no parental love at all, you don't spend any time searching for it, either in your parents or in

179

surrogate and successive sexual partners. You don't keep trying to please them, to live off the crumbs of praise or approval that you can then falsely interpret as a proof of their affection for you, their esteem.

Her next stop, Jason Brandt's office, added to the volatility of the emotional mix. She knew that she had to have a talk with the prosecutor and didn't want to acknowledge their physical intimacy of the night before in any way. And though she might have preferred to believe for a moment last night that they actually had potential to connect as people, Brandt had put the lie to that by getting up and leaving soon after the sex. Proof positive, she knew — she'd done the same thing herself — that all it had been was physical. Two consenting adults, thank you very much. In fact, rather than signal any kind of openness to see each other again, she thought this might be a good opportunity to score a few professional points, a payback for the grief she'd taken from him in the courtroom yesterday.

Brandt's work space was a reconverted closet that held his desk and chair, a bookshelf and nothing else. The door could only be closed because somebody had sawed several inches off the corner of the desk. One window, high up and tiny, provided neither light nor view. A bare lightbulb hung from a cord four feet above his desk.

Brandt was behind the desk, crammed amid his books and filing cabinets. The place was literally overflowing with binders, case files, periodicals. For a moment while Wu stood in the doorway, he didn't look up. When he finally did, in the first two seconds his face contorted through several iterations of arrangement — he was glad to see her; he wasn't sure why she was here; some kind of hope that they might get together again?

If it was that, Wu moved to quash it immediately. "Don't worry, I'm not stalking you. I was just up visiting my client and wanted to ask you if you thought I could get a little more time to plead him out."

Brandt's face instantly grew stern. "Why?"

Wu had decided upon a plausible explanation. "I'm having a slight problem with the parents. I doubt Boscacci would mind."

"He would. I talked to him just before the hearing yesterday and he was the soul of inflexibility."

"Really? That's funny, because when I talked with him, he didn't seem awfully concerned about timing."

"Provided Andrew admits."

"Right. Which he will."

"Shouldn't that be 'has'?"

"Tomorrow. That's 'will.' Beyond that, I'm talking only a few days' grace."

"Grace?"

"Courtesy. Whatever word you want."

Brandt leveled his gaze at her. "The word I want is 'now,' Amy. Anything beyond now — meaning tomorrow at the hearing, first thing, he admits — anything else makes me nervous as hell."

"Why?"

"You're kidding, right?" He stood up abruptly, coming out from behind his desk. "Excuse me," he said, squeezing past her, looking both ways down the hallway.

"What are you doing?"

His voice was quiet yet urgent. "I'm making sure nobody's out here to hear us, that's what." He turned and faced her. "You ask me why I'm nervous if we get delayed? Do you remember anything about last night?"

"What's that supposed to mean?"

He lowered his voice still further. "It means that when I walked into the Balboa last night and saw you sitting at the bar, you were a woman I had wanted to get to know for a long time. The case we were both handling was settled, so we wouldn't be squaring off in court anymore. We could do whatever we wanted. Now you're telling me it might not be settled? And you knew this last night? And still you let us go ahead?"

"It wasn't just me, if you remember, Jason."

"No, it wasn't. But you're the one who knew we might not be finished in court. If what happened with you and me gets out at all, and/or if this thing with Bartlett gets delayed, it's my *ass*. Don't you realize that? It's my job. And you knew it all along?"

The strength of Brandt's reaction caught Wu off guard. "No, but if I did, could you blame me, after how you treated me in court . . ."

He stared at her in shock. "I don't believe this. You're telling me you set me up on purpose? What's next? You blackmail me for your silence about us?"

"Come on, Jason. You're overreacting. It wasn't like that."

Brandt said aloud to himself, "I've got to call Boscacci. I'm out of this right now." Then he looked at her with a new flash of insight. "But if I do that, then you win, too, don't you? You get your delay. You knew this going in, didn't you? You've just been playing me."

"No, that's not true. I . . ."

But he wasn't going to be listening to any more excuses. In a fury, he put a finger to her face. "Don't you dare try and sell me on what's true or not, not after last night. You may have gotten me, okay, you win one. But that's the last time, I swear to God. The last fucking time."

He stepped back into his office and closed the door in her face.

8

Glitsky had meetings all morning.

The first was the bureau lieutenants' meeting, held in Department 19, a courtroom on the second floor of the Hall of Justice that happened to be dark for the day. Since there were thirty-two lieutenants within the Investigations Bureau and each was expected to present a short report on highlights in their respective bureaus since last week's meeting, this one tended to run long.

Glitsky sat up at the judge's bench, and after his initial remarks reiterating his stand in favor of quantifiable progress in police duties — arrests made, citations issued, investigations instigated, victim assistance and follow-up, and so on — for almost two full hours he listened and took notes on everything from the auto detail and home burglaries to homicide and hate crimes, from arson and the general work detail to bomb investigations and the gang task force, from narcotics and vice to sexual assault, domestic violence and psychiatric liaison.

All of this was numbing and tedious and, Glitsky suspected, not really necessary in the long run. He thought that within a few more months, he'd be able to let these meetings slide, once he had clearly delivered the message to his bureau chiefs that investigators needed to make arrests, take bad people off the street. That was the basic job. Patrolmen in uniform made the vast majority of arrests. Inspectors followed up to put the finishing touches on these cases. But the real inspectors' job was to solve cases. To assemble evidence and make arrests based on investigating crimes when no arrest at the scene was possible.

The new policy was showing signs of bearing some fruit, but nine of his bureaus had not made one arrest in the past week. There was still work to be done. Nevertheless, there had been a total of eighty-four arrests in that same period, up from seventy-eight the week before. This, he supposed, could be construed as progress, but mostly the cynical part of him believed it would turn out to be simply the manipulation of numbers, or cleaning out old, solved cases that they hadn't gotten around to filing yet. Speeding up the pipeline a little to rig the stats.

After the meeting, he stayed behind a moment with Lanier of homicide, passing along the Post-its with the names of Elizabeth Cary's brothers. Lanier might particularly want to have one of his inspectors on the case, Pat Belou or Lincoln Russell, check out Ted Reed, the crazy brother who lived down at Lake Elsinore. If he'd been in San Francisco last week, it might turn out to be something.

By ten-fifteen, he was up in Chief Batiste's office for a meeting of the Benefits Board, where he listened for another hour to the city's director of human resources talk in excruciating detail about the latest proposed improvements to the police department's pension and retirement plans, and its health and life insurance benefits. Like, what should be the deductible on sex-change operations? Like, should alcoholism automatically be presumed to be a job-related illness, entitling the officer to a full disability retirement for on-the-job injury?

At eleven-thirty, he was driven to the mayor's office. Smiling was a form of torture for Glitsky, but for most of another hour, that's all he did, while photographers took his picture with other local VIPs and the members of a Russian delegation here to explore business opportunities in the City by the Bay. As far as he could tell, there was no other reason for him to be present except that the mayor apparently believed that the Russians tended to be impressed by the presence of high-ranking, beribboned officers in uniform.

His driver, Sergeant Tony Paganucci, nagged him about getting some lunch. Wasn't he supposed to try and meet up with his wife and Clarence Jackman and some other folks at Lou the Greek's? But Glitsky had run out of time. He absolutely had to be back at the Hall of Justice for a one o'clock press conference, and that was in twenty-five minutes.

Paganucci dropped him behind the Coroner's Office. Glitsky came into the Hall through the back door. Taking the stairs two at a time for his only exercise of the day, rather than the elevators where someone would want to talk to him about something, he breezed through the outer office unmolested.

In the office adjacent to his own, the deputy chief of administration, Bryce Jake Longoria, a white-haired, soft-spoken patrician, was in uniform sitting at his desk, working at his computer. Glitsky stopped in the doorway until Longoria looked up, smiled, gestured at his monitor. "Just trying to get some real work done, squeeze it in during lunchtime."

"I hear you. I'd try the same strategy if I had enough time to boot up my computer, which I don't." Glitsky took a step into the room. "But I do have a quick question for you if you can spare a minute."

"One. Shoot."

"Say you know the name of somebody who served on a jury fifteen, maybe twenty years ago. Do you know if there's any database you could access to identify the case?"

Longoria pondered a moment. "You don't know the date, or the name of the defendant?"

"No. Just that it was a murder trial, and they found the guy guilty."

A dry chuckle. "Well, if it was during the Pratt administration, you could just go and manually look up every one. There couldn't have been more than three or four, maybe less."

"Unfortunately, I think it was way back before her. Maybe late seventies, early eighties."

Longoria clucked. "The Golden Years." He took another moment, then shook his head. "They may still have the physical records downstairs" — the cavernous basement of the Hall, larger than a Costco, that held many millions of documents, shelf after shelf after shelf, floor to twelve-foot ceiling, from cases stretching back to the city's earlier days — "but first you'd have to find them by going through every one individually."

"That's the other thing," Glitsky said, "it might not have been here. In San Francisco."

189

"Well, tell you what, I'd find that out first. If you had the case number, the defendant, maybe even the judge . . ."

Glitsky pursed his lips. "I know, but I don't."

"Well, then I'd say if it was a local case, it might be doable, but it'll take you most of a couple of years if you do it yourself. It would have to be pretty important, and if it was, I'd assign a good-sized team to it. Still, it wouldn't be quick."

"I don't know why it would be important. At the moment, it's just a question."

But Longoria had been a cop all of his life. He knew that any given question could turn into something critical, so he gave it some more time and passed on another thought. "Here's a real long shot, but maybe if your juror was foreman, he might have gotten his name in the paper. You could check. Other than that . . ." He shrugged. "Sorry."

"Not a big deal," Glitsky said. "Thanks." Closing the door to his own office, Glitsky went behind his desk and sat down. He had eleven messages on his answering machine, six on his Palm Pilot.

His press conference began in fifteen minutes. Its purpose was for him to explain why the police decision to allow a suspect in a gang-related multiple murder to leave the state had been the proper one. When they'd made the decision, Glitsky had had no doubt. LeShawn Brodie, considered armed and dangerous, had already taken his seat on the Greyhound bus to Salt Lake when they'd received the tip on his whereabouts. Rather than storm the crowded bus and possibly provoke a hostage crisis, Batiste, Glitsky and Lanier had decided to alert Nevada and Utah authorities to follow the bus in unmarked cars and have officers pick the suspect up after he got off, either in Salt Lake or en route. As it happened, LeShawn got out to stretch his legs and play a few slots in Elko, and authorities picked him up without incident. But it was now an extradition case, and Glitsky would be explaining all about it to the press.

Having put on dozens of these shows by now, he could imagine the questions already, and none of them improved his humor. Did Glitsky mean to say that the police knowingly allowed a dangerous criminal to ride for several hours with unsuspecting citizens? Did they have any assurance at all that LeShawn wouldn't take hostages as soon as he'd come aboard? Couldn't they have simply used a team of plainclothes cops and arrested him here, avoiding all the extradition hassles? Why did they let him get on the bus in the first place? Why couldn't they have used tear gas? Or a sniper with tranquilizer darts? Or beamed him directly to a jail cell?

Glitsky opened his middle drawer and popped three antacids. Pressing at the side of his stomach, he checked his watch again. He still had twelve minutes. He hadn't eaten a bite since his bagel at six-fifteen. He opened his peanut drawer, restored to its original position, and pulled out a small handful of shells, placed them on his desk.

The phone rang and, thoughtlessly, he picked it up. His secretary told him to hold for the Chief, and in two seconds Frank Batiste's tightly controlled voice was on the line. "Abe, I need you up here right away. The shit's going to hit the fan."

"What's up?"

"LeShawn. He's escaped."

When Clarence Jackman had first been elevated to the office of district attorney, he came from managing a private law firm and was relatively inexperienced in city politics. In fact, this was one of the reasons the mayor tapped him for the job — Jackman was a proven, results-oriented administrator, and this as opposed to an agenda-driven zealot was what the office required. In his early months, the DA had bridged the gap in his hands-on knowledge by convening an informal kitchen cabinet every Tuesday to get and keep him current on issues he might not otherwise have considered, the political implications of which he might not otherwise have been aware.

Now, gearing up for his first general election later in the year, Jackman had called together many of the original group again to feel out their respective interests in participating in his campaign. He had pretty much decided he would be announcing at the end of the week, and wanted to take the pulse of his core supporters on that timing as well.

The group assembled at the large, round table at the back of Lou the Greek's, a bar/restaurant across the street from the Hall of Justice, were all well acquainted. Dismas Hardy sat between Jeff Elliot, the wheelchair-mobile reporter for the *Chronicle*, and Allan Boscacci, relatively new to the group but apparently here to stay. Abe Glitsky's wife Treya, who had been with Jackman in his old firm and now worked as his personal secretary, sat on the other side of Boscacci to the DA's left. Glitsky would have been welcome, but obviously his work had kept him. Some of the old players were missing — David Freeman had passed away and Gina Roake had simply lost interest — and they'd been replaced by a couple of city supervisors, the young, ambitious, cheerily overweight Harlan Fisk and his aunt, a birdlike spinster named Kathy West.

But now the business part of the meeting, such as it was, had come to an end. No surprise — Jackman had assurances of undying support from everyone. Hardy was going to host his fund-raising kickoff party — they thought that for the best buzz and food they'd have it at Moose's — in about six weeks. Fisk and West would begin calling in favors, wheeling and dealing as necessary, to try to get at least a majority coalition of support from the usually divided Board of Supervisors. Boscacci, a political animal himself, was going to hire and oversee the eventual campaign manager, and funnel much of the day-to-day administration of the campaign across the desk of the abundantly capable Treya. As a supposedly objective and nonpartisan columnist, Elliot could only promise that he'd be inclined to continue and possibly even increase his sympathetic coverage of doings in the DA's office so long as Jackman maintained the same policies and programs that had been working so well during his first term; Elliot would also do his damnedest to use his considerable popularity and influence to get the *Chronicle* to support Jackman come November, something the paper would probably do on its own, although it never hurt to have an inside advocate or two.

So everybody was on the same team, and

a convivial spirit reigned at the table as people finished their coffee. Hardy had exchanged some easy pleasantries with the chief assistant DA when he'd sat down, but they hadn't talked to each other much since. Truth to tell, Hardy found Boscacci's perennially florid countenance somewhat forbidding — the collar at his neck, always buttoned to the top and festooned with a bow tie, seemed a half size too small; this in turn seemed to stretch the closely shaved skin on his face, to make his dark eyes bulge slightly, so that it always appeared that he might be on the verge of a stroke. Fifty-two years old, he wore his thick, black hair slicked with some kind of hair lotion and pulled straight back off his prominent forehead. But Hardy knew he could be an affable enough guy when he was on your side. He took the opportunity, as though he'd just remembered it, to thank Boscacci for the courtesy he'd shown Amy Wu yesterday in the Andrew Bartlett matter.

Boscacci waved off the comment. "Ah, that was nothing. She's an easy person to want to do something nice for." Then, leaning in a bit and lowering his voice, he added, "Besides, she didn't know it, but she couldn't have timed it better for us."

"Us?"

He included the group at the table.

"Clarence. All of us. We chalk up the two convictions before the end of the week, when Clarence announces he can say he's had fifty murder *convictions* so far this term, not even four years."

"You're kidding me. Is that the number?"

"With your associate's two, it is. And fifty sounds so much *bigger* than forty-eight, you know what I mean?"

"I don't know, forty-eight sounds pretty good to me."

"Don't get me wrong. Forty-eight is a fine number. But we figure fifty is easier for the man in the street to get his arms around. Pratt's administration, she didn't even *charge* fifty murders."

"I remember it well," Hardy said. "I doubt if she charged fifteen."

Boscacci lowered his voice. "Twelve, if you want to get precise. Which is one of the reasons we've got such great numbers. Between you and me, we're recycling some leftovers." He grinned in triumph. "So, anyway, your Ms. Wu comes to me with a reasonable and some might even say charitable request, we find a way to make it win-win. She says it's not even out of the question the kid's stepfather — you know Hal North? North Cinemas? — will be so grateful for saving the kid thirty plus of hard time, he might want to express his gratitude to Clarence in a more tangible way."

"She mentioned the same thing to me, but I wouldn't be expecting that check soon."

Suddenly the forbidding aspect of Boscacci's personality appeared. His face darkened perceptibly. Hardy was half-tempted to reach over and undo his bow tie, let him get a breath, but he spoke clearly enough, without any difficulty. "Why? Is there some problem? North should be slobbering in gratitude."

Thinking fast, and realizing that he'd inadvertently almost tipped Boscacci to his own concerns about Wu's disposition of the case, Hardy said, "No. I don't see any problem, Allan. It's just that eight years is eight years that his stepson is gone. It's not likely that North's going to see the deal in quite the same way as you do."

"Well," Boscacci said, "somebody ought to go and explain it to him. Given the case against his boy — *and it's a deuce,* remember that — it may be the best deal we've ever agreed to from a suspect's point of view. Time we get around to serious fund-raising for Clarence, I'd hope he'd come to understand that. I'd bet your Ms. Wu could even have a little chat with him come fall if she was so inclined, draw the picture a little more clearly." He paused.

"Anybody could do it, she could. She put her mind to it, I believe that woman could charm the skin off a snake. You're lucky to have her, but you already know that, don't you?"

Hardy nodded, affable as he could force himself to be. "It's why we pay her the big bucks, Allan. All that charm and a legal whiz on top of it. If I didn't believe the cosmic truth that we were always on the side of the angels, I'd say it was close to unfair."

9

A small jungle of dieffenbachia, rubber trees and other more exotic plants thrived in the corners and against the back wall of the firm's conference room. Opening to a sheltered outdoor atrium, complete with grass and fountain, the entire outer wall and part of the roof jutted from the line of the building, creating a greenhouse effect, and giving the room its nickname of the Solarium.

Now, at a few minutes after six, Gina Roake, the building's owner, in a conservative gray business suit, sat with a cup of coffee at the head of the large table that commanded the room. Roake was closing in on fifty years old, but few people would have guessed it. She'd always had good skin and a youthful face. A recent diet and exercise program had accented her chin and cheekbones and slimmed the rest of her down significantly, though she remained a bit zaftig. To her left, Dismas Hardy, emulating his old mentor Freeman, sipped some Baystone Shiraz from an oversized wineglass. Across from him, Wes Farrell was trying to tell what had supposedly just been voted the funniest joke in the world. But he was having some trouble getting to it.

"Who votes on that kind of thing?" Hardy asked. "It's got to be bogus. Nobody asked me, for example. Gina, anybody ask you?"

"No."

"See? And we're both famous for our senses of humor."

Farrell wasn't to be denied. "It's a very prestigious group of joke researchers based in Sweden or someplace. They wouldn't ask people like you and Gina."

"So it's a European joke," Hardy said, "which strikes me as pretty arrogantly Eurocentric. Okay, so now it's like, in some Swede's opinion, the funniest joke in the world. Those wacky Swedes, with the highest suicide rate in the world and all."

"Can I tell the joke?" Farrell asked. "And then you decide."

"All right," Hardy said. "But telling us up front that this is the funniest joke in the world, it's guaranteed to be forty percent less funny."

Farrell persisted. "You'll still get sixty percent of it. It'll be worth it, I promise."

"I can't wait," Roake said.

But Hardy wasn't through yet. "Did you

laugh out loud when you heard it, Wes?"

"No, but I never laugh out loud at jokes."

"You laughed at Dirty Harold."

Farrell broke a grin. "True. I did."

"So based on your own response, this new funniest joke in the world isn't as funny as the Dirty Harold joke."

"Fucking lawyers," Farrell said. "Everything's an argument."

"What's the Dirty Harold joke?" Roake asked.

Hardy turned to her. "This little kid with a filthy mouth, so the teacher won't ever call on him. Then one day they're going through the alphabet, finding words that start with a given letter and then they use the word in a sentence. They finally get to 'e' — Harold's hand has been up the whole time on every letter — but she figures there aren't any filthy words that start with 'e,' so she calls on him . . ."

"Elf!" Roake exclaimed, smiling. "I know an elf with a big prick."

"That's it." Hardy drank some wine.

Farrell seized his chance. "So Holmes and Watson go camping and set up their tent and they go to sleep. Two hours later, Holmes goes, 'Watson, what do you see?' and Watson goes, 'I see millions and millions of stars.' And Holmes says, 'And what do you deduce from that?' Watson says, 'I

201

imagine each star has planets around it just like our own, with a chance of life on each one.' And Holmes goes, 'Watson, you fool, someone's stolen our tent.' "

"So." Roake maintained a poker face. "Having heard the joke, maybe now we can begin. I've got a handball game in forty-five minutes."

They were gathered for their monthly partners overview — business, after all — and Hardy spent the next twenty minutes going over the firm's numbers. The associates were all well utilized — the firm was cranking along, racking up substantial fees almost as though it were on automatic pilot. Hardy's concerns about Wu's deal with Boscacci might have been a legitimate topic for discussion on another day, but so far nothing had actually gone wrong, and he elected to keep his qualms under his hat.

Under "other business," Hardy mentioned the firm's upcoming involvement in support of the Jackman campaign, which he considered an opportunity as good as any to broach the one sensitive topic they needed to discuss. Might the Jackman candidacy entice Roake back to work, Hardy wondered. To something approaching regular hours?

Roake straightened up in her chair. Her eyes flicked between the two men. "I resent the hell out of that question, Diz. What I do with my time is my business."

Hardy's gaze didn't flinch. He kept any sign of edge out of his voice. "I'm not arguing with that, Gina. You've earned whatever time you feel you need. But as a business matter for the firm, you're drawing a decent salary for yourself and your own private secretary and you've got a big corner office that's essentially sitting unused."

Roake clipped off her words. "How about if I just quit and start charging the kind of rent for this building that another firm would have to pay? I could give up my decent salary and I'd still be making more money than I am now. How about that?"

Hardy shook his head. "That's not what I want. I don't think it's what you want. I wasn't speaking critically. If you don't want to do any more billing, you've got my complete support. Wes's, too. But when we started up together, we had a business plan that included the three of us bringing in business and billing our own time. And that's not happening. Even with our otherwise good utilization, we're struggling to make those original numbers."

Hardy came forward, his hands clasped on the table in front of him. His voice was still soft, almost caressing. "I'm just trying to get a sense of your plans, Gina, so I can know what we're dealing with. As it stands now, you're an expense item and not a profit center, and we didn't plan for that. The firm has to come up with the difference, which is not insignificant. I owe it to us all to tell you about it. Times are good now, but if they get tight, we could find ourselves in a heap of trouble."

Roake scratched at the yellow legal pad on the table in front of her, staring down at her scribblings. "All right," she said, without looking up. "I'd like to think about this for a few days, if you don't mind."

"Not at all," Hardy said, "and Gina? There's no wrong answer here. The firm needs to know, that's all. We've talked about some capital improvements on the horizon. We've got to know if they're feasible, that kind of thing."

"I hear you," Roake said. "Really, I do." Then, with a crisp smile, she pushed back from the table, gathered her notes and told them both good night.

After the door to the Solarium had closed behind her, Hardy let out a long breath and met his partner's baleful eye over the table.

"Okay, then." Farrell drew a palm over his brow. "All in all, I'd say that went pretty well. You want to pour me some of that wine?"

★ ★ ★

Hardy put his briefcase down by his reading chair, then walked down the long hallway in his house. Before he'd remodeled it, the old Victorian had been in the railroad car style, with all the downstairs rooms opening to the right off the hall. Now a large, recently renovated kitchen opened up in the back, and behind that was a family room and then the bedrooms for the two kids. They didn't keep the television on much as a general rule, so he was somewhat surprised to hear the low drone. He poked his head into the family room. "What's on?"

Frannie looked over from where she sat on the couch. "Abe."

He walked over and joined them. "What's that loopy guy done now?"

On the tube, Glitsky frowned into a battery of microphones. "No, that's not true," he was saying. "I consulted with the Chief and Lieutenant Lanier, but the decision was mine. At the time it seemed the best one. No one could have predicted that Mr. Brodie would escape. And in fact, the capture itself took place without incident."

The picture flicked back to the pretty anchorwoman, who wore the same cheerful face whether she was reporting on terrorism or bake sales. "But in spite of Deputy Chief Glitsky's comments, the fact remains that LeShawn Brodie, still considered armed and extremely dangerous, and a suspect in several local murders, remains at large after he allegedly stole one of the officers' weapon and engaged in a dramatic shoot-out with arresting authorities this morning in Nevada. Critics are calling ill-advised at best Glitsky's decision not to arrest Brodie while he sat on a bus in the Greyhound terminal in downtown San Francisco early this morning. And considering the suspect's escape and record of violence, it's hard to disagree with them."

"Hard, but not impossible," Hardy said. When the male anchor appeared and it was clear that the news had moved on to its next sound bite, he grabbed the remote and turned off the set. "You notice she never mentioned who the critics were. Did I miss that? 'Yet, it's hard to disagree with them,' " he intoned in the anchor's voice. "What kind of reporting is that?"

"Bad," Vincent said. "They weren't even listening to what Uncle Abe said."

"How long was he on?" Hardy asked.

"Long enough." Vincent's voice was breaking with adolescence. He cleared his throat and went on. "What did they want him to do? Shoot up the whole bus to get the one guy?"

"You got the gist of it, I think." Frannie put a hand on Hardy's knee. "Maybe you ought to call him, though. He's taking a lot of heat. How was your day?"

"Evidently better than Abe's, though it had its moments." He glanced at his watch. "You think he's home?" But he was already punching numbers on the telephone. "This is your best and possibly only true friend," Hardy said, "and if you get this . . ."

"What?"

"Monitoring your calls, I see."

"You would, too. It's been ringing off the hook."

"TV'll do that. Instant fame."

"Great, but I don't want to be famous."

"There's your problem. You're the only person in America who doesn't. The media doesn't know what to do with you. Maybe you ought to get a new makeup guy. Wipe away those frown lines. Did you know you had a scar through your lips? I'm sure they could airbrush that out, too."

There was a pause. Then Glitsky asked, "Are you calling for any real reason?"

"Not exactly. You were on the news just now. I thought you'd enjoy the sound of a friendly voice. Also, for the record, Vin's on your side."

At his side, Hardy's wife said, "Frannie, too."

"I heard that," Glitsky said. "Tell them both thanks."

Frannie squeezed Hardy's leg. "Ask him . . . No, wait, let me." She grabbed the phone. "Abe, what are you and Treya doing tonight? I've got a big pot of spaghetti sauce going. Why don't all of you come over here? Get away from these people who don't love you like we do."

Wu had planned all along to get back to Andrew, get the plea locked up, before tomorrow. She wasn't about to enter Arvid Johnson's courtroom in the morning with any sort of question still hanging about her client's disposition. But before she went in to see Andrew again, she found that she still needed some time to gather herself.

She sat at a table in the street window of what had probably once been a nice little boutique espresso shop half a block from the YGC. But the place had been servicing the juvenile hall clientele for so long that it had given up hope and lost whatever charm it may have once possessed. Now the bulletin board by the door bristled with lawyers' business cards, photos of missing kids, ads for bail bondsmen and private investigators. Stacks of assorted newspapers lay piled on a table by the sugar and cream. A pit bull, chained, slept on the floor in the back of the shop. Behind the counter, a young woman with a peg in her tongue and a ring in each eyebrow was wiping down the back counter, putting things away.

Outside, long shadows stretched up the hill, but the faces of buildings across the street glowed in the last blast of blinding evening sunlight. The wind had picked up and was all but howling, flinging any trash that weighed less than a pound along the nearly deserted street.

Wu's day — from waking up hungover and alone, to her meeting with the Norths, then Andrew, then the fight with Jason Brandt — seemed to have lasted about a week so far, and the hardest few moments were no doubt still ahead of her.

Well, maybe not the hardest. For a combination of guilt, anger and shame, she knew that it would be tough to top the half hour or so after Brandt had stormed away from her. What made it even worse was that she found she couldn't even blame him. For it was true. Even when she'd first begun flirting with him the night before, she *had* known that her deal with Andrew wasn't consummated. If she wanted to have any claim to calling herself an ethical attorney, she would have disclosed her conflict about Andrew to Brandt first thing. You simply did not have sex with your courtroom opposite number.

Sipping her coffee, she was still sick with herself, appalled at what she'd done and at the situation in which she and Brandt now found themselves, a situation that she had orchestrated.

She had risked both of their jobs — still risked them, if the truth came out — to satisfy some undefined and pathetic need to connect. It was beneath her, she knew, or at least beneath the person she had been until her father's death had kicked the foundation out from under her, turned her into the kind of unstable, needy, manipulative, *dangerous* woman she'd always hated and resolved never to become. And the scariest thing was that the lapse with Brandt had completely broadsided her — she'd never even considered discussing Andrew's case with him. There had been that spark, the attraction, and lubricated by drink, she'd just gone for it.

Never mind that he was a colleague, a good guy, a no-bullshit attorney she felt she could really come to like and admire someday. Maybe more than that. Of course, now all of that possible future was out of the question. And that, too — the waste of it, the sheer stupidity — made her sick.

And now — she looked at her watch — *right now,* she had to face her young client and wrest a final agonizing decision from him, one that shouldn't have been his to make in the first place. She should have left the original disposition to fall where it would — with Andrew filed as an adult. Then there would have been an adult trial and he'd all but certainly have been convicted of some degree of murder, but it all would have been according to the system. Now, because of her arrogance, stupidity, blindness, she had placed the entire burden of choice on an unhappy, miserable kid. She wondered if it was a burden he would have the strength to bear. Earlier, when he'd broken down, she'd even viewed that as a positive thing — he'd be persuaded to do what she wanted. But what if he simply couldn't deal with it?

She shook her head, finished the last of her coffee and left the mug on the table.

As was the case with Jason Brandt, this was yet another example of where she'd acted — committed herself, really — before she'd considered the implications of what she was setting in motion. She could only pray that Andrew was in fact guilty, as she'd assumed and believed all along. As she'd convinced his parents. That would make Andrew's admission, though still difficult, acceptable, even preferable, as a strategy.

As she turned up the walkway to the cabins, she stopped and looked up at the razor-wire fence. After she got Andrew's admission sewed up tonight, she vowed she would change and never put a client in such a position again. But first she had to get his admission. First that. Then begin work on fixing herself.

But she couldn't lose sight of her objective in the short term. Too much was already riding on Andrew's admission. She couldn't let the accumulation of this day's terrible events weaken her resolve or blind her to her first duty.

"Don't wimp out now," she said aloud to herself, and started up to the cabins.

"Who was that?"

Frannie took off her reading glasses and put down her P. D. James. She was in bed, propped against her reading pillow. She had let her red hair down and now it hung to her shoulders and shone in the room's light.

Hardy turned from his desk by the room's door. "Amy."

Frannie checked the clock by the bed. "At eleven-fifteen?"

"She didn't want me to worry and lose any of those precious minutes of sleep that are so important to men of a certain age."

"What were you going to be worried about? That now you're not, I presume."

He spent a minute filling her in on his concern that Wu might find herself having to renege with Boscacci. "But she just got back home from what must have been a marathon session with Andrew down at YGC. She wanted me to know that she had nailed down the plea."

"Well, there's a relief. I would have tossed all night." Frannie went to pick up her book, stopped. "It took her twenty minutes to tell you that?"

"To do it justice."

"And how old is this boy?"

"Seventeen."

Frannie made a sad face. "Seventeen."

A nod. "And, unfortunately, a killer. A double killer, actually. Eventually, apparently, he gave that up to Amy."

"Confessed, you mean?"

"Well, agreed to admit the petition, which is pleading guilty. And since that's the deal Amy cut with Boscacci, I'm glad he finally got religion around it."

"So what was the deal with Boscacci?"

Hardy filled in the particulars for his wife, concluding with the comment that Amy had been smart to keep Andrew's parents away while she put the pressure on the kid.

"Why is that?" Frannie asked.

"Because he'd been telling Mom and Dad he didn't do it."

"But he did?"

"Yep, if he's pleading, which he is."

"So then tell me again why he wouldn't

agree to plead guilty if his parents were there."

Hardy stopped and turned by the closet. "Because, my love, he continues to scam them. The dad's paying the bills. First he can be a good boy and assure them to their face that he's innocent, then he can save his own skin by telling Amy the truth. And — the real beauty of it all — he can then go back to his parents and tell them that Amy talked him into the whole thing. She coerced him. It wasn't his fault. He didn't really kill anybody. He's a good boy."

A long moment passed, his wife staring into the empty space in front of her. "You are so cynical."

"Life makes smart people cynical," he said. "It's a sad but true fact."

"Not all of them." Frannie let out a deep sigh. A shadow of distaste crossed her face.

"Cynical's not so bad," Hardy said. "It saves a lot of heartache down the line."

"Right. I know. That's what you think." She closed her eyes for a second, drew a heavy breath, weariness bleeding out of her. "I guess I'm just worried about you."

"Me? *Moi?* I?"

Tightening her lips, biting down against some strong emotion, she said, "Never mind," and turned away from him.

"That was a little humor, Frannie. Just

trying to lighten it up."

Her chest rose and fell twice. Finally, she faced him. "That's what I'm worried about. Everything being a joke."

He tried to keep it light, josh her out of whatever it was. "That's funny," he said, "I wish more things were jokes."

When suddenly, none of it was a joke at all anymore. She threw off the covers and was out of bed, nearly running across to the bathroom, closing the door behind her. The lock clicked.

Hardy stood stock-still, his head down. After ten seconds, he went over and knocked. Whispered. "Fran? Are you all right?"

He thought he heard a sob.

"Whatever it is, I'm sorry." He waited a moment. "No more joking if you come out. Promise."

Finally. "In a minute."

It was more like ten.

He was lying on the bed, hands behind his head. He barely dared look at her, afraid he might scare her off. The two of them hadn't had a cross word since before the shoot-out nearly a year and half ago. He didn't want anything to be wrong between them now. He said nothing while she got into her side of the bed, pulled the blankets up over her. "I didn't mean to be so dramatic," she said. "I'm sorry."

"You can be dramatic anytime you want."

He waited for another minute, perhaps two. A very long time.

Finally, she sighed. "I don't mean to be critical of you," she said. "It's just that I am so worried about you."

"You don't need to be. I'm fine."

"Maybe you are, but you're not the same person you always said you wanted to be." She shook her head. "I'm not saying this right."

"Okay. Take your time. I'm not going anywhere."

She wrestled with it for another minute or more. Finally, she sighed. "I just don't know if there's anything you care about anymore."

"I care about you. And the kids."

"No. I know you love us, but I mean with yourself, with your life. Are you happy with your life?"

A million glib answers, the usual grab bag, sprung to his mind. But that, of course, was what she was getting at. He sat up and half turned away from her. "Am I happy? What makes you think I'm not?"

"It's not what I think."

"But something, just now, made you ask."

She reached over and touched his back. "It's not just now. And maybe it's the same something that's making you not answer."

He shifted to face her. "I honestly don't know what that is, Frannie." Then: "I don't feel like I'm doing anything different."

"You don't?"

"No. Not consciously anyway."

"No? What about this boy Amy just called you about? Andrew?"

"What about him?"

"You're happy with him going to jail for eight years?"

Another shrug. "It beats the alternative, which is life in prison. It's also the deal Amy made. It seemed like a good one."

"If he's guilty."

Hardy shrugged. "Amy says he's admitting, so he probably is. Either way, though, the deal gets him out not much later than if he went to trial and got acquitted anyway."

"So eight years for an innocent person is okay with you?"

"Well, first, as I said, he's probably not innocent. And second, he's already in the system. So he's looking at a year or two, minimum, before anything shakes out anyway."

"Which leaves six years. In six years, your own little boy is twenty."

Hardy ran a palm over his cheek. "So

this is about Andrew Bartlett?"

Frannie shook her head. "It's about . . ." She started over. "It just seems everything you do nowadays has to do with manipulating the rules somehow. It's all just cynicism, and money, and cutting the deal."

Hardy's voice hardened perceptibly. "Maybe you don't remember last year too well, Frannie. When you and I tried to play by the rules, and got Polaroids with gunsights drawn on over our kids. The experience hasn't quite paled on me. So yeah, I guess I've gotten a little jaded on the whole play-by-the-rules concept. If I'm good at bending them and that makes life easy, I'm a sap if I don't."

"That's what you tell yourself?"

He turned now, frankly glaring. "Yes, it is. And I do very well at it."

Frannie glared back. "And that's also why you drink all the time now? Because it helps you forget how you're living?"

"What I'm doing is supporting this family, Frannie. The best way I know how."

Frannie watched a muscle twitch in his jaw. "Look," she said, "you cut a deal on this child molester guy the other morning, when you know there was a time you wouldn't have gotten within a mile of him."

"That was fifty thousand dollars' worth of —"

"Stop. Then you go to lunch, have a few drinks, and make a deal for your firm to help elect the DA. Then you have some wine at your partners meeting and try to cut a deal to make poor Gina come back to work when you know that her heart's gone out of it . . ."

"Let me ask you this, Frannie — tell me someone whose heart hasn't gone out of it, especially after . . ." He let it hang.

Frannie waited until he met her eyes again. "I don't mean to make you mad. I just don't believe that the person cutting all these deals is who you really are."

"Who I am." His laugh rang dry and empty. "Who I am is a guy who's lost faith in the process. But the bills keep on coming, the kids' college is around the corner. What am I supposed to do? Just stop?"

"Maybe you could do something you care about." She moved over toward him, put her arms around his shoulders. "Here," she said, "lie down with me. Close your eyes. You don't have to make any decisions right now, tonight. But a blind person can see how unhappy you are, how it's all frantic and manic and going going going just to keep busy."

"Eat, drink and be merry, for tomorrow we die."

She kissed him. "You're not going to die tomorrow."

She felt him growing calmer next to her, his breathing more regular. He put his arm around her and she lay up against him. After another minute, he said, "I think maybe I am drinking a little too much."

She noted the repetition of the disclaiming qualifiers — "I think," "maybe," "a little." But it was nevertheless an admission of sorts and, she hoped, a start.

After another couple of minutes, his body seemed to settle next to her. Sleep trying to claim him. "I'm tired," he said. Then, "I'm worried about Abe, too." The words were a barely audible mumble.

Then he was asleep.

Back at her apartment, Wu changed out of her lawyer clothes and chose a black leather miniskirt, a diaphanous red shirt over a skin-colored bra, a heavy leather jacket against the cold wind. Fifteen minutes after she'd hung up with Dismas Hardy, she was among the packed bodies at Indigo's, another bar at the triangle. At a dinner-plate-sized table, twirling her first cosmopolitan of the night with a well-manicured hand, she perched herself on a high stool and showed a lot of leg. The volume of the music — an endless bass and drum loop — made conversation impossible, but she didn't mind.

She didn't want to talk. She didn't want

to think about Jason Brandt, either. Or Andrew Bartlett.

Wu shrugged out of her jacket, put it across her lap, straightened her back and turned to survey the groups of men who were drinking and laughing all around her. She caught one of the guys — good-looking in a grungy way, long blond hair, couple of earrings — checking the assets she so artfully displayed.

He was very much interested.

She smiled, slipped off the stool, got her drink in one hand and her jacket in the other, and moved in to cut him out.

10

The wind blew itself out overnight, but it was still unseasonably cold. A high, clear sky, bright sun. A rare city frost bloomed on every patch of green — admittedly not many of them — that Wu passed as she drove up Market Street.

Her hands shook and her eyes burned, but she was still thankful about the timing of the hearing this morning. The ten o'clock call meant she didn't have to go by the office and check in before driving to the YGC, and this had allowed her to grab an extra hour or two of sleep, badly needed after all the cocktails that had gone with last night's adventure. She hadn't made it back to her apartment until sometime after 3:00 a.m. She hadn't fallen asleep until nearly dawn, and was jarred awake by the alarm two hours later — disoriented, depleted, wrung out.

Still, by the time she entered the holding cell behind Arvid Johnson's courtroom, the mixed jolt from the Dexedrine and the espresso had kicked in. Handcuffed, Andrew sat on a cement bench built against the wall. He seemed subdued and nervous, shrugging a greeting of sorts, then going back to studying the pattern in the floor between his feet.

Wu put on a brave face, sat up close next to him. He smelled of disinfectant and soap. "Are you holding up all right? Did you get some sleep? How do you feel now? Are you still comfortable with our decision?" To each question, she got a shrug, a nod.

She tried a few more conversational gambits, telling him that the judge was going to want to hear him admit the petition himself. All he had to do was follow her lead and it would all be over before he knew it. He nodded some more, then at last shut her up with a curt "I know what I've got to do."

She had to take that as an assurance. He was going to be okay.

Hal and Linda North were at their place in the first row, holding hands. Wu nodded to them, got a response from Hal, nothing from Linda but a blank stare. On the opposite side of the room, Jason Brandt directed his complete attention to the contents of some binders that were open in front of him. He avoided any eye contact with Wu. The two "rays of sunshine" had taken their respective positions again, Nelson by the back door to the holding cell, Cottrell in the otherwise-empty jury box. The court recorder and probation officer chatted amiably, and then suddenly the door to Arvid Johnson's chambers opened and the judge, in his robes, was on the bench.

Again, there was little sense of ritual. The probation officer simply got a nod from the judge, stood and began. "Good morning. This is Petition JW02-4555, the matter of Andrew Bartlett, who is present in the courtroom. Also present are the minor's natural mother, Linda Bartlett North, and his stepfather, Hal North. The minor's attorney is Ms. Amy Wu. Mr. Jason Brandt is the district attorney."

Judge Johnson thanked the officer and peered down over his glasses. "Ms. Wu, it's my understanding that your minor client Mr. Bartlett and the district attorney have agreed to a mutually acceptable disposition in this matter. Is that correct?"

Wu put a hand under her client's arm and the two of them rose. "Yes, your honor."

Johnson had done this innumerable times, and although Wu was tuned to a high pitch of anxiety, for him it obviously held all the excitement and drama of a quilting bee. "Mr. Bartlett, I want to ask you if you understand the decision that's been reached here on your behalf."

Andrew's voice was firm. "Yes, your honor, I talked about it with Ms. Wu last night." He turned halfway around, gave a small nod to his parents, then came back to face the judge.

Johnson nodded. "And you understand, Mr. Bartlett, that by admitting this petition filed against you by the State of California that you in fact claim full responsibility for the murders of Michael Mooney and Laura Wright? And that immediately following this proceeding, you will begin serving a term at the California Youth Authority, and will remain in custody until your twenty-fifth birthday?"

Andrew hesitated for an instant and Wu, jumping in, spoke up for him. "Yes, your honor. Mr. Bartlett understands."

But Johnson shook his head. "I'd like to hear it from him, Counselor. Mr. Bartlett?"

Andrew looked at Wu, then up to the judge. When he began the first time, he was almost inaudible, so he cleared his throat and started again. "I understand about the sentence. That's what we decided I had to agree to." Clearing his throat again, he went on. "But I'm not really comfortable . . ." He stopped, turned back to his parents again, came back around to Johnson. "But I can't say that I

225

killed anybody, because I didn't."

Wu had a sense of the world spinning before her. She reached out, put her hand on her client's arm. "No, wait, Andrew!" Then, addressing the judge: "Your honor, if I may —"

But Johnson gaveled her to silence. He removed his glasses, squinted out over the podium. "No, Counselor, you may not, not for a minute anyway." He pointed a finger at Andrew. "Mr. Bartlett, I want to hear you say it yourself one more time. You're not admitting the petition?"

"Your honor." Wu spoke up in a panic. She couldn't let this happen. "I'd like to request a short recess."

Over on her right, she heard Brandt close his binder with a sharp snap.

"Request denied," Johnson said. "We just got here." Back at Andrew. "Mr. Bartlett? Repeat your plea."

This time Andrew's voice was much more forceful. "I'm just saying that I didn't kill anybody."

Behind her, Wu could hear the Norths reacting with a muted enthusiasm. Needing to undo what Andrew had done, she turned to him, whispered urgently. "You can't do this, Andrew. You're looking at life in prison. Don't you understand?"

The judge brought his gavel down again. "Ms. Wu, Mr. Brandt." He motioned with his head. "Chambers." And he was up in a swirl of black robes.

Johnson was waiting, facing them as they came through his door. No trace of anything avuncular softened his countenance as he reached around and closed the door behind them all. He came right to the point. "I don't tolerate being trifled with in my courtroom, Ms. Wu. What is this supposed to be, some kind of publicity stunt? Or delaying tactic?"

She tried to swallow, get a breath. "No, your honor."

"No to which?"

"Neither, your honor. I'm as surprised as you are."

Johnson looked to Brandt — who wisely stood at respectful attention — then came back to Wu. "This is unacceptable. What do you expect me to do now?"

"I'll go talk to him."

"And what good will that do?"

"I'll get him . . . He's just afraid. He was on board with this last night. He just couldn't go through with it, that's all."

The judge crossed his arms. "Stop wasting my time. As far as I'm concerned, he's denied the petition. This is really unacceptable, Counselor," he added. "Wholly unacceptable." Then, making no effort to hide his anger and disgust, he continued.

"All right, let's get the show back on the road, go back in there and get this done as fast as we can."

Brandt spoke. "Your honor, if I may?"

Johnson turned his glare on him. "What?"

"I just wanted to say that Ms. Wu isn't as naive as she's pretending to be. She knew the conditions when she cut her deal. Andrew admits or he goes up as an adult."

"I think we all knew that," Johnson said. "So now we're going to have him tried as an adult. Ms. Wu should agree to that." His stare at her brooked no denial.

Brandt nodded, satisfied. "Then we want him certified today, your honor, unless the plan all along was to get him to juvenile court by misrepresenting his intention to admit."

Wu, holding her temper in check, talked to the judge. "Your honor, I promise you, I don't know what he's talking about. I had no such plan. I didn't want Andrew to have to run the risk of an adult trial. An admission, to me, seemed like the right thing."

Johnson's face remained grave, his color high. "I'm just wondering if it's possible that you are actually this ill-prepared, Ms. Wu. Agreeing to plead out a case before securing the client's agreement?" But he didn't wait for her to answer. "It doesn't matter. The point is that Mr. Bartlett, as you undoubtedly must be aware, is already in the juvenile system, you see. Now he *can't* be tried as an adult without a seven-oh-seven hearing first. Do you expect me to believe you didn't know that?"

Suddenly the enormity of her miscalculation came into much clearer focus. Wu had been acting as though she needed Andrew's admission to secure his place in the juvenile system. But this was not, strictly speaking, the case. What she needed his admission for was merely so that the sentencing could proceed. In fact, Boscacci's initial filing had assured that, legally, Andrew was already in the juvenile system, and hence protected from LWOP as long as he stayed there. "I didn't think . . . ," she stammered.

"All right," Johnson snapped at her. "You didn't think. So can I now assume that you will agree to waive the seven-oh-seven hearing and have Mr. Bartlett recertified an adult today, as Mr. Brandt here has requested?"

"I . . . I can't do that, your honor."

"No," Brandt exploded. "No, of course you can't." He obviously, justifiably, thought she'd planned to have her client deny the petition all along. This would not only delay Andrew's eventual trial as an adult, but place another administrative hurdle — the 707 hearing — in the middle of his path. He appealed to Johnson. "I don't believe for a moment, your honor, that this wasn't her plan all along."

"That's not true. That's just not true, your honor."

Brandt ignored her. "Your honor, the only way to read this is she set it up so that she could stall down here for months. But I'm certain that the district attorney is going to want to get this matter back into adult court, so I'd like to ask that the seven-oh-seven be calendared at the earliest possible time."

Johnson gave a last withering look at Wu, then nodded. "I'm inclined to agree with you, Counselor. Let's go out and put it on the record."

11

"Look at the bright side," Wes Farrell was saying. "She's convinced the clients that she did it on purpose. She planned it all along. Now the kid catches a break in the seven-oh-seven, maybe he never has to go to trial as an adult, and everybody wins."

"Except the DA never trusts anybody from the firm again."

"Picky, picky." Farrell, on the couch across the room, shrugged. "They probably didn't trust us all that much anyway. Remember, we're *defense* attorneys, a bare evolutionary step above pond scum."

"That much, you think?" Hardy could joke, but he wasn't amused.

"Maybe not, if you want to get technical. The thing is, though, we're going to help get Jackman elected again, so we're his pals, or will be again soon. It'll all blow over in a few months, and they'll be trusting us as much as they ever did, which — don't kid yourself — is not close to the world record anyway. Meanwhile, Amy's got the Norths thinking she's a latter-day Clara Darrow, snatching victory from the jaws of defeat."

"Swell." Hardy pushed his chair back from his desk. His elbows rested on the arms of the chair, fingers templed at his lips. "So she spins it to deceive the people who are paying her?"

"Paying *us*, you mean. Just keep repeating the paying part and you'll feel better."

"I won't feel better. I don't want to get paid to lie to my clients."

"Well, fortunately, they're not your clients, they're Amy's."

Hardy straightened himself up in his chair. "Precisely the opposite point you made about one sentence ago, you notice. When the Norths were paying, they were our clients; when they're being lied to, they're Amy's."

"You've stumbled upon my specialty, honed in years of debate. Answers tailored to justify any course of action." Farrell broke a smile. "It's a modest enough talent, but it's seen me through some dark days. And what do you mean, you don't want to get paid to lie? I thought that's what we *got* paid for."

But Hardy held up a hand. "Wes. Enough. Okay?"

The smile faded. "Okay. So what's she going to do? Amy?"

"First thing, I had her go down to Boscacci and apologize in person. Tell him the truth, which is that the kid decided on his own not to admit."

Farrell sat back and crossed a leg. "And why do you think he did that?"

Hardy gave it a minute. "He's young. Eight years sounds like the rest of his life. But for now, I guess he'd rather take bad odds at pulling life than no odds at eight years." He sighed. "He's going to find out."

Inspector Sergeant Pat Belou stepped out of the elevator on the fourth floor of the Hall of Justice. She had ridden up from the lobby with her partner Lincoln Russell, a well-dressed mid-thirties black inspector. Also in the small enclosed elevator had been about ten other citizens, at least one of whom badly needed a shower, some new clothes, a toothbrush, maybe industrial disinfectant and certainly deodorant. Lots of deodorant.

"That was the longest elevator ride I've ever taken," Belou said when the door closed behind her. "We ought to arrest that guy as a health hazard."

"Not till he kills somebody," Russell said. "We're homicide. He's got to kill somebody first. Those are the rules."

"Well, he almost killed me. That ought to count. Anybody goes with him all the way to the top, their life's in danger."

"Maybe we catch him on the way down," Russell said.

Belou blew out through her mouth, waving the air in front of her nose. She was a thirty-year-old, tall and rangy woman with an outdoorsy look, a bit of a heavy jaw, some old, faded acne scars on her face. But her large mouth smiled easily, she laughed as though she meant it, and her shoulder-length hair, a shade lighter than dirty blond and with a perennially windblown look, set off lovely blue eyes.

The inspectors turned into the hallway, and Belou stopped suddenly, hit her partner on the arm. "Glitsky," she said. "Good a time as any."

Russell said he'd see her in the homicide detail, and she turned around and came back to the double doors by the elevator lobby that led to the admin offices. She was just asking the receptionist at the outside desk if she could have a word with the deputy chief when the man himself appeared from somewhere in the back. He wore a deep frown and was accompanied by a sergeant in uniform, Paganucci by his name tag.

She spoke right up. "Sir? Sergeant Belou. Homicide."

Glitsky, obvious frazzled, came to a full stop. "I'm running to a meeting," he told her. "If you'd like to leave a message with Melissa here, I'll get back to you as soon as I can."

"Yes, sir. But this is short. Ted Reed."

"Ted Reed?"

"Elizabeth Cary's brother. Lake Elsinore."

"What about him?"

"He's been in custody on an arson charge down in Escondido for most of the last month. The public defender down there told me he must have decided he liked the food in jail, didn't want to waste his money on bail. His trial's in a couple of months. Bottom line is he didn't kill his sister."

Glitsky nodded. Something else was distracting him, but he said, "Okay. Thanks. Good job."

Then, to Melissa: "I'm at the Young Community Developers ribbon cutting out on Van Ness. I won't talk to any reporters before the next scheduled press conference. Tony." He turned to the sergeant who accompanied him. "How fast can we get there? We're late already."

"Lights and sirens, five, six minutes."

"If they call," Glitsky told Melissa, "tell them we're on the way."

Then they were gone, jogging through the elevator lobby, hitting the stairs at a run.

Behind the reception desk, Melissa looked up at Belou, shook her head in commiseration. "Man don't belong doing this. Gonna make hisself sick." The phone rang and she picked it up, said without ceremony that the deputy chief wasn't available, hung up. She smiled at Belou, pointed at the telephone. "One of the reporters he didn't want to talk to. They eatin' him up."

"What about?"

"This LeShawn Brodie thing. You following that?"

"The Greyhound guy?"

"That's him, sugar."

"What about him?"

"So you ain't heard? He was headin' back this way, but they pulled him over up in Colfax. Now he's got hisself twenty hostages in some diner up there, already killed two of 'em." She pointed to the phone. "Them reporters. They wantin' his hide."

Hardy asked Phyllis to hold his calls. He locked his door, took off his shoes, loosened his tie and lay down on one of his couches. He'd had a good breakfast with the family and wasn't remotely hungry, and he decided he would start to break the bottle-of-wine-with-lunch habit by skipping lunch entirely. Eliminate the temptation.

He fell asleep instantly, and awoke nearly

three hours later. Alone in his office, he threw water on his face, brewed a cup of espresso and drank it down as soon as it didn't scald.

Replaying Frannie's monologue from last night in his mind, he realized that all of his friends involved in the gunfight had been wrestling with their long-term reactions and demons ever since. He shouldn't have been surprised that he had his own issues, and that he'd been ignoring them as best he could. But from today on, he resolved that things were going to change. It was just a matter of will, and that had always been one of his strengths.

But today, after he'd finished his coffee, he got up to pour himself another cup and noticed the bottle of Rémy Martin in his bar. Without agonizing about it too much, he poured a shot into his cup and added coffee. He'd never entertained the thought that he intended to quit drinking altogether, and after all he'd not had any wine for lunch. He deserved that shot as a reward for his earlier abstinence, and one shot wasn't going to affect him adversely in any event. It would just take a little of the edge off.

Raising the cup to his mouth, though, he hesitated.

Maybe Frannie's point last night was that his normal response to conflict or inner turmoil lately had been to round off the edges. He was literally dulled, and in that state, nothing was really that serious. You could take the easiest course, ride it out, have a few drinks, and usually things tended to work out acceptably. You couldn't spend your whole life worrying about the what ifs, the small stuff. And that was counterproductive, too. At least as debilitating as drinking.

In fact, seen in that light, drinking had enabled him to function better. He came to work every day, drummed up mega-business with whoever could pay his fees, used his natural talent for schmoozing. He was good with people, that was all. And with a bit of a load on, even more charming.

Like Wu. Charming.

The thought stopped him cold.

Like Wu. Screwing up. Hiding behind that old glib shit. Ultimately failing those who might be counting on you.

Leaving the cup untouched on the counter, he instead walked over to his dart area, opened the cabinets and pulled the three tungsten customs from the board. It wasn't so long ago that he used to throw his darts to clear his mind as a relaxation technique, and now he got to the line in the floor, turned and threw. Threw again. Again. One round.

Before he moved forward to pull the

round from the board, he went over to the counter, picked up the coffee cup and poured it down the sink.

It was nearly four o'clock by the time he knocked on Gina Roake's door.

She had the corner office, an altogether different work space than Hardy's. There were a few stuffed chairs and a sofa, an old wooden coffee table, a computer table and chair, but no formal desk to speak of. Instead of hardwood floors, Gina went with wall-to-wall carpet, a shade darker than champagne. Cheaply framed posters of old movies — *Giant, Casablanca, Gone With the Wind, Citizen Kane* — decorated the one big wall. The other, by the door, mostly held her law books, although there was one shelf of David Freeman memorabilia — an empty bottle of La Grande Dame champagne (from the day he'd proposed to her); a picture of the two of them outside on the deck at the Alta Mira in Sausalito, the bay shimmering in the background; a hand-blown blue and red glass perfume bottle; some erotic if not frankly obscene porcelains from Chinatown; a clean ashtray with an unlit cigar and a book of matches from the Crown Room at the Fairmont. Then there were the windows, six of them to Hardy's two. In the afternoon, now, the light suffused the room with a golden glow.

He stopped just inside, carefully closed the door behind him. "You busy?"

She was at the computer, work showing on the screen. "I decided you were at least a little bit right. If I'm going to have my name on the door, I should pull some of the weight."

He drew around one of the folding chairs, flipped it open and sat on it. "That's funny, I decided I was at least mostly wrong. The firm's making a fortune. I was a horse's ass. Am." He gestured vaguely around the room. "If you don't want to work, you've earned the right not to." He waited a moment. "So how are you?"

She turned to face him. Thought a moment. "I'm all right. I think if I exercised any more, I'd self-destruct. Which is maybe what I was trying to do. I'm damn sure already the strongest woman my age I know, if any man has the guts to want to find out." But the smile faded. "But it wasn't physical strength, though, after all, was it? It was bullets."

"It was bullets," Hardy agreed.

A silence ensued. In only a few seconds, Gina's face tracked through several variations on the themes of grief, revenge and regret. Last year she'd killed a man, and the experience had scarred her. "So what brings you down to this neck of the woods?

If it was just your apology — unnecessary, but nice."

"It wasn't just that. It's Amy."

He gave Gina a brief recap of the events leading up to this morning's fiasco in juvenile court, and by the time he finished, Gina had turned and was facing him, her face set with worry. "She made the deal before she had the client's consent?"

"Right." Then he added, "It's possible she thought he had given it."

"How's that? Did she have him sign a statement?"

"I don't think so, no. She called me last night and said it was locked up. Solid."

"But didn't get his John Hancock? And then he went sideways?"

"Last minute, in the courtroom." Hardy shrugged. "It happens."

"Not as often as you might think if you do it right. So. What do you want me to do?"

A pause. "For Amy? Nothing. For me, I could use some guidance. I'm the managing partner, and I've managed this whole thing wrong up until now. I knew her client hadn't signed off. I kept convincing myself that I should trust her judgment that he'd come around. That was irresponsible enough, but it was more than that, really."

Roake cocked her head. "What, though, exactly?"

Hardy took a minute deciding what he should say. "You may remember, Amy's father died a few months ago. Since then she's been . . . distracted. And her work's been suffering, today's problem being the best of several good examples." Again, he paused. "I can't help but feel that a lot of where this has gotten to is my fault. I should have stepped in at the git-go, and three or four other stops along the way. But the point is, she's been playing fast and loose with this boy's life and it probably feels relatively okay to her because she's playing fast and loose with her own."

Roake leaned back into her chair, let out a heavy breath. "People are going to do what they're going to do, Diz. Do you think she's competent? Legally?"

"I don't know. She's got a good mind. But the only bright spot right now, if you want to call it that, is that she's somehow conned the parents, who are paying the bills, that this has been her plan all along, to pretend to go along with the deal to get Andrew declared a juvenile."

"Which, I take it, isn't true?"

"Right."

"So she's still lying to her clients?"

Hardy tried a weak grin. " 'Spinning' is the preferred term of art, I believe. But it's going to unravel fast enough, you watch. Boscacci's going to demand a seven-oh-

242

seven before she knows what hit her. And if she loses there, which is a good bet because not only does she have the burden of proof, but the judge already hates her, then her boy's looking at adult murder with specials." Hardy found a chair and sat. "I'm thinking I have to step in, take her off it. That would mitigate the personal issues with Boscacci and the judge anyway. Although the paying customers currently think Amy is a genius. If I yank her, they quit. Maybe she quits, too. Did I mention the fees here? It's going to go adult murder, and that's six figures, high profile. We don't want to lose it."

Roake crossed her arms over her chest, whirled halfway around in her chair, and stared out toward one of the windows. Finally: "If memory serves, the seven-oh-seven's not about evidence, is it? It's only a question of whether the child can be rehabilitated in the juvenile system or should be punished in the adult. Isn't that about right?"

Hardy nodded.

"Okay, then. And how is Andrew's record otherwise?"

"Nothing to speak of. One joyride, community service and a fine. Expunged."

"Well, then." Roake considered a moment. "In that case, she might have a shot. The court can't say that the boy's already a hardened criminal and needs to spend the rest of his life locked away. She might pull it off."

"Maybe." Hardy had his doubts. He knew perhaps better than Roake that the last of the five criteria in determining whether a defendant was legally a juvenile or an adult was the gravity of the offense, and there was nothing more serious than murder. On that alone, Hardy thought, the 707 hearing was doomed to failure.

He ran a hand down his cheek. "I don't want to step on her, Gina, or God knows, fire her. But her focus has been off on this since the beginning, and now, especially after she reneged on Boscacci, he's going to want to take her down." He sat back, crossed his arms in a pensive mode, looked from window to window around the room. Suddenly, he came back to Roake, his eyes bright with an idea. "How about if I tell her I'd like to sit second chair?"

Roake gave it some thought. "She might resent that, too. She might even quit. And your hours on top of hers? Would the clients go for that?"

"I don't care about my hours," Hardy said. "I wouldn't charge for them. Long term, getting Amy straight and on track is worth more to the firm than I'd bill, don't you think?"

Roake smiled, spoke gently. "You don't

have to ask me, but that doesn't sound like the managing partner I know and love. He's been pretty tough on billing lately, even with some of our partners."

"Touché," Hardy said, smiling.

But Roake was back to business. "She still might quit, though. Take it as a vote of no-confidence."

"Except that she knows she's screwed up. I think it might be more likely, especially with the other pressures she's feeling, that she'll be grateful she's not fired."

Roake, warming to the idea, was nodding. "Okay. You could certainly say you've got every right as managing partner to demand a closer accountability. You can't let another mistake happen on your watch. What's she going to say? No?"

"She could. She might."

But Roake shook her head. "Sure, but I don't think so. I think she'll thank you for offering. So, assuming she'd be okay with it, how would you handle it logistically?"

Hardy came forward, suddenly pumped up at the prospect. "The way I see it, I get up to speed on the evidence while she's arguing the rehab criteria at the seven-oh-seven. That way, even if we lose at the hearing, we're stronger for the adult trial. Plus, between you and me, if her personal problems become too much for her, I'm already on board. The clients now know me.

It's good insurance." He dropped his head for a moment, stunned at how right this decision felt.

Frannie's message the night before had struck a reverberant chord. He needed something to reconnect himself with who he was — an officer of the court, a justice freak, a guardian of the law. What he needed for his own good was a pure case, where you defended your client because the presumption was innocence. If the prosecution couldn't prove otherwise, couldn't prevail against a spirited defense, the client walked.

This was neither cynical nor manipulative — it was the essence of the system. And though Hardy had lost some faith, a great deal of faith, in the mechanics, in the way it sometimes played out in the real world, suddenly it was crystal clear that this imperfect system, if he still believed in anything, was what he believed in. More, it was an opportunity for his own redemption that he couldn't let pass.

He hadn't taken a murder case in over three years. They were too time-consuming, too physically grueling, too emotionally demanding. They played hell with his home life.

There was better money to be made quicker and more fun to be had cutting deals. You could skim along the top of things and not worry too much — hell, not worry at all. You laughed until your face hurt, and you'd be damned if you'd ever have to internalize any of your clients' problems. You just fixed their messes.

And yet at some level, Hardy never lost his awareness that the fun was about as ephemeral and nourishing as cotton candy, and often left a worse aftertaste. And the money often felt dirty.

He might not have wanted to face it squarely, but once he did, it wasn't any mystery to him why he'd been drinking too much. He could see where it would all lead if he continued. The picture wasn't pretty. No, more. It was so ugly that, thank God, it had made Frannie cry.

Maybe it was time to engage again, to let himself care.

He lifted his head, broke a weary half grin. "So. Second chair? You think?"

Roake nodded. "It's got your name on it."

Amy Wu hadn't been able to face the idea of going back into the Sutter Street office and facing Dismas Hardy and her other colleagues again, not after the brutal dressing-down she'd taken at the hands of Allan Boscacci, who'd first kept her waiting for almost two hours, then informed her that he had already filed a motion for a

707 hearing on the Bartlett matter, to have the boy declared an adult.

He hoped she realized what she'd done, and wanted her to be under no illusion — she wasn't getting away with it. Oh, and by the way, if she ever wanted to communicate with him about any case ever again, she should do it in writing, signed by her, no "dictated, not read" bullshit. And he didn't mean e-mail. And she would find this to be the policy for every assistant district attorney in his office.

Badly shaken, fighting tears, she'd crossed Bryant, then descended into the dark and ripe-smelling stairway under the bail bondsman's office that led down to Lou the Greek's. She'd taken her stool at the bar and ordered straight vodka.

No cosmopolitans today. No frou-frou little cocktails. She wasn't here to party. She was drinking.

By five-thirty, Lou's was jammed and Amy's immediate troubles had mostly been drowned. The bar was Mecca for the lawyers and cops who worked out of the Hall of Justice, and Amy's situation with Andrew Bartlett was as nothing compared with the shit storm that had developed over Deputy Chief Glitsky's handling of the LeShawn Brodie matter.

During the late morning and early afternoon, Brodie had taken the lives of seven of his hostages, one every twenty minutes while the local cops and the highway patrol argued over who had jurisdiction to provide a helicopter that would take him to the Sacramento airport. There, Brodie evidently had been convinced that authorities would also supply him with a plane to take him to Cuba. In fact, a police sniper shot him in the forehead when he'd gotten one step outside of the diner's entrance, while the helicopter waited, its rotors twirling, in the parking lot.

Both of the televisions over the bar at Lou's had been carrying nothing else for the past several hours, while the pros and cons of the original police strategy had fueled an endless and passionate debate among the clientele.

By the time it had gotten dark, Amy had had six vodka martinis and was ready to go home and get some sleep. But an aggressively clever young defense attorney named Barry had outlasted the other hopefuls around her, and now he had his arm around her as they negotiated the doors and came out into the suddenly full-dark night.

At the top of the stairs, Barry turned to her and she found herself being kissed. Then they were walking together down the alley that ran alongside Lou's. She had herself tucked inside the jacket of his suit against the chill. She'd already told him she didn't think she should drive, but he said he was sober enough and could drive them both.

He was parked where she had parked. Where every visitor to the Hall parked. In the All-Day just up at the end of the alley.

The lot was one block wide, bounded by three-story buildings on both sides, closing the place in. Every spot, alley to alley, was filled during business hours every day. Now the place held only three cars — Amy's by the near building, and then Barry's car and another one parked in adjacent spaces on the far side. One light, burning from high on a pole by the deserted pay station, cast its pool over the area, leaving the borders in deep shadow.

When they got to his car, Barry opened the door for her and she lowered herself, taking care lest she collapse into the seat. As they backed out, the car's headlights raked the building in front of them, then washed over the car in the adjacent parking space.

Following the beam through heavy-lidded eyes, Amy sat up abruptly. "Wait a minute. Stop!"

"What?" Barry slammed on the brakes.

Before the car had fully stopped, Amy opened the door. She was halfway out, staggering. She fell once, cut her knees, then got up and moved forward again.

"What are you doing?" Barry, still in the car, called from behind her.

She turned and pointed. "Get your lights next to that car, over by the wall." She kept moving over toward a dark amorphous mound on the pavement up against the building. As the headlights hit it, its shape became obvious.

Barry came running up next to her. "Jesus Christ!"

The body was dressed in a business suit under a trenchcoat. It lay skewed on its side, the face visible now in the headlights. A dark pool had formed under the head, but Amy wasn't able to pay any attention to other details. She stood transfixed, unable to tear her eyes from the awful, vacant stare of the victim.

The dead man was Allan Boscacci.

Part Two

12

"Excuse me, are you a Mr. Hardy?"

It was all he could do to remain polite with the sweet young waitress. It was Date Night and he was out with his wife, having the world's best chicken at the Zuni Cafe. Everyone in his world orbit knew that Wednesday night with Frannie was the one time he was absolutely not to be disturbed. To further that end, he had taken to leaving his cellphone and pager at home. He put down his fork mid-bite, used his napkin, nodded and forced a polite smile. "I have that distinction," he said.

"You have a telephone call."

Frannie, thinking the same thought as Hardy — that it must be one of the kids and if they were interrupting Date Night it was a true emergency — was halfway out of her chair when the waitress added, "An Amy Wu."

Glitsky, in his uniform and on his way to the ring of police cars in the lot, stopped in his tracks, changed directions and walked over to a subdued group who stood in a knot under the pool of light from the pole lamp by the pay booth. He nodded all around, said to Hardy and Frannie, "What are you two doing here?"

Hardy motioned to the circle that was now crawling with police. "They asked us not to leave until they'd talked to us. We're waiting." He half-turned. "You remember my associate, Amy Wu." Hardy paused, came out with it. "She discovered the body."

Wu came forward, still a bit unsteady, and gave Glitsky her hand. "Good to see you again, sir."

Glitsky held onto her hand, squinted down into her face. "Have you been drinking?"

"Yes, sir," she said. "A few down at Lou the Greek's. Barry and I. But we're fine now."

The other man came forward, introduced himself — Barry Hess — said he was who'd called 911. Glitsky took that in, stepped toward the crowd by the body, stopped again. "Anybody get statements from you two yet?" he asked both Hess and Wu. As the people who'd discovered the body, both could probably look forward to a long night in a small interrogation room.

"No, sir," Hess replied.

"I'll try to get somebody over here soon," Glitsky said. Then he closed in on Frannie. "I can see your husband, who lives for parties like this one, but why are you here?"

She forced a weak smile. "It started out as Date Night."

"Right. Of course. Great timing," Glitsky said. "You okay?"

Frannie nodded. "But maybe we'd be more comfortable in a car with the heat on."

Glitsky tossed his head toward Hardy's car. "Go on ahead. I'll send somebody over."

After Wu's short interview at the scene with Sergeant Belou — she had promised to come and give a better, more coherent statement at the Hall tomorrow — she didn't want to be with Barry anymore. It was obvious to Frannie that, badly shaken by the murder, and still very drunk, she didn't want to go home alone, either, so she asked Wu to come and stay with them at their house tonight. Then Dismas could take her down here tomorrow, where she could do any more business that needed to be done at the Hall, pick up her car.

Wu passed out on the drive home. They had to wake her up to let her off at the house with Frannie while Hardy drove around the neighborhood — a constant ritual — and tried to find a parking place. By the time he got back to the house, she was asleep again on the fold-out bed in the family room behind the kitchen.

Hardy couldn't sleep. Sometime well after midnight, he swung quietly out of bed, pulled on a pair of drawstring gray sweatpants and went downstairs.

A bulb over the stove threw out about fifteen watts in the otherwise dark room, and Hardy opened the refrigerator and stared into it. What he craved was some alcohol, get his brain to stop its endless looping. Today there'd been the long nap in the afternoon, no wine with lunch, an interrupted dinner. The drunken condition of Amy Wu, passed out on the fold-a-bed, and Frannie's lack of interest in a nightcap, had somehow constrained him from a drink when they'd gotten home.

Nightcap. A harmless little old nightcap.

Maybe he'd have it now — a couple of fingers of gin and peppermint schnapps over crushed ice. It would help him sleep, finally. And God knew he had to get some sleep if he was going to be any good at work tomorrow. Sleep had to be the first priority. If he had one short one now, the only effect would be sleep. He'd wake up refreshed, strong for whatever challenges the day might bring.

And with Boscacci's murder, there would be lots of them.

But something kept him from opening the freezer, from reaching for the crushed ice.

They kept a three-legged stool in the kitchen because Frannie needed it to reach the higher shelves, and suddenly, the refrigerator still open, Hardy found himself sitting on it, leaning over, elbows on his knees.

In the dimness — stove light, refrigerator light — he turned his hands over, looked at his palms. There was no shake. Closing his eyes, he dropped his head, sighed audibly.

"Sir? Are you all right?" Wu was a spectral shape in the doorway. Barefoot, wrapped in the comforter they'd provided, she came into the light.

He looked up, raised his hand in greeting. "I'm trying to make the critical midnight snack decision. Could you eat something?"

"Do you have some aspirin first?"

"Sure." Hardy reached into the top drawer right next to the refrigerator, where he'd taken to storing the bottle so he could get it with his coffee, so he wouldn't have to walk the extra steps to the bathroom.

"How many you need?"

"What's the legal limit?" she asked.

"I'm impressed, sir. I didn't know you could cook."

"I can't, really. If it's not in that one black pan, I'm hopeless. But that pan, I know all its secrets. I treasure it, for what that's worth. No soap, just salt and a wipe. Nothing ever sticks. It's magic."

Hardy had grabbed one of his daughter's bathrobes and Wu had put it on to come and eat. Now they sat kitty-corner to each other at the dining room table, splitting a very runny four-egg omelette of fried salami, artichoke hearts, cheddar cheese. Sourdough bread. They both had cups of hot Ovaltine.

Hardy had closed the connecting door to the kitchen so his family wouldn't wake up, but still he whispered. "And you can drop the 'sir' if you want. I realize that my august personage is intimidating, but somewhere beneath the awesome authority figure beats what Mr. Buffett calls a schoolboy heart."

"Warren Buffett talks about a schoolboy heart?"

Hardy shook his head. "No. But Jimmy does."

Wu couldn't quite get to a smile. "I've got a searing headache and you've got a schoolboy heart. Want to trade?"

"No, thanks. But they can remain our little secrets." Hardy tore a piece of the bread and sopped up some melted cheese. "Anyway, that pan. My mother got it from *her* mother and gave it to me when I went away to college."

"I bet she missed it."

"Not for long." Hardy pushed some egg around. "My folks both died my freshman year of college. Plane crash."

"I'm sorry. I didn't know that."

"Well, it was a long time ago. I'm over it by now."

Wu squeezed her eyes shut, fighting her hangover, then put down her fork. "You are? Really?"

"Pretty much. Sometimes I have to concentrate to remember them at all. Even what they looked like. And their voices, forget it. That's what I wish the most I had some memory for, their voices. But I can't hear them."

"Do you mind if I ask you how long that took? Before you felt, I don't know, normal again?"

"It was a while." He met her eyes. "Certainly more than four months."

Wu blinked a couple of times. "I keep wishing I'd done something more, somehow. Something my dad would have approved of."

261

"He didn't approve of your being a lawyer?"

"I don't know. More, I think, he didn't approve of how I lived. You know?"

"No. I don't."

"I mean, being almost thirty, not married, no kids. Oh God, I hurt." She pressed her hands up against her temples. "And the great irony is that one of the reasons I stayed in school and became a lawyer was to make him happy. Even if he didn't like me, I could always be a good student, and I thought that pleased him, so I kept at it. But it really didn't matter."

"Why do you think he didn't like you?"

"I don't know. Maybe I was too much like my mom. She left him — left us both, really — when I was thirteen. Another guy she divorced a year later. Then a few after that." She fell silent, pushed again at her temples, drew a pained breath.

"Eat some eggs," Hardy said. "Nothing's worse than cold eggs. Is your mom still around?"

Wu took a bite, shook her head. "No. She got emphysema. She died about ten years ago, but really she hadn't been in the picture for so long, her dying wasn't so hard for me, even though that sounds bad. But my dad . . ." She swallowed, took another bite, drank some chocolate. "Oh, man," she said.

Hardy waited while she ate and gathered some strength.

"Anyway, my dad. He regretted that he didn't marry a pure Chinese. Instead, he marries Mom, you know, a black woman, and his family just hates her, and then I come along and look like her, at least color-wise . . ." She stopped. "And it wasn't like he didn't try to be nice to me, but you can tell if your parent doesn't like you, you really can. Nothing you do is right. And I guess I lost patience with trying all the time and getting nothing back in return and so then I got mad at him, and then . . ." She swiped a finger under one eye. "And then he dies before you can fix it up." She shook her head. "I'm sorry. I don't mean to dump on you."

"It's all right. I knew something was bothering you. I thought it might be something like this. You lose your dad, it's not trivial. Then with the extra baggage. Have you thought about maybe taking some time off, letting some of this settle out?"

"From work? God, no. Work's the thing that's keeping me sane."

"Because it keeps you so busy you don't have to deal with the other personal stuff?"

She started to say something, then pushed back from the table, pulled the robe close around her. She dropped her head, shook it slowly side to side, side to side.

★ ★ ★

They remained at the dining room table, the dishes pushed to one side. Second cups of Ovaltine, now forgotten, had grown tepid in front of them.

Hardy didn't want to add to Wu's pain right now by criticizing her performance in the Bartlett case, but she introduced the topic herself, laying it all out in a torrent of words. She had loved the idea of finessing Brandt, of snookering Boscacci. These arrogant men would see that she was good, could hold her own in a fair fight. Take that, Dad! It should have all worked out.

"Still, you really should have nailed down Andrew's plea before you even tried to make any kind of deal with Allan."

"I realize that now. I just got caught up in the rush of it. If I could do it. I couldn't believe that once Andrew saw the evidence, he wouldn't realize he had to lose."

"Except if it wasn't about the evidence, to him."

"But it's always about the evidence!"

"No. Not always. O.J. wasn't about the evidence. Patty Hearst. Mark Dooher — you remember Wes's famous case? Ask him if it was about the evidence. No. It was about the passion and commitment of the defense. The vision thing."

"But you don't need that if you already have an out. And Andrew had an out."

"You call that an out? An eight-year top?"

Her arms crossed, she sat back, defiant. "The other alternatives were too risky. I still believe it's madness to let him go to trial."

"Not if he didn't do it."

Wu closed her eyes, pushed on the lids with her fingers. "Please, sir. Not you, too. It's not whether he did anything. That's Law I-A. It's whether they can prove it. And they probably can, because he probably did."

Hardy jumped on that. "Aha. You said 'probably.' At last. Doubt enters."

Wu shook her head. "Not really. Not reasonable doubt, anyway. Not enough doubt to gamble his life away."

"Which brings us back full circle. All right," Hardy said. "Let's even go on the assumption that he's guilty. What else do you know about him? I mean, personally."

"With all respect, who cares? It's not who he is, it's what he did."

"No. Sometimes it's who he is. Who the jury sees. If you can make them believe he's somebody who literally wouldn't hurt a fly, they'll never believe he killed a human being. Or if you gave him a compelling enough reason . . ."

"It's jealousy, sir. Diz. I mean, he probably thought it was a good enough reason at the time, but no jury in the world, not even in San Francisco, is going to buy it enough to let him off. You don't get to kill people you're jealous of."

"All right. How about his home life?"

"He's a spoiled rich kid. Not a good sell."

"But abandoned by his father long ago, right? And *pissed* about it. Haven't I heard about him needing anger management therapy? Maybe he did it, but it was literally out of his power to control. You yourself got abandoned by your mother. You can certainly sell a jury on the rage." Hardy saw his cup of chocolate, lifted it and took a drink, made a face. "Look at Dan White. He sneaks into city hall and shoots the mayor and a supervisor dead one fine afternoon, and a jury of his peers basically lets him walk because he ate too many Twinkies that morning."

"He didn't walk."

"No. But he got less than the eight years Andrew didn't want to give away. My point is, now you're in it. You've got an opportunity with the seven-oh-seven to get a preview of what the witnesses will say at the trial . . ."

She stopped him. "How do I do that? That hearing's not about evidence. It's . . ."

"Wu. Listen to me. It's about whatever you can make it about. You're entitled to call witnesses about the boy's amenability to the juvenile system. The judge isn't going to stop you from calling just about anybody you want. He doesn't want to make a mistake and give you that issue on appeal. So you call Andrew's best friend. You call the guy who identified him in the lineup. You call his school principal, his counselor, his parents, his sister. You call his shrink. You're just trying to find out what happened. Not just that night, but to Andrew. You don't know what happened that night. Andrew doesn't know what happened. *He wasn't there for the murder!* How could he know? Hell, he called nine one one. Why would he do that?" Hardy sat back himself, crossed his own arms, dared a smile. "At the risk of sounding like David Freeman, you can actually have fun with this."

He came forward, intent now. "But you've got to *commit,* Wu. Whether or not he actually did it, your job is to get him off, any legal way you can. If he'd have copped the plea, okay then, you got him a deal he could live with. But he didn't. He couldn't live with it. Have you asked yourself why that might have been?"

"He's got to think he can get off."

"And why, looking at all the evidence arrayed against him, would he think that? Is he stupid? Does he think a jury won't convict him somehow?"

"No. I don't think he's stupid."

"Well? Could it be that he believes the system will work because he's innocent? I mean, is that even a possibility?"

"If it is, then he's a very unlucky guy."

"Okay. And if he's unlucky, what does that mean?"

She frowned, shrugged. "I give up, what?"

"It means someone else killed these victims."

She rolled her eyes. "The famous other dude. But —"

"Don't say it. It doesn't have to be a real person. It just has to be a *believable* story that a jury can take as an alternative. Let's say the teacher, what's his name?"

"Mooney."

"Okay, Mooney had another girlfriend before Andrew's, Laura is it?"

"Yes, Laura."

"Right. So this other girlfriend might have been jealous, too. As jealous as Andrew was. And maybe she also told a friend of hers. And, lo and behold, her father also owns a gun, and she had no alibi that night." Wu started to reply, but Hardy held up a hand. "I'm not saying there's any of this. But there's something out there somewhere, I guarantee it. There's always something." He paused, looked directly into her face. "At any rate, Wu, that's what I'm going to be looking for."

It took her a minute for the message to sink in, but then Wu sat up straight. "You? What do you mean, you?"

"Me. Your boss. I'm going to sit second chair with you on this."

"But . . ."

"No. No 'but,' I'm afraid."

Her mouth hung open for an instant. She swallowed hard, looked down then up. "If you don't think I can do the job, sir, then you might as well fire me."

"No. Although honestly, we considered it. You realize that nearly every decision you've made with this client from the beginning has been dead wrong, don't you? That you've compromised the firm's reputation to a significant degree?"

Unable to deny it, she could only nod.

He let her live with the harsh reality for a minute, then softened it somewhat. "But everyone makes mistakes, Amy. Everyone. And we don't want the firm to lose you. Beyond that, on a personal note, I've got to bear my own share of the blame for where this has all gotten to. I didn't do my job."

"And what was that?"

"Supervising you. Advising against your deal right from the first minute I heard about it. Letting you go ahead afterwards.

You want more? I've got 'em, believe me. But now we've got an opportunity to right those wrongs, both of us." He leaned in toward her. "Listen, by turning down the plea, Andrew basically bet us that he didn't do it. Whether or not we believe him, the firm signed on to keep the DA from proving he did. I still like to think that we can get this kid off."

"You and me, together?"

"Yes."

"Get him off completely?"

"Maybe even that. It happens sometimes. You prepare the seven-oh-seven hearing on the kind of person Andrew is, whether he was temporarily insane or had a lousy childhood or organic brain damage from braces that didn't fit right. Or if he's got uncontrollable rage that should put him in a program instead of jail. Me, I try to find a good alternative story. Time the trial comes around, we've already seen the DA's case at the hearing, so we choose the best option and run with it."

"So he goes to trial after all? I was hoping there was some chance with the seven-oh-seven that I could at least keep him down as a juvenile."

"Not likely," Hardy said. "Murder one with specials goes to adult court every time."

"Well, then, why wouldn't *every* murder go adult?"

"Murder one does. Some homicides don't, but they've got to be really close to an accident, or a retarded kid, or an abused kid who kills his dad, something like those. A righteous one-eighty-seven" — the code section for first degree murder — "the kid goes up, I don't care if he's fourteen years old."

"So why are they having this hearing in the first place, if the outcome is foreordained?"

Hardy broke a sad smile. "Because you made them, Wu. It might not have been your original plan, but you made them."

13

Before they'd even come close to removing the body, the city's power elite had descended upon the All-Day Lot — besides Glitsky, his boss and his underling, Police Chief Frank Batiste and Homicide Lieutenant Marcel Lanier appeared within fifteen minutes of each other. Of course Clarence Jackman needed to be on hand — the victim, after all, had been his chief deputy. Even a tuxedo-clad Mayor Washington himself, called from whatever party he'd been attending, showed up in his limo.

Everyone agreed that this was no ordinary homicide — the tendrils of Boscacci's career extended near and far in half a dozen directions. Over the course of his life, he'd either personally or administratively been involved with the prosecution of a wide range of wrongdoers — gang members, white-collar criminals and drug dealers; scam artists, rapists and murderers. But he'd also been extremely active in the city's hyperactive and often acrimonious labor negotiations. Politically, he had

been slated to run Jackman's next campaign, and his abrasive, no-nonsense style
had not enamored him to any of the DA's
six or eight challengers.

By the time all these heavyweights were
ready to go home, they'd unanimously
agreed to assign an event number to the investigation. The police department, like all
city departments, had a budget and was expected to stay within it. But when something extraordinary happened — an
earthquake or a papal visit, say, the mayor
would agree that the event would get a
number, and extraordinary expenses would
come from the General Fund. Practically,
this provided nearly limitless funds to allow
the work to proceed. Inspectors wouldn't
have to worry about their overtime; the
crime lab could run any sophisticated tests
it needed beyond the routine; the whole
apparatus — for a welcome change —
working in unison toward a common goal.
Abe Glitsky, not only as deputy chief of inspectors, but as a former head of homicide,
was the logical choice to take point.

Now, before the building had come alive,
before any other staff had come in, Glitsky
sat in his office, door closed, with Jeff
Elliot, the influential writer of the
"CityTalk" column for the *Chronicle*. Elliot
and Glitsky were both members of
Jackman's informal kitchen cabinet, and

had a lengthy and decent history between them. Not exactly close personal friends, they nevertheless got along about as well as a cop and a reporter could.

Maybe part of that was because, in spite of Glitsky's hatred of the reporter's basic prying function, he couldn't help but admire Elliot's essential bravery in the face of his ongoing struggle with multiple sclerosis. The bearded columnist lived and worked without reference to his wheelchair, his crutches, his specially designed car so he could get around. There was no hint of victimhood about Elliot, who had more claim to it than most. He was a true mensch, and Glitsky respected him.

"At least," Elliot was saying, "we don't have to talk about LeShawn Brodie, which was the original plan for today's interview, as you may recall."

Behind his desk, Glitsky sipped at his tea. "I'd be curious to hear your take on that, though, just as a matter of interest."

"What's to take? Your call was the only thing that made any sense. And in fact, until the clowns who picked him up let him escape . . ." He let the statement hang. "What were you supposed to do, storm the bus?"

"Apparently. But what I don't understand is all the vehemence, the rush to lay blame. Not that I feel anything personally, of course. I'm a cop, and therefore have no feelings."

"Of course," Elliot said. "That goes without saying. Why would you need them? But you know as well as anybody how these frenzies develop. It's lucky for you that you're not an elected official. Brodie could have done you in."

"In spite of the fact that it was the right decision? No, don't answer that. It wasn't really a question. But off the record, it makes me think I've about Peter Principled out. I'm not cut out for spin. I must have the wrong genes or something."

"I don't know. Some of us Neanderthals in the media find it quaintly refreshing. You say something, you mean what you say; most of the time it even makes sense. The public can either deal with it or not." Elliot shifted in his wheelchair. "You don't watch out, you might become a cultural hero."

Glitsky ran a finger over the scar in his lips. "Unlikely," he said, "but give me an event number and a murder to investigate, I may not be totally useless."

"Which brings us back to Allan."

A brusque nod. "It does. Although I have to tell you, this is too soon for me to have anything you could use. We're nowhere. We sent a couple of inspectors out last night to canvass the neighborhood.

Nobody heard or saw anything. I was actually hoping you might have something for me."

Elliot considered for a moment, then shook his head. "He wasn't everybody's favorite guy, but I never caught a whiff of anything particular that would make somebody want to kill him. I hope to get a chance to talk to Clarence, who's got to be devastated by this."

"He is. But we talked last night, and he's as mystified as anybody. Allan was a rock. Came in early, stayed late, great administrator, loyal as a dog."

"He fire anybody lately?" Elliot asked.

"A couple. We're checking them." The purging of the deadwood from the earlier DA's administration had been an ongoing, albeit low-key program for the past three years. To the affected parties, though, Glitsky would bet the termination was probably not as low-key as it seemed to others. "But to tell you the truth, Jeff, we're going to find out about everything in Allan's life. This is something I know how to do, as opposed to going to meetings and eating lunch with businesspeople. And for a change we've got the manpower and budget to do it right. If this killing wasn't completely random, and I can't believe that it was, we'll find who did it." He looked up, slightly startled. "Did I just say something quotable?"

Because the All-Day parking lot was cordoned off with police tape and he couldn't park there, Jason Brandt had to find a place nearly six blocks south of the Hall of Justice and walk up. He was standing in the hallway outside of Clarence Jackman's office at eight-thirty when Treya Glitsky got to the door.

"Can I help you?" she asked, introducing herself unnecessarily. All the assistant DAs, even those who worked mostly off-site, knew who she was.

Brandt pulled his hands from his pockets and introduced himself as well. He feigned an easy smile, but it was clear that he was wound up. "I was hoping to get a minute with Mr. Jackman."

She made a face of regret. "I don't remember an appointment . . ."

"It's about Allan."

Treya drew a heavy breath. "Well, then." She put her key into the door. "That poor man," she said. "It seems so . . . so completely unbelievable." She shook her head, clearing the thought, then came back to him. "I don't know when or even if Mr. Jackman will be in this morning. I know he was at the crime scene until well after midnight, then went to Allan's home after that. So it might be a while, if at all. You're welcome to wait, if you'd like."

Brandt thanked her and took the chair next to Jackman's door. Treya opened the blinds, turned on her computer, checked her voice mail, then the wall clock. The telephone rang and she picked it up. "District attorney's office." She lowered her voice. "Hi. No, not yet. I'll call you as soon as he does. No, really." A pause, the hint of a smile. "Me, too. Bye."

When she hung up, Brandt asked, "Was that your husband?"

"So much for subtle."

"I read that he was in charge of the investigation."

"I read that, too. He was gone before I was completely awake this morning. I can't imagine who would have done this. Can you?" She sat up. "Is that what you wanted to see Clarence about?"

Brandt shook his head. "No." He hesitated. "It's a little weird to talk about Allan's work and not his death, but with him gone now . . . I don't know, it seemed important to tell Mr. Jackman what was going on in this case so it didn't fall through the cracks. It doesn't have anything to do with Allan's murder."

"What's the case?"

Slightly embarrassed now, Brandt started to shrug it away, then spoke anyway. "Just up at the YGC . . ." He went on to tell the story — Andrew Bartlett, the juvenile proceedings, the scotched plea bargain deal. Amy.

Treya nearly jumped at the name. "Wait a minute. Amy Wu?"

"Yes, ma'am."

"And this plea deal, it was between her and Allan?"

"Right. She was coming down here to explain it to him, how the kid — Andrew, her client — had screwed her, or screwed them both. Anyway, Allan probably would have gone ballistic." Having noticed something in her expression, he stopped. "What?"

"Nothing. I'm sure it's nothing." Then, after another pause, she said, "Did you know that Amy was the one who found his body?"

"Pardon?"

She nodded. "Really. Abe — my husband — mentioned it last night when he got home, only because we both know her a little. They were all down there at the scene."

Brandt's eyes went inward while he processed the information. "Was she hurt, too?" he asked with real concern. "Is she all right now?"

"Who?"

"Amy." From Treya's expression, she wasn't following him. "I mean, was she around when Allan got shot? Is she okay?"

"I think she's fine. I'm sure she is."

For a moment, Brandt felt light-headed with relief. The feeling surprised him, and it must have showed.

"Is Amy a friend of yours?" Treya asked.

"No," he answered, perhaps too quickly. "Just a colleague. We're in this case together, on opposite sides. Anyway, I knew she was planning to talk to Allan yesterday. When you said she found him, I thought she might have been with him when it happened."

"No," Treya said. "She was with another guy at the Greek's and they found him when they went to get their cars."

"Who was the other guy?"

"I don't know. I think just some guy. Abe's going to talk to both of them. He'll find out."

Hardy came out of the elevator into the lobby at his office. In the reception area, Phyllis, with a pinched and pained expression, her hands clasped nervously in front of her, stood up and said, "I'm sorry, sir. I told him he couldn't just walk in, but he said you wouldn't mind. If you didn't like it, he said, you could call the police."

"Who are we talking about, Phyllis?"

"Lieutenant Glitsky."

Hardy showed a bit of teeth, the ghost of a grin. "He's a deputy chief now, Phyllis.

He thinks the rules don't apply to him anymore."

In the office, the deputy chief was on the couch, elbows on his knees. As soon as Hardy closed the door behind him, Glitsky started in. "Why didn't you tell me last night that Amy Wu had had a major fight with Allan Boscacci yesterday afternoon? About three hours before he died? At the Hall of Justice, which if your memory fails you is about two hundred yards from where he got shot? Did you imagine that this would not be relevant to his murder investigation? Or were you afraid that we would have sweated her on videotape last night, which we absolutely would and should have done?"

"It's good to see you, too," Hardy said. "How's your morning been?"

"Long. Already."

"You want some tea?"

"I want some answers."

"Not mutually exclusive. I'm having some coffee."

"Of course you are. Where's Wu now?"

From the counter, fiddling with his ingredients, Hardy turned. "I just this minute dropped her at the Hall. I turned her in directly to Lanier so he could get the murder collar and make you look bad, not that you seem to need much help on that score lately. Who put the bee in your bonnet about her?"

"Jason Brandt told Treya about the fight. Evidently a pretty good one."

"I don't know him. Brandt."

"Ask Wu; she does."

"Oh wait," Hardy said. "DA up at Youth Guidance? The Bartlett case?"

"Now the Boscacci case."

"Not." He turned, pushed the button for the espresso machine, came back around. "Look, Abe. I'm sorry I forgot to mention it last night, but if you recall, there were other things going on at the time. You saw Amy out at the lot. She could barely walk she was so drunk. Ten minutes after you let us go, she passed out on the way home in our car."

He grabbed his cup, walked over to Glitsky and sat kitty-corner to him. "You know how she got drunk? After her fight with Allan, she went over to Lou's and started pounding vodka, which she continued to do without pause until she left to go home with Barry or Larry or Jerry or whatever the hell his name was about five minutes before they discovered Allan. Lou's got six, eight, ten guys who were all trying to get into her pants for four hours in a row and will severally and individually swear that she didn't sneak out and shoot Allan. I, too, personally promise you that she didn't either."

"You still should have told me about this last night. Who we interview, and how, is not your call, Diz."

Hardy sipped his coffee. "I thought I already had apologized for that, but if not, I hereby solemnly do so again."

"I'm still going to want to talk to her. Soon. On tape."

"And she, no doubt, will be thrilled to cooperate in any way she can. Did Mr. Brandt actually accuse her of murder? Did he give you any kind of motive?"

"No. He didn't even know what he was telling Treya. But when I heard about the fight, I asked around at the Hall. People heard Allan yelling at her way out in the hallway. This was a couple of hours before he got hit."

"All too true, I'm sure. But I guarantee a complete waste of your time. Wu did not kill Allan, Abe. Is that really the best you've got?"

Glitsky sat back, crossed a leg. "We don't have anything yet. Nothing from the scene except the slug, too deformed for comparison, at least using the computer. Not that we have anything to compare it with. No casing. One witness says maybe a car peeled out of the lot just before it got dark, but he couldn't even swear to the color."

"How about Allan's family?"

"How about them? The wife is sedated right now. Clarence broke the news to her and she dissolved on him. Two kids, eight and ten. Lost. Destroyed. Nothing there."

A pause. "What was he working on?"

"One active case, that's it. A murder." At Hardy's questioning look, Glitsky explained. "He's been mostly assigning cases since he moved up to chief assistant."

"Okay, what's the murder?"

"You remember, the old guy — Matosian — who poisoned his wife and himself in a suicide pact, but miraculously survived? But the point is there's no witnesses around that case who'd want him dead. Otherwise, Allan's played a role in putting away a thousand people over the years. Although you know they never blame the prosecutor. He's just doing his job."

"Almost never."

A weary nod. "I know. We're going to look anyway. We're looking at everything."

"Then you'll probably find it."

"Let's hope," Glitsky said. "Even though it's undoubtedly a complete waste of time for everybody, would you please tell Ms. Wu we want to see her at the Hall, as in now? Could that be arranged?"

"Probably. I really did drop her off down there an hour ago to get her car. She was planning to go home and get some sleep, but she might be in your outer office even as we speak, hoping to chat with your august personage-hood. Though you might want to ask around at Lou the Greek's first. She was evidently the main event there last night. People will remember her."

"I'm sure they will." He took a beat. Then: "Do you think it could have been political?"

Hardy's mouth went tight. "I don't know, Abe. It's a reach. The campaign hasn't even begun yet. And if you want to take somebody out, you take out the candidate, not his eventual campaign manager, wouldn't you think?" He put his cup down, looked into Glitsky's face. "But no physical evidence, huh?"

"One deformed slug."

"Do you ever wish you'd let yourself swear once in a while?"

Glitsky stood up, brushed some imaginary lint from his uniform. "All the time, Diz," he said. "All the darned time."

The pale, polished wood of the door to Hardy's old office upstairs displayed a patchwork of bumper stickers. "Imagine Whirled Peas," "Kill Your Television," "Practice Random Acts of Kindness," "Wouldn't It Be Great If Schools Had Everything They Needed and the Govern-

285

ment Had to Hold a Bake Sale to Build a Bomb?" "Support the Right to Arm Bears," "Jesus Is Coming and Boy, Is He Pissed." Perhaps twenty more in the same vein, all of them to go with Wes Farrell's collection of T-shirts.

For not the first time, as he stared at this monument to the First Amendment right to freedom of speech and expression, Hardy wondered if they'd been smart to bring Wes Farrell aboard as one of the firm's founding partners. As a business move, it had seemed defensible enough at the time. Farrell had come up the hard way in the legal profession, taking one bleeding heart case after another, forgiving nonpayments even while he was going broke himself.

But, almost in spite of himself, he'd built a practice with solid referrals, a few retained accounts, lots of estate and trust work. Plus, he practiced good lawyering. He helped his clients, cared about them, found his own motivation in their interests. In many ways, leaving his superficial lack of professionalism aside, he was the perfect attorney. He dressed well in court, deferred to judges, respected the clerical staff. And there was no question that now he more than carried his own weight in the firm.

But if Phyllis thought Hardy was slightly out of the lawyer mode, Farrell was well into the lunatic range, although due to his good manners, Phyllis had not yet caught on. And, fortunately for Wes and perhaps the rest of the firm, Phyllis's entire range of migration at work consisted of the receptionist's station and the strip of floor between that and the women's room. She ate and took breaks in her chair in the lobby, surrounded by her phones and the waist-high, polished mahogany, circular cubby Freeman had built for her back in 1985, when he'd originally bought and renovated the building.

So far as Hardy knew, Phyllis had never walked up the fourteen steps to his old office, now Farrell's domain. He was sure that if she had, they'd have known it because she'd have screamed in dismay before dying of chagrin and mortification on the spot.

Hardy heard Farrell talking within, a telephone call. He tapped once and opened the door. He'd worked in this space for most of a decade and the move from it had been if not traumatic, then at least portentous. A Rubicon of sorts. He'd jettisoned his old desk, his metal filing cabinets, the Sears furniture. He'd come up once after all the stuff had been taken out and stood in the empty room, turning a page in his life.

Now, with Farrell's furnishings, the place

belonged heart and soul to the new guy, and reflected some sense of who he was. The first change — the desk — was so fundamental that Hardy had never even considered it. To him, a desk obviously went in the middle of the room, facing the door. It was the podium from which you conducted business. You could use it to create a sense of distance or formality. Most simply, it held your work stuff.

Farrell didn't think so. He had placed his in one of the room's corners, underneath one of the Sutter Street windows. There was a chair behind it, but Farrell almost never sat in it. At the moment, the chair along with the surface of the desk was cluttered with paper — red folders, three-ring binders, yellow legal pads, mail opened and unopened, a month's worth of newspapers — everything overflowing onto everything else.

The corner desk placement left a relatively vast open space that Farrell had essentially made into an informal living room. When Hardy came in, Farrell was stretched out — tie and shoes off — on the longer couch portion of his green, matching sectional set. In one corner, an overgrown rubber tree draped itself over an arm of his wing chair. A brass and bamboo magazine table held a small television in the other corner. On the wall, where

Hardy's dartboard had presided, Farrell had mounted a smallish hoop for his Nerf balls. Over by the bar/counter, there was still lots of room behind the couch for up to four people to play at the foosball table. On the other wall, by the desk, Farrell tended to use butcher paper on which he would draw flowcharts to track his various cases.

Farrell held up a finger, indicating he'd be a minute. Hardy crossed over behind the couch, picked up two Nerf basketballs from the floor, and took a shot, then another. He retrieved the balls, did it again. After a few rounds, Farrell said good-bye to whoever it was and sat up. "What's up?" he asked. "Though you've got to be quick. I've got a client coming up here in ten minutes."

"So you cleaned up for him?"

Farrell checked all around, looking for a problem, couldn't find one. "The guy's been in jail ten of the last twelve years and I'm afraid that in spite of my best efforts, he's going back soon. This will be the nicest room he's seen. I like my clients to feel comfortable. So how can I help you?"

Hardy tossed him the ball he was holding. "I can't find my darts. I wonder if you might have carried them out inadvertently."

Farrell shot, patted his pockets. "I don't think so." He went over and grabbed his jacket, made a show of a search. "Nope, not here either. When did you miss them?"

"Just now. A few minutes ago. I was going to meditate, as I like to do . . ."

"You check your desk?"

"Everywhere. I can't understand it. I don't know where they'd go."

Farrell looked at his watch. "I'm sure they'll turn up. What were you meditating on?"

Hardy rested a haunch on the back of the sectional. "Allan Boscacci, mostly. Amy a little bit. I've hooked up with her on this juvenile case she's been handling, and not a minute too soon, either."

"How's she connected to Boscacci?" Farrell had sat down and was tying his shoes. "Hell of a thing, though, wasn't it? I think I'm in the minority — I usually am — but I kind of liked the guy. Straight shooter, no bullshit."

Hardy nodded soberly. "I know. I felt the same way."

"Anybody have a clue who did it? Or why? Or anything?"

"Not yet. Abe was by here this morning. We exchanged a few bon mots." Hardy hesitated. "He seemed to entertain the thought that it might have been Amy."

Farrell stopped with his shoes, snapped his head up. "Get out."

"That's what I told him. You know the

deal that went south? Allan yelled at her and people heard. But, fortunately or not, Amy was at Lou the Greek's getting picked up and pasted about the time Allan must have walked by outside."

"So she's clear now, right?"

"I don't think she ever wasn't. But Abe will get her statement on tape anyway because that's what he does." He was still holding one of the Nerf balls and dropped it onto the couch. "But still, on Amy, Clarence also called. He was his usual low-key and polite self, but said that given the history of this Bartlett affair to date with Amy and Allan and all that, he was sure I'd understand why he was pushing for the seven-oh-seven to get Bartlett back into adult court as soon as possible. He couldn't let people — even my good, well-meaning associates — get away with manipulating his office. Think of the precedent."

"Think of it," Farrell said. "How soon?"

"What's today? Thursday?" Hardy asked. "Next Tuesday. Five days."

"Five days?"

"That's what I said."

"He can't do that. He'll hand us an appeal."

"I said that, too, but I just now checked and there's no rule says he can't. So he can. On the appeal, he says there can't be one since he could have filed on the kid directly as an adult to begin with. He's taking the position that we can't base an appeal on some inadequacy in a hearing we should never have had to begin with."

"But nobody can prepare for any kind of hearing in five days. It's just not doable."

"That was more or less his point, Wes. Clarence wants the boy back upstairs where he belongs, and he wants him there now, to remove the taint, as he so delicately phrased it. After that, we can waive time for the Px" — the preliminary hearing — "and take as long as we want preparing for trial. But Andrew's out of juvenile next week if Clarence has anything to say about it. And then he's looking at life without."

"You don't want to let him get there."

"No," Hardy said. "I've got that part figured out. The rest of it's a little murky."

Farrell got to his feet, tucked in his shirt, buttoned up and grabbed his tie. "So. Are we still throwing that campaign kickoff party for our good friend Clarence?"

Hardy wasn't laughing. "Nothing's easy," he said.

"Stop the presses. You're onto something."

Phyllis buzzed, telling him his client was here, on his way up. "Sorry, but you've got to go," Farrell said. "This guy — my client? — he really hates lawyers."

14

Wu awoke at Hardy's house to another hangover of staggering proportions. Stabbing pain wracked every cell and joint in her body. Pinpoints of flashing light hovered in the periphery of her vision. How many drinks had she had at Lou's? She thought she'd counted six, but it might have been seven or eight, even nine. More than one guy was buying, hoping to get lucky, and Lou was famous for his heavy pour.

Nine drinks? Eighteen to twenty ounces of vodka. She weighed about a hundred and thirty pounds. She was lucky to be alive.

After Hardy had driven her to the All-Day and she'd picked up her car, he had recommended that she take yet another sick day, go home and sleep. And that's what she'd done. After a six-hour rest, at around three o'clock, she called work and left the message that she'd be back in the office tomorrow.

Then, in jeans and a turtleneck sweater, she walked from her apartment down to the Marina green. The sun sparkled off the Bay, and though the breeze was light, it carried a chill. She crawled over some enormous breakwater boulders and sat invisible down in among the stones, facing the water and hugging herself for warmth. There, she cried herself out.

When she came back to her apartment, she found that Hardy had left a message. Glitsky really for truly did want a statement from her right away. The 707 hearing would be in five days, next Tuesday.

Five days.

She played the message again, thinking she couldn't have heard it right. But it sounded the same the second time. She sat in her chair and stared blankly out her window. Five days was impossible. She couldn't possibly prepare.

But apparently, that's all the time she had. The DA and perhaps the judge were sending a very clear message to her, venting the system's righteous pique. It wasn't going to be a matter of choice anymore, of what she'd prefer, of what she could work out with Brandt or Jackman. With the clock now ticking, she had to meet with the Norths, get together with Hardy, above all find out more about who Andrew really was. If she had only five days, she had to start *now* on some real defense that would be worthy of the name.

Her hangover wasn't forgotten — her head still throbbed with a dull and persistent pain — but she couldn't allow herself the luxury of suffering. She had to go to work. Lifting the phone, she punched in the Norths' number.

Glitsky's demand for her statement, to the extent that it had registered as important at all, was nowhere among her priorities.

Linda North greeted her phone call warmly enough. After all, Wu had partially convinced them that she'd played a significant role in keeping Andrew in the juvenile system for the time being. At least he wasn't going to adult court yet and he still wasn't looking at life in prison. Wu's strategy had been harrowing and tense, but ultimately successful. They still had confidence in her.

But Linda had been just leaving the house to get her hair done when she picked up Wu's call. She told her that this wasn't really a good time. It was her regular weekly hair appointment, and if she missed it, Michael would simply give away the time forever to someone else and she'd have to rearrange her entire schedule. It was a pain, but that was how he was. All these *artiste* hairdressers were the same. She was sure Wu understood.

In any event, Hal couldn't come home right now anyway. He'd already missed a lot of work because of this whole problem with Andrew. And when he wasn't in the office, Linda told her, there were always problems. But if it was important and time-sensitive, Wu should just call Hal at work and meet with him there. He'd fill Linda in when they got together later.

Wu, trying to be flexible, had suggested that she meet them both at their home when Hal's work was done and she'd finished with her hair. But no. It wasn't a good night for that, either. Hal had some black-tie stag food-and-wine event. Linda was planning to see Andrew later on at the YGC, but if Wu needed to talk to one of them right away, she should really just go to Hal's office and talk with him there. That would work out. There wasn't any real crisis with Andrew or anything, was there? If not, Hal was better at details anyway. He would be the one to talk to. He and Linda had great communication and he'd keep her informed of anything Amy thought was important.

The headquarters of North Cinemas was located on Battery Street near the Embarcadero. The three-story building itself was large — it took up most of the block — with a long and low, modern look, brick and glass. Wu parked on-site under the building, in a reserved spot next to Hal's to which the attendant had directed her.

Still in her jeans and sweater — the Norths might not have been anxious to meet with her, but she'd left her own home in a hurry — she took the elevator to the top floor, then turned right and walked a long hallway covered with a soothing green industrial carpet. The walls were adorned on both sides with framed movie posters, dozens of them. Having checked in and been told by the polite, spike-haired young blond woman at the desk that Mr. North was expecting her and would be able to meet with her shortly, she waited in the cool and spacious reception area, flipping through the pages of *Entertainment Weekly*. Through the floor-to-ceiling tinted window, she looked across the bay to Treasure Island, then to Berkeley beyond. In the clear afternoon light, under the breeze-swept sky, both looked close enough to touch.

When she finished a cursory perusal of the magazine, she looked at her watch and frowned. Giving it one more minute, she ran out of patience, got up and walked to the reception desk again. "I'm sorry. Is Mr. North being held up?"

The young woman looked up. "I'm sure he's busy. He said he'd be right out."

"Yes, but I wonder if you would mind checking again. It's been fifteen minutes."

The woman lowered her voice, spoke conspiratorially. "Fifteen minutes is *nothing.*"

Wu forced a tolerant smile. "I'm afraid it is to me. Would you mind trying him again please? Amy Wu."

She popped her gum and shrugged. "Sure. I remember." Pushing a few buttons on the console in front of her, she spoke into her headset. "Hal? Ms. Wu's still waiting." A pause. "Okay. Sure, I'll tell her." She ended the connection, looked at Wu. "He says two more minutes." But she held up her hand, opened and closed it twice slowly — the message clear. It was going to be closer to ten.

It was eight.

Projecting energy and command, Hal appeared from out of nowhere and suddenly was standing in front of where Wu sat. "Amy, sorry to have kept you. All kinds of madness going on back there. As usual. We're supposed to open the new Disney tonight and somehow somebody over in Walnut Creek lost six reels. Tell me where the hell you mislay six reels, I'd like to know. I gotta think somebody's stealin' them." She stood and they shook hands. "Anyway, I'm here now. What's the problem? I thought we were coasting on the legal stuff for a while until we got this next hearing scheduled. Is everything okay with Andrew?"

Wu was somewhat gratified to hear that both parents at least asked about Andrew's welfare. "Yes, sir. I think he's fine. I'm planning to go on up and see him after I leave here."

"Good. He told Linda he thinks you're upset with him, about what he did. He'll be glad to see you."

"So Linda already visited him today? She said she was going tonight, too."

"Did she? I don't know. What's today, Thursday? Thursday is normally her bridge group in the morning, I think, but maybe she went up. You'd have to ask her. Anyway. So what's up you need to see us all the sudden? You want to stay out here, by the way? Go in to my office? Whatever."

"Here is fine. I just wanted to tell you that they have scheduled the next hearing." She paused. "And it's for next Tuesday."

The slab face went into a shock riff. "Next Tuesday?" He counted silently to himself. "Five days. That's like it might as well be tomorrow, isn't it? I thought the courts liked to move slow on this stuff."

"Most of the time they do. In this case, the DA's mad Andrew didn't admit when he thought he was going to. He's expressing his displeasure."

"That's bullshit. Fuck him."

"Yes, sir."

Hal's scowl deepened, his voice suddenly harsh. "And I thought the plea change was part of your strategy all along. Now here we are sandbagged again. What's that about?"

Wu, expecting something like this, had prepared her reply. "It's about Allan Boscacci getting shot, sir. The whole thing would have rolled off his back I'm sure, but now we've got Clarence Jackman himself with his shorts in a twist. He's just asserting his authority. Anyway, I'm going to appeal the date, but my boss says it's not likely to change."

"Your boss?"

She nodded. "Dismas Hardy, you might have heard of him. He's good. And this is really very good news. If the hearing goes ahead on this accelerated time frame, he's going to come aboard to help out."

"And I pay extra for that?"

"No. The firm covers his time and expenses. We didn't make this problem with the DA, but we don't think it's right to ask you to pay for it, either. I'll be putting in a lot of hours, though. Just to let you know. We may be looking at another retainer payment, especially if Andrew goes up to adult."

"Which we're going to fight."

"Tooth and nail. Yes, sir. But on the assumption that the seven-oh-seven is going ahead as scheduled on Tuesday, I wanted to bring you and Linda up to speed on how it's structured so we can be prepared how to proceed."

"Jesus," Hal said. "It never ends." He threw a glance over his shoulder — all the work awaiting him behind one of those doors — then came back to Wu. "Maybe we want to sit down." They did. "All right," he said. "Shoot."

Over the next twenty minutes or so, Wu gave him the short course.

For all of its apparent complexity, a 707 proceeding concerned itself with only one question: is the minor "amenable to treatment" as a juvenile? From the perspective of the courts and the justice system, this determination was critical. Despite the insistence by some that one of the goals of adult incarceration should be rehabilitation of the inmate for an ultimate return to society, in practice, adult jail and prison time was essentially punishment. By contrast, the juvenile system's ethic took on a far more hopeful and optimistic cast. Though incarceration was part of the process, the goal was primarily to rehabilitate, not punish, the minor.

If you were in the juvenile system, the bureaucracy contemplated your eventual redemption. You still had a chance to turn out all right, to be a good citizen and a productive member of society, your youthful sins forgiven. So the system provided not just the stick of incarceration, but the carrots of education, psychological and career counseling, job training and a host of other social welfare programs. Because of these programs and treatments, each minor in the juvenile system would typically interact with an assortment of counselors, educators and social workers, and not just his warden and guards.

But this vast, bureaucratic apparatus of hope was not to be wasted on those it could not help, who were not "amenable to treatment." These were juveniles who, by virtue of their callousness, cruelty, history and crimes, must in justice be viewed as adults. Society would rightfully treat them as incorrigible and not squander its limited resources in a doomed and hopeless bid to try and rehabilitate them. And further, these lost causes wouldn't be permitted to contaminate the salvageable kids by their sophisticated and fixed criminality.

But first, the courts needed an objective formula to identify those who might be helped, and those who must be abandoned.

To that end, for violent crimes, five criteria for amenability had evolved. If in the court's judgment the minor failed the test for any one of these criteria, then that person would be found not amenable to treatment in the juvenile system and handed up to Superior Court to be tried as an adult. These criteria were (1) degree of the minor's criminal sophistication, (2) the likelihood of the minor's rehabilitation prior to the expiration of the juvenile court's jurisdiction (i.e., the minor's twenty-fifth birthday), (3) the minor's previous delinquent history, (4) the success of previous attempts by the juvenile system to rehabilitate the minor and (5) the circumstances and gravity of the offense for which the minor has been charged.

"Okay," North said. "So what's all that mean?"

"It means we're going to have to talk — you and me and Linda — about which if any of these criteria apply to Andrew. I mean, we've got a pretty good idea about number five, the gravity of the offense. It's murder, so it's serious. But we fight that one when we get to it. Meanwhile, I've got to know about all the others, so that if any of them seem to apply to him, we work up a defense, or at least an explanation for the court."

North was frowning deeply, sitting all the

way back in the couch, his hands in his lap, his legs straight out and crossed at the ankles. "Haven't we already done that? Remember that second day at the house, I think it was. When you wanted to know all about the blowups, and we talked about his shrink and all that?"

"Sure. I remember. But this is getting down much more to the nuts and bolts. Individual events. Reasons he shouldn't really be considered an adult."

"Character issues?"

"Right."

He turned his head to face her. "But didn't you say the other day that we didn't want to bring up character? Once we did that, then the prosecution could introduce their own stuff and jump all over us?"

"You were listening." Wu didn't seem very happy about it.

"Damn straight. I'm a good listener. So now you're saying we need character?"

"Maybe it's a bit of a risk. Certainly it's a different situation. But the bottom line is we need to defeat all the criteria. Every one of them, or Andrew goes up."

North sighed heavily, cast his gaze out to the view. "I'll talk to Linda. Maybe between us we can come up with something. You got those things, the criteria, written down?"

"Yes. Right here."

"Okay. Leave them with me, and if we can come up with something concrete you don't already know, we'll get back to you. How's that?"

Wu arrived before her client did in the cold and tiny room — the scratched table, the ancient chairs, the antiseptic old-school smell. Suddenly, she noticed the bars of sunlight high on the opposite wall, and she realized that she'd been awake only for a little over three hours total today, and the daylight was already nearly gone.

And wouldn't her father have been proud of her for that? For wasting the day? Or the past weeks? She rested her head in her hands as a fresh wave of nausea and revulsion rolled and broke over her. An unconscious moan escaped.

"Are you all right?"

She hadn't heard the key, hadn't been aware that the door had opened. Now Bailiff Cottrell — the young one with the old eyes — stood in the entrance, holding a restraining hand up for Andrew, waiting for a sign that the interview was still on. It wasn't immediately forthcoming, so he asked, "Are we good here, ma'am?" Eventually she nodded, and the bailiff lowered his hand, let her client come in, closed the door.

Andrew warily kept his eyes on her as he

pulled his chair over, sat on the front inch of the seat. "Are you mad at me?" he asked.

Wu's mouth was dry, her face clammy. She closed her eyes for an instant, ran her hand over her forehead. "No. I'm not mad at you, Andrew."

"I thought you would be because I didn't do what you wanted me to." He had his hands clasped together between his knees. "But I couldn't say I did it."

"I know," she said. "I wouldn't worry about it now. It's done. The thing we have to do now is prevail at this hearing, get you mandated in the juvenile system so you stay here."

"But I thought that was already over with." Confusion played itself all over his features. "I mean, that's what everybody is so mad about, right?"

"Not really. They're mad that now they have to go through the hassle of trying to move you back up to adult court."

"So you're saying your deal, even though I didn't agree to it, got me another chance anyway?"

"Yeah."

Suddenly, the look of confusion cleared. Her client tentatively smiled. "Well, then, if your job is my defense, how could it have been wrong? Maybe the guy you made the deal with wasn't as careful as he needed to be, either. You ever think of that? Maybe it wasn't all your fault?"

Wu wouldn't think ill of the dead, especially not today. But Andrew's rationale released some small bit of the tension she felt. "Well," she said, "at least some of it was my fault. But that's very nice of you to say, and I could use a little nice." For the first time with Andrew, she felt something like a connection.

But there was still the business, the five criteria for amenability to the juvenile system. After she had painstakingly gone through the list for him, she sat back with her arms crossed over her chest. "We need to talk about each of these individually, Andrew," she said. "If the court finds you not amenable on any one of them, you go up."

"Any one?"

"That's the rule. And I'm afraid we've got less than a week to prepare."

"But these criteria." Andrew scratched at the tabletop. "Most of them don't apply to me at all. I don't even know what they mean by criminal sophistication, or if I can be rehabilitated. Rehabilitated from what?"

"Your violent criminal past."

He looked a question at her. "I don't have one."

"I know. But I don't think sophistication is the problem. Neither is rehab."

"But gravity is."

Everyone seemed to understand that one immediately. "Yes."

He gestured around the small room. "If it helps me get out of here . . . but I was saying, even on gravity, if I didn't do it . . ." He raised his eyes, hopeful.

But she didn't want to raise those hopes. She came forward and reached across the table, a hand over his forearm. "This hearing isn't about whether you did it, Andrew. I need you to understand that. It's only about whether you go up as an adult or not. They're going to pretty much assume the gravity criteria."

"And they only need the one?"

"I'm afraid so."

"So I'm going to lose?"

"We may lose, yes. For now. But we'll get a real chance in adult court."

"We ought to just go straight there, then. If this hearing is just a formality."

"No," she said. "We've got to try. Anything that keeps you down here even for one extra minute is what we want to do." In his eyes, she saw real worry — perhaps he was starting to realize where his refusal to admit had left him. Left them both. "So we've got to talk about some real issues, Andrew. My partner, Mr. Hardy? He's got a few ideas about gravity. We're not just going to give that to them. But the other criteria, we don't want any surprises with those either."

"I don't know what they'd be."

"No. I don't either, but that's why they call them surprises."

He started with some marginal enthusiasm as they discussed possible witnesses for the various criteria — the psychologist he'd seen for anger management, his school counselor, one of the probation officers up here. But before they'd gone too far, the enormity of what he was facing seemed to drag him down.

His focus wavered, then abandoned him entirely, and Wu — not at peak performance levels herself — found it difficult to humor him. From her perspective, his primary emotion was sorrow for himself. He stopped every few sentences, stared straight ahead or down at the table. He fought back tears a couple of times.

"Why should we bother doing this?" he'd say. "We're never going to win."

Or: "I'm such a loser. This isn't going to make any difference."

Or: "It'd be better for everybody if I just killed myself, wouldn't it?"

That last one stopped Wu. "Why would you want to do that, Andrew? What good would that do?"

"It'd end all this stupidity. If they're going to put me away anyway."

Wu scratched at the table, summoning

her patience. "That's what we're trying to avoid."

"It won't work, though, will it?"

"Not if we don't try."

But even to her, the words sounded condescending, the kind of adult pablum he'd been forced to eat a hundred times. "Or even if we do," he said.

She tried to keep him on track, but it was a long, uphill slog until they finally summoned him for dinner. After he left, she felt she had no reserve of strength and remained sitting, elbows on the table, on her papers and notes. She rested her head on her palms, the heels of them pressing into her eyes.

She heard a knock. "Excuse me? Ms. Wu?" Bailiff Cottrell, come to close up the room, stared down at her from the doorway. She must have nearly let herself doze off. "Are you feeling all right?"

"Fine. I'm fine."

"You don't look well. Can I get you something? Some water?"

Moving slowly, she leaned back in her chair. "How about a head transplant? And maybe a new body to go with it."

"You couldn't get a better face," he said, "and you definitely don't need a new body."

At the moment, she felt about as attractive as a garbage truck, and she almost laughed at the compliment. But he was, she thought, just trying to be nice. "Thank you," she said. "I'm sorry to have kept you waiting while I just sat here. It's been a long day." She started gathering the papers and folders she'd spread out over the table.

"Ms. Wu, let me help you," he said.

"No, thanks. I've got it. And you can call me Amy."

"Ray, if you didn't remember," he said, then stood waiting at the door while she finished up, throwing everything into her heavy lawyer's briefcase, snapping it closed. When she stood, then leaned over to pick the briefcase up, he said, "That thing must weigh a ton. At least let me take that."

Exhausted, her head still pounding from her hangover, she finally nodded. "That would be nice."

He stepped into the room, picked up the briefcase, gave her some support with a hand under her elbow. "You're sure you're okay to walk?"

In fact, she had some question about that, but she took a step and then another and in a minute they were outside in the hall and then at the main entrance to the cabins. Cottrell accompanied her outside to the razor-wire gate and opened it for her. They stopped there and he put down her briefcase. Turning to say good-bye, she looked up at him. Their eyes met for an instant, and she thought she caught a glimpse of that earlier wariness she had noticed in the courtroom. Again, his eyes seemed old and somehow empty, but — it was as though he had a switch he could throw — suddenly a bit of life came into them. "Your client seems pretty down," he said.

She blew out heavily. "I don't blame him," she said. "He's screwing himself."

"How's that?"

"I dealt him an eight-year top and he turned it down. Now he's looking at LWOP."

"They're moving him to adult?"

"Not yet, but it's probable. I'm trying to get him to help me, but he doesn't seem to know the word 'cooperate.' "

"Maybe he's just scared."

"I'm sure he is. And he should be. Oh, God!" She brought a hand up to her head, squeezed at her temples. With her other hand, she grabbed the side of the gate for support. Cottrell stepped up, grabbed both of her shoulders. "You look like you're going to faint. Maybe you want to sit down."

She nodded and leaned into him. He put his arm around her and walked her back toward the cabins.

From the lobby of the admin building,

down the hill Jason Brandt saw the bailiff carrying her briefcase, walking with her to the gate, where they stopped and spent a minute talking. He didn't want her to see him, at least not until she was alone, and so he remained where he was, pretty much out of sight.

Wu hadn't left his thoughts since the night they'd spent together, and now Brandt was unable to take his eyes off her. He had wanted to get to know her since the first time he'd seen her, back right after his law school days. But one or the other of them had always had other relationships going or big cases and she'd more or less slipped from his consciousness until she showed up in his courtroom last week, when finally — he'd thought — there had been no impediment.

Then he really believed that running into her at the Balboa had been a sign. There had been real chemistry between them that night, something uncommon and, he believed, maybe even a little magical. As a general rule, he didn't do one-night stands. The encounter, like it or not, had seemed as though it meant something. Maybe something important.

Then, this morning, thinking for a moment that because she had been near Boscacci when he'd been shot that she, too, might have been physically hurt, made him realize that he'd been way too harsh with her the other morning. Okay, she'd made a mistake by not telling him right away that Bartlett's case wasn't really settled, but maybe it had been innocent after all, something he'd never really given her a chance to assert. Maybe they'd just started talking at the Balboa and in all the personal stuff they'd shared, including the sex, the professional business between them had receded into the background. It certainly had for him.

So he didn't want this antagonism between them to go on any longer. He wanted to apologize for his overreaction, at least see what she had to say to that. And just now, when he'd first seen her coming out of the cabins, he thought he'd take the opportunity to talk to her. One way or another, he thought that the Bartlett matter was going to be over in a few weeks at the most, at least as far as Wu and he were concerned. If Bartlett went to adult court, they wouldn't be adversaries in the same courtroom anymore. Maybe they could pick up where they'd left off. If he could get her to talk to him.

Although if she had gone off on him as ballistic as he had with her, he wasn't sure if he would talk to her.

But then suddenly, as Brandt was watching them, he saw the bailiff put his

314

hands on her shoulders. Then she leaned into him, her face against his chest, and he put his arm around her, keeping it there until they had both disappeared back into the cabins.

His stomach went hollow. He turned to take the long way out the front door of the admin building, where there was less chance that they would inadvertently run into each other.

Cottrell stayed with Wu until she told him she felt better, and then he told her to take care of herself and went inside, back to work. Still, Wu didn't move for a few minutes. She sat on the bench just outside the entrance door to the cabins, trying to summon enough strength to get up and walk to her car. When the cellphone in her briefcase rang, she considered not answering, but then realized that it might be, in fact probably was, the Norths. After all that had transpired so far, she felt that however exhausted she might be, at least she owed them accessibility. She got it on the third ring.

It wasn't the Norths. It was her boss. "Amy? So you're up and about. Where are you?"

"Up at the YGC. I just talked to Andrew."

"Good for you. How's he doing?"

"He's depressed. We talked about starting a club. Not really. That was a joke."

"Well, this isn't. Did you get the message I left at your house about talking to Glitsky?" It came back to her in a flash. "Oh, shit."

"Right," Hardy said. "He's still at his office and he called me at home just now, which I really try to discourage. He was wondering how he could get in contact with you, like immediately. Since I had more or less promised him that you'd see him today, he wondered what was going on. You want his direct number?"

"I guess I'd better."

"Good guess."

By now it was nearly 7:00 p.m. There was no one at any of the desks in Glitsky's reception area at the Hall of Justice, so Wu walked back through the conference room and down the small hallway to the deputy chief's door, which stood ajar.

Some natural light from outside made it through the drawn blinds, but with the electric lights off, the room seemed dim. Glitsky sat in one of the chairs in front of his desk. He was canted slightly forward, his elbows resting on his knees, his head down. He might have been napping. Wu was surprised that he didn't seem to have heard her approach, and she stood a moment in the doorway, waiting for him to turn and acknowledge her. When that didn't happen, she tapped lightly on the door.

He didn't exactly jump, but he'd clearly been somewhere else. Now, back in the present, he stood and came toward Wu, checking his watch as he did so. "You made good time from the YGC," he said. "I appreciate it."

"No traffic for a change," she said. "I'm sorry about the mixup around this interview, sir, me not coming down here. It's all my fault, not Mr. Hardy's. He called my home and told me you wanted to see me, but I have a client who's in big trouble and I went to see him first. I didn't realize that this was so urgent, even though Mr. Hardy said it was."

Glitsky seemed to find a little humor in her explanation. "Next time I talk to him, I'll tell him you tried to cover for him. But I know the truth. He forgot to tell you, didn't he?"

"No, really. He —"

But Glitsky held up a hand and stopped her. "Kidding, just kidding." He didn't seem to take much joy in it, though. Awkwardly, he shrugged, half turned. "Well, you're here now," he said, pointing. "Why don't you take that chair and we'll get going."

Wu sat while he got his tape recorder out

of his desk, tested it, set it down and recited the standard introduction, identifying himself, his badge, the case and event number, his subject, where they were. Three or four years before, in her first year out of law school and before Treya and Abe had gotten married, Wu had played a small role helping Hardy and Treya learn the identity of the person who'd killed Glitsky's grown daughter. They hadn't all exactly socialized — last night at Boscacci's death scene was the first time Glitsky had seen her since — but there was a definite sense of familiarity and even goodwill still between them. Nevertheless, Glitsky was a procedure freak, and this was a formal interview pursuant to the death of an important person. He wasn't going to phone it in.

"Ms. Wu," he began, "where and when was the last time you saw Allan Boscacci alive?"

"Yesterday afternoon, here at the Hall of Justice. In his office."

Pre-supplied with Hardy's version of events and Jason Brandt's information conveyed through Treya, he walked her through the history and intricacies of the Bartlett matter. Then: "Mr. Brandt mentioned that there might be some bad blood between you and Allan because of this blown deal."

"Not really bad blood. I don't know why he said that. It wasn't personal."

"But the meeting was rancorous?"

"A little, yes."

"Were voices raised?"

"His. Yes, sir. I had been wrong and didn't do much except sit and take it."

"Did he threaten you?"

"Physically? No. Professionally, he made it clear we wouldn't be doing many more plea deals together."

"And how did you feel about that?"

"It wasn't much of a surprise, after what had happened. I just let him vent, and couldn't really blame him."

"You had no reaction?"

"No. Of course I was upset. But more at myself than at Allan."

"All right. And after that, after this heated interview with Mr. Boscacci, what did you do?"

She gave him the details, as much as she remembered them, of the rest of her afternoon and early evening at Lou the Greek's.

"And you were there continuously? You never left the premises?"

"No, sir. Not until about eight, eight-fifteen, something like that."

"Accompanied by Mr. Barry Hess, is that right?"

"I think so. I mean, I think that was his name. Whatever it is, he was with me when

I walked out of Lou's and went to the All-Day."

"So what is your relationship with Mr. Hess?"

"We don't have one. He picked me up at Lou's and I may have let him kiss me once or twice on the way to the parking lot. I really don't remember too clearly."

"Okay. To get to the place he was killed from the Hall, Mr. Boscacci very probably walked by Lou's. Did you by any chance notice him walking by?"

"No."

"Do you recall hearing a gunshot?"

"No."

"All right. After you discovered the body, what did you do?"

"We called nine one one on Barry's cellphone, and got the police."

"And then what? Did you call anyone else?"

"I called Mr. Hardy at his home, but he wasn't there. His kids told me where he was, and I reached him at a restaurant."

"And why did you call him?"

"Because he's my boss and I thought he'd want to know about Allan right away."

"Is he also acting as your personal attorney in this matter?"

"My personal attorney?"

"Yes."

"I'm sorry. In what matter?"

"Mr. Boscacci's death."

"No. Why would I need . . ." She stopped.

"He pretty effectively protected you from having to do this interview with me or someone else last night. Did you discuss that between you?"

"No. I was drunk. That's why I didn't talk last night. You were there. I talked to you, remember? We said today would be fine."

"Right. Did you talk to Mr. Hardy about your statement today?"

"Just that I ought to get down here and give it."

"Nothing about its substance?"

"No."

"So last night, you didn't call Mr. Hardy to come down to the crime scene to act as your attorney?"

"No. No, of course not. I didn't need an attorney."

"All right, Ms. Wu. Thanks for your cooperation."

The bailiff wanted Linda to meet Andrew in the general visitors' room, which was much larger than the other room they'd used the last couple of times, but far less private. She told the bailiff that she'd really prefer the smaller room, as she wanted to have a sensitive conversation with her son. But there was nothing the bailiff could do. The smaller attorneys' visiting room was currently in use. There were a lot of kids here, and all of them had lawyers and parents.

So she waited, and waited — there were only twelve stations — until she got to the front of the line in the gymnasium, and then until a chair cleared. Sitting between two other women, one Hispanic and one African-American, she was hyper-aware of being the only Caucasian visitor.

Eyes down, Andrew entered in his protective shuffling teen gait, exaggerated shoulder movement, his feet kind of sliding along. She wondered why teenage guys considered it so cool to be sullen and silent, then tried to remember when Andrew had begun to adopt that walk. She thought it was about the time he'd stopped talking to her — to anyone in the family, really — three or four years ago.

But what could she do? It wasn't as though parents could control their children or exert any discipline. Not in today's world when everyone grew up so fast, when between television, the movies and the internet all kids were plugged into the same culture, the same clothes, the same slang, even the same walk. Linda believed that there was no way that she could have any impact against such a relentless and ubiquitous force. If you tried to teach them manners, discipline them, influence their behavior at all, they just shut you out. It didn't even make sense to try; they'd just resent you for it. The thing to do was be their friend when they let you and otherwise leave them alone. The best you could hope for is that they'd eventually grow out of it, and somehow turn out okay. But that sure wasn't anything over which she had any control.

The partition prevented her from giving him a hug. She missed the contact. It might embarrass him, but thank God he still let her hug him sometimes. Not that it wasn't somehow grudging, not that he hugged her back with any enthusiasm. But he was still her baby, and she didn't know any other way to reach him.

Andrew pulled out his chair and sat down across from her. They didn't have him in handcuffs. They could reach across the counter and hold hands if they wanted, although she knew that Andrew probably wouldn't go there.

"Hey," he said.

"Hey."

Silence.

"Aren't you glad to see me?"

"Sure." A pause. "Thanks for coming down."

"Hal and Alicia say hi."

"I'm sure."

"Don't you want to tell them hi back?"

His eyes were flat. "Sure."

For a minute, she feared that neither of them would find anything else to say.

She forced herself to keep trying. "How are you holding up?"

"Okay."

"Really?"

A shrug.

Another silence.

"You look a little tired. Are they feeding you all right?"

"Yeah." He drew a heavy breath, finally said something. "My lawyer was by earlier."

"I know. She called us, too."

"What'd she tell you?"

Linda tried to sound upbeat, but the news didn't lend itself much to that. "That she was bringing on another lawyer from her firm to help with your case. Supposedly he's really good."

"What else is she going to say? That he's shit?"

"Well." She wished he wouldn't use that kind of language, but she wasn't going to say anything he might take as a reprimand. Not with everything else he was going through. "She also told Hal about these criteria to keep you here."

"Yeah," he said. "The Ritz."

Linda sighed. "Do you like her?"

"Who?"

"Amy. I mean, Hal and I feel she's doing a really good job, and now she's brought on this senior partner to help. But if you didn't feel good about her . . ."

"I don't really care. She's all right. It doesn't really matter."

"Of course it does, Andrew. Don't lose hope now."

"Okay."

"Really," she said. "Don't."

He shook his head. "Okay, sure, good idea, Mom. Except that it's starting to look I'm never going to get out of custody."

"Don't say that." She reached out over the counter. "Here, hold my hand," she said.

"That's not going to help anything."

"Please," she said. "Humor me, okay?"

He sighed again and put his hand in hers. "So there's this hearing on Tuesday to see if I stay here. Did she tell you it doesn't look too good?"

"Not really so much that. She said it was kind of like a dress rehearsal for the trial, where we get to see what they've got. Which is really an advantage."

"I bet."

"It is."

He shrugged again. "Either way, Mom, I

didn't do this and still they got me in here. If they can do that, I don't think they're ever going to let me get out."

Linda didn't want to argue with him. "Well," she said, "let's just wait for Tuesday and hope for the best."

"Mom, the best, even if we win on Tuesday, is *eight years*."

"No. If they have the trial down here, then the *worst* is eight years."

"Great," he said, "maybe we should throw a party."

"Andrew."

"All right, all right."

"Let's just see, okay. Keep your chin up." She gave him a quick buck-up smile, squeezed his hand.

"Sure."

A longish silence settled. Finally, she said, "I want to ask you something."

"Okay."

"And I want to know how you really feel."

"All right."

She took in a lungful of air. "Well, you know the Newport Open . . ." This was a tennis tournament in Southern California that they'd attended for the past several years. "It starts tomorrow and —"

He pulled his hand out of hers. "Go."

"You're sure?" She searched his face for any sign of wavering, and saw none.

"You won't mind?"

"Why would I mind?"

"It's just we won't be able to visit you."

"That's all right. I'm going to be working with Amy most of the days anyway. It doesn't matter."

"You keep saying that."

"That's 'cause it's true. It doesn't matter."

"We'd stay here if it made any difference to you at all, you know. *At all, even the tiniest little bit.* No question."

"I know that."

"But we've had these tickets for months. They're really expensive, you know, but we'd give them up gladly. We would."

"You don't need to."

"And even if we do go, we'll be back by Monday, in plenty of time for the hearing. We'd be there for you for that."

"Mom, I said go. I mean it. It's no big deal."

"You're sure? I mean completely positive?"

"Completely," he said. "A hundred percent. Go. Have a good time."

It wasn't yet completely dark out, but Wu had drawn the blinds in her apartment and turned out the lights. She was completely wrung out and badly shaken by the thought that Glitsky might actually entertain the thought that she could have killed Allan. When she had at last gotten home after the interview, she'd swallowed more aspirin, brushed her teeth twice, then taken a shower.

Her head still throbbed, but she let herself believe that it was marginally better. By the time she woke up in the morning, she might be halfway to human again. Collapsing into bed, she had just pulled the covers up over her head, turned onto her side and closed her eyes when the doorbell sounded. This time she was going to ignore it. She'd already had the day from hell and all she wanted it to do was end, which it would when she slept. Whoever it was would go away.

Another ring.

Leave me alone! She pulled the covers tighter around her.

The knock, when it came, was authoritative. Three sharp raps. "Amy! Come on, open up." Brandt.

She threw her blankets off and padded over the hardwood to the door, spoke through it. "What do you want, Jason? I'm trying to sleep. I don't feel good."

"I want to talk to you."

"Talk to me in the morning."

"Two minutes, that's all."

"You can apologize through the door."

"It's not just that."

"No? Well, it should be." She hesitated another moment, then sighed. "All right, let me get some clothes on." Hitting the light switch by the door, she grabbed her jeans, stepped into them, then tucked in the yellow spaghetti strap cotton blouse she'd gone to bed in.

She considered taking thirty extra seconds and putting on a bra — she didn't want to send any kind of sexual signal — but if it was going to be two minutes, she might as well hear it and then get back in bed. Besides, she wore no makeup, her hair was still damp, her eyes must be ravaged. She was a train wreck.

She opened the door.

In a gray business suit, white shirt, rep tie, Brandt stood awkwardly. Hands in his pockets. He cleared his throat. "Can I come in?"

Stepping back without a word, she let him pass, closed the door behind them.

He crossed over to her all-purpose table, pulled a chair around and sat in it, looking around, getting his bearings, really seeing the room for the first time. The other night they hadn't paused for the grand tour before dragging each other into bed. Afterward she didn't think he'd even turned on the lights, just pulled his clothes on and let himself out.

Arms crossed, waiting, she leaned against

the counter by the sink.

"I was down in the street for a while and saw your shadow moving up here, then the lights went out. I thought if I was going to get you, it had to be now."

"Okay, you got me." Then his phrase caught her. "You were down in the street for a while? Doing what?"

"Just standing there." He shrugged again. "Deciding whether to come up and try to talk to you."

Something in his tone stopped what would have been another harsh reply. She cocked her head. "All right. Talk."

"First," he began, "I wanted to apologize."

"Okay."

"But beyond that, I guess I'm having trouble figuring you out." He took a breath, pushed on. "I don't understand what's happening exactly, first the other night with us, then the next morning at my office —"

She cut him off. "Then you accuse me of murder. Talk about not understanding what's happening."

"Amy, I swear to God. I never accused you of anything like murder. I didn't accuse you of anything at all."

"That's funny. I just got back from the Hall of Justice, where Abe Glitsky said you told him there was bad blood between me and Allan. He seemed to think I was some kind of a suspect."

"That couldn't have been me."

"You're saying you didn't talk to him?"

"No. I talked to him. But just telling him about what's happened with Bartlett —"

"And me and Allan."

"Okay. But never even implying . . . I mean, come on. If Glitsky came to that on his own . . . If you want, I'll call him tomorrow. I never meant anything like that. I'm so sorry. I didn't mean . . ." He looked up at her. "I'm sorry," he said again.

Her tone softened. She was too exhausted for another round. "All right, apology accepted, okay? Now if you don't mind, I'm exhausted and your two minutes are up."

But he didn't move. "I didn't just want to apologize." He scratched at the table, took a quick breath. "I wanted to ask you about you and me."

"You and me?" She pulled a chair around and sat on it. "First you accuse me of screwing you for advantage in a case, then you go to Glitsky and somehow give him the idea I might have killed Allan. I don't see any 'you and me' in this picture." She paused, let out a breath. "Look, I don't expect anything from you, Jason. That night was that night. I'm not telling anybody about it, so our jobs are both safe. So now you can go. In fact, you really should go now."

"That's not it," he said.

"No? Then tell me what it is." Sighing again, she shook her head. "Look, if it makes you feel any better, I thought it was a game to you, too."

"No. Okay, maybe it started that way at first." He walked over to one of the windows, turned back to her. "For a minute, I thought we had something going. I mean personally." He tapped his chest. "In here." He waited, eyes on her. "I guess not."

She didn't contradict him. Did he really think she was going to fall for this line now? If he would have said something that night, maybe. Because he was right. There had been a real moment between them. They'd both realized it. Beyond the physical stuff, something that had felt to her like a deeper connection. Then in the morning, he'd been gone.

Fool me once, okay. But twice? She didn't think so.

A tense silence gathered, until she finally broke it. "I think you'd better get out of here right now. I mean it."

15

Hardy didn't want to go out after dinner at home, but with the 707 hearing looming, he felt he had no choice. Since Frannie had suggested he put his heart into his work again, she couldn't very well object. They both knew the strains that Hardy's work ethic had placed on their marriage in the past, and both saw the irony in her position. If Hardy was going to care, he was going to put in the hours. That was who he was. That was the trade-off. So when he told her he had to go out and have a talk with Mike Mooney's neighbor, she kissed him with a tolerant humor. "Husbands," she said. "Can't live with 'em, can't kill 'em."

He had conceived of a strategic idea that he thought stood a long shot, but still possible, chance to play at the 707 hearing if all the stars lined up just right. He'd already told Wu that she could confidently call any witnesses she wanted. Jackman's insouciant attitude notwithstanding, Judge Johnson would be concerned about the risk of having the case reversed on appeal. He wouldn't hurt the defense any more than he already had done. And it would be greatly to Wu's advantage if she knew how some of the witnesses were going to testify at trial.

But it had occurred to Hardy that he might be able to take it a step further, and convince Johnson that justice demanded he allow witnesses to the crime itself. This would be decidedly unusual, since in this type of hearing, the prosecution only had to make a prima facie case that the crime had been committed, and there wasn't any doubt that *somebody* had killed Mooney and Laura. But Clarence Jackman had never practiced as a criminal lawyer in his pre-DA career, and even after three years in office, he was sometimes embarrassingly inexperienced in the nuts and bolts of how things really worked. And Hardy's hope was that Brandt, young and relatively green himself, by pushing the super-charged rush to the 707 after Boscacci's murder, had goaded Jackman to a tactical blunder.

Judge Johnson would be nervous that the defense had only been given five days to prepare for the hearing. No doubt feeling angry and abused himself, he would be inclined to grant the DA's wish to get Andrew moved downtown — he'd want to slap Wu as badly as either Brandt or Jackman did — but Hardy and Wu would file motions by Monday making sure the judge knew that the defense considered this unseemly hurry an appealable issue. After that, if Johnson let the hearing proceed as planned, he'd be extra sensitive to the threat of appeal, and might let the defense get away with calling witnesses related to the case in chief as a function of the fifth amenability criterion — the gravity of the offense.

If Hardy and Wu could make that happen, then Andrew would get himself not just an administrative hearing, but a de facto juvenile trial. If he lost at the 707, then worst case Hardy and Wu would get two chances to hear the prosecution's case. And to beat it. And even if Andrew then lost again in adult court, Hardy might still be able to appeal, saying that they'd been forced to go to the 707 before they could adequately prepare.

Hardy knew this wasn't just a long shot, it was a full-court bomb at the buzzer. But occasionally, he knew, they went in.

So as he turned into Beaumont Avenue, in the first block off Geary Boulevard, he felt some small grounds for enthusiasm. Twenty feet of free, legal curb space yawned open on his right, and he pulled over and parked. He'd driven out with the top down on his convertible — there was no fog and the last days' winds had finally abated — and now he sat, headlights off, letting a sense of the crime scene seep into him. He forced himself to wait, to observe, to listen. There was no hurry. If his coming out here was going to do any good at all, he had to slow down and take time.

It was a short block. Eleven relatively small two-story housing units squatted between the major thoroughfare of Geary and the next street south, which was Anza. The address he sought was the fourth building down from Anza, and, at least from the outside, by far the smallest residence on the block. Set back a little from the street, it was also the only building with a lawn in front and a driveway with a separate garage on the side. Lights shone from the upstairs windows while the bottom unit — Mooney's old place — was dark.

Finally, he put up the hood on his car, grabbed his legal pad from the seat next to him, got out of the car and went to lean against one of the streetlights on his side of the street. With six of these, all miraculously functioning, the area was surprisingly well lit. This wasn't the most unusual thing in the world, Hardy thought, but it almost never happened on his own block, which was in a similar suburban, high-density neighborhood.

He made a note to check and see if Public Works had come out to install new lights since Mooney's murder. Sometimes a station captain or one of the beat cops, called to a crime scene in one of these nice neighborhoods, would take the opportunity to check the city's housekeeping and let somebody know. If the street had been significantly darker two months ago, it might make a difference to eyewitness testimony.

Standing there on the curb, Hardy became aware of a subtle rhythm. He timed it out of curiosity — he didn't think it was really worth writing down. About every forty seconds, the street noise from Geary, less than two hundred feet away, increased dramatically as eastbound traffic, released from its last red light, sped past on the way to the next one. The sound wasn't anywhere near deafening, but once Hardy became aware of it, he waited through a few cycles, trying to determine how loud it could get.

Loud enough to cover gunshots? He didn't think so. Certainly not for the closer neighbors. And it would be quieter as it got later.

The gunshots were a question and he jotted it down.

Andrew's walk was critical to his story and Hardy wanted to see if it made sense, so he checked the time and started moving south a few blocks to Turk, where he then turned east along the periphery of Lone

Mountain College. This time of night, the road was quiet enough and might be conducive to memorizing lines. Certainly, this was a better route for that purpose than anything along Geary would have been. There was also quite a bit of street parking — it was where Andrew said he had parked on the night of the murders.

Rather than go all the way to another busy street, Masonic, Andrew said he had turned south again, crossed the campus of the University of San Francisco by the baseball diamond, then come out through a little cul-de-sac. Andrew hadn't known the name of this street when he'd traced his route for the detectives, but Hardy was glad to see that it fit his description — a paved walkway allowed foot access to the campus at the end of the street.

When he turned back west at Fulton, Hardy found the uphill going a little slower. There was also a significant increase in traffic — it might have been more difficult for Andrew to concentrate or memorize his lines on this part of the walk, but maybe not. There simply was no way to tell.

He passed St. Ignatius Church at the top of the hill, continued down a couple of blocks to Stanyan, then turned right and made it back to his car. He checked his watch. He hadn't been particularly pushing himself, and he'd made the circuit in eighteen minutes — rather far from the half hour it had supposedly taken Andrew. Although Andrew might have stopped once, twice, several times, to set a line or perhaps just to think, he'd never specifically mentioned stopping. Hardy didn't feel comfortable with the twelve-minute difference. He made another note.

Crossing the street, he stood under the streetlight and looked up at the Salarcos' unit. From reading the police reports, Hardy knew that the involvement of this critical witness had been reluctant at first. Salarco was a mow-blow-and-go gardener with an INS problem — no green card. Ironically, the Salarcos were only involved in the case because Andrew himself had told the detectives about them. Sergeant Taylor had asked him if he had any idea who might have called nine one one before he had — that person had had a thick Mexican accent.

Andrew had volunteered that he bet it was the people upstairs — they had definitely been home that night. Their baby had been crying incessantly, and it had been distracting to the max. Andrew had told Sergeant Taylor that it was one of the reasons he couldn't just go into one of Mooney's back bedrooms to work on memorizing his lines. He'd had to get out where it was quiet enough to concentrate.

So Taylor had asked Salarco if he'd seen or heard anything, or had called nine one one. At first the neighbor had said no. He and his wife had a sick baby. That's all they were concerned with. But Taylor had a hunch and asked about Salarco's immigration status, then explained that he was not with the INS, that Salarco's testimony might be crucial to a murder investigation and might in fact mitigate in his favor with *la migra*. Hardy knew this was probably a cynical lie on Taylor's part, but it did accomplish its goal — Salarco talked.

At the sidewalk in front of the house, Hardy took a deep breath, hoping he could make the man talk again.

The door to the Salarcos' upstairs unit was around the driveway side in the back. A small flatbed truck took up most of the space between this building and its neighbor. There was no light over the door, and Hardy heard nothing when he pushed the doorbell, but after few seconds, he heard footfalls within, coming downstairs. Then, *"Sí? Qué es?"*

"Señora Salarco?"

"Sí. Policia?"

"No. Habla inglés?" Hardy dug for some words that he hoped were close enough. *"Soy abogado de Señor Bartlett."*

"Momento."

The footsteps retreated. Hardy had time to turn around and examine the truck and the building. Wooden fence posts lined both sides of the empty flatbed. He saw no tools. The windows in the cab were up. The house was old, ramshackle, very small — less than half the size of the other buildings on the block. Hardy had wondered how an illegal handyman could afford the rent to even a doghouse in this neighborhood, and the answer was that it wasn't much bigger than a doghouse, and from the outside at least, not much nicer.

Another set of footsteps on the stairs. This time the male voice, though heavily accented, spoke English. "Yes."

"Mr. Salarco?" he said through the door. "My name is Dismas Hardy. I'm the lawyer for Andrew Bartlett. About the murder case?" No response. "If you've got a few minutes, I'd like to talk to you if I may."

Salarco didn't ponder for long. Perhaps, Hardy thought, he considered anyone involved with the case a potential official who could turn him in. If so, Hardy was happy to let him keep believing that.

With bright red skin and an unlined face, he struck Hardy as much younger than his stated age of twenty-eight. A little above medium height, in his T-shirt and jeans, Salarco could have been a weight lifter,

341

with his massive arms and well-developed shoulders, tiny waist. But the face — Hardy came back to it — it was the face of a boy. "*Tardes, señor* . . . what is it, please, your name again?"

"Hardy. Dismas Hardy."

"Deezmus. I don't know that name."

Hardy kept it genial. "Nobody does. I wouldn't worry about it."

They ascended a narrow stairway that ended in another door that opened into Salarco's living room. It was little more than a cubicle, but nicely furnished in Salvation Army. A beaded bottle of Modelo Negro rested on the coffee table, along with a paperback book — *Cien Años de Soledad.* So the gardener was a reader, perhaps with intellect. It was good, Hardy thought, to find out early.

The television was tuned to a Spanish station. Salarco turned it off, indicating that Hardy sit on the upholstered couch. *"Cerveza?"* he asked, and Hardy nodded. When he came back with the beer, Salarco took the opposite end of the couch. "So what do you want to know?" he asked.

Hardy put his beer down on the table, took a relaxed position. "I'd really just like to walk through the events of the night of the murder, when you called the police. I've got a copy of your statements here, and I just wondered if you'd mind telling me again what you did that night, in your own words. Would that be all right with you?"

"*Sí.* Sure."

"Before we begin, though, I want to ask you if you've talked to any lawyers with the DA's office about your statements, or your identification of Andrew Bartlett."

He thought about it for a second, then shook his head. "Not any lawyers. I have talked to the police three, maybe four times. But no lawyers."

This made sense to Hardy. In the normal course of events this case wouldn't come to trial for the best part of a year. Whoever pulled Andrew Bartlett for the adult trial wouldn't even have had a chance to review his own discovery yet. With all the dealing and then the hurry to move Andrew up out of juvenile court, Hardy doubted whether Brandt had, either, since he didn't have to know all the facts about the crime — he wasn't trying the case.

So Hardy had a clear field. But before he started to run, it was important that Salarco understand his position. He had already gotten it out, and now he handed him his business card, as required by statute. "I want you to know that I represent Andrew Bartlett, the boy you identified as the killer of Mr. Mooney and the girl, Laura Wright. I'm his lawyer. I want to hear what you have to say because I'm going to have to try to find out what happened."

The seriousness of the little speech hit a mark. Salarco drew his arm off the couch and onto his lap. His brow clouded a bit. "I will just tell the truth," he said, "as I have."

"That's all I can ask. Thank you." He took a hand-held tape recorder from his jacket pocket and placed it on the table. "Do you have any objection if I record what you say?"

It wasn't clear whether Salarco knew he had the option to refuse. He nodded, then waited. "How do you want me to start?"

"Just what happened that night."

Another nod. "The main thing is Carla, our baby, she was sick. High high fever. She is crying crying, but finally, maybe about nine o'clock, we finally get her to start to sleep." He uncrossed his legs, reached for his beer and drank. "But then downstairs, you know, just down there, right below, we hear this . . . this *fight*."

"A physical fight?"

"I don't know. I couldn't see, but I heard loud yelling — a man, two men, and a woman. *Loud! Really loud!* And of course then it wakes up Carla. She started crying again and . . . You have babies?"

"Two," Hardy said. "Older now."

"Well, you know, then . . . when they cry. At least me, it makes me . . . I don't know the word. *Impaciente.* Crazy to have it stop."

"Impatient," Hardy said. And thought, To say the least.

"*Sí.* Impatient. So then Carla starts again and I am impatient with the noise from below. So I stomp on the floor like this" — he brought his heel down — "boom, boom, and it's quiet for another few minutes, then the yelling starts again, and Carla is crying."

"And what happened then?" Hardy asked.

"Then, when it started again, I went downstairs to ask them to stop."

"Just a minute, please." Hardy sat up straight. This was not in anything he'd read. "You're saying you went downstairs at a little after nine o'clock and talked to the people down there?"

"*Sí.*"

"And who was there?"

"The girl, Señor Mike, and the boy."

"Andrew? The boy you identified in the lineup?"

"*Sí.*"

Hardy took a breath. This wasn't good. If Salarco had seen Andrew at the house, close up, there was much less chance that he'd been mistaken at the lineup, or would recant at the trial. He sipped some beer to get his concern under control, and the question came out almost casually. "And what then? Did they tell you they'd stop fighting?"

A questioning look crossed Salarco's face.

"What is it?" Hardy asked.

But it passed. "Nothing," Salarco said. "I don't know. But yes, they said they'd stop."

"And then it was quiet?"

"Yes."

"For how long?"

"No *se.* When the baby is crying, time just goes, you know. But again, we just got her to sleep again and Anna and I, we come out here, to this room, and turn on the TV, real quiet, but then there is this . . . this scream, the girl, and then a . . . a bump. You could feel it up here, like something dropped. The house shook. Then right after, a crash, the sound of a crash, glass breaking. And a few seconds later, suddenly *boom* again, the house shakes another time, somebody slamming the front door under us."

Salarco on his feet now, acting it out. "Anna goes to this window, here, and I am behind her, and there is the boy running away. He stops under the light there, and turns, and Anna starts to put the window up to . . . to yell at him I think, but then Carla starts again with crying. *Madre de dios!*" Salarco, living it again, turned to Hardy and put both hands to his head. "Is it never going to end?"

"And then?"

"Then I . . . remember, I am . . . I have no sleep and my baby has been crying for ten hours straight. I run downstairs. I go to yell at them all, but when I hit the front door, I hit it with a fist and it . . . it opens." His hands hung at his side. "And I see them."

"Mooney and the girl?"

"*Sí*. On the floor, with so much blood. I walk in. The girl is shot, I think, in the chest, and is by the back wall. There is a big stand-up lamp knocked on the floor, broken, all smashed, next to her, but there is still light above and from in the *cocina*. And Señor Mike is on his back with a hole in his face. I will never forget."

"No," Hardy said. "I'm sorry."

Salarco crossed back to the couch, sat now on the edge of it. He seemed to remember his beer and picked it up, drained it, looked across to Hardy. *"Otros?"*

Hardy hadn't put much of a dent in his first beer, and didn't want another, but he wanted to keep Salarco talking. *"Gracias. Sí."*

When he came back with the two cold ones, he put them on the coffee table and began without any prompting. "So the phone is there, and I go to it and push nine one one, and tell what I see, where I am. And while I am talking, I notice the gun on the little table in front of the couch." He leaned forward, knocked wood. "Just the same as this one."

"And then what did you do?"

"Then I see how bad this looks, me in this room with the gun. I think the boy, maybe he's going to come back. If he sees I am there, he can say it was me."

"What was you?"

"Who killed these people."

"Why would you have done that?"

Salarco turned his palms up. "The noise. I already come down one time to stop it. Maybe next time, I bring the gun and make sure. Then the woman on the phone, she tries more to get my name, and the other thing comes to me, *la migra*. I know I have to go. I cannot be there when the authorities come. So I come back up here and watch out the window until the boy comes back, and the authorities."

"You mean Andrew again?"

"*Sí.*"

"You saw him under the streetlight there out the window?"

"*Sí.*"

"The same boy? You're sure."

Salarco put down his beer bottle, turned and faced Hardy directly. "I'm sorry, *señor*, but it was him. The same hair, the same clothes . . ."

"And what were they, the clothes?"

"Like all of them wear. I don't know how you say . . . loose?"

"Baggy?"

Salarco nodded. "*Sí*. The pants, baggy. And then the . . ." He made a gesture of pulling something over his head. "Like Eminem in the movie."

"You mean he had a hood? A sweatshirt with a hood?"

"*Sí*. That was it."

"And even with the hood, you saw his face? And it was the same face?"

After the shortest pause, Salarco nodded. "*Sí*. Of course. It was the same boy, I say."

Hardy believed him. In fact, it had to be Andrew returning from his walk, or from wherever he had gone. Perhaps having run away and then realizing he'd left the gun, which could be traced back to him. Looking up, Hardy caught a glimpse of Salarco's wife hovering in the doorway back to the kitchen. He might have to talk to her one day as well, but for tonight, he took a last pull from his beer, then stood up. "I want to thank you for your time.

You've been very helpful."

"I am sorry about the boy, *señor*. Truly I am."

"Thank you," Hardy said. "I am, too."

16

It was well past nine o'clock by the time Glitsky sat down to dinner at the small table in his kitchen.

Treya had gotten good at meals that took fifteen minutes to prepare, and she waited until she heard his tread on the steps up to their duplex before she threw the halibut on to broil in the oven. When she turned it the one time, she would smear it with jalapeño jelly, which would melt, forming a fantastic glaze. The asparagus sat in a shallow covered pan with a quarter inch of boiling water. She'd finish that with olive oil, balsamic vinegar and a pinch of sea salt. A small, still warm, dense loaf of homemade bread-machine bread — roasted-garlic with Asiago cheese — would round out the meal, after which they'd split a plate of frozen grapes for dessert.

Glitsky had fed Rachel in her high chair and for the past few minutes had been doing magic tricks, making a quarter disappear. Now Treya put the adult plates down. "Arranged yet," he said. She'd garnished with a few sprigs of fresh rosemary. A crystal vase sat between the place mats on the small wooden table, and in it bloomed one perfect daffodil.

Glitsky put a finger on his daughter's nose, turned to his food and picked up his fork. "Do I thank you enough for doing all this?"

Treya kissed the top of his head. "Every day." She touched her baby's cheek. "You gave me her, didn't you?" She came around the table and took her seat. "Now shush and eat your fish. It's brain food."

"I'd better, then. I'm going to need it." He chewed, swallowed. "This Boscacci thing."

"At least it's not LeShawn Brodie. I checked, and you'd dropped right off the news tonight, just like it never happened."

"Fresh kill," Glitsky said. "Anyhow, you'll be glad to hear Amy Wu's almost certainly out of it."

"She was never really in, though, was she?"

"No, not really, although she could have timed her last meeting with Allan a little better. The real story, though, is that because of her, I got to give Diz a little grief."

Treya smiled. "Always a plus."

"And even more so because I swung by his office to give him his earful of righteous cop, and while I was there, I found a way to repay him for his little caper with my peanut drawer."

"I thought you weren't sure who that was."

"I wasn't, then I realized it had to be Diz. No one else is that immature."

"I can think of one other person," she said.

The corners of Glitsky's mouth rose a fraction of an inch. "Thank you," he said. "Plus, anybody at the Hall, it's too risky if I catch them. They're flayed, then fired. Diz, I get him red-handed and he says, 'Ha ha, you got me, so what?' It was him."

"Okay. So what'd you do to him?"

"First, you have to promise not to tell under penalty of death."

"That goes without saying."

"Diz or Frannie. You'll be tempted."

"I'll resist, I promise. What?"

A spark of mischief flashed in his eyes. "I stole his darts. You want to hear the best part?"

"That wasn't it? What could be better?"

"Next time I'm there, I'm going to put them back. Then steal them again. My hope is that eventually he'll go insane."

"And that would be so that you two could play together as equals?" Treya put her fork down and looked across the table, her own eyes alight. She turned to Rachel.

"Do you know how lucky you are that you can't understand any of this?" she asked.

An hour later, the baby was in bed and the two of them sat in their living room with their after dinner tea. "But that poor man . . ." Treya was talking about Boscacci. "Do you have anything at all?"

"Well, if you count that we're fairly certain it wasn't Amy, we've got that."

"Well, yes. But we knew that this morning before you even talked to her."

"True. But now we know with more certainty," he said. "And not because she works with Diz. Because she couldn't have done it."

"So who could have?"

Glitsky pulled at the scar at his lower lip. "My best guess now is someone he fired in the last three years. Maybe one of them took it personally."

"So how many people did he let go? Allan?"

"Seventeen."

Treya whistled softly. "That's a lot."

Glitsky sat back into the couch. He reached down near his belt and probed, perhaps unconsciously, at his side. "Well, fortunately," he went on, "I've got a lot of resources for a change. I've got two inspectors from General Work for the canvassing and alibi checking, then Belou and Russell from homicide, and they'll basically be full time to find and interview the folks Allan fired. Then Marcel asked to be part of it, too, back on the street if he had to. And, of course, my own magnificent self."

"What are you going to be doing?"

Glitsky drew a sharp breath. "Well, mostly, given the lack of any forensic evidence, I'm going to be developing theories. But I'm not complaining. At least it's a homicide. Something I know how to do."

Treya put her cup down, reached over, put her hand on Glitsky's shoulder. "Is your side hurting you again? Maybe you should see a doctor."

"No."

"No to what?"

"Both."

"You won't see a doctor?"

Glitsky grunted. "I've seen enough doctors. You start in with doctors, it never ends. They looked when this started and couldn't find anything. I'm not about to let them cut on me again just to look."

"But it's still hurting you, whatever it is."

"I know what it is." He softened his tone. "I'm uptight. I'm waiting for the other shoe to drop, and till it does or I decide it's not going to, I've got to tough it out."

"So what's going to make you decide that? Do you have any idea?"

"I don't know," he said. "Maybe doing something I'm good at."

"What does that mean? You're doing a great job as deputy chief. Everybody says so."

"Nobody was saying so yesterday with LeShawn."

Treya waved that off. "Those were just the media vultures, Abe. You know that. You can't take them seriously. I'm talking about people like Clarence, and Frank Batiste. The mayor. Kathy West. I hear nothing but good things and where I work, that's saying something."

A shrug. "I make my numbers. I show up on time. My brass shines. But inside I'm not like these people."

"What people?"

"Frank, Clarence, the mayor — all the people who have these meetings." He pushed at his side again. "They're politicians. Plus I've got this little secret and can't help thinking that someday somebody's going to find me out."

Treya spoke with some care. "Maybe you want to talk to somebody?"

"What do you mean, a shrink?" He barked out a black laugh. "So then word goes out that the man is cracking up? And everybody starts to check out my office furniture? Half the folks would think I really am crazy and the other half would figure it's a scam to get disability. I'd kiss my credibility good-bye forever."

"It wouldn't have to be a psychiatrist. Maybe a psychologist. Or a career counselor."

"And what's this person going to do, talk me out of the pain?" He took her hand. "Besides, I talk to you."

Treya wasn't going to be conned. "And I can't help. I *haven't* helped. I'm just saying maybe someone else could get somewhere."

"Not if I couldn't tell them about it. And I can't. You know I can't."

"That's what you keep saying. But there *is* such a thing as doctor/patient privilege, you know. That's a real thing. They couldn't tell."

"Right, in theory. But in real life, they tell all the time. A rumor gets started, and you know cops, they ask questions. And then where are we?"

"At least you're not in pain."

"Wonderful. Except that now I'm ruined, even in jail. How does that sound? There's no statute on murder."

"It wasn't murder. It was self-defense. You keep saying it was murder, and it wasn't."

"All right, but it killed a cop. And I was a party to covering it up. Whatever happens, if that comes out, even if I never go to jail, it's the end of my career." He exhaled with some force. "I've got to live with it, that's all. It's not that bad."

But as he said it, he tightened his lips, the scar through them going white with the pressure. Treya, her own face tight with concern, laid a palm on his thigh and he covered it with his own hand, squeezing hard. When the spasm had passed, he released his grip. "Not that bad," he repeated.

He came into the bedroom and Treya put down her book. "Who was that?"

"Marcel."

She checked the bedside clock. 10:42. "This time of night?"

"I told him he could call anytime."

She smiled at him. "Of course you did." She patted the bed next to her. "Here, sit down. What did Marcel find?"

"Well, again, it's more what they didn't find. Nobody heard anything."

"What do you mean?"

"I mean, Marcel sent out our team to knock on every door within two blocks of the All-Day Lot. Have another go at them, catch the people who weren't home earlier. They got forty-four hits, which is the jackpot. Nobody heard a shot, not even the shoe repair folks still at work just around the corner, like fifty feet away."

"Maybe they just didn't want to say."

"Maybe. Some percentage wouldn't give away their trash to save humanity. But you've got to hope that with forty-four people, maybe a couple are good citizens. But these folks were there, admitted they were there, talked to our people. Nobody heard anything."

Treya sat up. "Is that so unusual?"

Glitsky shrugged. "You know what a nine-millimeter sounds like? Close up, a cherry bomb. A block away, you hear it and you stop a second and go, 'What was that?' "

"And nobody heard anything? Maybe he was inside a car and rolled the window down?"

"Maybe that," Glitsky said. "Or maybe he had a suppressor."

"A what?"

"A silencer. Suppressor."

"And what does that mean? Other than the shot doesn't make much noise?"

"It means he's probably a pro. In which case he's probably in another state by now. But if he was a pro, that also means somebody hired him. It's another place to look, that's all."

Hardy owned a one-quarter interest in one of San Francisco's oldest bars, the Little Shamrock, at the corner of Ninth and Lincoln, just across the street from Golden Gate Park. The majority partner was Frannie's brother, Moses McGuire, another emotional casualty of the shoot-out. By jogging just slightly from the direct route to his home from Juan Salarco's, Hardy could pass right by the place, check up on his brother-in-law, maybe have a short nightcap.

It had gotten late. After saying good night to Salarco, Hardy had gone out to his car and, with the interview still fresh in his mind, listened to the tape of it twice through again. With the sometimes lengthy time-outs he took for making notes, both as the witness talked and as ideas occurred after each listening, he worked for most of an hour that felt to him like five minutes.

The Shamrock's bar ran along one wall halfway back to where the room widened out slightly. At the front door, it was wall-to-wall people, five or six deep. His first glance told Hardy he had no chance to claim a stool anywhere near the bar itself, and even if he was successful at that, the crowd would keep Moses too busy to talk. Nights like this, Hardy would sometimes take off his jacket, grab a bar towel and help out behind the rail. He'd been a bartender once, and a good one.

But tonight he wasn't in the mood. It was too crowded, too loud, too hot. The jukebox was cranked up with some old Marshall Tucker music. Maybe he ought to go home.

He was just turning to leave when Wes Farrell and his live-in girlfriend, Sam Duncan, pushed their way in. Sam was a petite, feisty, pretty dark-haired woman, forty-ish, who ran one of the city's rape crisis counseling centers not far away on Haight Street.

"You're not leaving?" Farrell said. "Not when we're just getting here."

"It had crossed my mind. It's going to take an hour to get a drink."

"We've got that knocked," Sam said. "We know the owner. Come on."

Sam took Hardy's hand and led the way, jostling them through the crowd. Once they'd cleared the bottleneck up front, there was adequate room to stand and even move as long as nobody wanted to polka. Hardy noticed that Farrell was his out-of-the-office casual self, wearing one of his trademark T-shirts, which read "Be More or Less Specific." At Hardy's shoulder, Sam was saying that since he was buying, she'd have a Chivas rocks and Wes would have a pint of Bass Ale. Hardy could have whatever he wanted.

"Thanks," he told her. He ducked under the bar, gave McGuire a half-salute and called down that he was getting his own

361

drinks, Moses shouldn't worry about him.

When Hardy got back with the drinks, Farrell nudged Sam and said, "Tell him."

"Tell me what?" Hardy said.

Sam sampled her Scotch, nodded appreciatively. "I don't know how it came up," she began.

"At dinner," Farrell said. "I started telling you about this situation with Amy."

"That's it." She came back to Hardy. "Well, the point is he mentioned this boy Andrew Bartlett and I said I knew a little about it. I'd been following it in the papers. I was interested because back when I was young and foolish, I used to hang out sometimes with Linda." At Hardy's uncomprehending glance, she added, "His mother."

"What do you mean, hang out?"

A shrug. "Just that. Go to bars, meet guys. This was before I met my true love here, of course. But if you wanted to pretty much guarantee you'd get lucky of a given night, you wanted to hang with Linda if you could. She could materialize men out of a vacuum. You're thinking 'so what?' Aren't you?"

In fact, that's what Hardy was thinking. Sam could make almost any story listenable. But the wild child Linda Bartlett was now the married Linda North, and other than the fact that San Francisco continued to be a small and self-referential little world, there wasn't anything particularly fascinating about the fact that she'd hung out and picked up men with Sam Duncan when both of them had been younger. But Hardy said, "Go on."

"Well, since it's the law and by definition must be endlessly enthralling, I say to my darling here, 'I'm not surprised the little kid didn't turn out right. His dad ran off and his mother didn't give him the time of day.' "

"So Andrew was around when you and Linda were hanging out?"

"He was around in the sense that he was alive. He must have been three or so about this time. But Linda would dump him with anyone at the drop of a hat. I even kept him with me for a couple of weekends when she went away with somebody. He was the cutest little guy, if you like three-year-olds, which, you know, are not generally my favorite. But even given that, this was a woman who shouldn't ever have become a mother. The boy was nothing but inconvenient to her. She was going to have her fun and all he did was get in the way."

Sam drank more of her Scotch. "Actually, that's one of the reasons I stopped hanging out with her. It just became obvious, the kind of person she was. I like to think I'm as shallow as anybody —

it's why Wes loves me, after all — but she just wasn't going to be involved with her own son, and that was that. After a while it got so I couldn't stand to see it."

Farrell jumped in. "The reason this might be important to you, Diz —"

"Hey!" Sam hit him on the arm. "It's my story, all right? I understood your point at dinner. I'm getting to it."

"I'm listening," Hardy said.

"Thank you. The *point*," she shot a glare at Farrell, "being that the boy really has had a difficult life, especially in his early years. So in spite of the pampered rich boy he might seem to be, he was essentially an abandoned kid, raised, if you want to call it that, by an emotionally removed if not outright abusive mother."

"She abused him, you think?"

"I don't know if she actively abused him, like beat him or anything like that, but I guarantee you he's deeply scarred. And, finally, the point is . . ."

"Ahh," Farrell said, "the point."

". . . is that in many jurisdictions, but especially in San Francisco, the wise defense attorney, such as my esteemed roommate here, will take every opportunity to present his criminal client as the victim of something, childhood abuse being perhaps the all-time favorite."

"It is a good one," Hardy said.

"And Andrew is legitimately in that club."

"If you can get it into the record," Farrell said. "It may not get him off, but it sure as hell couldn't hurt in sentencing."

"No," Hardy said. "I don't imagine it could."

17

"We've got a problem."

At his desk, Hardy motioned Wu in. She'd taken some care dressing and making up this morning. She often did, so this wasn't unusual in itself. But the two-piece pin-striped dark blue business suit she wore was such a far cry from the way she'd looked in his daughter's bathrobe, nursing the mother of all hangovers, that Hardy blinked at the transformation. He'd been listening again to the tape he'd made at Juan Salarco's — something about it bothering him — and now he removed his headphones, gave Wu his attention. "Hit me," he said.

"He's a writer."

"Who is? Andrew?"

She nodded. "On his computer. They delivered more discovery here yesterday while I was out. This disk," she held it up, "is not good. You want to see?"

"It would make my day." He took the disk from her and slipped it into his computer.

" 'Perfect Killer Dot One,' " she said. "Love the name."

Hardy's fingers moved over the keyboard. Wu came around behind him as the document appeared on the screen. Quiet and intent, together they read Andrew's short story about a young man filled with jealous rage who kills his girlfriend and his English teacher. For over ten minutes, the only sound in the room was the tick of the computer's cursor as Hardy scrolled through the document.

When they got to the end, Hardy found his heart pounding. He had also broken a sweat. He pushed his chair back from the computer, stood and went over to open one of his windows, get some air. After a minute, he turned to Wu. "I'd better go meet the client."

"Can I ask you a question?" Wu asked. They were driving out to the YGC in Hardy's car, the top down. "Do I come across as some kind of monster?"

"Not at all." Hardy didn't know exactly what to say. He looked over at her. The light changed and he pulled out. "Why do you ask? Did somebody say that?"

"More or less. That I didn't feel anything. That there wasn't anybody real inside of me."

"Who said that? Somebody in the firm?"

"No. A colleague."

"Well, whoever it was can ask me. The other night, talking about your dad, that was real enough."

"But I was drunk then, with my guard down."

"I've done research on that exact topic. It still counts."

"I don't know." She turned in her seat. "But I'm thinking if that's all people can see in me, then maybe that's all my dad saw, too."

Hardy kept it low-key. "Or maybe it wasn't you at all. Maybe your dad just wasn't able to show what he felt."

"No, he really didn't approve of me. Or like me very much."

"Or maybe the idea of showing you terrified him, so he was extra-tough so you wouldn't ever find out and take advantage and hurt him." Trying to lighten it up, he added, "And if that's the case, you better watch out. It's genetic, that kind of thing." Hardy flashed a quick look at her.

Abruptly, Wu had turned straight ahead in her seat, her eyes on the road.

"Are you all right?" he asked.

Her lips tight, her jaw set, she nodded. But said nothing.

Throughout all of his schooling at the best institutions in San Francisco, Andrew had been inculcated into the sensitive, educated modern child's nutritional paradigm of healthy eating. Sutro had both a juice and a salad bar, and that's where, for a mere $4.45, he bought his lunch every day. Over the years, like most of his classmates who'd been forced to witness the brutal slaughtering of some food animal on videotape in school, he had come to believe that humans shouldn't eat meat. A few days of real hunger after his arrest, though, had conquered his qualms. Besides that, the YGC vegetarian alternative meal was total slop.

Wu didn't think it was the food, though, that accounted for his pallor and lethargy today. He'd shaved, showered, and combed his hair, but in the jail outfit — blue denims, gray sweatshirt — he showed no sign that yesterday afternoon's depression had lifted at all. If anything, it seemed worse.

He greeted Hardy with a bored and sullen silence. He only shook, no grip, after a pause long enough for Hardy nearly to withdraw his own offered hand. Wu started to explain that Hardy was here because he had more experience with murder cases and . . .

"You said that yesterday. So we're going to adult trial?"

"Maybe not," Wu said. "We're hoping

369

that this hearing . . ."

But he cut her off again. "No you're not. Yesterday you said that was hopeless. They get one of the criteria, it's over, right?"

Andrew had stuffed himself into the old school desk. Wu sat at the table. Hardy was standing in the corner, leaning against one of the walls, arms crossed. He spoke matter-of-factly. "You can always go back and admit the petition. I'll bet you I could talk Johnson into accepting that if you wanted to change your mind. You want to do that?"

Andrew kept his eyes on the table in front of him. "That's eight years automatic."

"That's right," Hardy said.

He looked up. "I didn't do this."

"Well, then," Hardy said, "you don't want to do those eight years, do you?"

He didn't answer.

"Which, like it or not," Hardy said, "leaves us with an adult trial, unless we can win this hearing next Tuesday."

He pointed to Wu. "She says we can't do that."

"We've got some problems," Hardy admitted, "but we've also got some strategies. To make them work, though, we're going to need your help. If you think it's even worth it to try."

Andrew shrugged.

Hardy came forward, his voice hardening up, pressing him a little. "You do? You don't? I'm not reading your signals very clearly. You want to try using some words?"

It was clear that Andrew hadn't had too many people talk to him so harshly. "All right," he said finally. "What do you want me to do?"

"Let's start by you telling me about the gun," Hardy said.

"What about it?"

"I'm curious why you brought it to your rehearsal that night."

Andrew didn't have to think about it. "It was just in my backpack. I'd been carrying it around for a few weeks."

"But you took it out that night. At Mr. Mooney's. Isn't that right?"

"Yeah."

"So how did that happen?"

He shrugged. "It was a prop, that's all. We were doing *Virginia Woolf*, you know. That was the play. And Mike — Mooney — he thought it might add to the tension if we had a gun on stage. It's not really in the script, but he just wanted to see how it would feel."

"So he asked you to bring a gun to rehearsal?"

"No. I had it with me anyway, so I brought it up. It was my idea. I thought it might be cool."

Hardy thought this would be a good time to shake things up. He forced an amused little chuckle, walked up to the table, looked down at Wu. "The boy's good, Amy," he said. "This is some brilliant delivery. I can see where he got the lead in the play."

"What are you talking about?" Andrew asked.

Hardy kept his tone easy. "I'm talking about acting, Andrew. What else?"

"I'm not acting. This is what happened." A pause. "Really."

Hardy nodded, chuckled again, talked to Amy. "Damn," Hardy said. "Impressive. I mean it. I'd be pretty well swayed if I were on a jury."

"Me, too," Wu said. "We put him on the stand, he flies."

Hardy looked down at him. "It's always a big decision whether or not to put a defendant on the stand himself. But we get a world-class performer like yourself, it's a real bonus."

"Why are you saying this? I'm not performing. I'm telling you the truth."

Again, Hardy spoke directly to Wu. "And the award goes to . . ."

"*I'm telling the truth, goddamn it!* What are you saying?"

Hardy didn't rise to the challenge. Retreating to his neutral corner, he leaned against the wall again, crossed his arms. "You tell him, Amy."

She took the cue. "Andrew," she said. "Andrew, look at me."

He dragged his pained expression back down to the table.

"Why Mr. Hardy is skeptical is that in 'Perfect Killer,' you tell that same story as the —"

Andrew jumped as if he'd been stung. "How do you know about that? I never . . ." He shot a look to the corner, where Hardy was the picture of nonchalance. Nothing there. He came back to Wu. "I never even printed that out."

"No," Wu said. "I don't suppose you would have. But it was still on the disk."

Hardy spoke up. "It's pretty standard procedure now, Andrew. The police get a search warrant and dump your computer files, read your e-mail. That's the one thing I'd criticize about your story. The writing was good. It reminded me a little of Holden Caulfield, but you hadn't done your research on the latest tech stuff. Didn't you know they'd served a warrant at your house? Didn't it occur to you that they'd look for everything they could find?"

Andrew slumped at his desk. His arms hung straight down, his head bowed. They let him live with his new reality for a minute or more, a very long time under those circumstances. Finally, he sighed and raised his head. "Look," he said, "I'm not acting. I'm telling you guys the truth. What I made up was that story. I had my guy, my character —"

"Trevor," Wu said.

"Right, Trevor. I had Trevor —"

Hardy cut in. "Andrew," he said. "That's the most incriminating document I've ever read and I've been in this game a long time. No judge in the world is going to let you off if he gets a look at that, which he will. How many other stories like that are in your computer?"

"None just like that."

"Thank God," Wu said. "What in the world were you thinking, Andrew?"

Unbowed, he snapped back. "I was thinking about writing a story. You know, fiction?"

"We know all about fiction," Hardy said. He hadn't moved from his spot in the corner by the door. "But this just . . . Well, it isn't fiction. I flat don't believe it."

"You can believe what you want. Haven't you ever read *Crime and Punishment*? Or John Lanchester's *The Debt to Pleasure*?"

"I've read them both," Wu said. "What about them?"

"Well, I had just read *Debt to Pleasure* earlier in the year, when I was starting to have some problems with Laura." His eyes went back and forth between his attorneys. "When we first started rehearsing with Mike, she . . . well, like Julie in the story, she was just all impressed with him, that she'd gotten the part, all that. It got to me. We actually broke up about it."

"That wasn't in the story," Hardy said. "The breakup."

"No," Andrew said. "That's because I *made up* the story. Have I already mentioned that? I thought I had."

Hardy's mouth grinned, but his eyes didn't. "I don't know who convinced you that sarcasm was a powerful debating tool, Andrew. But whoever it was didn't do you a service. I understand that you made up your story. It's not that tough a concept to grasp. But you have to admit that there's a lot of it that seems pretty closely based on your own experience. Now, do you want to tell us about that, or not?"

Andrew tried stewing for a moment. He turned to Wu, who might show some sympathy, for support, but she stonewalled him. At last, he spoke. "When I wrote it, I was jealous of Mike with Laura. I was going for a weird-guy feel like Lanchester did."

"You got that," Wu said. She turned to Hardy. "*The Debt to Pleasure* again."

Hardy deadpanned. "I've got to read it."

"In the end," Andrew said, "that's why I didn't send out the story anyplace. It was too derivative. I mean, a really really bright guy who's basically insane. It's been done a million times now. Plus, I don't think the ending worked really well. I wanted Trevor to find a really unique way to commit these murders, but in the end, I fell back on the gun."

Hardy had to fight a disorienting sense of surrealism. Here's a client up for murder and what he wants to discuss are plot points in a story that might hang him. "Have you published before?" he asked.

"No. But I've sent out a bunch. I did get a nice note back from *McSweeney's* on one of them, not a straight rejection."

"I'm happy for you." Hardy finally moved up to the table, pulled around a chair and sat in it. "Listen, Andrew, whether or not you made this up, we've got to work on some kind of spin for this story. You've got to see that it casts you in the worst possible light."

"It wasn't that bad," Andrew said.

"No, it's peachy," Hardy said. "But I'm not talking about its literary quality. I'm talking about the events and motive around these two murders that have actually taken place and that you're charged with committing and that you pretty much exactly mirrored in the story you wrote two months earlier. Two murders — your teacher and your girlfriend. Your dad's gun. Even down to your alibi."

"Don't forget my favorite moment," Amy said. She'd printed the thing out at the office, and now had found the page, and read aloud. "Talking about the gun now. Here's your narrator. *But what if I get rid of it after? Then, even if they can recover the slugs, they won't be able to compare the ballistics marks. I double-check and make sure the gun isn't made in Israel, where they shoot their guns before they sell them. Then the ballistic readouts are computerized and matched with the weapon's buyer, so even if the gun itself is unavailable, they can identify its owner.*"

"That's true," Andrew objected. "That's what they do. I found it in my research."

"Good for you," Hardy said. "But not the point. Here, Amy, let me."

She handed the pages across to him. He flipped to the end. "How about this part, Andrew? How do you think a jury would feel about you if the prosecutor got this admitted, which he will, and reads it out loud? *I come back and find the bodies. I call nine one one. They're going to think there's no way I'd come back and do that if I'd done the shooting.*

"Will the cops suspect me? Yeah. But I've gotten rid of the gun and the gloves. The night

I do it, I pack a change of clothes just like the ones I was wearing in a plastic bag in my trunk. Shoes, too. I adios the whole package before I come back and discover the carnage.

"*The cops look, but I'm clean. And Mike and Laura are gone.*"

"No! That's wrong." Andrew came halfway out of his chair. "I didn't write Mike and Laura. I wrote Julie and Miles. The characters."

"Oh, that's right, you did. I guess it seemed like you meant Mike and Laura, so that's what I read. Honest mistake." Hardy turned the pages facedown, looked across the room at his client. "Listen, Andrew. Not only is this pretty much exactly what happened, it shows premeditation and planning. It's also sophisticated stuff. You may remember that as another one of the criteria we're supposed to avoid — criminal sophistication."

Andrew slumped back into his chair, crossed his arms over his chest. Given the magnitude of disaster he was looking at, his expression was almost serene. "Look," he said. "You start with my character in the story, remember, not me. You put him in a situation that you know something about. That's what they tell you, to write what you know."

"That's what you say in the story, too. So all right, you picked jealousy."

"I hadn't ever felt anything like it before. It was just . . . overpowering. Laura would get to going on about Mike, and after a while I just couldn't listen to it anymore. I suppose I started acting like a jerk . . ."

Wu jumped on it. "How?"

"Every way I could, really. Coming on to other girls around her. Cutting her down in front of other people. Dissing Mike . . ."

"But nothing physical?" she asked.

"No."

"Nothing?" Hardy repeated. This was the kind of fact about which you wanted no ambiguity. "You never hit her? Nobody ever saw you hit her?"

"I never hit her," he said. "I would never hit her. I loved her."

"Okay." Hardy thrummed his fingers on the table. "Let's go back to the story. Do you have any idea how we deal with it, or get around it?"

Andrew sighed. "It's fiction. I don't know what else I can say. The character isn't me. Julie isn't Laura, Miles isn't Mike. There's tons of stuff in the story that didn't really happen."

"Name me something important," Hardy said. "Something that will make any difference to a judge or jury."

"Well, the main thing, in the story, Trevor had had a lot of sex with other girls. That wasn't me."

379

"You're a virgin?" Hardy asked. "That didn't read like a virgin wrote it."

"I was then," Andrew said, a hint of pride in the admission. "I imagined what a guy like Trevor would have felt and done."

"All right." Hardy wasn't giving him much. "But it's a stretch to call that the main thing, Andrew. Maybe you could tell us something about the crime that's different in the story from real life."

The boy looked to Wu for help, but she, too, was waiting for what he'd say. "Okay," he said finally. "Okay. In the story, I have Trevor almost decide not to use his father's gun, right? He understands that if he does that, the cops have got to see that he's tied to the crime. So if I understood that clearly enough to write about it four or five months ago, would it make sense that I'd just go ahead and use Hal's gun?"

Hardy shrugged. "Maybe you figured out some way you could make it work?"

"But I didn't. It wouldn't have worked. So I wouldn't have done it. Not in real life."

Wu came forward. "But Hal's gun *was* there, Andrew."

"But that was — I mean, look, I got the idea from writing the story — we have the gun there on stage . . ."

Hardy butted in. "We've already done this. Let's go to something a little more personal. Your best friend — Lanny is it? — Lanny has testified that you thought Mooney and Laura were intimate. That's why you brought the gun to school in the first place, and . . ."

"That's another one!" Andrew's expression was alight with triumph. "My character Trevor never would have showed the gun to anybody at school. I wouldn't have shown it to Lanny if I'd been planning to use it. I mean, think about it, would that make any sense? Would a guy smart enough to write the Trevor character be dumb enough to show the gun around?"

"Smart guys do dumb things all the time," Hardy said. "The question is did you believe that Laura and Mooney were having sex?"

Deflated, Andrew sat back. "I thought maybe. That's why I wrote the story. But then we got back together . . ."

"You and Laura?" Hardy asked. Between the fiction and the reality, he almost felt he needed a scorecard. "I guess I missed the breakup. What was the timing on that?"

"Before Christmas. A couple of weeks after we got on the play."

"And why did you break up again?"

"She broke up with me. Over me being so jealous."

"But then after Christmas, you got back together?"

"Right."

"How did that happen?"

Again, the lick of pride. "She convinced me there was no reason for me to be jealous."

"In other words," Wu put in, "you started having sex."

Andrew nodded.

"But in the story," Hardy wasn't letting this go, "Julie having sex with Trevor didn't make any difference. In fact, it only fueled his jealousy."

"Right. But that's not what happened with us." Suddenly, he brightened. "In fact, ask Lanny about that. He'll tell you."

"What?" Wu asked. "About you having sex with Laura?"

"No." The question rankled him. "I didn't tell him about that." He read doubt in both their faces. "That's the truth! I didn't brag about it. Laura and I . . . that was private. It was nothing like in the story at all. That was another reason I didn't think I could send the thing out — those descriptions, they would have hurt Laura's feelings. That's not how we were. That's how Trevor was. Don't you guys see that?"

Hardy prompted him. "We were on Lanny."

"I never said a thing to Lanny. I've never

told anybody about me and Laura, in fact, until right now. Nobody even knows we'd gone that far. It was only between us."

"Okay." Hardy, unimpressed with Andrew's vision of his own virtue, pressed the inquisition. "So what do we ask Lanny about?"

"Whether I was jealous anymore after we got back together. I didn't have to tell him why, about the sex, I mean. But I did tell him that all the jealousy was over."

"But you still kept the gun in your backpack? And while we're at it, you want to tell me how a spent shell casing, I'm assuming from your father's gun, got into your car?"

"I think that must have just been bad luck. When I first took the gun, I wanted to see what it felt like to shoot it, so I drove out to the beach one night and fired it a few times."

"From inside the car?"

"Just outside. One casing must have kicked out and gone back in through the window."

"It must have," Hardy said. "But it still leaves you with the gun in your backpack for at least several weeks after you say you had no intention of using it, except of course," Hardy paused, "for your motivation."

"I should have put it back. I see that

now. Oh, and another thing I just remembered . . ."

"You just remembered?" Hardy said. "Don't start remembering things now, Andrew."

"No, about the story, another thing I would have done, definitely, that Trevor did when he went for his walk. He made it a point to talk to the clerk in that store. Remember that?"

"Vividly," Hardy said. "What of it?"

"On my walk, on my *real* walk that night, I didn't do that. I didn't stop in some store and establish where I was. And I would have, don't you see? Trevor thought of it, so I would have."

"Terrific," Hardy said. "There's progress. The problem we're on, though, is still that you didn't put the gun back in your father's drawer. And Mr. Salarco happened to see it at Mooney's." He paced three steps to the wall, turned around. "Andrew, I promise you I'm a lot gentler than anybody else you're going to talk to in the courtroom. I want to get your answers down here so we can have an opportunity, perhaps, to . . . give them a more positive slant if and when you get up in front of the judge. Are you with me?"

"What's my other option?"

Hardy snapped his reply. "I've already told you that. Your other option is plead-

384

ing guilty as Amy suggested at the beginning if — and this is a big if — they'll still do the deal. You want that? No? All right, so here's my last question. Did Laura in fact wind up staying at Mooney's once in a while after you left? To your knowledge, did he ever drive her home?"

"Yeah."

"Just like in your story?"

"Well, except they didn't . . ." He hesitated.

"Have sex? Are you sure about that?" When he didn't answer immediately, Hardy pounced. "Yes! The answer's yes, Andrew. You're sure about that. If you ever get on the stand, there is no doubt at all. Do you understand?"

Cowed, the client nodded. "If I'm not sure, the jury will think I've still got a motive."

His mouth a tight line, Hardy nodded. "Good, Andrew. That's correct. And you know for sure they didn't have sex because you and Laura talked about that, the way you talked about everything, isn't that right?"

"Yes, sir. That's right."

"And because you talked about everything, you knew everything important about her and her life, isn't that true?"

Andrew sat back in his chair, suddenly wary. "Pretty much everything, yeah," he said. "Everything important."

"Andrew." Wu couldn't wait any longer. "What Mr. Hardy's getting at is that Laura was pregnant. Did you know that?"

"That's what they told me, after the autopsy."

"But before that? Didn't you know she was carrying your baby?"

Hardy asked him, "You know that DNA sample they took when they booked you? They called with the results before we came up here today. It was yours."

"It had to be," Andrew said. "I know that."

"But you didn't know it while she was alive?" Wu asked. "That she was pregnant? She didn't tell you?"

"No. She didn't."

Andrew's face went slack and told the whole story. He'd just told his attorneys that he and Laura shared everything — their most intimate secrets — but he'd had no clue she'd been pregnant. Hardy, certain that he'd never had a client who was less inherently credible, cast a quick glance at Wu.

Andrew must have seen it. "It's really bad, isn't it?"

Hardy rubbed a hand back and forth across his forehead. "This might be a good time to take a break," he said.

18

Hardy left for a lunch meeting, and Wu stayed with Andrew, preparing her witness list, revisiting his alibi, playing devil's advocate for what she guessed would be Brandt's attack at the 707 hearing. It continued to be dispiriting work. Getting information and/or cooperation from Andrew was like pulling teeth without an anesthetic. It was early afternoon by the time they finished.

Ray Cottrell was coming up the hill to the cabins when Wu walked out into the sunshine. He got to the gate a few steps before she did, and held it open for her.

When she thanked him, he took it as an opening. "So how'd it go today?" he asked.

She made a face, shrugged. "All right, I guess."

"Curb your enthusiasm."

"You really want to know, he's pretty depressed."

"He's looking at life in the joint. You'd be depressed, too."

"I guess so." She paused. "Can I ask you something?"

"Sure."

"You were in court when Andrew wouldn't plead. When he said he didn't do it? Well, that's what's got him looking at life without."

"Okay. What's the question?"

She considered her phrasing. "You pretty much know how things work up here. You've seen a lot of these kids. I'm thinking Andrew's got a lock on an eight-year top; he's got to take it. He doesn't understand that whatever the actual truth is, *it looks like he did it*. Almost any jury is going to find him guilty. I don't understand why he can't see he can still get out of this. Johnson might still take a plea. Andrew doesn't have to be looking at life."

"He probably thinks it matters that he's innocent. If he is."

She shook her head, frustrated. "That's *so* not the point."

"He probably thinks it is."

"Well, that's my question. Why can't he see it isn't? What matters is playing it to your best advantage. There's a system here, a way that it works, and it's not going to work to let him out. So he should take the best deal they offer, right? Is it only because I'm a lawyer that I see that so clearly?"

Cottrell stared off somewhere behind her. "Maybe."

"Okay. But look," she said, "even if he's in fact innocent, he could take the plea and his dad could buy a team of private investigators who might find something that could get him out."

" 'Might' and 'could.' Not exactly a lock. Eight years, a kid his age, it's the rest of his life. You ask how he feels, he just wants to get back out. He doesn't care how it works."

She set her jaw. "Here's how it works, Ray. There's one rule. Maybe you could help Andrew with it if you two talk."

"What's that?"

"You listen to your lawyer. Ninety-nine times out of a hundred you're better off."

"But there's that one," Cottrell said. "If you think the one chance where you're not better off happens to be *you*, it's hard to take."

"You still play the odds. You deal with it."

For a second, he seemed almost angry with her view of it. But then he shrugged. "Or not," he said. "Anyway, it looks like you're feeling better today."

The reference took her a minute. "Oh. Than yesterday?" She broke a smile. "I *always* feel better than I did yesterday. That was the low point of my life."

"That's good news then."

"The low point of my life? How's that?"

"It's behind you. Everything's better from now on."

"That's a nice way to look at it." She paused, then added, "Though I may never drink again."

"Darn," he clucked with disappointment. "I was going to ask if I could buy you a drink sometime."

The comment stopped her cold. Glancing quickly up into the pockmarked face, she cocked her head, sighed as though she meant it. "I'm flattered, Ray," she said, "I really am. But I've got a policy about seeing people with whom I have a professional relationship. I've found it's just not a good idea."

"Sure," he said, "No sweat. It's cool."

"I'm sorry. I really am. It's nothing personal at all."

"No," he said. "Why would it be?" He pointed at the cabins. "Well, I've got to get in to work. See you around."

If she thought cabs were few and far between downtown, they were an endangered species up here on the hill. Now she waited at the corner of Market, berating herself for more stupidity, being friendly to the bailiff. But again, her actions had been misinterpreted. This was becoming a goddamn trend. She was tired of it.

No cab.

She checked her watch. Quarter to two. She'd been standing here for nearly fifteen minutes. She should have called and ordered one. Now she reached down into her briefcase, pulled out her cellphone, flipped it open. Suddenly a purple PT Cruiser pulled up to the curb. She stepped back as the window came down. Brandt was leaning over. "I couldn't help but notice you standing here when I left the building five minutes ago. Are you waiting for somebody? Where are you going?"

"Downtown."

"Me, too. You want a lift?" He pushed open the passenger door. "Professional courtesy," he said.

She started to hesitate, then realized she was being foolish. She could take a ride downtown with him.

Ray Cottrell was outside on guard duty, watching an inmate basketball game. The court was on the far side of the cabins, at the highest point of the grounds. The fence, topped with more razor wire, ran along a ridge that fell off in about a hundred-foot cliff to Market Street, just below.

He turned around for a minute and happened to see something familiar in the woman standing on the corner down there.

Squinting in the bright sun, he moved to the closest spot on the court for a better look. It was her, all right.

Uptight lawyers. He should have known.

"I don't see people with whom I have a professional relationship."

But still, he watched her. Even at this distance, she was a lot easier to look at than anything else he was likely to see today. All dressed up today, but yesterday with the jeans and sweater, he'd seen what she packed under that business suit.

Man.

The basketball slammed into the fence a foot in front of him, rattling the chain link, maybe one of the players noticing he didn't have his eye on them, taking the opportunity to shake him up a little. He shot a glance at the court, everybody getting a kick out of making him jump.

He ignored them, looked back down for another glimpse of Wu. Still there.

Then suddenly, he saw Jason Brandt's car — no mistaking it, that yuppie piece of shit — pull up from around the corner, come to a stop in front of her. Cottrell watching as she steps back, talks into the passenger-ride window. The door opens, she gets in.

She doesn't *see* people with whom she has a professional relationship, does she?

Cunt, he thought.

For the first several blocks, neither of them spoke. Finally, Brandt said, "So where's your car?"

"Back at the office. I drove up this morning with Mr. Hardy, but he had a meeting. I told him I'd get a cab."

"We don't see too many cabs up here."

"I noticed."

They went another block in silence.

Brandt finally broke it. "So what did your boss want?"

"To meet Andrew. He's coming on second chair."

Brandt threw a look across the seat. "You okay with that?"

"We didn't vote on it." She forced a small laugh. "I haven't exactly impressed him at every turn, you must admit."

He didn't comment.

After a minute, she said, "Anyway, I've been distracted."

Again, he looked over. She was looking straight ahead, her big briefcase lying flat on her lap, her hand clasped and resting on it. "You might as well know that my dad died a few months ago. I guess I haven't been myself."

"I'm sorry," he said. "You should have told me when . . ." The words stopped.

"Yeah. Well, it's not the kind of thing you talk about when you're getting picked up. Especially if you think it's why you're letting yourself get picked up."

He let that thought hang in the air between them for a minute. "You could have told me," he repeated.

"Maybe," she said. "But I didn't want to find out."

"Find out what?"

"If you'd want to deal with baggage."

"Yeah, I try to avoid that at all costs."

"Me, too."

"As you said, we're the same." After a moment, he reached out his hand across the seat. "Friends?" he said. "Tentatively."

She gave it a second, then nodded. "Okay," she said. "I guess so."

They shook on it.

19

During the previous administration, the pre-ferred firing method for the DA's office had been a pink slip on your chair while you were out at lunch, or even making a quick court appearance. Just so long as there was no direct confrontation or discussion. You've had your job for sixteen years and you've got three kids, two just starting college, and you go down to department 22 for fifteen minutes and come back and surprise! You're an "at will" employee and now you're fired. Thanks for the memories. The terminated tended to take this so badly that for a period of time the DA actually had an armed investigator posted outside the office in case somebody wanted to lodge a violent, personal protest.

Boscacci's more straightforward manage-ment style in this regard was making it easier for Glitsky and Lanier. He had held exit interviews for every assistant district attorney he laid off under Jackman, and he'd filed the records of those interviews, as well as other personal data, alphabetically in his secretary's credenza. This narrowed the list of truly disgruntled ex–assistant district attorneys down from seventeen to three, and Glitsky had assigned those three to the homicide inspectors Belou and Russell.

The other fourteen would be interviewed and otherwise checked out by the General Work officers, although hopes were not high that these interrogations would lead to a break in the case. The last of the Boscacci layoffs had been nearly a year ago. In a back booth under the windows at Lou the Greek's, Glitsky was telling Marcel Lanier that he didn't consider it likely that at this remove in time, someone would suddenly get mad enough to kill Allan for it. ". . . but I think we've got to look there anyway. Eliminate the obvious, then move down the list."

Lanier chewed at today's special — potstickers cooked up in some kind of yogurt sauce with garlic and paprika over rice. "I'm not sure that these guys are even the most obvious anymore," Lanier said. "Although yesterday they seemed like a good place to start. If nobody heard the shot, it probably was silenced. And if it was silenced, it was a pro."

Glitsky sipped iced tea. "The lab says the Boscacci bullet has scuff marks that could be from a silencer. Not certain, but possible. And if it was a pro, I agree, we lose. But since that's out of our control . . ."

For years, Lanier had been a homicide inspector under Glitsky's supervision, and now they fell into an old and familiar routine. "It wasn't a robbery," Lanier said. "So it's someone he knew. So it's about motive."

"Right. And we eliminate the family?"

"Yeah."

"I agree. And no caseload to speak of. Just one murder, and that one kind of self-enclosed. He mostly assigned cases. That's the job."

"True. But he might've been riding herd on some actives. He was also pulling guys to trial who'd been waiting around in the system for a while. He was ramrod for that program."

Lanier had a small notebook out and jotted. "That's real," he said.

Glitsky nodded. "Maybe we want to look at who's coming up the pipeline. Somebody with mob connections — Russian, Chinese, Vietnamese, regular Mafia. I'm not up on the latest. Do any one of them use suppressors more than the others?"

"Any of them would. Simple business."

"All right. Speaking of business, what about the union stuff?"

Lanier forked some special, nodded. "I

don't see someone with the union getting so bent out of shape about the negotiations that he takes Allan out. He's just watching Clarence's back. He probably leaned toward giving the union a lot they wanted anyway."

"Agreed. Not worth pursuing without some kind of tip."

"Okay, who's that leave? With motive, I mean."

"Our professional? He's getting paid. That's motive." Glitsky shook his head. "But we're counting him out as hopeless. Somebody else."

"The rest of the known universe?"

Tempted to smile and ruin his reputation, Glitsky sipped tea. He looked up as Lou himself stopped by the table. "Abe, you don't like the special?"

Glitsky had taken one bite and realized he wasn't that hungry. "It's great, Lou, but I didn't realize it had yogurt in it. I'm allergic."

"Hey. Whyn't you say so? I'll have Chui whip you up something else. She's got a whole tray of pot-stickers still hot back there on the steam table. She could throw some soy over 'em, vinegar, hot flakes. You'd swear you were in Chinatown."

"Thanks, Lou, but me and Marcel are out the door in a minute. We've got a meeting. In fact, we were getting the check just now."

"All right. I'll run and ring it up." He pointed to the untouched dish. "But I don't like this. It happens again, you've got to let me know right away. And I'll tell Chui. She uses yogurt all the time, gives her stuff that Greek taste everybody loves, but she'd cook up something special for you, Abe. I mean it."

He went off to get the bill and Glitsky said, "The awful thing is, I think she would. So where were we? The known universe? How do you feel about checking out everybody he's put away? As a prosecutor, I mean."

"In like what, twenty-five years? When's the last time you've heard anybody did that?"

"Not recently. But it's a few less than the whole universe. And we've got the General Work people to look. They start with anybody's who's gotten out of the joint recently."

"You mean somebody that Boscacci sent away?"

"Right."

Lanier shook his head. "It's not what they usually do, Abe."

"I realize that." Glitsky thought a second. "Okay, we put that on hold for a few days and instead check the gun shows."

"For what?"

"For somebody selling silencers." Glitsky cut off Lanier's reply. "You never know. We might get lucky. At least we're doing something. Maybe I'll go do one of the shows myself."

"You think somebody's going to talk to you at one of those places?"

"Well, it's either that or we start slogging through twenty-five years of old records and find every case Allan ever won. And they'll talk to me at the gun shows. I won't wear my uniform."

"Yeah," Lanier replied, "that'll fool 'em."

Glitsky's Friday afternoon had originally been scheduled to be taken up with addressing the Pakistan Association of San Francisco at the Bay Area Band Shell Music Concourse in Golden Gate Park. When he got back to his office from lunch, he debated with himself for the better part of five minutes before placing a call to Frank Batiste.

He told the Chief that there had been a possible development in the Boscacci matter and he personally wanted to look into it. Perhaps, he suggested, one of the department's senior press officers could stand in for him at the Pakistani gig and deliver some poignant remarks, which were certainly to be better received than his own in any event. On his way out the door to his office, Deputy Chief of Administration Bryce Jake Longoria called out and stopped him. Although he ran around as much as any deputy chief, Longoria was again behind his desk, again at his computer.

"I'm out the door, Bryce. What can I do for you?"

"Don't let me slow you down. I was just wondering if you'd had any luck with your jury question."

"My jury question?"

"The last time we talked? Somebody who'd been on a jury somewhere a hundred years ago?"

Glitsky closed his eyes, trying to bring it back. He shook his head, about to give up when the name came. "Elizabeth Cary," he said.

"Maybe. I don't know if you ever told me."

"That was it. Shot at her doorstep last week."

"Still nothing, though?"

"Not with her. Last time we talked, I recall, was about five minutes before LeShawn Brodie broke, and since then Boscacci. Those two washed Mrs. Cary clean out of my brainpan and she hasn't had much opportunity to come back. But why? You got an idea?"

"No." Longoria shook his head, lifted and dropped his shoulders. "It just seemed vaguely like real police work, so it got my attention."

A chuckle tickled at Glitsky's throat. "You, too, huh?"

Longoria waved a hand at his surroundings. "The desk," he said. "You know."

"I hear you."

"So where are you off to?"

Glitsky took a step into the room. "Between us, Bryce, I'm cutting school. Checking out a gun show."

"What for?"

"See if I can pick up a line on somebody selling suppressors illegally. Nobody heard the shot that killed Boscacci."

Longoria held up a finger and turned to his computer, tapped a few keys. "Look at this first," he said. "I may save you a trip."

Glitsky, not particularly wanting to save himself a trip, crossed to the desk and leaned over it. "What am I looking at?"

"I just ran a search for 'gun suppressor.' You know how many hits I got?" He scrolled down to the bottom of the screen. "Five thousand eight hundred twenty-eight. And you're going to a gun show?"

"Got to be quicker than checking all of those."

"Plus, you're not stuck in the office."

"There is that." Glitsky was stuck on the screen. "When did suppressors get legal?"

"Oh, they're not," Longoria replied with a breezy air. "All these listings, they clearly state that sale of suppressors is only permitted for government agencies and police departments."

"Police departments? We don't use 'em."

"Yeah, we do. TAC has a couple. The tactical unit. You don't know that?"

"I haven't done much business with TAC."

"Yeah, well, they're on the roof of a building with hostages downstairs, they want to zap bad guys they meet on the way down without waking up the whole block. That's legal, at least under federal law. But these websites. Check 'em out."

Longoria scrolled through several screens. "Here. These journals on how to make your very own sweet little suppressor from common items in your home shop. 'For information purposes only,' of course, or 'academic study.' I'm sure no one has ever bought one of these books and actually made a silencer."

"No," Glitsky said. "That would be wrong." But he'd already decided that he was going to do some old-fashioned footwork, outmoded though it was. He told Longoria good-bye, then at the door turned around. "You think of anything I can do about Elizabeth Cary, I'd love to hear."

"I'll keep it in mind."

On any given weekend, gun shows are common in Northern California. Glitsky had checked the internet, then made a couple of calls, and discovered that this weekend would feature Gun & Doll shows in several communities — Santa Rosa, San Jose, Fremont, Sacramento and the San Francisco Cow Palace, which was actually in Brisbane, in San Mateo County. The more he thought about the idea — given that they weren't going to waste time looking for a professional hit person — the more he liked it. The suppressor angle might actually give him a lead. And at least, as he'd told Longoria, he was away from his desk and the endless meetings on one of the first truly lovely days of the year.

In his hiking boots, Dockers and a camouflage blouse, he was far more comfortable than he would have been in uniform. Beyond that, he didn't think he much resembled a cop — the camo actually worked to his advantage that way. On his way down to the Cow Palace, he finalized arrangements for his event number detail to hit their snitches and cover all the shows over the weekend, then report back to him on Monday. If everybody struck out, Glitsky might have them begin culling the internet suppliers for their mailing lists and customers. Even if he could get the not-automatic cooperation of Alcohol, Tobacco and Firearms, it would be an enormous and tedious job, pretty much comparable to assembling the list of Boscacci's convictions over the past twenty-odd years. Still, it was early afternoon and he was on the road. An added bonus was that he still had the services of his driver. Paganucci pulled the black Taurus up to the Cow Palace parking lot and Glitsky gave him two hours off.

The right half of the huge, hangarlike structure boasted well over three hundred booths, with ordnance of nearly every conceivable type, as well as all the ancillary clothing, equipment, ammunition and literature. From the smallest imaginable single-shot pistols to shotguns to assault and sniper rifles, to every type of hand-held six-shooter and semiautomatic gun, the sense Glitsky had of the place was that if it fired bullets, you could buy it here. And, of course, the weapons displays weren't limited to firearms — dealers were showcasing a spectacularly wide assortment of personal-use and paramilitary gear, including cross-bows, slingshots, hunting and/or combat knives, leather accessories.

The NRA had a booth at each end of every aisle. Business seemed to be brisk. Glitsky couldn't help but make the observation that in spite of an apparently continuous assault from the antigun lobby, the Second Amendment seemed to be holding its own, even in the liberal mecca that was San Francisco.

He was glad to see it.

As a cop, although concerned with the idea of loaded guns getting into the hands of children and/or burglars, he was comfortable enough with the idea of home protection and private weapon ownership; somewhat less thrilled with the assault rifle booths, the really vicious-looking knives, the weapons whose only function was essentially military, their only potential targets human beings.

But no suppressors.

Silencers were illegal in all fifty states, but then again, so was marijuana. Glitsky didn't believe that the former were nearly as commonly available as the latter, but the street snitch he'd called on his cellphone, a two-time loser named Walter Phleger, had set him straight. At the Cow Palace, you had to ask for Mort. You had to have a hundred-dollar bill, then about another grand in cash.

In the first hour, he wandered, stopped, handled many weapons up and down the aisles. He stopped and chatted with sales-people at five booths, smaller manufac-turers. Getting comfortable. He hadn't done any street work in a very long time.

After the shoot-out last year, Moses McGuire had disposed of all the guns they had used in the firefight, including both of Glitsky's Colt .357 revolvers. In the in-terim, he hadn't really missed them — he wore his Glock .40 automatic with his uni-form every day — but now he had a hunch and on impulse he stopped in front of the Colt booth. There were two other cus-tomers, but the man behind the counter stepped to Glitsky as soon as he ap-proached.

"How are you doin', sir?" Jerry, by his name tag, was in his mid-thirties. He was buffed under his shirt and tie, and wore a clipped red mustache and jarhead haircut. "Are you interested in buying a gun today?"

Glitsky slowly looked to one side, all the way around to the other. Guns for sale ev-erywhere he looked. He came back to Jerry and nodded. "It appears so, doesn't it?"

"Are you familiar with Colts?"

"Moderately. I used to own a couple. Somebody took them." Technically, this was not a lie. "I thought I'd see if one of these spoke to me." He pointed down under the counter. "This Python looks like the brother to the ones I lost. Three fifty seven."

"Yes, sir." The man was lifting it out, placing it on the counter.

"May I?" Glitsky asked, reaching for it.

He hefted it in one hand, passed it to the other, flipped open the cylinder, removed it entirely, then held the gun up to his eye and squinted down the barrel.

"What line of work are you in?"

Glitsky checked the sight, replaced the cylinder. "Security." His smile did not reach his eyes, and lowering his voice, he cut to the chase. "What kind of suppressor works on this, Jerry?"

Jerry had heard the question before. He turned, rummaged in a drawer at the desk behind him, and a few seconds later placed a professionally designed, full-color brochure on the counter. "The only problem with what you've chosen here, sir, is that if you're going to go with a suppressor, Colt recommends its M1911 handgun, which takes your forty-five-caliber ACP cartridge. The M1911, of course, is semiautomatic and takes the S0S-45 suppressor once its been threaded for —"

Glitsky interrupted. "The guns that got taken from me, they were these three fifty seven revolvers, and I had suppressors to go with them. They also got taken."

"Well, yes, sir. But —"

"It sounded like you were telling me if I didn't shoot a semi, you couldn't help me."

"No. Not at all. Although we can't authorize any sales of suppressors out of the show today. We can't even carry them, as I'm sure you realize. But if you're interested . . ."

"Maybe you haven't been listening to me, Jerry. I'm interested in this gun, right here, right now, and I happen to have the thousand dollars to buy it. I don't like to use a semiautomatic. They jam, you notice that? Now, are you telling me you can't help me locate a silencer in this brochure of yours here for this exact weapon that I'm interested in putting down some money for? 'Cause if that's the case, I think maybe I can find another dealer nearby who might be willing to."

He put the revolver down on the top of the glass counter. "On the other hand, you put me in line with a top-quality suppressor for *this gun,* I give you my credit card, come back later on after the ridiculous fifteen-day cooling off period has expired, and you've got at least one sale, maybe a few more after I talk to some of my friends. Are you hearing me?" He leaned in and lowered his voice. "Someone told me if I had any trouble I should ask for Mort."

It was, indeed, the magic word. Jerry glanced at his other customers — nobody paying any real attention. "Give me a couple of minutes," he said.

It was more like twenty, during which Glitsky wandered some more, checking back at the Colt booth at five-minute intervals. The fourth time, Jerry was talking to a heavy, short, bald man and motioned Glitsky over. "This is, uh . . ."

"Abe." Glitsky extended the hand that held the C-note.

"Mort." The man's grip was weak and sweaty, but he palmed the bill like a master, glanced down at it quickly, apparently was satisfied. "Let's go," he said.

They walked out back toward the main entrance, Mort a couple of steps ahead of Glitsky, never looking back. Glitsky got stamped for readmission. Outside, they turned right and walked in the bright sun through the parking lot. Hard up against the chain-link fence, a white van with a dash full of dolls in the window squatted in the meager shade of a lone eucalyptus. Mort knocked once, then twice, on the back door, then turned and, without a word or a nod at Glitsky, headed back across the lot.

When the door finally opened in a fog of cigarette smoke, Glitsky stepped forward.

If he'd thought that Mort was overweight, the man who sat on the swivel seat in the rear of the van put things into perspective. He must have gone close to three hundred, although the untucked Hawaiian shirt may have added twenty pounds or so. He was still smoking, and every breath wheezed out of him like a bellows. He squinted through the smoke and out into the sun and said, "It's nine hundred dollars. Cash."

Glitsky fanned away some of the smoke. There was no ventilation in the van itself. "That's what I heard. I'm looking at a Colt three five seven revolver." He took out his wallet and started counting out the bills, laying them out on the filthy shag rug.

The huge man wheezed again, put out his cigarette, then swiveled and grabbed one of the thick black leather briefcases that lined a shelf behind the front seats. Pulling it onto his lap, he opened it, studied a moment, then took out one of the long, heavy metallic objects. "This isn't just a flash suppressor," he said, handing it over. "This will eliminate noise in excess of seventy-five dB. I can thread it and mount it here whenever you pick up your weapon, a hundred dollars, or you can take it with you and mount it up yourself. I recommend you let me do it here. I've got all the equipment as you can see. You fuck it up, it might kill you."

The left side of the back of the van was a low metal work counter, with a vice and array of tools neatly mounted against the side wall. He grabbed a metal box off the counter, wiped his brow and, wheezing with the effort, reached down to pick up Glitsky's bills. After counting them again, he placed them in the metal box. When the box was back on the counter, he pulled a small spiral notebook from his pants pocket. "You got a number? Cell's best. I change the setup, I like to keep my customers in the loop."

Glitsky's hands had gone damp with nerves. So far, everything that his snitch had told him about this operation had turned out as advertised, but if this fat man had a partner sitting in any one of the hundreds of nearby cars, covering him, this is where it would get ugly. He put the suppressor down on the rug and reached behind as though for his wallet or a belt-worn cellphone. Instead, he pulled his Glock from where he'd tucked it in at the small of his back.

At first, the fat man's face registered a mild surprise, as though Glitsky had brought along the weapon for which he wanted the silencer. Then, realizing how and where the gun was pointed, he lowered his hands into his lap, then raised them slightly. "You can take your money back," he said. "And whatever else is in there. I'm absolutely cool with this. You can take the truck, too. I don't care."

"Keep your hands where I can see them and crawl on out here."

He backed up as the man slowly got himself off the mounted swivel chair and pathetically, on all fours, made his way across the gross shag. His dark hair hung in greasy shanks down around his face.

"All the way out," Glitsky said. "Then over to the fence, hands on it over your head. Okay, now slowly lift your shirt — I want to see your belt — and turn around. All the way. Pants. Up at the ankles."

"I'm not armed."

"That's what they all say. I'm happier making sure."

Glitsky had him step back from the fence and, still facing it, lean against his hands, his legs spread wide. After patting him down, Glitsky told him he could straighten up and turn around. "What do you want?" the man asked.

The gun never left the man's midsection. "Let me see some ID please."

The man's driver's license identified him as James Martin Ewing, of Redwood Shores, about fifteen miles south of where they were. Glitsky stuck the wallet into his back pocket. "What do you want?" he said again.

"I've been trying to make up my mind about that," Glitsky said. "I decided it's pretty much your lucky day. I'm San Francisco police."

This brought an outraged rise. "Bullshit! All by yourself?"

Glitsky was calm. "All I want from you right now is that little book of your clients' phone numbers. That and my money back, of course. You think we can handle that peaceably?"

Ewing's eyes were slits as he tried to figure out the angle. "What else?"

"How many silencers have you sold here in the past few months, would you guess?"

"I don't know."

"James." Glitsky steadied the gun on the man's kneecap, his voice calm and thrumming with menace. "Don't push this. You make most of these suppressors yourself, I take it?"

"Yeah. I got a metal shop at home."

"There. See? You're cooperating already. So I ask you again while you're still in the mood. How many of these have you sold in, say, the last month?"

"Say ten."

"Ten a month. Is that about your average?"

"Close. Look, man, if you really are a cop, you're screwing up big time."

"I appreciate your concern," Glitsky

said. "Now let me see the notebook. Just toss it on the ground near my feet." Glitsky picked it up, opened it. It was a small book, two by three inches, with about ten lines on a page. It was about a third filled with phone numbers. Ewing had been in business awhile. Glitsky put the book in his shirt pocket. "Okay, James, here's what I want you to do. Let me have the keys to your van. Okay, now I want you to start walking across this lot here toward that exit way over there, the farthest one down. Go ahead now; the exercise will do you good."

"You're going to shoot me in the back."

"I doubt it, but either way, you start walking and don't look back. Go."

"You've still got my wallet."

"That's right, I do. I'll leave it in the car."

Ewing scanned the lot, possibly looking for some help, but it was a slow and peaceful Friday afternoon, not much going on. Finally he started to walk. When he'd gone maybe a hundred yards, Glitsky closed the back doors, climbed into the driver's seat, opened the windows and started the motor. Checking the rearview mirror — Ewing was still walking away — he turned and lifted the metal box from the counter, extracting his money. He picked up the bills that remained, estimated the amount as close to two thousand more, closed the box with the money still inside, and put it back where it had been.

Putting the van in gear, he drove to where two empty Brisbane police cars were pulled up by the entrance. He stopped in front of them, blocking them intentionally, and got out, leaving the motor running and Ewing's wallet on the front seat. Then he walked out the exit gate and hopped into the backseat of his waiting ride — Paganucci's timing was perfect — and told him to step on it, lights and sirens if he had to. He had a date with his wife and didn't want to be late.

". . . most fun I've ever had as a cop."

Treya put a soft hand to his face. "It's good to hear you talking about fun again."

"You think talking about it is good? Try *having* it. I was beginning to think it had all left the planet."

"Says the man who just recently stole his best friend's darts for fun."

"That was revenge, not fun. My sacred honor was at stake."

"Ah."

They had eaten borscht and sandwiches in a booth at a no-name deli on Clement, and now were pushing Rachel along in her stroller, taking advantage of the soft dusk light and the unseasonable warmth. "What I really love is that I'll have reverse listings on everybody in Mr. Ewing's book by Monday at the latest. These are real people we can work on, every single one of them in violation of the suppressor law, and I'll have the troops to go after them."

"And you really think one of them may have shot Allan?"

"No, it's not likely. But at least it's somewhere to look. Maybe one of the names will intersect with another part of the investigation."

"And meanwhile you're hip deep in a murder and all's right with the world."

Glitsky didn't answer, but he knew Treya was right. He put an arm around her, drew her in next to him. "I don't love feeling like I'm dancing on Allan's grave, but looking for his killer is how I ought to be spending my time. Not going to meetings." A thought struck him and he stopped. "How about this? I've been trying to figure out how to get the ATF to help us out here. They've got to have access to mailing lists from the net, people who have ordered silencers or the handbooks to make them. They won't be inclined to share, but once I get the names from Ewing's list, I've got something to trade, right?"

"This is what you need to be doing, Abe.

Working cases. Really. You know that?"

He walked a few more steps, then stopped, turned and kissed her. "You think?" he said.

20

Laura Wright's parents wouldn't see Hardy. They didn't buy his opening gambit that he and they were working toward the same goal — to find Laura's killer. They did not even want to talk to anybody who had anything to do with defending the murderer of their daughter. Lanny Ropke's parents were wary, too, but ultimately allowed the interview. June wanted Mark to be home for any discussion Hardy might have with their son, so they scheduled it for 6:30.

Hardy rang the doorbell exactly at the stroke.

Now the four of them sat around a Pottery Barn wrought-iron table in a screened patio off the kitchen door of the Ropkes' Victorian. Irving Street, out here on Twenty-sixth Avenue, supported the occasional large home on a big lot, and the Ropkes' was one of them. A tall and well-trimmed laurel hedge hemmed the backyard on all sides, and long shadows fell across the deep lawn in the back. They'd also had room to erect a playground set by the back hedge — swing, slide, sandbox — and half a basketball court. To Hardy's left, there was another redwood porch off what he assumed was a bedroom, and on it was a large, covered hot tub. Hardy had been introduced to the rest of the family — two cute and well-mannered young adolescent girls named Kim and Susan — but they'd disappeared by the time Mark suggested the patio for the interview. June poured heavily lemoned iced tea from a beaded pitcher.

They were a handsome family, with a strong resemblance along gender lines. June's button nose and athletic figure were reflected in her two daughters, and Mark and Lanny — both lanky and big-boned, with prominent Adam's apples, milky blue eyes and ruddy cheeks — might have been brothers. Hardy had a copy of Lanny's transcript and he got it out of his briefcase and came right to the point.

"The situation is this. Lanny, when you talked to the police, you told them about Andrew bringing his father's gun to school, and then talking about maybe using it on Laura and Mr. Mooney. I'm not going to try to get you to say anything that's not true, but I do want to ask you a few questions that might clarify some things for the defense. I'm assuming you're okay with helping us out if we're trying to help Andrew."

"Sure. He was my best friend. I mean he still is."

June said, "He wants to go visit him in jail, but after they arrested Andrew, the police said it might not be good to let the two of them talk, since he was going to be a prosecution witness."

"I wouldn't change what I said, Mom. I'm not going to lie."

"No. Of course you're not, Lanny. No one's suggesting that," June said.

"We thought it seemed like a reasonable suggestion," Mark added. "That's all."

Hardy smiled tolerantly at the parents. He was starting to see why they both wanted to be here while he talked to Lanny. "Well, my opinion," he said, "is it really wouldn't do any harm to either of them, but that's of course your decision." He shifted to the boy. "So, Lanny, what we're facing immediately, this next Tuesday, is a hearing to see if Andrew gets tried as an adult or not. And I'd like to call you as a witness to talk about the kind of guy Andrew is."

"I'd do that."

"Good. Let's talk about the gun. When you first saw it, what was your reaction?"

Lanny considered for a moment. "I don't know what you mean, exactly. It freaked me out. I mean, a gun at school is not a good idea."

June spoke up. "We don't understand why he didn't tell . . . well, at least *somebody* about it right away."

"I didn't want to get Andrew in trouble." His eyes implored Hardy to ignore his mother. "We've gone through this a hundred times. I didn't think he was going to use it."

"Why not?"

"It's just not who he is. When I talked to the police, they just wanted to hear about how Andrew had the gun and talked about using it. Which he did, I'm not denying that. But that was like way back in December, definitely before Christmas, while they were still broken up. By the time of the killings, it wasn't an issue at all anymore."

"But he still had the gun?"

Lanny shot a quick look at both of his parents, came back to Hardy. "I mean, you've got to know Andrew. He's a little . . . dramatic sometimes. He liked to play with, I don't know . . . ," he searched for the right word, ". . . ideas? After he'd gotten away with it for a while, he got to thinking it was cool, I guess, that everybody thought he was this nerdy good student and he carried a gun around. He didn't have to use it. It just made him feel like he was putting something over on everybody. I think, if you want to know the truth, Mooney might have had something to do with that."

Mark cleared his throat. "Now, wait a minute, Lanny. I thought we agreed that it wasn't Mr. Mooney's fault that somebody shot him."

June concurred. "He didn't bring it on himself."

Lanny let out a breath of frustration, talked to Hardy. "But Andrew's idea of keeping the gun for when they rehearsed, Mooney thought that was neat. He wanted it out there. I think, otherwise, Andrew would have put it back. He was starting to be afraid he'd get caught."

Hardy sat back. "So there was no blowup in the last day or two?"

"No. Not that I knew."

"And Laura and Andrew were solid. Together."

"More than ever, I think." He flashed to his parents. "I guess everybody knows she was pregnant by now."

"Andrew says he didn't know it while she was alive."

"That's true," Lanny said. "He would have told me."

Mark came forward, his eyes alight with a possibility. "Hey, what about this? Maybe Laura told him she was pregnant that night and Andrew thought it was Mooney's . . ."

Lanny turned on him, raised his voice.

"He wouldn't have thought it was Mooney's, Dad. She wasn't sleeping around. She was with Andrew and he knew it."

"Maybe it *was* Mr. Mooney's baby, though," June said. "Maybe they did have a relationship, Mr. Mooney and Laura, back when Andrew was first worried about it . . ."

Hardy put a stop to the argument. "Even if they did," he said, "the baby was Andrew's. They took his DNA when they booked him. He was the father."

"And Mooney didn't do it with Laura, Mom, for God's sake. He just didn't!"

"How do you know that?" June asked. "I don't see how you can be so sure."

"If I may," Hardy interjected. "Mrs. Ropke, do you have some reason to think he did?"

Silence descended. June Ropke's eyes had gone wide with surprise, and an embarrassed giggle escaped. "Well, no, of course not. I mean . . ." Her eyes went to her husband, then Lanny, finally to Hardy. "Except, well, the rumors, you know. That he'd slept with students before."

Hardy brought a hand up to his mouth. Andrew's short story had introduced this basic topic, but this was the first corroboration of it he'd heard in the real world. Earlier in the day, he'd talked to the principal at Sutro, and Mr. Wagner had scoffed at the idea. Mr. Mooney was a charismatic and relatively young teacher, and girls undoubtedly got crushes on him, but he had never to Wagner's knowledge had a breath of scandal surface. From Hardy's perspective, though, if rumors about Mooney were even circulating, then regardless of their substance this would add credibility to the prosecution's theory of Andrew's motive.

"I haven't ever heard anything like that," Mark said. "And if there was even a shred of truth to it, Sutro would have kicked him out. I'm sure of that."

"That's why I've never believed them, either," June said. Although Hardy was not sure this was the truth.

He turned to the young man. "What about you, Lanny? Were there rumors? Did students think Mr. Mooney slept around?"

"I'd never heard that," Lanny said. But, of course, Hardy reasoned, Lanny had come to understand the damage he'd done to Andrew. Now he wanted to protect his best friend if he could, and that's what he'd have to say.

Hardy knew that if he were going to introduce any plausible alternative theory of the murders for either a jury or a judge to consider, he had to get more of a handle on the lives and circumstances of the two victims. If he could somehow establish that someone else had a strong motive to kill either or both of them, Hardy might be able to create some doubt about Andrew. At this stage, he'd take almost anything. But Laura's parents had already shut him out.

That left Mike Mooney. He'd thought that Lanny Ropke might give him some insight into the teacher beyond what he'd already gleaned from Andrew and his damned short story, but if anything, Lanny had only strengthened Andrew's apparent motive — this was doubly damning because clearly that was the last thing he wanted to do.

Any thought of spending time this weekend with Frannie or the kids had to be banished to the exigencies of the case, and they'd opted to get in one last ski weekend before the slopes closed. Now, full dark on this warm Friday night — Hardy pulled up to an address on Poplar Avenue in Burlingame, fifteen miles or so south of the city. He found he could park in an empty driveway — what a concept! — and then walked on stones placed in the lawn to a craftsman-style bungalow's porch, where a light burned and where he pressed the bell, which echoed within.

The door opened. "Mr. Hardy?" A practiced, formal smile. "Please, come in." He offered a hand. "I'm Ned Mooney."

Mooney's father lived on the property of

the Baptist church which he served as minister, although he wasn't wearing a clerical collar tonight at home, but a black V-neck pullover and black slacks. Hardy followed him into a dim, well-furnished semi-sunken living room with a baby grand piano in one corner and a lifetime of books and magazines on the dark wood built-in bookshelves. He took the deep red leather chair — one of a pair of them — that Mooney indicated. The reverend took the other one, sat back, smiled his professional smile again, threw one leg over the other and clasped his hands on his lap.

There were deep bags under his eyes, a sallowness to the skin which wasn't just the poor lighting. A few strands of gray hair covered his scalp. Reverend Mooney looked to be at least seventy years old. Though his handshake had been firm and his walk to this room steady, Hardy sensed a deep fatigue, as though he were drawing upon his last reserves of strength. "You said you're defending the boy accused of shooting Michael," he began in a very quiet voice, "so I'm not sure what I'll be able to do to help you."

"I'm not, either, Reverend, though it might help you to know that what I'm most interested in is no different from the police. I want to identify your son's killer. I don't believe that's my client."

"You don't? Why not? From what I understand, the case against him is very strong."

"Actually, there are any number of problems with it, not the least of which is that there's no physical evidence tying him to the murder weapon, no evidence that he fired a gun at all that night. And they have to prove he did. Andrew doesn't have to prove he didn't."

Mooney rubbed his weary eyes. "And they don't have that?"

"No, sir."

"What about all the yelling? Didn't the man upstairs say they'd been fighting all night?"

Hardy leaned in closer. "I talked about this with Andrew just this morning. Do you know what play they were practicing?"

"Yes. I think it was *Who's Afraid of . . .*" He stopped. "Where the characters are yelling at each other for half the play, aren't they?"

"Yes, sir." He paused. "They weren't fighting. They were rehearsing."

Mooney eased himself all the way back into his chair, slumped low. Eyes closed, he templed his hands over his mouth and blew into them. Finally, he opened his eyes again. "It doesn't really matter," he said. "It won't bring him back."

"No. But the wrong man shouldn't be

punished. Would your son have wanted that? Would you?"

He sat low in the chair, nearly horizontal. "I've spent all of my life in the service of God, Mr. Hardy. I don't understand how He could have done this to me. After He took Margaret, Michael was all I had left." The man's sincerity was heartrending. "He was my pride and joy." He pointed with an unsteady hand. "You see that piano over there? You should have heard Michael on it, playing like an angel and singing along, ever since he was a child. He just had an immense and God-given talent. He was such a wonderful boy. Then those tapes. Do you see them? That whole second shelf? Those are the acting jobs, the television, even parts in some movies. I tell myself that someone born with that much, God only lets us keep them a short while before He wants them back. I tell myself . . . ."

Hardy understood what he was saying. He'd lost an infant son over thirty years before — also named Michael, he suddenly realized, but he wasn't going to let himself get sidetracked down that path now. He was here for his client.

"Reverend Mooney." His voice barely intruded on the room's stillness. "Aside from his performing, what was his life like? I'm trying to get a sense of if there might have been someone who would have a reason to want to hurt him."

The old man shook his head. "He didn't have any enemies. Everybody loved him."

"Do you know if he'd had a run-in with one of his students? Maybe gave somebody a poor grade?"

"You really didn't know him, did you? He was the softest grader in the school. I'd ask him sometimes if he shouldn't be harder on the kids, if he wasn't doing them some kind of disservice, being so easy. He wasn't preparing them for real life. But he always said I didn't understand the importance of grades nowadays. You get one 'B,' half your college options disappear. He wasn't going to do that."

"So you saw him a lot, still?"

"Once a week, at least. He'd come for Sunday service and stay for lunch. Every week. We were very, very close."

"So you'd know about his social life. Did he talk about that? I know he lived alone . . ."

Mooney dragged himself back to upright, eager to talk about Michael in spite of himself. "He'd pretty much given up on dating. He was married twice, you know, and neither one worked out. I think this was the biggest disappointment in his life, especially after the wonderful life we all had while he was growing up. Me and

Margaret, our marriage, was his model I'm sure. When he didn't succeed in either of his, I think . . . This sounds a little strange, but I think it broke him in some way. Anyway, after the second marriage ended, he just kind of gave up on the idea of having his own family. Said if it was meant to happen, God would take care of it."

"How long ago were these marriages?"

"Both when he was in his twenties. Both lasted a couple of years. And two fine women, too. Terri and Catherine. It seems they all just wanted different things. And of course, the artist's life is never easy. He wasn't making much money . . ." He sighed. "I think those failures, and the constant worrying about money, that's a big part of what made him turn to teaching, which finally made him happy. I know he loved his work — the kids, the plays, all of it. It was his life now, maybe not the one he'd chosen when he was young, but the one God had chosen for him. It was good."

Hardy took a last look around the dim, ordered, cultured room. If there was anything in Mike Mooney's life that had played a role in his death, Hardy was certain that Mooney's father knew nothing about it.

Driving up the freeway with the top down, listening to the news to check for traffic problems and determine whether he should take the 101 or the 280 back home, Hardy suddenly leaned forward and turned up the volume.

"Police in San Francisco tonight are looking into two separate shootings that occurred within fifteen minutes of each other earlier tonight in the Twin Peaks District. Both victims were shot in their homes, apparently at close range, and both died at the scenes. Police are unaware of any immediate connection between the victims, a middle-aged man and an elderly woman, but have not ruled out the possibility that both shootings may have been the work of one gunman. Neither shooting appears to have been gang-related. Police are advising residents in the area to be especially cautious opening their doors to strangers. So far, no witnesses have come forth with even a tentative description of the suspect in either shooting."

Hardy pushed the button on his dash and flipped over into CD mode. In a minute, he was listening to Nickel Creek again, the haunting and beautiful "Lighthouse's Tale." He was tired of hearing about murders in the city, although vaguely aware that it seemed to be turning into an unusually bloody month. As it was, he had his work cut out for him with Andrew, and for the moment he was out of ideas.

★ ★ ★

Wu didn't go home.

She'd missed eight hours of billing the day before, and after Brandt dropped her off, she went to her office, and closed the door behind her. By six, she'd drafted the sixteen-page memo of points and authorities that Farrell had requested on the "notice rule," a question of whether or not the statute of limitations had run on a client's malpractice claims against his wife's doctor, who in spite of several physical examinations had failed to properly diagnose her breast cancer until it had been too late. Wu got into it — it was a fairly sensitive analysis of when the statute began to run, at the time of the original non-diagnosis, or when the damage had been "noticed." Plus, Farrell had given her twenty billable hours, and for a change, she thought, she could be efficient.

Sometime afterward, they delivered her order of takeout Chinese and she ate her carton of lo mein at her desk while she studied the files of two conflicts cases she'd picked up — one computer identity theft and one meth sales, complicated by a concealed weapons charge — that were coming up for prelim. In neither of these cases did she entertain the slightest doubt that her clients had done what they'd been accused of.

Nor did either of them deny it. She hadn't even asked them yet — it would be unnecessary and even a little rude before the prelim to press them too hard about what had happened. Better they should hear the evidence and then decide what their respective stories would be. Her meth guy was looking at a third strike if he was convicted, and life in prison, so he had nothing to lose. The computer geek didn't think the rules actually applied to him. He was tedious and whiny and kept complaining about how his court appearances were inconvenient, and why hadn't Wu gotten the charges dismissed yet? He was a long way from being ready to face the music.

Now it was ten o'clock and she was alone in the office. Yesterday's hangover had become a dim memory and she pushed herself back from her desk, thinking that it was Friday night, she'd worked more than a full day, expiated her demons. Now it was time to party, to forget, to score and prove again how desirable she was, how charming, fun, worthy of love.

Her eyes fell upon the picture of her father, framed on her desk. She wondered if he was seeing her now, watching from wherever he might be. Sitting back down, she pulled the picture near. To her knowledge, her father had never gone out and "partied" in his life. He did his job, he took care of his responsibilities, raised his difficult daughter all by himself.

She stared at his likeness. Well, if he wasn't going to like her anyway, she'd show him. She wouldn't need him anymore, either. That was the greatest punishment she could inflict on him. She could be completely independent, financially secure on her own, emotionally untouchable. Alone.

Alone.

"Come on, Dad. Talk to me," she said aloud.

It wasn't her father's voice, but Jason Brandt's that she heard. *For a minute, I thought we had something going. I mean personally.* She saw him tapping his chest. *In here.*

She sat back and gathered herself, her eyes closed. When she opened them, her gaze fell upon the cardboard box containing the files in the Bartlett case. She reached down and pulled it over to her. Hard on the heels of the two cases she'd just been reviewing, she was suddenly struck by the qualitative difference between both of them and this one. Between all of her previous clients, in fact, and Andrew.

She'd been completely blind to it at the beginning, assuming that her client was guilty, as all of her previous clients had always been. But now as she turned the pages in the files — the police reports, autopsies, photos of the crime scene, transcripts of interviews with Andrew and every witness in the case — she tried to take everything fresh, but this time with the prejudice that he might actually be innocent.

Certainly Andrew himself hadn't deviated from his original story; even when he'd been presented with new evidence that seemed to damn him, he always had an explanation that fit the facts. Andrew was an intelligent young man — "Perfect Killer" illustrated that clearly enough. His stubborn insistence on his own version of events, when he had no illusions about how bad it made him look, had a certain perverse authority. She found the quote from his short story:

Would a smart guy like me admit to these damning lapses if I had done it? No, I'd lie about them, too. I'd make up a more consistent story. Think about it. Doesn't that make more sense?

And, in fact, she had to admit that it did.

She pulled her yellow legal pad over in front of her and on the top of the first page wrote "First Criterion: The Minor's Degree of Criminal Sophistication." Lifting the rest of the pages of "Perfect Killer" out of its folder, she chewed on the end of her pen, trying to recall every instance where Andrew's story, which, she reminded herself, was *fiction*, which *he'd made up*, pointed more to his innocence than his guilt.

Tomorrow — Saturday — she'd be in here writing the motion to Judge Johnson on the impropriety of the rushed timing on the 707 hearing, giving notice they would be cutting him no slack. They had not yet truly begun, and were already laying the groundwork for an appeal. Maybe even a writ — get the Appellate Court involved before the 707 even took place.

She'd already made appointments to talk to, recruit and perhaps even get time to prepare some reasonable number of the seven witnesses she and Hardy had preliminarily identified to testify on the various criteria. She had to nail down addresses, phone numbers, schedules.

She desperately wanted to talk to Jason Brandt again — her hand had gone to the phone half a dozen times while she'd been working. Each time she'd drawn it back. But she felt she had to apologize. She had to let him know how she really felt about all of her mistakes, the seemingly endless series of them. She wanted to tell him that she was beginning to get some understanding of what had been driving her. The ghosts that had haunted her. Her hand went to the phone again. If he answered, they'd just talk. It wouldn't be about Andrew.

She pushed the numbers, heard the ringing, got his machine. Of course. It was Friday night. Of course he was out. She hung up before the message ended, sighed and opened another folder.

It was going to be a long weekend.

21

On Saturday morning, alone in the house, Hardy showered, dressed in jeans and a blue workshirt and went downstairs to the kitchen. He poured himself a mug of coffee and took the first essential sip. Lifting his eight-pound black cast-iron pan from where it hung from the hole in its handle on a marlin hook, he put it over a high gas flame on the stove. They were out of eggs — he'd used them all up with Amy the other night — and this slowed him down for a second, but he hadn't eaten dinner last night at all and was famished. So he cut a half inch of butter, threw it in the pan, let it start to melt.

With an English muffin going in the toaster, he opened the refrigerator, found some luncheon ham and cut it up with a can of new potatoes, half an onion and a red pepper. After it had browned up a little, he added a tablespoonful of flour and a bouillon cube, and stirred it all together into a dark paste, into which he then poured a coffee mug full of water and stirred again. After it had thickened up, he tasted it, added Worcestershire and Tabasco, stirred again, and turned down the heat while he went to get the paper.

Poured over the muffin halves, he figured his breakfast was at least as good as most of the specials at Lou the Greek's. Maybe he'd even type up the recipe, drop it by there. Chui would serve it over rice instead of English muffins, and probably use soy sauce instead of Worcestershire for the gravy, but it would be cheap to make and, at least for Hardy this morning, it was satisfying enough. He could call it "Hearty Bowl," a pun. Abe would love it.

The two homicides last night made the front page. The coincidences they'd mentioned on the radio had blossomed into a tentative theory — it had been the same shooter. They'd recovered 9mm slugs from both scenes and police were running ballistics to see if they came from the same weapon. But in both cases, there appeared to have been no sign of forced entry. The woman, Edith Montrose, was seventy-two years old, and lived alone on Belvedere Street, while the man, Philip, the fifty-five-year-old owner of Wong's Fine Produce, lived in a duplex on Twin Peaks Boulevard with his wife, Mae Li. The article noted that the two murder scenes were less than four blocks apart. There were other similarities as well: both victims were shot at very close range, in the chest. Nothing was apparently stolen from either domicile.

Hardy finished the article, then came back to the front page and found a follow-up story on Allan Boscacci. So far, Glitsky and his special task force didn't appear to have accomplished much.

He washed his dishes and poured another cup of coffee. It wasn't much after 7:00 a.m., still too early to call anybody on a Saturday. And who was he going to call upon anyway? He was beginning to think he should have gone up to Northstar with the rest of the family after all. Certainly, he hadn't helped Andrew's case by either of his visits last night. It wasn't really too late. He could hop in his car now, and if he flew, he could still ski a run or two before lunchtime.

Instead, he came back to the table and finished reading the rest of the newspaper. He'd think of something to do here. There were still several people he hadn't talked to, notably Hal and Linda North and their daughter, Alicia. He told himself he should just show up at the Wrights', Laura's parents, and try again to get them to talk to him. He thought his best bet, though, might be Juan Salarco. He was a nice enough guy, and something about their talk the other night had seemed somehow unresolved, although Hardy hadn't been able to put a finger on what it had been. Maybe if he went back there, went over the whole night one more time, talked to the wife . . .

Glitsky got the call back from Hardy at 9:15.

"Where have you been? I've been calling you for an hour."

"You only left one message."

"That's because if you hear that one," Glitsky said, "you won't need the others. Which apparently you did, since here you are, calling me back."

"True enough. I was taking a walk, clearing my brain. It didn't seem to do much good. What can I do for you?"

"You can listen to my adventure yesterday. Treya's getting a little tired of it after the fourth time, I can tell, but I think you'll appreciate it."

"All right. Hit me," Hardy said, and listened to Abe's version of his single-handed Cow Palace bust, leaving the van, loaded with illegal suppressors and paraphernalia, not to mention Ewing's driver's license and address, with the engine running, and blocking the unmanned Brisbane police cars into their places.

When the story ended, with Glitsky ducking into his car and making a clean getaway, he waited a minute for Hardy to say something. When he didn't, Glitsky did. "I said, is that cool or what?"

"Yeah."

"Yeah? That's your complete response to one of the great moments in my career?"

"Right," Hardy said. Then, with a small show of interest: "Sorry, Abe. I missed the end of it. What were you saying?"

As soon as he hung up, Hardy grabbed his telephone book and looked up Juan Salarco's number, which was listed. The phone rang four times, then he heard a message in Spanish.

"Juan," he said at the beep. *"Soy Dismas Hardy, abogado de Andrew Bartlett. Importante, por favor."* And he left his number in both English and Spanish.

He'd stopped listening to Glitsky about halfway through the saga, when it occurred to him that maybe his friend had inadvertently supplied him with what had been nagging him about Salarco's testimony all along. It was a small enough point, perhaps, but it could prove important.

He'd already listened to the Salarco tape several times all the way through, but to be sure now he got his briefcase, put it on the dining table and took out his notes and the tape. With some chagrin, he realized he'd even written a comment about street noise,

443

and whether the gunshot could have been heard over it. But he'd never followed up. Now he put in the tape and started running the interview through another time. This time, knowing what he was listening for, it was even less ambiguous.

Salarco's voice. *". . . and turn on the TV, real quiet, but then there is this . . . this scream, the girl, and then a . . . a bump. You could feel it up here, like something dropped. The house shook. Then right after, a crash, the sound of a crash, glass breaking. And a few seconds later, suddenly boom again, the house shakes another time, somebody slamming the front door under us."*

Stoked up now, Hardy ran it back, played it yet again.

A bump. *"You could feel it up here, like something dropped."*

A crash. *". . . the sound of a crash, glass breaking."*

Boom again. *". . . somebody slamming the front door under us."*

A bump, a crash, a boom. But no gunshot.

Paper-thin walls, where even the sounds of Andrew's and Laura's rehearsals could wake the baby upstairs, and yet Salarco did not hear, or did not comment upon, the explosive percussion of two 9mm automatic rounds fired probably within eight feet of him? Could it have been possible

444

not to hear them?

The telephone rang, and Hardy leapt to it, perhaps Salarco getting back to him already, pulling a break on this case at last.

"Dad." Something wrong with the voice. Something wrong altogether.

"Vin. What's the matter?"

"Um, it's not bad. I mean, everybody's alive . . ."

"Jesus Christ, Vin, what?"

"It's Mom. She didn't want you to worry, but . . ."

"Vin. What about her? What's happened?"

"She had an accident. Somebody hit her."

"In the car?"

"No, on the slope. Skiing."

"Is she okay? Where is she now? Can I talk to her?"

"She says she'll be okay, you know? You're not supposed to worry. But you can't talk to her. They had her on a backboard to the ambulance and now they've got her in the emergency room and the Beck's waiting outside in case . . . Anyway, she said I ought to call you."

"Where are you?"

"The hospital in Truckee. By the emergency room."

"I'm on my way up. I'm on my cellphone the whole way."

"Okay. And, Dad?"

"Yeah, bud?"

"Hurry, huh?"

Frannie was going to be okay. As Vinnie had said, nobody was going to die. But okay was a relative thing.

They let him take her home on Sunday, but as soon as she got there, Hardy was to make sure she got in bed and stayed there until her local doctor told her she could get up. She'd definitely sustained a concussion. It was very much out of character for Frannie, who didn't like to acknowledge physical pain, but she didn't argue with him at all. She'd be wearing a neck brace and sporting an arm sling for at least six weeks. After that they'd do some more tests and have a clearer picture of what, if any, further damage had been done to her spine and/or neck. She'd also cracked two ribs on her left side and sustained a Ping-Pong-ball fracture of the left shoulder socket in the course of dislocating it.

By the time he had fed her some soup and settled her into bed, it was full dusk, but the Beck still hadn't made it home. She'd been driving his hot little sports car, following close, but they'd lost sight of her in the traffic just outside Sacramento, and now they'd been home for almost an hour and still no sign of her.

For dinner, Hardy and Vincent cooked up two cans of corned beef hash — the black pan again, but without any romance — and quartered a head of iceberg lettuce with a mayo and ketchup thousand island poured over it. They amused themselves, and kept the unspoken fear about the Beck at bay by inventing tortures for the person who'd run into Frannie on the slopes, who of course didn't even slow down and had never been caught.

Finally, they heard the front door. Hardy put down his fork and prepared himself not to speak harshly. He'd almost been unable to swallow for the second half of his meal, as the minutes had passed. His beautiful, smart, clever seventeen-year-old was never late, and if anything had happened to her, too . . .

She stood at the end of the dining room. "I'm so sorry, Dad. I got a flat tire in Sacramento, and you had both cellphones with you, and I wasn't anywhere near a gas station. And then I couldn't figure out where they put the spare . . ."

"It's under the rug in the trunk," Vincent said.

"Thanks, dear brother, I know that now. And I even know how to change a flat tire. But, Dad, look, I pulled over and some guy stopped and . . . I mean, an older guy, and he helped me, but then he asked for my number, and I got . . . Anyway, I didn't think . . . I thought if he followed me . . ."

"Wait, wait, wait." Hardy held up a hand. "Did he follow you?"

"No. I don't think so. But I was afraid when I was parking . . ."

He stopped her again. "Are you okay now? Is the car okay? Good. Are you hungry? Sit down, I'll make you something." He stood up, put his arms around her, kissed the side of her face, the top of her hair. He kept his arms around her, tight around her back. "I love you. Everything's all right. Your mother's upstairs sleeping. Thanks for driving my car down. I'm sorry about the flat tire. They happen."

They separated and she looked up at him. Getting her bravery together. "But, Dad," she said, suddenly breaking a smile, "what a great car!"

Finally, finally, the kids both relatively calmed and catching up on their weekend's homework, he got to the Sunday paper. While they'd been gone, things had developed rapidly in the double homicides, and by this morning, "Executioner Stalks City Streets" was the banner headline. Ballistics had confirmed that both victims in the Friday night shootings had in fact been shot by the same weapon. Because of the nature of the attacks — the execution-style, point-blank shot to the heart — Marcel Lanier of homicide had told some reporters that he was afraid that what we had here was some type of executioner, and judging by the headline, the idiotic name looked like it was going to stick.

Hardy never even looked at his answering machine until the kids were asleep. He hadn't had a drop to drink since at least Thursday night, and was somewhat surprised to see that he hadn't missed it a bit. Still, now he thought he could use a beer. He opened a Sierra Nevada and, turning off the overhead, finally noticed the blinking light on the far end of the kitchen counter.

Salarco, getting back to him.

It was 11:15 on a Sunday night. The gardener undoubtedly got up at or near daybreak. Hardy wouldn't be doing himself or Salarco any favors by calling back this late.

For a minute, he cursed himself for all he'd absolutely had to do this weekend that he'd left unaccomplished. His client's hearing was now only two days away, and he'd made no progress of any kind. It had been through no fault of his own, true, but he knew that other lawyers might have found a way to proceed on the case even

449

through two such difficult days. They
might have called in partners or associates,
hired private investigators, even pled hard-
ship to the judge. He might have thought
to do something, but all he'd been able to
think of was the suffering of his wife, the
worries of his children, the needs of his
family.

"So sue me," he said aloud. Put down
his unfinished beer. Went up to get some
rest.

22

Hardy got the phone before it finished its first ring. Next to him, Frannie moaned but did not wake up. It seemed to be sometime in the middle of the night, pitch out the window.

"Hello." His sleep-edged voice cracked. He cleared his throat and said it again. "Hello."

The voice was urgent, yet controlled, the words hastily strung together. "Sorry to wake you up, sir. It's Amy. I just got a call from the YGC. Andrew's tried to kill himself."

"Give me a second." He was up, moving to the bathroom, where he closed the door behind him and turned on the light, blinking in the glare. "What do you mean, tried? Is he alive? What happened?"

"All I know is they called me about ten minutes ago. They said he tried to hang himself in his cell, but the guard heard something and got to him in time to cut him down. Or maybe the shirt he used ripped, it wasn't clear. It doesn't matter."

"So where is he now?"

"They were bringing him to SFGH." San Francisco General Hospital. "I'm on my way down now."

"I'll meet you there."

Dressed now in the same clothes he'd been wearing yesterday, and Saturday before that, down in the kitchen, he stopped to write a note to Rebecca and Vincent, telling them where he was going. They'd been getting themselves ready for school, making their own breakfasts, their bag lunches, for some time now. Beyond that, Hardy didn't know the Monday morning routine, but he was confident they could work it out themselves. He reminded them to check on their mother upstairs, make sure she got some food and liquid and her pain medication. He'd be back home, hopefully, by mid-morning if he could. Again, he'd be on his cellphone. Call with any questions or problems.

He grabbed his briefcase, glanced at the clock on the kitchen wall. 4:30.

Outside, he paused in thin fog at the sidewalk just outside his gate, realizing that he didn't know where Rebecca had parked his car last night. Well, fortunately they had two of them. Now if he could only remember where he'd parked the 4Runner. After a minute's reflection, it came to him and he turned up toward Clement. Half-

452

jogging now, he covered the two blocks down to Thirty-second, then turned right — the car was about midway down the block, under a burned-out streetlight.

The front seat was dew-drenched and cold. Inside the car, in fact, it seemed exceptionally cold, but the reason for it didn't really register until he turned to look over his shoulder as he put it in reverse so he could pull out. The backseat window on the passenger side wasn't there anymore. Neither, he suddenly realized, were the skis they'd left the night before.

Now in a flash, his actions last night came back to him. Double parked in the street right out front of his house, he and Vincent had helped get Frannie inside. Then he'd gone on the daily search for a parking place, finding this spot a couple of blocks away — not too bad, considering. In his rush to get back to his wife, he'd locked up, of course, but hadn't unpacked this car, thinking to return soon with his son. But then the Beck hadn't shown up, and . . .

Knowing what he'd find, he got back out of the car and walked around to where the broken glass covered the sidewalk, crunching under his feet. He opened the door and peered over the backseat into the storage area in the back and verified that they'd not only taken the skis, but the poles and boots and luggage bag they used for the rest of their stuff — gloves, goggles, extra clothes, everything. The deck was bare, cleaned out.

Sick at the world, he got back in behind the wheel, started the engine, put on his lights and pulled out into the still-dark street.

Wu wore a dark blue jogging suit and tennis shoes, a black and orange Giants warm-up jacket, no makeup. Her hair was back in a ponytail. Hardy thought she could have passed for about Andrew's age. ". . . because it's my fault, that's why," she was saying.

"How could it be your fault?" Hardy had had enough of hospitals over the weekend with Frannie to never want to see one again, and yet here he was now, outside the emergency room at SFGH, aptly nicknamed the San Francisco Gun & Rifle Club by the law community. He and Wu sat on red molded-plastic chairs and he was drinking vending machine coffee from a paper cup.

"I spent almost all day yesterday with him, going over the criteria, ways we might be able to beat them. It wasn't too heartening. By the time I left, he was pretty down."

"Did you tell him about our plan to call

454

witnesses on the crime itself?"

She nodded. "Sure, but by that time we're on number five. He figured we couldn't win on any of the first four, either, not after his short story got out. So he was going up, that was his opinion. We couldn't do anything to stop that." She hung her head wearily, came back up to Hardy. "I keep thinking if only I wouldn't have gone in to talk to him, it wouldn't have come to this. But what was I supposed to do? Who else except Andrew could have . . . ?"

A young Asian woman in bloodstained blue scrubs and a stethoscope was approaching them. Wu stopped talking and they both stood up.

"The officer who brought him in told me you were with the hanging victim," she said. "He's going to have trouble talking for a while, and he'll be in some discomfort, but fortunately whatever he used — evidently his shirt — couldn't hold him and the fall didn't break his neck. He's going to live. The officers want to take him back to the YGC, but I told him we're going to hold him here for observation for at least a day."

"Thank you," Hardy said. "Under the circumstances, I'd make it a close watch."

"We will," the doctor said. "Do you know where his parents are, by the way?

Does he have parents?"

"They're in Palm Springs, I believe. At a tennis tournament," Wu said. Then, including Hardy: "But I'm concerned about his sister. The YGC called his home first and there was no answer at all. They called me next."

"So no parents," the doctor said. "And people wonder where kids go wrong." The young woman's face was set in frustration.

"Can we talk to him?" Hardy asked.

She shook her head no. "He can't really talk. Also, I've got him sedated for now. He'll be out for a couple of hours. And he really won't be able to talk normally for at least a few days." A pause, then a gentler tone. "Do you know why he might have tried to do this?"

"He's got a hearing coming up soon," Wu said. "He thinks he's looking at years in prison."

The doctor nodded. "What did he do?"

"The charge is murder," Wu said. "But there are questions."

This was the first time Hardy had heard Wu say something like that, and he shot a glance at her.

Wu nodded back.

Hardy and Wu were walking across the parking lot. Out in front of them, the sun still hadn't cleared the hills across the bay, and wisps of fog still hung in the air, but the chill had already gone out of it. Overhead the sky was a clear blue and there was no wind.

"What did you mean in there? There are questions — which hasn't exactly been your mantra since you got on this case. I was wondering if something had happened."

"Nothing specific. I just decided that I needed to adjust my attitude if I wanted to keep on defending him. His position hasn't budged — he's innocent." She shrugged. "So I guess I decided to try on believing him, see what it felt like. At least it's got me thinking that it might be possible after all. Otherwise, why would he persist in all these insane contradictions? Until I read his short story, I thought he just might not be too bright, but we know it isn't that."

"No. We know it isn't that."

"Right. So now I'm kind of leaning the opposite way, thinking he's just too smart to have made up so much dumb stuff. He wouldn't have shot them and left the gun on the table, for example. Period. He just wouldn't have done it. Anyway, once I decided maybe he wasn't lying about everything, it gave me some hope."

"That's funny." Hardy told her that some similar thoughts had been surfacing for him since he'd started to consider the

457

fact that the upstairs neighbor, the state's prime witness, hadn't said he'd heard any gunshots. But as soon as he'd said it aloud to Wu, he immediately backpedaled.

"It's nowhere near certain," he said. "I've got to talk to him again. Salarco. About the gun. What it looked like. If it had any kind of silencer on it, he would have had to notice. But if not, then I've got to find out if the cops found any kind of muffling agent at Mooney's. Maybe the shooter shot through a pillow or something."

They'd both stopped walking. Wu faced him. "There's no indication of that from the crime scene pictures. I didn't see anything in discovery."

"I know. I double-checked them myself. And Salarco probably would have mentioned something like a silencer if he'd seen one. It's a big old protruding tube stuck on the end of the barrel, you know. It's not something you'd miss."

"So what are you saying? If all of this gets borne out?"

"Well, the simplest interpretation, which is always the best, is that if Andrew's gun didn't have a silencer on it, and he didn't use anything to kill the sound, then that gun — the purported murder weapon — never got fired that night." Hardy's eyes were bright with the possibility. "It's not quite exactly the other dude that I must say there's no sign of, but Andrew's gun is a big part of the picture. If I can get Johnson to listen, or get Salarco to testify that he got a good gander at the gun and it looked normal . . ."

". . . then . . . wait a minute."

"What?"

"Well, being devil's advocate, Andrew could have used a silencer, killed Mooney and Laura, then taken the silencer off and ditched it before he came back to call nine one one."

"Then got rid of the gun? A second trip? I don't see that happening. I can't see Andrew doing that."

"I don't either. But Jason Brandt will see it, and the argument's then refuted and we're back where we started."

"No. Not exactly," Hardy said, "at least I'm not."

"What would be the difference?" Wu asked.

"You mean if everything is just as I described it to you now? Salarco didn't just miss the two shots? No muffling agent in the house, no silencer on the gun?"

"Yeah. What then?"

Hardy's eyes were out of focus while the idea worked itself into something like resolution in his mind. The matter settled, he came back to her. "Then I'm pretty sure I

459

don't have to pretend to myself anymore. If Salarco didn't hear the gun, then Andrew didn't shoot it. And you know what that means? What I've got to believe?"

"What's that?"

"He's innocent. Somebody else killed them."

Part Three

23

Hardy's medical business with Frannie — taking her to the doctor, getting her back home, into bed and fed — trumped any interaction he might have had with Juan Salarco, and took up a good portion of his morning. Rebecca, the dear, had told her mother that since Dad had taken the regular car, she had no choice but to drive herself and Vincent to school in the convertible. So after he'd changed into his business suit, then called to speak with the principal at Sutro, he swung down to their high school, found the S2000 in the lot and switched cars on her, leaving a note about the broken window on the 4Runner so she wouldn't think it had happened at school.

He drove by Salarco's, saw that the truck was nowhere to be seen, and realized he'd have to come back after the workday. As far as he knew, Juan's wife Anna spoke only Spanish. Beyond that, he doubted if she would know the precise residence where her husband was working at any given moment. Anxious though he was for

Salarco's information, he had to pass for now. He had other questions, and precious few answers.

It wasn't far to Sutro and he made it there by the end of the school's lunch hour. The outer administration office was empty, but Hardy knew where he was going and went right to it. The principal was in his office, behind his desk doing some paperwork, and stood when Hardy poked his head in. "Mr. Wagner? Sorry to barge in but time is short and there isn't anybody out front. Dismas Hardy. Andrew Bartlett's attorney?"

Wagner, portly and slightly foppish with a bow tie and suspenders, reached a hand out over his desk. "Certainly. How's he doing?" In his earlier call, Hardy had told him about the suicide attempt.

"He's alive," Hardy said. "Which is good enough for now."

Wagner swiveled in his chair, looked out the window behind him at the play yard, still packed with students. "This has been a terrible tragedy for the school," he said. "To think that he was coming here every day for weeks after . . ." He sighed. "Our counselors are a little overwhelmed, you know. Students realizing they'd been walking around, or even taking classes, with a murderer."

"An alleged murderer," Hardy said.

"Alleged or otherwise." Wagner spun back around, gave him the man-to-man. "Mr. Hardy, please. Do you really think it's possible Andrew is not guilty?"

"Yes. Possible. Although proving I'm right may be a different story."

"I must say it's refreshing to hear someone say they don't think he's guilty. Pretty much all I heard after the arrest was that it was open-and-shut."

"I'd heard the same thing myself. I keep hearing it, in fact."

Wagner moved some papers around on his desk. "You know, it would be so wonderful for the school if that weren't the case. It's bad enough that the two victims were members of the community. But if somehow Andrew were found innocent, it might go a long way toward starting the healing."

"Well, you know, sir, that's the reason I came by here today. I've got a hearing for Andrew scheduled to begin tomorrow and I wondered if I might ask you a favor. I understand his sister goes here, too."

"That's right."

"Well, I know it's unusual, but I've got some questions for her, and for the two other people that were in the play with Andrew, that really might be of some use. I know I could wait and see all of them at home with their parents" — and maybe their lawyers, he thought — "tonight, but I'm in a time crunch of major proportions. Would it be possible to borrow a room here in the office and pull those three people out of class for a few minutes?" When he saw that Wagner had a problem with the idea, he added, "Mr. North assured me that I would have your complete cooperation in the defense of his son."

Wagner considered a moment. "I'm sure we can do that." A bell rang and he looked up at his wall clock. "Fifth period," he said. "Together or separately?"

"Separately would be better," Hardy said.

But it wasn't to be that simple. Wagner's desire to see Andrew cleared because it would benefit Sutro might have blinded him to the fact that he should not under any circumstances be allowing his students to talk to an attorney without parental permission. But obviously he couldn't let Hardy be alone in a room with one of his students, either.

Hardy was obliged to let him sit in. He couldn't help but think that this changed the dynamic dramatically — he had been planning a gloves-off discussion with each of the kids, but he had no choice. If the meetings were going to happen at all, they'd be in Wagner's office with the principal in attendance.

Alicia breezed in first. Hardy had heard next to nothing about her, either from Wu or from Andrew. His only preconception was that she was probably the model for the sister in Andrew's short story, locked in her room listening to death music and smoking dope. His first look at her — very pretty with beautiful long dark hair, clear skin and eyes, designer clothes — was a bit of a shock and brought him up short. Andrew's story, he reminded himself, was fiction. If the judge wound up having trouble with that concept, Hardy thought he could bring in Alicia as a witness and win the point without any further debate.

She took a few confident steps into the office, threw at glance at Hardy — a stranger to her — and spoke to Wagner. "You wanted to see me, sir?"

"Alicia, this is Mr. Hardy. He's one of the lawyers representing Andrew. He'd like to talk to you for a few minutes if you don't mind."

Her face grew serious, and she nodded first at Wagner, then at Hardy. "Sure. Okay. Why would I mind? Although Andrew and I aren't exactly what I'd call close."

"Why not?" Hardy asked.

"Well, I don't know. He's just . . . We don't have that much in common, I suppose."

"So you don't know much about what's

467

happening with him?"

"Just of course the basics. What Dad and Linda have told me. I thought it must be some misunderstanding or something that Dad would have to work out."

Hardy found that an interesting turn of phrase. He asked her, "Would you be surprised to hear that Andrew tried to kill himself this morning?"

She stared. All the vivacity drained out of her face. She looked to Wagner. "Is that true? Is he dead?"

"No, but Mr. Hardy was at the hospital this morning."

"He tried to hang himself," Hardy said. "He didn't succeed."

The news derailed her for a beat. Without asking permission, she went to a chair and sat. "I guess I could see him doing that," she said. "He's just always so intense and so unhappy. And then when Laura . . . was killed, it got so much worse." She turned and faced Hardy full on. "But I don't think he killed her. You don't think he did, do you?"

Hardy shook his head no. "There might be some facts about that night that don't work if Andrew did it."

"See? I didn't think he did either."

Hardy hadn't quite said that, but he'd take it. He stood up, hands in his pockets, and began to pace the room. "But the problem I've got is that I don't know what else was going on in Andrew's life, something that might have had some connection to Mr. Mooney or Laura and given someone else, perhaps, a reason to have killed them."

"Surely not another student here," Wagner said.

"I'm not implying that. There's no evidence implicating anyone else here at Sutro." Hardy came back to Alicia. "But you're his sister. You may have heard Andrew say something that didn't seem to mean anything at the time, but now when you think back on it, it might have been important."

He thought that given the different crowd Alicia hung out with, the odds were against her providing some alternative theory of the crime, but at least she might start thinking about her brother's situation differently. In Hardy's experience, schools — like companies and coffee groups and men's clubs — always had secrets. If Andrew hadn't killed Mooney and Laura, then the person who had done it might have had some connection to Sutro. At least, from Alicia or one of the other students, he might get some rumors, something to wave in front of a judge or jury, as opposed to what he had now.

Which was nothing.

Nick and Honey are the character names of the young couple in *Who's Afraid of Virginia Woolf?* who become foils for the vitriolic outpourings of George and Martha as their relationship implodes. Mooney cast Andrew and Laura as the leads, with the secondary couple's parts going to Steve Randell as Nick and Jeri Croft as Honey.

If Alicia North was the norm for the "popular" look at Sutro, Jeri was something else again. She'd dyed her hair a dark henna, rimmed her eyes with black kohl shadow. Waif-thin, the pajama bottoms she wore hung low enough on her hips to reveal a hint of pubic hair on her belly under the black T-shirt. In addition to the silver rings adorning both of her ears, she'd pierced her nose, eyebrows and tongue. When she got to the office, she greeted Wagner and then Hardy with an ill-disguised wariness. She tugged her pajamas up an inch or two. "So why again am I here?"

Wagner went through the explanation for a second time. The girl scanned Hardy up and down, clearly pegged him as another meddling adult in the Wagner mold. Suit and tie. A dork who started out by saying, "I'm trying to get at the truth of what happened that night."

She rolled her eyes, an actress all right.

"I don't think so," she said. "If you're Andrew's lawyer and you're any good, you're trying to get him off, whether it's the truth or not. So give me a break, all right? And that night? I don't know what happened. I wasn't there."

"Okay," Hardy said. "Thanks for coming down, then." Dismissing her. Two could play at that game.

She threw a confused glance first to Hardy, then at Wagner. "That's it?"

Hardy, stonewalling, shrugged. "You obviously don't want to talk about it. I want to help Andrew and I'm sure there are other students here at Sutro who feel the same way I do. So why waste each other's time. Sorry to have interrupted your class."

She shifted her weight, hip cocked. "Who said I didn't want to help Andrew?"

Hardy, giving her nothing, looked up from scribbling on his legal pad as though surprised she was still there. "I got that impression. It's not a problem. Thanks again." He went back to his notes, spoke to Wagner. "Let's try Steve Randell."

"Wait a minute! Steve doesn't know anything either."

Patiently, Hardy said, "Well, if that's true, I'm sure he'll let us know."

"What could he tell you? He wasn't there either."

"I don't know, Jeri. What do you know,

say, about Laura?"

"You mean she and Mooney?"

"We can start with that, sure."

"Well, the main thing, they didn't have anything going. Sexually."

"But Andrew thought they did?"

"Maybe. I mean, yeah, sure, the first couple weeks of rehearsal, Laura got a crush on him. So did I, you want to know the truth. He was just so there, you know?"

"This is Mr. Mooney now?" Hardy ventured an encouraging smile. "Just keeping the players straight. Mr. Mooney was so there, you said. You want to talk about that?"

A sigh. "Have you met Laura's parents?"

"No. They wouldn't see me."

"There you go. They wouldn't see her much either. I'm going to sit down." She folded herself down onto the floor. "The thing about Mike — Mr. Mooney — is there was no . . . like barrier, you know. I mean, at school he was a teacher and all, but when you got acting, you were with him. Just completely equal. He'd get inside your space and you'd just want to stay there. It was just total acceptance."

"Of what, though, exactly, if you can say?"

She paused, thinking. "Of who you are, of what you were doing."

"And Laura? How did she react to that?"

"What do you think? Like a desert to water. She bloomed, man. Everybody did."

"And this is when Andrew became so jealous?"

Jeri didn't answer right away. "Okay," she finally said, "let's get this part straight. At first, yeah, Andrew kind of freaked. But you've got to remember that this was like in November or something, four months before the shootings happened. Four months. You know how long that is? That's half the school year."

"All right. But you said Andrew freaked? What do you mean by that?"

"First, though, you had to know Laura."

"Were you and she friends?"

"Like, best." On the floor with her legs crossed, Jeri bent over at the waist, stretching, came back up. The movement seemed unconscious, but it bought her some time to get her emotions in check. "You know she was seriously depressed?"

"No. I hadn't heard that."

"That's the key, though. She'd been in therapy forever. She tried to kill herself two years ago. Did you know that?"

Hardy and Wagner exchanged glances, and Wagner gave a small nod, acknowledging it.

"Do you know why?" Hardy asked.

"A million reasons. The world, you

473

know? But mostly the home scene sucked."

"What sucked about it?"

"Basically, clueless parents. They're heavily into the social thing here in town, you know? The Wrights? Wright-Way Components? Anyway, she had this whole wing of her house that was all hers? So she comes home from school, goes to her room and gets loaded, listens to all, like, you know, metal and death music."

"Like who?"

Jeri shook her head. "You wouldn't know them. They're not playing for guys like you. Let's just say the music's dark. So anyway, she's popping valiums and ludes and anything else she can get her hands on, but nobody notices. I mean, her parents see her every day, right? And Laura's fine, she's pulling A's and B's. And Mom and Dad are all, 'Whatever, as long as you don't bother me, 'cause I've got a party.' You know? Same as Andrew."

"You mean with the drugs, too?"

"No. Andrew's uptight about drugs, but the home thing. Gone parents. That's how they connected."

Hardy found himself working the fictional angle again — the sister in "Perfect Killer" hadn't been based on Andrew's sister, Alicia, but on his girlfriend Laura. *He made it up.*

Next, wondering if the Wrights had discovered their daughter's pregnancy and, because of the rumors about Mooney's promiscuity, attributed it to him. And what they might have been tempted to do about that. He scratched a note, came back to Jeri. "So how does all this relate to Mr. Mooney?" he asked.

She scrunched her face puzzling it out. Hesitantly, the words started to come. "I guess, I think Laura needed somebody to notice she was alive. Maybe Andrew needed the same thing. That was kind of the baseline, you see?"

Hardy didn't exactly, but wanted to keep her talking, so he nodded.

"Okay, so you've got two needy kids — Andrew and Laura — hanging on to each other, right? Then, all the sudden really, one of them wakes up. Now she doesn't just need anymore. Suddenly, she's . . . I don't know if happy is the word, maybe . . . *validated*. Mike — Mr. Mooney — makes her feel that way, all on her own, without Andrew. If you ask me, that's what Andrew freaked about. Laura just had this new confidence and went flying away. Not with Mike, by herself. But Mike had made it happen, and Andrew didn't know how to handle it."

"So how'd they get back together?" Hardy asked.

"That's what's funny. The same thing, I

think, happened to Andrew. Mike really thought Andrew was a great actor. I mean, he gave him the lead. And I think Andrew finally just got it. He'd been stupid and he apologized. So next time he and Laura got together, it was . . . I don't know . . . it seemed like it was on a different plane, if that makes any sense."

"So you're saying you don't think Andrew was jealous of Mr. Mooney anymore, at least not by the time the shootings happened?"

"No way. He just wasn't. I knew them as well as I know anybody. They were tight."

"But she didn't tell him she was pregnant? Did you know that she was?"

Jeri glanced down to the floor. "Yeah. But she was getting an abortion. She didn't want to screw things up with Andrew again by getting him involved in all that. It would be better if he just never knew. That's why she was staying later with Mike those nights, getting all that worked out. He was going to help with the arrangements. She sure couldn't go to her parents."

"All right. But what if Andrew found out about the baby and wanted to keep it? Might they have fought about that?"

"I doubt it. And so then because he wants the baby to live, he kills it? I don't think so. And while we're at it, Andrew didn't shoot Laura, either. Or Mike. There's no way. That's just not who he is."

Hardy leaned forward. "Then do you have any idea at all who might have?"

"This is going to sound weird, I know," she said, her dark eyes shining now, "but I don't think it could have been anybody who knew either of them." A tear track, black with kohl, coursed her cheek. "They were too great," she said.

24

First thing that Monday morning, Glitsky
had put out the word with Marcel Lanier
that he would like to see the field notes
from the weekend work of his task force investigators on the Boscacci investigation.
Because of the Twin Peaks killings on
Friday night, Lanier himself, as head of homicide, had been otherwise employed and
had not been able to participate, but Pat
Belou, Lincoln Russell and the General
Work inspectors had covered all of the gun
shows in the Bay Area that weekend except
the one in Fremont. Maybe because these
San Francisco cops didn't have reliable
snitches in some of the outlying counties,
nobody came back with anything remotely
resembling Glitsky's phone book from Mr.
Ewing's truck.

Frustrated by the lack of data, Glitsky
still believed he was on to the only possible
lead, albeit a remote one, to Boscacci's
murder. So before he ran out to his 8:00
a.m. chiefs' meeting, he called the ATF liaison for San Francisco, got a recorded

message and left one of his own. He gave a Xerox copy of Ewing's phone book to the guys from General Work and told them to get names and addresses for everyone in the book from the phone company's reverse listings. He wanted them by the time the ATF got back to him so that he'd have something to trade — the names and addresses of known suppressor buyers — in exchange for the ATF's cooperation in supplying still other, much larger lists of similar buyers. He had the personnel and the budget, for once, and he was looking for the nexus, if any, of suppressor buyers and people who might have had dealings with Allan Boscacci.

After chiefs', he met with the mayor's representative, Celia Bonham, at City Hall, to discuss some jurisdictional issues between the SFPD and the officers and administrators of Homeland Security. After that, Paganucci drove him halfway home, out to Fillmore, to talk to the new executive director of the African-American Art & Culture Complex about some mutual impact issues, such as the use of the city's finest as private security for the complex at the city's expense. Back at the Hall of Justice, he fielded questions from reporters on all three of the major events currently transpiring in his domain — the handling of the LeShawn Brodie matter, Allan

Boscacci's murder (which some reporter had now called an assassination) and the double homicides of the Executioner on Friday night. Since he had nothing good or even mildly productive to say about any of these, it was a dispiriting news conference. Glitsky couldn't seem to get much of a spin going about the fact that between the chiefs, the homicide detail and his own special event number task force, he had nothing to show, and very little to say, about crime in the city within the past six days.

He finally checked into his office. The General Work guys had done a good job while he'd been going to meetings, and they'd compiled a neatly typed name and address list from the Ewing phone numbers, which now lay under a stapler on his desk. For lunch, he washed two rice cakes down with a Diet Coke. When his receptionist buzzed to tell him that two ATF agents were here, he felt reasonably prepared.

But that didn't last long.

The two of them — Aitkin and Drew — struck Glitksy as having come straight not from their offices but from the street, perhaps a bust. Both still wore their black field jackets with the oversized initials "ATF" across the back; both were packing in obvious, bulging shoulder holsters. Drew made the introductions for both of them, and they sat without any fanfare in the chairs in front of Glitsky's desk.

Glitsky had planned to open the discussion by expressing his appreciation that they'd come down on such short notice and so on, but Drew barely gave him the chance before he interrupted. "We just wondered, sir," he began in a terse tone, "if you're familiar with the joint task force we've had working with local officers in each county and through which we're all supposed to coordinate our activities?"

"Sure," Glitsky said. "I called Sergeant Trona last Friday and he told me he could get me hooked up with one of your agents by early next week, which is now. I'm heading up an event number force on this Allan Boscacci homicide. I didn't have that kind of time." He reached for his list. "But I think you'll be pleased with my results."

Aitkin, who so far hadn't said a word, came forward and took the sheet of paper. Drew glanced over at it without much show of interest. "And these are what?" he asked.

"Names and addresses of people who've bought suppressors illegally from a man named James Martin Ewing out of the Cow Palace. Or at least that's where he was working out of last Friday."

"How did you get to him?" Drew asked. "Ewing?"

"I had a snitch. It was easier than I thought it should be."

Finally Aitkin spoke, turning to Drew. "Imagine that."

"I beg your pardon." Glitsky didn't much appreciate the tone. "Do you gentlemen have some kind of a problem?"

"Yes, sir. I'm afraid we do." Drew sat back, linked his hands over his belt.

Aitkin had carried in with him a flat leather briefcase and now he opened it on his lap and withdrew a photograph, which he handed over to his partner. Drew, in turn, handed it to Glitsky. "I'd like to ask you, sir, if this looks familiar to you."

The picture was of him. The photo was taken last Friday, no doubt from the camera Ewing had concealed somewhere inside his van. "Ewing is your snitch," he said.

Drew nodded. "Didn't you wonder why it was so easy getting connected with him? You got a guy looking at twenty years if he gets caught at this stuff and you drop one name to a more or less random dealer at a gun show and you're talking to him in fifteen minutes? Any warning bells go off for you?"

"I thought I was having a lucky day."

The two agents' heads turned, briefly, to

each other. Drew came back at Glitsky. "So what are you looking for?"

"Background. I need to know if any of these guys are connected to Boscacci." He pointed to his list. "It's long odds, but we're not working with much."

The problems of any local police department were of no concern to the ATF. "We've busted two-thirds of Ewing's people already," Drew said. "The others we're watching to see who they hang with, how they hook up. You know the drill, which is why we're asking you not to pursue . . . this any further."

Glitsky passed the photo back to Drew. His stomach was doing a mariachi dance and he put a hand over it. "I'd still be interested in getting some background on anyone who has bought suppressors, see if we can get a match."

Drew and Aitkin exchanged a glance and nodded. "We can provide that," Drew said. "Probably be a couple of days."

"Sooner would be better."

"Always. Of course."

As the two men were standing up, Aitkin spoke for the second time. "It's always our intention to work with local agencies, sir. That's why we set up the joint task forces, for mutual communication and cooperation. So in future, if you plan to freelance out of your jurisdiction, you might check in with local authorities to find out what you might be getting into."

"I get it," Glitsky said.

When they had gone through the door and out of the office, he heard one of them say, "Fucking locals."

"I need to talk to you." Wu hadn't changed since the hospital. She still wore her blue jogging suit, tennis shoes, the Giants warm-up jacket. She stood in the doorway to Brandt's mini-cubicle at the YGC. Her mouth was dry and her palms wet. Even after the ride they'd shared to downtown, which had seemed to break the ice a little, she didn't know how he would receive her. But she felt that coming here to him could be read as an apology of sorts. She was playing straight with him now, keeping her opposite number up on developments in the case. She knew she was here with the best of intentions. "You're not going to like it."

Brandt had his hand on the telephone receiver, halfway to his ear, but he replaced it. He wore a neutral expression. "I already heard," he said. "Did he make it?"

"He's going to."

"I'm glad. I really am."

"Which leaves us some business." She leaned against the doorjamb. "I'm requesting a continuance on the hearing tomorrow. I wanted to tell you about it beforehand."

"I figured you would," Brandt said, "when I heard about the suicide attempt. You ought to know, since we're being up front with one another, that I heard Warvid this morning talking to his clerk about that very thing. I wouldn't get my hopes up."

"He said he wouldn't continue?"

"That's what I hear from the clerk. If Andrew's bipedal, we go."

"Maybe he won't be."

"That remains to be seen then. But let me ask you something. If Warvid continues on these grounds, what's to stop everyone from feeling suicidal the day before their hearing?" Brandt leaned back in his chair, put his hands behind his head, his feet up on the desktop. "Let's be straight here, okay? This hearing is a formality. You know it, I know it, Warvid knows it."

"My client went sideways, Jason. Hasn't that ever happened to you?"

"Of course. All the time. But right now, the only thing Warvid wants is to restore order to the cosmos, and to do that, he's got to get Bartlett back upstairs. Which he'll do. Tomorrow."

Wu went from one doorpost to the other, arms crossed. "I'm calling witnesses, you know. I've filed a list."

Brandt's feet came off the desk. He straightened in his chair. "You're not fighting the criteria?"

"Every one."

"All I need is one, you realize that?"

"Sure."

Brandt sighed. "I've got to assume you've read his short story."

"I have," she said. "I can mitigate it."

"All right, mitigate. But you can't believe that a double homicide won't strike the court as of sufficient gravity?"

"It isn't if he didn't do it."

Brandt's mouth stood half-open. When he finally spoke, his voice hummed with concern. "Amy, listen. Last time we were in court, you were admitting the petition. Now you've got one of the world's fairest judges seriously upset with you. And what are you going to argue, that the homicides didn't happen? 'Cause that's all I've got to show — that they did. There's no burden of proof. You know this. I make a prima facie case and I've got gravity and circumstances. You even get a step into arguing the basic facts and Warvid's going to shut you down."

She smiled. "Good. You're worried."

"I'm not worried," he said. "Or rather, I'm worried for you. There's no argument to be made here. Warvid's going to walk in with his mind made up, as it should be."

"Maybe not, after he's seen my motions."

"But Amy . . . Bartlett isn't a juvenile!"

"He's seventeen, Jason. He's a boy."

Brandt threw his head back, brought his hands to his face, finally looked at her over them. "I don't believe you're doing this."

Wu took a step, about the limit she could trespass without coming behind Brandt's desk. "Jason, listen to me. You know when Andrew said in court that he didn't do it? He might have been telling the truth."

"No, he wasn't."

"But what if he was?"

"So go to trial downtown and get him off. But for God's sake, do yourself a favor and get it out of Warvid's courtroom first."

But she shook her head. Intense now, she leaned in to him. "He's already suicidal, Jason. As it is now, he thinks he's going to be in prison the rest of his life."

"That's where he should be. He killed two people, Amy."

"Maybe, but he's innocent until —"

Brandt barked a laugh of pure disdain. "Oh, give me a fucking break."

"You read his stuff, Jason, you know —"

"I know he's dangerous; that's what his writing shows me. He's a sophisticated criminal mind who thinks he can use you, and is on his way to proving it."

"He tried to kill himself to manipulate me? Is that what you're saying?"

Brandt shrugged. "I heard the shirt he used ripped. Maybe he tore it a little first."

Wu reacted in a blaze of rage. "Bullshit, Jason! That's just such *bullshit!*"

Suddenly, behind them in the hallway loomed the imposing and, to Wu, increasingly sinister form of bailiff Nelson, knocking on the door behind her. "Is everything going along okay with you people?" He moved in closer, lowered his voice. "The sound's traveling pretty good in the hallway here."

Brandt spoke over Wu's shoulder, the voice relaxed and friendly. "We're fine, Ray. Just a friendly little pretrial conference between two country lawyers."

Wu's eyes were flashing, her color high. She whirled and brushed by Nelson. "Excuse me, please." Jogging, in her tennis shoes, she disappeared around the corner of the hallway.

Brandt found her car, the last in a long line of them parked at the curb downhill from the front entrance to the YGC.

She was in the driver's seat, sitting with both hands on the wheel, head down. From the sidewalk, Brandt hesitated, then touched the passenger window with a knuckle, leaned over so she could see who

488

it was. She reached over and unlocked the door. When he'd closed it again behind him, they both sat in silence for the first seconds. Finally, Brandt, eyes sideways, let out a long sigh. "I shouldn't have said that in there. I don't think your boy faked it."

She kept her own eyes forward, her hands back on the wheel. "I came down here as a courtesy to you, Jason. I wasn't playing any more games." She paused. "With this case or with you. The other night . . ." The words stopped. She looked over at him.

"We don't have to talk about that."

"Yes, we do, I think." Then. "You were right. There's something wrong with me."

"I didn't say that."

"You didn't have to." She moved her hand from the steering wheel as though she were going to touch him, but stopped, dropped it into her lap. "Can I tell you something?"

"Sure."

"That night, at the Balboa . . . I didn't go into that thinking about Allan or Andrew or the deal I thought I'd made. That was just us. That was real."

"All right."

"That's all I want to say."

"Okay, then, I've got one. If it was so real, why'd you kick me out?"

"I didn't kick you out. You left."

"After you said, and this is a direct quote, 'You'd better be out of here by morning or we're in trouble.' You don't remember saying that?"

Wu shook her head slowly from side to side. "I didn't mean legal trouble. I meant . . . I meant if this was supposed to be a one-nighter and neither of us wanted to get serious, you had to leave before we went any further."

"But we already —"

She turned on him. "I didn't mean the sex."

Brandt blew out heavily. "No. I know. I know what you meant." A long silence. Then. "You figured I was playing you." He chuckled. "I love this."

"Me, too. It's perfect."

"A microcosm of life itself," Brandt said. "Makes me think, though, that maybe we want to go in and get out of Bartlett now."

Wu shook her head. "We can't. I can't abandon him, and if you drop out, the seven-oh-seven gets continued, plus you'd have to give a reason, which would probably get you fired."

Brandt suddenly saw something over Wu's shoulder, and he swore. Across the street, Ray Nelson was leaning over the roof of his car, lighting a cigarette. Seeing them both now looking at him, he raised a hand in greeting, then opened the car door and got in.

"He saw us," Wu said.

"Yes, he did. But so what? We're sitting in a car, having a discussion."

"Do you think he followed us out?"

"I don't know. Why would he?"

"I don't know. To have something on us." Wu looked after Nelson's car, now driving away. "The guy creeps me out."

"Ray? He's a pussycat after you get to know him," Brandt said.

"I don't want to get to know him."

"No, honestly, you probably don't. But maybe him seeing us out here was a good object lesson, after all."

"In what?"

"The wisdom of being seen together outside the courtroom."

25

Top down on the convertible, with coat and tie off and the top button of his shirt undone, Hardy with his headphones on might have been mistaken for a stressed-out executive zoning out to his relaxation tapes. In fact, he was waiting across the street from the murder scene, listening again to the tape of the other male actor in the play, Steve Randell, to whom he'd talked at Sutro after he'd finished with Alicia North and Jeri Croft.

When Juan Salarco pulled into his driveway at a little after three o'clock, Hardy sat up, slipped the recorder back in his pocket, put up the car's hood and got out. Across the street, Salarco exited his truck and immediately went to the small garage and opened it. By the time he turned around, Hardy was standing by his driver's side fender. He raised a hand with an exaggerated nonchalance that he didn't come close to feeling.

He realized that ever since he'd concluded his careful review of the tape he'd made with Juan, he'd begun to imagine that Andrew Bartlett might be innocent. But, he reminded himself now, that belief hinged on what Salarco told him in the next ten or fifteen minutes. If he had in fact heard two gunshots, or even what might be interpreted as two gunshots, Hardy's hopes and maybes would be out the window. He hadn't recognized before this moment how invested he'd become. "Hey!" he said, low-key.

Salarco's boyish face broke into a ready smile. "Deezmus," he said, coming forward to shake his hand, crushing it effortlessly. "I try to get you this weekend, after you call, *sí?*"

"*Sí,* but my wife had an accident skiing. She's okay, but it took up some time. Now I'm wondering if I can take up a little more of yours."

Salarco took a minute, perhaps translating the request, then nodded. "Sure." He pointed. "First, I unload though, the truck, okay?"

The sun was bright overhead, but a light breeze kept the day cool enough, and Hardy decided to pitch in. It seemed the natural thing to do, lifting the rakes, shovels and wire trimmer from their positions in the wooden slats on either side of the truck while Juan wheeled the mowers and heavier gear down his makeshift

493

wooden ramp and around into the garage. When they finished, Juan locked up the garage and the truck, and then they walked up the indoor stairs together.

At the door, Salarco called out, *"Hola,"* got a female response and went straight through the living room, past the television with its American soap opera on the screen, to the cheerful kitchen. Hand-sewn curtains — bright yellow cotton with a red and orange floral print — cast shade over the back counter and the Formica table, but they only covered half the windows, and allowed in bright shafts of sun.

Anna turned as they entered. Hardy saw her light a smile at her husband, then extinguish it when she saw him. She had a large pot going on the gas burner — olive oil and garlic — and was cutting more vegetables — onions, red and green peppers, tomatoes — on the counter, while Carla, the baby, sat contentedly jailed, spinning the plastic letters on the sides of the playpen.

Salarco picked up the baby, tucking her in his arm. He then kissed his wife, whispering something to her, and went to the refrigerator for a couple of beers. Hardy took his, pulled at it, tried with a grin to break some ice with the wife. "It smells great in here." She nodded politely and went back to her vegetables. Still holding

Carla like a football under one arm, Salarco walked over to the table and sat in one of the chairs, indicating that Hardy should take another one. Moving forward, he took his tape recorder from his pants pocket and held it up, getting tacit permission.

Salarco nodded. "So, how can I help you?"

Hardy had been waiting so long to ask that he pushed the record button and was talking before he'd sat down. "Something we really didn't get clear last time that might be important."

Salarco moved the baby to his knee and began bouncing her up and down. "Okay."

"The noise of the gunshot."

"What about it?"

"The last time we talked, and I listened to the tape of our conversation a lot, you were talking about the noises downstairs when the fighting was going on. This is after you'd gone down the first time to ask them to be more quiet. Do you remember?"

"*Sí.*"

"All right. If you don't mind, I'd like to go over those few minutes again with you. From the first noise that woke up Carla again. Do you think you can put yourself back there and try to remember exactly what things sounded like? What you thought at the time?"

"All right."

"We can take a minute," Hardy said. "We're in no hurry. I want you to think back to that night if you can. Carla had a high fever and she'd been crying all night, and then finally you got her to sleep. You and Anna went out to the living room and turned on the television, quietly. Do you remember all that?"

Salarco was concentrating, the perfect witness who wanted to recall the exact truth. And with no one to object if Hardy led him back to the scene, to his state of mind. "*Sí,*" he said. "I am there."

"Okay." Hardy had memorized the sections. "Last time we talked, you said you heard a scream, the girl scream."

"*Sí.*"

"And then the first noise you heard — a bump, you called it — where you said you could feel it in the floor, as though something heavy had dropped downstairs."

Salarco was paying careful attention. He had stopped bouncing Carla, put one of his fingers into her mouth, a pacifier. His face took on a faraway look.

"Is that about right?" Hardy asked. "The first noises, then, were a scream, then a bump?"

A nod.

"Now the next noise, the second one.

You said it sounded like something crashing with glass breaking." Anna, Hardy noticed, had stopped cutting her vegetables, although she didn't turn around.

"Yes. I hear that," Salarco said. "The glass breaking. Okay."

Hardy threw another quick glance at Anna. She hadn't moved a muscle. "Finally," he said, "the last one was a boom again. You didn't say it *sounded like* somebody slamming the front door under you. You said it was the door slamming."

"*Sí*. Okay."

"You mean yes? That's what it was?"

"Right. Yes."

"So would you now describe any of those sounds — try to remember exactly if you can — would you say any of those sounds could have been a gunshot?"

A spark of surprise, or perhaps it was something else — recognition of a mistake? pure fear? — shot through Salarco's eyes. He licked his lips. The youthful face suddenly aged.

"It's all right," Hardy said. "You've never testified that they were. You've said what you've said, and people assumed. Now I'm asking you. Were they gunshots?" He was sure for a moment that he'd spooked him by springing an unseen trap. And he couldn't afford to lose Salarco's cooperation. If that happened, Andrew would be tried as an adult and probably convicted. Hardy, himself, might never know the truth of what happened downstairs that night.

He had been subliminally aware of the television in the next room — in English — throughout the entire course of his questions so far with Juan. And now, needing to somehow redirect the energy and keep these witnesses talking, he had to take a chance. "Mrs. Salarco?"

Her shoulders tightened; then she sighed and she turned around. *"Si?"*

"Wouldn't you say that's about right? The way your husband described the noises? Did any of them sound like gunshots to you?"

She didn't even have to think about it. "No. I never thought about that before, but there was no sound of any shots. Just the other sounds." She turned to her husband. *"Cariño? Si? Es verdad?"*

He nodded and seemed to take some strength from her. Taking a breath, he came back to Hardy. "When I sit back and listen, I cannot say any of the noises sounded like shots."

The relief almost made Hardy dizzy. Not only had he gotten the critical admission, but they'd both put it on tape. Now, instead of being the prosecution's star witnesses, the Salarcos' testimony would work if not to exonerate Andrew, then at least in his favor.

Anna came over, picked up the baby and stood holding it, leaning against her husband.

"Your English is very good, Mrs. Salarco," Hardy said.

She wasn't happy or, at the moment, proud of it. "Three years," she said. "Juan and I — me? — we try at home."

"And pick up a little here and there on TV?"

She flashed a glare into the living room, went and placed the baby gently back into her playpen.

Hardy let them get used to the change in the dynamic. He took a sip of his beer, then spoke to both of them. "As I said before, I'm not with the INS. I will do nothing to involve you with them, no matter what you say or do. If they come to me with any questions about you at all, I won't answer them. The only person I'm interested in is Andrew. I'm starting to believe he may not be a killer."

"But I . . ." Juan stammered. "It was him. I saw him with these eyes."

"Yes, you did," Hardy said. "In fact, you saw him twice. Once when you went downstairs the first time to complain, the second time when he came back after you'd called nine one one. Isn't that right?"

"Yes. But there was also the other time."

Hardy clucked, folded his arms, sat back a moment. He picked up his beer as a prop. He didn't want to risk alienating Salarco for good, but he had another point to drive home, perhaps more critical than the first. And to get to it, he had to expose something much worse than Salarco's gunshot misperception, or lack of precision.

"That other time is what I wanted to talk about," he began. "The time after the door slammed downstairs, when you and Anna jumped up from the couch and looked out the window and saw somebody turn around on the walkway out by the street."

"It wasn't 'somebody,' " Juan said. He pushed back a little from the table, straightened himself in his chair, his back stiff now, and crossed one leg over the other. He'd picked up on Hardy's direction, and didn't like it. "It was the boy. Andrew. I saw him."

Afraid of losing him, Hardy twirled his bottle, took a beat. "I'm not saying you didn't, Juan. If you saw him, you saw him, and that's the end of it."

Salarco nodded, an abrupt bounce of the head. Suddenly *impaciente* with all this, and equally afraid of where it might go. When he picked up his bottle and drank, Hardy seized the opportunity. "It's just that when we talked the other night . . . I've got a copy of the tape right here if you'd like to hear it . . . but I also wrote down exactly what you said." He took the folded sheet of yellow paper from his shirt pocket, opened it, and spread it out in front of them. "Here. Listen: *'Anna goes to this window, here, and I am behind her, and there is the boy running away. He stops under the light there, and turns, and Anna starts to put the window up to . . . to scream at him I think, but then Carla starts again with crying.'* " That's what you said, Juan. Isn't that how you remember it?"

Salarco put his bottle down and stared out through the curtains.

Hardy pressed him. "The reason it's so important, Juan . . . the reason that *this particular identification* is so important . . . ," he brought Anna into it with his eyes, "is that there's little doubt that the person that both of you saw out the window was the person who had killed Mr. Mooney and the girl. Very little doubt."

Salarco pouted, his visage frankly dark now. "It was Andrew," he said.

"I'm not arguing with you. It may have been Andrew. Certainly it looked like Andrew, with the same cowled sweatshirt he was wearing that night. But listen to what you said in your own words. You said

501

Anna went to the window, and you were behind her."

"*Sí.*"

"So you weren't *at* the window exactly, were you? Could you have been maybe a couple of feet behind it?"

No answer.

"Then the boy runs down the walkway," Hardy kept up his pace, measured yet urgent. "He stops for a second under the light, and turns. This is the moment that you see him. He's under the light, he turns, the cowl over his head . . ."

Hardy looked to Anna, who stood transfixed.

"This is when Anna goes to put the window up, to yell at him. She's angry, you're angry, and just at this second, your baby starts crying again. You're behind your wife, who is standing at the window, trying to pry it open, and suddenly your baby screams, and you turn, cursing and swearing, and go back to her."

"Yes," Salarco said softly. "Yes. That's how it was."

"Well, then," Hardy said. "If you were behind your wife, a few feet back from the window, and she was standing in front of it, trying to get it open, and the boy with the cowl sweatshirt over his head was thirty feet away, in only the dim light from one of the street lamps, please tell me how you

502

could possibly have seen his face?"

Salarco stared at a spot in the middle of the table, not meeting Hardy's eyes. Finally, he looked up. "I'm sorry, *señor,* but it was Andrew," he said.

26

Monday afternoon, Lanier told Glitsky that this would be a good time to come down and talk to the troops. With the rash of killings lately, Lanier felt overwhelmed. It was bad enough when it was the usual gang-banger mayhem and carnage, but when regular citizens got killed, it felt to him like another matter entirely. And regular citizens were taking an especially serious hit over these past two or three weeks, first with Elizabeth Cary, then Boscacci, and now this Executioner and his two victims last Friday.

Hanging up with Glitsky, Lanier stood, stretched and walked out into the inspectors' area. The desks of his twelve people were placed back to back, in team pairs, and over the years a line of metal filing cabinets had slowly grown like a vine out from one of the walls so that it now nearly bisected the space, isolating the inspectors area from the lieutenant's office. Even so, over the past half hour, Lanier had been aware of inspectors drifting back in for their paperwork, or simply to get the decks clear for tomorrow.

Now, he got himself a cup of coffee in the main room. He hadn't yet taken his first sip when Glitsky showed up. In another minute, eight homicide cops stood or sat casually around the partnered desks of Dan Cuneo and Glen Taylor.

Lanier wasted no time. "I know all of you are busy with your own cases, and a couple of you are on the Boscacci force, but in light of these Executioner killings, Deputy Chief Glitsky thought it might be helpful to do some brainstorming. Abe?"

Glitsky looked over the inspectors' faces, realizing with some surprise that most of them had never worked personally under him. Of the assembled group, only Sarah Evans and Darrel Bracco had been homicide inspectors while he'd run the detail. Of the other four — Belou, Russell, Glen Taylor and Dan Cuneo — two were almost complete unknowns. The other two, Cuneo and Russell, had actually investigated Glitsky in the weeks before last year's shoot-out. It was common knowledge that they still weren't among his fans. So it was not as congenial a group as Glitsky might have hoped.

Still, he needed their cooperation. "First, I'm only here because Marcel asked me to come down. I've been working with a small team on the Boscacci killing, and frankly, we haven't made much progress. Marcel tells me it's basically the same situation with these Executioner hits, although we've got the ballistics match, that connection between the victims. My question is whether there's another one."

Sarah Evans spoke up. "Nothing's leaping out at us, sir. The elderly woman, Edith Montrose, lived alone, and has no local survivors, although a son and a daughter have both flown in from out of state for the burial. Neither of them had ever heard of the other victim, Philip Wong. And Mr. Wong's wife, Mai Li, didn't know Montrose."

Evans's partner, Darrel Bracco, added his voice. "We're close to eliminating robbery, too. We wouldn't know for sure with the Montrose woman, but Mai Li hasn't found anything missing. Both of them look like, pardon the phrase, executions."

"Am I missing something?" This was Dan Cuneo, sitting at his desk, playing some imaginary bongo drums between his legs.

"What's that, Dan?" Lanier asked.

The inspector stopped drumming. "Well, you've got this Boscacci thing on the one hand, and the two executions on the other." He turned to Glitsky. "Aside from the fact that we've got very little on any of them, I don't see any connection at all."

"I don't either," Glitsky said. "But along with no connection, I see total evidence of two slugs. No witnesses, no prints, no forensics, no motives, no nothing. Am I wrong?"

"No, sir," Evans admitted, speaking for the rest of them.

"This spark any ideas for anybody?" Glitsky asked.

"Does what spark any ideas?" Cuneo asked. "Nothin' from nothin' leaves nothin'."

"Wait a minute," Belou stepped out from behind her partner, Russell. "We do have another open case with that profile."

"Hell, Pat," Cuneo said, "I've got about a dozen myself if you want one."

"Yeah," Lanier interjected, "but are any of them citizens?"

"Elizabeth Cary was," Belou said.

"Yes, she was." Glitsky filled in for those who didn't know. "Couple of weeks ago now, Elizabeth Cary, a middle-aged, white housewife, was gunned down at her front door, one bullet in the heart. The shooter left no sign except a nine-millimeter casing."

"Was there a slug?" Cuneo asked.

Belou shook her head. "No. Through and through, then through the drywall and stucco out the back of the house. We had

CSI look for a whole day. They couldn't find it."

"So we don't know if it was this Executioner or not?" Russell asked.

"Right," Glitsky said. "He left us nothing. Now my question to all of you is: why does this sound familiar?"

"Excuse me, sir." Cuneo had straightened up in his chair. "So you're saying you think because we got nothing on these separate cases, that they're related. With respect, that seems like a stretch." He got agreeing nods from at least Russell and Taylor, and went on. "It's like saying beer isn't water, and milk isn't water, therefore beer is milk."

"I realize that." Glitsky, knowing what he'd come down here to propose, was prepared to remain unruffled. "And of course it's a good point. But on the other hand, since we've got nothing on these four homicides in this past fortnight, maybe the only way we'll catch a break is to go outside the box. We can expect this Executioner to hit again, and until he's kind enough to leave us a clue, maybe we ought to work with what we've got."

"Which," Evans said, "I thought was nothing."

"No, Sarah, not quite," Glitsky said. "We've got only the ballistics connection if we're looking at the Twin Peaks killings.

But if we go on the assumption, first, that Boscacci may have been an Executioner victim . . ."

Cuneo nearly jumped out of his chair. "Wait wait wait! You're really losing me here, sir. You're saying maybe the Executioner killed Boscacci? Next is Kennedy maybe, too, huh?"

Lanier came to Glitsky's defense. "No one's denying it's a reach, Dan."

"If we had anything else at all to follow up on the Executioner's victims," Glitsky said, "I wouldn't waste anybody's time talking about this. But the fact is, we don't have anything."

"And nothing with Boscacci either," Cuneo said.

Glitsky: "Not quite. We believe it's likely he was shot with a silenced weapon. In fact," he turned to Lanier, "that's why we need to have the lab reexamine the slugs from Twin Peaks."

"They already ran ballistics," Lanier said. "And the Boscacci slug was deformed so they couldn't cross-check."

"I know," Glitsky said. "I'm not talking about ballistics." He talked to the group. "Boscacci's slug had a fairly distinctive scuff. Sometimes, if a silencer isn't fitted properly, it scuffs a slug as it leaves the barrel, and normal ballistics wouldn't pick it up, especially if the slug is deformed.

509

But," he added, "they get a visual match with the Twin Peaks's slugs, maybe we're in business."

"So these are pro jobs," Taylor said.

"Maybe," Glitsky said. "In any case, it would be worthwhile to find out if anybody in Twin Peaks heard a gunshot. Or," he turned to Belou, "near Mrs. Cary's home?"

"Yeah, but so what?" Cuneo asked. "Every witness says they heard nothing, which is the answer every time I ask anything. They didn't hear nothin', they didn't see nothin', as far as they can recall if their memory serves them at that particular point in time they were out of the area code if not the hemisphere when the incident occurred. Then what? We're going to consider that some kind of positive evidence?"

Glitsky remained calm. "At least positive enough so that the ATF will supply us with people who bought silencers. These we interview and try to find some connection between any one of them and any of the victims. At least it's doing something, instead of just waiting for another strike."

"And meanwhile," Taylor said, "when the Executioner does hit again, then what?"

"Then, if he leaves us anything at all, we move on that, of course. But until we've got something better, we've got to eliminate other options, the best one being that a silenced weapon has killed four people instead of two."

"And," Lanier said, "we can know the answer to that by, say, tonight, if we all go out and canvass now, when witnesses are likely to be home."

Evans chuckled softly. "That was subtle, Marcel."

Lanier smiled all around. "Thank you. I like to think it's the key to effective management."

"So we're approved on the overtime?" Russell asked.

This was always a thorny issue. Lanier hesitated, looked over to Glitsky, who nodded. "Put it all on the event number," he said.

"One more thing," Cuneo said. Everyone turned to him. "When we started talking about Boscacci, you said, *first,* you were going on the assumption that he was one of these Executioner victims. Was there something else?"

A muscle worked in Glitsky's jaw. "I said *first?*"

"I believe so. Yes, sir."

Another minute. "Sorry," he said, "it's gone."

When Hal and Linda North came out of their son's guarded room at the hospital,

Wu and Hardy were there in the hall to meet them. After Wu introduced Hardy, Linda smiled and said, "Dismas? Wasn't that the name of the good thief on Calvary?"

Hardy forced a smile. He didn't feel remotely friendly. "That was him," he said. "Not too many people know that. He's also the patron saint of murderers."

Linda tightened, drew herself up. "Andrew isn't a murderer."

"No, ma'am, he isn't."

Hal spoke up. "After all we've been through on that score, it's good to hear somebody say that. So you're telling me we've got a chance?"

"Don't get me wrong. We've got some tough days ahead, but there's some reason for guarded hope. There have been some developments in your absence. Besides, of course, this suicide attempt." He fixed them both with flat eyes.

Linda read his look. "You probably think we're horrible to have gone away, don't you?"

"It doesn't matter what I think," Hardy said. "Maybe I wondered a little."

"About what?" Hal stepped protectively in front of his wife. "About what?" he repeated. "Us going south?"

Hardy said nothing.

"I *asked* Andrew and he said he was fine.

He knew that we'd had the reservations for months and he was adamant we should just go. It was only for three days. He said he'd be fine. He was getting used to Youth Guidance. We didn't know he'd do anything like this. How could we have known?"

"Mrs. North," Hardy said, "Mr. North. I'm not accusing you of anything. It's none of my business how you run your lives. For Andrew's sake, though, it might be helpful if we knew where we could find you if we need to contact you while this is going on, but . . ."

"He knew where we were." Hal was growing hot. He turned to Amy. "I was sure he'd have told you."

"No, sir. He didn't."

"He can talk to us anytime," Linda put in. "Both of our kids can. Hal and I, we're always there for them if they need us."

"There you go." Hal took an aggressive stance between them, but spoke to Wu. "You could have called Alicia at home. You have that number. She could have reached us. Easily."

"How did you find out?" Hardy asked. "About this?"

"I called the YGC to talk to Andrew as soon as we got home this morning. They told me. Then I called Hal and we came straight here."

But Hal continued at Wu. "I still don't understand why you didn't think to call the house. Alicia could have called and gotten us back here hours ago."

Wu matched his gaze, tightened her lip, turned to Hardy, who came to her defense. "Your daughter wasn't home, sir."

"What? Of course she was. We both talked to her."

"We did," Linda said. "She was home. Absolutely. She called us."

"On her cellphone?" Hardy asked.

"Yes, I think so." Linda looked from Hardy to Wu, then back to Hardy. "You're saying she could have called from anywhere."

"I'm telling you," Hardy said, "that when they found Andrew in his cell this morning, they called your home first, then sent a squad car by — this is at four a.m., remember — and nobody was there. The first person they could reach with any connection to Andrew was Amy, at her apartment."

"I don't believe that," Hal said.

"You check it out," Hardy replied. "Won't take you five minutes."

"Now you're calling my daughter a liar." Hal directed his ire at Hardy. "Hey, you know what? We don't need to take any more of this crap from you or anybody else." He turned to Linda, grabbed her by the elbow. "Let's go. That's the end of this."

But she held back. "I want to know the truth about Alicia."

"You just heard it," Hardy said.

"It doesn't matter," Hal snapped. "It's another ploy to make us feel guilty and ultimately, I'm sure, to pay him more."

"Pay me more? Here's a flash for you, pal, if you haven't already heard. I'm doing this for free." Hardy was by now so mad at the man's blindness and arrogance that he was tempted to throw a punch. Blood pounded in his ears. He felt he had to raise his voice to get above it. "And firing Amy? There's a brilliant idea! Never mind how Andrew is going to feel if the one person who's been standing by him since his arrest deserts him, too. You think that's going to help his state of mind? His self-esteem? Of course, worrying about what Andrew's feeling isn't something you do much, is it?"

Linda stepped in front of her husband. "How can you say that? I love my boy. I do."

Hardy forced himself to some semblance of calm. "You know, Mrs. North, I'm sure you do. But doesn't last night tell you that maybe he's not getting the message? That maybe he feels alone and deserted in the world?"

"That's not because of us," Hal said.

"Our kids have had everything they need their whole lives, every opportunity." He looked to his wife, took her hand, came at Hardy. "You keep wanting to bring this back to me and Linda. We are not at fault here. This is all because of Andrew — the lies he told, how he acted, who he is. He's always been such a difficult kid. This is not me and Linda. We have been damn good parents."

This, Hardy realized, would never go anywhere productive. "Look," he said, "I've got two kids myself. Teenagers. I know what you're talking about. My wife and I get a chance for time alone, we take it, too. But I might suggest — and this is true with me and my wife and maybe every other set of parents on the planet — that maybe you're not as in touch with your son's feelings as you think you are. He did, after all, just try to take his own life."

After a short and tense moment, Linda broke the silence. "I'm going back in to him," she said, "for when he comes out of it. Come on, Hal. Are you coming?"

With a surly look back at both Wu and Hardy, and no comment, Hal took her hand, and together they turned back toward Andrew's room.

27

". . . And people wonder where they go wrong raising children," Frannie said. She was already chafing at the bedrest edict, and against her doctor's orders had been planning on coming downstairs to dinner. But Hardy had finessed her by bringing up the fettuccine Alfredo and serving her in the bedroom. Now he sat next to the bed, eating his own pasta from a television table.

"I don't know if Hal and Linda wonder about that so much," Hardy said. "Ask them and they'll tell you. They're not doing anything wrong. They're great parents. They've worked hard and now just want to have some fun."

"You can't argue with the basic concept."

"Okay, but getting it even a little bit right takes some energy. You check up on them from time to time, get in their faces when they need it; once in a while, God forbid, you say no. You make sure they know they're loved all the time, even when you hate 'em."

"Especially when you hate them."

"That, too. See, it's not that complex."

"Although I've heard you say more than once that raising the little darlings is the hardest thing in the world."

"That's because I only speak in revealed truth." Hardy went back to his food.

Frannie fell pensive. Time passed. Then: "Maybe they just got tired. The Norths."

Hardy put his fork down. "Who doesn't? But you're still in their lives a little. Not that some percentage of them wouldn't make it if you left, even a large percentage. But somebody like Andrew who's already got obvious issues, it might occur to you he's at risk, wouldn't you think?" He shook his head, forked some pasta, chewed thoughtfully. "One of the kids I talked to at Sutro today was this girl, Jeri, pierced everywhere you could stick a needle, tattoos — the look, you know? Not my first choice for fashion consultant, but a really good kid. Solid, grounded, helpful. She was in the play with Andrew."

"What about her?"

"Well, when she walked in, she was the one who fit the poster child image of troubled youth. But you hear her talking about Andrew or Laura, these kids who look like they've got everything, and she's got the answer. She calls them gone parents. Even if they're right in the house, they're gone.

And Hal and Linda aren't even in the house all that much."

Frannie reached over and put a hand on Hardy's tray table. "So what happens now? With Andrew, I mean?"

"Well, they're sending him back up the hill in the morning. Meanwhile, it looks like Amy's on tomorrow."

Frannie took a breath and let an involuntary moan escape. Closing her eyes, she let herself back down onto her pillows. "And what about you?"

"No. What about you? That didn't sound too good."

"I'm a little sore, that's all."

"That's all. You didn't by any chance forget to take your pain medicine, did you?"

She shook her head as far as the neck brace let her. "It's not that bad. I don't want to be drugged up."

"If you weren't already so hurt, I'd whup you upside the head." Hardy got up and went into the bathroom, found her medicine and brought it back. "Here. Take these, would you? Give yourself a break. Tomorrow you can get up and suffer all day if you want."

"What are you going to do?"

"Clear dishes, check on kids, take the rest of the night off."

"On the day before a hearing? You're kidding."

"Yep," he said.

"So what? Really?"

"Really? I don't know exactly. I've got some phone calls. I've got to find something that might help this kid. Especially after what he tried last night." He leaned over and she put a hand behind his neck, held him in the kiss for an extra second. When he straightened up, he said, "On the other hand, I could close the door and get these silly dishes off the bed, although with your medical condition we'd have to cut back on the usual acrobatics."

"It's a nice offer, but with the concussion and all, I really do have a headache." She offered him a weak smile. "I hate to say that."

"It's fine. I really do have stuff to do anyway." He sat down on the side of the bed. "But for the record, that was a nice kiss."

"Thank you. I thought so, too. You know why?"

"Why what?"

"Why suddenly I thought a good kiss was in order."

Hardy shrugged. "I thought it was just the usual animal magnetism."

"That, too," she said. "But also I'm liking this guy who showed up again recently. Caring for his clients, interacting with his kids. All that sensitive stuff." She touched his hand. "Really," she said. "If he wanted to stick around, that wouldn't be so bad."

"He's thinking about it," Hardy said. "No commitments, though."

"No, of course not. No pressure, either. But just so he knows."

Hardy leaned over and kissed her another good long one. "He'll take it under advisement," he said.

As a matter of course and of habit, Hardy had left his card — home and business numbers — with all of today's interview subjects. He had also asked for their own numbers and told all of them that he might need to call them as witnesses for Andrew, but this really didn't seem too likely at the moment. None of them had given him a shred of evidence, and without that no judge would let him introduce even the most compelling alternative theory of the murders. Hardy had to have something real, and he had nothing at all, not even a reasonable conjecture of his own.

This last fact, considering that he'd come very close to actually believing in Andrew's innocence, was the most galling. If someone else had killed Mooney and Laura Wright, he had no idea who it might have been, or what reason they might have had. Perhaps the most frustrating element was that Hardy now believed that Juan Salarco — or, more precisely, Anna Salarco — had actually seen the murderer as he fled from the scene and turned to look back at the house.

But because of the promises of the police for some kind of intercession on his behalf with the INS — promises Hardy knew to be empty — Salarco couldn't admit that he'd made a mistake on the identification. Maybe he didn't even accept that fact himself. Maybe all Anglos looked pretty much the same to him, especially young ones wearing cowled sweatshirts.

He was just finishing up a telephone discussion with Kevin Brolin, the psychologist who'd treated Andrew for his anger problems when he'd been younger, and whom Hardy wanted to testify the next day on the second criterion, Andrew's rehabilitation potential. Brolin had been called by the Norths before they'd even flown home after the suicide attempt, and Hardy had talked to him earlier that evening at the hospital right after his little contretemps with Hal and Linda. Brolin seemed knowledgeable and sympathetic and, more importantly, convinced that Andrew had resolved the problems with his temper — in Brolin's opinion, he was not a candidate for physical violence. He'd learned to channel that negative energy into creative outlets, such as writing and acting. Brolin even understood that he'd stopped eating meat out of compassion for the suffering of food animals.

Hardy didn't tell him about Andrew's jailhouse conversion on the vegetarian issue. Nor was he particularly convinced by Brolin's professional opinion about Andrew's current commitment to a nonviolent life. In Hardy's own experience, he'd known people who had directed their "negative energy" toward creative outlets, and who were still capable of heinous acts of violence. The two were not mutually exclusive. But if as a psychologist and expert witness — at a thousand dollars per court day — Brolin thought they were, and was willing to say so, that was all right with Hardy. It might not convince the judge, but Brolin would certainly make a damn strong argument that would be hard to refute, especially if Jason Brandt had not thought to present a rebuttal witness to testify to the opposite.

Hardy was still on the kitchen phone when the front doorbell rang. He checked the wall clock. It was 9:40. "Anybody want to get that?" he called out.

"In a second!" Vincent called from his room.

Rebecca gave her constant refrain. "I'm doing homework!"

The doorbell rang again. Hardy said, "Excuse me a minute, Doctor, would you?" Covering the mouthpiece. "Now!" he called out, "as in right now!"

"Beck!" Vincent yelled.

"I'm doing homework, I said." Her final answer. She wasn't budging.

"So am I! It's not fair!" Hardy heard a slam from Vincent's room — a book being thrown down in a fit of pique? — then a chair perhaps knocked over. Anger anger everywhere. His son went running by down the hallway. Hardy came back to the phone. "You work with children all day?" he asked. "How do you do it?"

"I'm a very, very old forty-five," Brolin said.

From the front door. "Dad! Somebody for you."

Covering the phone again. "Tell him I'll be a minute."

Hardy heard Vincent's steps coming back up through the house, then passing through the kitchen. His put-upon fourteen-year-old son didn't so much as favor him with a glance.

Hardy cut it off as quickly as he could with Brolin, told him he'd see him at the YGC the next morning and walked up through the dining room to the front of the house. No one waited in the living room and the front door was still closed. Was it possible, he wondered, that Vincent had left the caller to cool his heels outside and closed the door on him? Surely between him and Frannie, he thought, they'd covered, at least once, some of the basic etiquette involved in answering the goddamned front door?

But evidently not.

A shadow moved behind the glass and Hardy opened the door.

The young man looked familiar. Recently familiar, but Hardy couldn't quite place him. "Mr. Hardy," he said. Then, reading Hardy's uncertainty: "Steven Randell, from Sutro?"

"Sure, sure. Sorry. Didn't my son invite you in?"

"He said you'd just be a minute."

Hardy sighed, backed up a step, opened the door all the way, summoned him inside and closed the door behind him. "You want to come in? Can I get you anything? Something hot to drink, maybe?"

"No, that's okay, thanks."

He went to the window seat. Neatly groomed and as tall as Hardy, with brown hair and a good complexion, closely shaved, he hailed from the opposite fashion camp as his costar Jeri. He wore tan cargo pants and a black leather coat over a blue work shirt. During the session they'd had earlier in the day at Sutro, he hadn't volunteered much, his position being that he hadn't known either Andrew or Laura very well. But if Andrew had killed Mr. Mooney, Steve hoped that he'd be punished for it. Hardy had given him his by now pro forma song and dance about Andrew's innocence, but had gotten the impression that it had rolled off. But, obviously now, if he was here, something had stuck.

"You mind if I ask you how you knew where I live?" Hardy asked.

Randell shrugged at the no-brainer. "I had your phone number. I just got directions to here on the web."

"You can do that?"

Another shrug. Had Hardy climbed the evolutionary ladder all the way up to Cro-Magnon? "Sure," he said. "You can find anything on the web."

Hardy wanted to ask him how he'd found this particular and unnerving bit of information, and if there was a way he could remove it from the public domain, but he guessed it would be impossible now. Besides, the young man hadn't come here to talk about cyberspace.

"So what can I do for you, Steven?" he said.

He sat straight up, rather stiffly, his hands folded in his lap. The window seat was really more of a bench with cushions.

There was nothing to lean back against, no real way to get comfortable. And now that they were down to the nub, Randell seemed suddenly reticent, even confused. "Um . . ." Wrestling with it.

Hardy helped him out. "Did something we talked about earlier come back to you?"

"Something like that."

Hardy waited through another lengthy silence. In the street out front, a couple of cars passed, and from up on Geary came the wail of a siren. City noises. Finally: "Steven."

"Yeah. I know." He let out a heavy sigh, took an audible breath. "But before I tell you anything, I need you to promise me that it stays between us."

Hardy narrowed his eyes, cocked his head. "Do you know who killed Mooney and Laura?"

"No. But I know something. I just don't know what it might mean, if anything. I almost told you at the end of our talk today. And maybe I should have, but then Wagner would have known, too, and he might have felt like he had to go to my parents. Anyway, then tonight I couldn't get it out of my mind, that I should have told you. I'm not even sure it matters, but there are things about it that definitely matter a lot to other people. And to me. Personal things. Do you know what I'm saying?"

"I don't mean to be dense, Steven. But you have my word that whatever it is, I'll keep it between us. How's that?"

Another sigh. "It just seemed like you really might believe that Andrew didn't do any of this."

Hardy finessed that admission, which was still just slightly too strong. "I believe that somebody else might have come to Mooney's while Andrew was on his walk. If that's true, I'm trying to find out who, or why, or both."

"Okay. What if I told you . . . and this is the thing I was talking about, the secret. What if I told you that Mr. Mooney was gay?"

The perverse obviousness of it brought a lightness to Hardy's head. He'd been standing by the fireplace, and now he crossed the room and sat down on the ottoman by his reading chair. "Then I'd say he did a good job of keeping it hidden."

"Yes, he did. That was on purpose. Do you know his father?"

"I've met him. Yes."

"Well, Mike loved him more . . . more than almost anything, I think. He couldn't let him find out, his dad. It would have broken his heart. He couldn't have dealt with it."

"The dad, the Christian minister, couldn't have dealt with it?"

"The Southern Baptist minister. Right."

"How is that possible? I mean, this is San Francisco in the two thousands. Mooney's dad must have seen hundreds of people come out."

"Yeah, but not his own son. Not Michael. And he isn't a San Francisco minister, putting together an AIDS quilt. He's a nice enough man, I guess, but his church is down on the Peninsula, and his brand of preaching is, uh, more conservative. The sons and daughters of Gomorrah being turned into salt, and rightfully so. I've heard him." Steve pitched his voice differently. " 'Homosexuality is always sin, and always a choice. It's not a matter of genetics, as some would have us believe, but a degenerate lifestyle for those unfortunate people who can muster neither the strength nor the grace to reject it.' Straight out of the fifties, huh? And that's Michael's dad. Still."

But Michael's dad or no, Hardy immediately saw the incalculable strategic value of this information for Andrew. If he could bring it out at the hearing — or the trial if it got to that point — then all he and Wu would have to do would be to keep their defendant from testifying, which was always the defense's option. Meanwhile, the jury would naturally assume, especially in San Francisco, that Andrew and everyone else at Sutro knew that Mooney was gay. This would, in turn, eliminate the prosecution's primary motive of jealousy.

It would also not only open up an alternative theory of the crime — the "soddit," or "some other dude did it" defense — but also allow Hardy and Wu to question the original police investigation that had resulted in Andrew's arrest. They certainly should have interviewed people from this aspect of Mooney's life; a failure to even identify Mooney as gay must surely argue for a shoddily handled case from the outset. If Hardy could then get Salarco's no gunshot testimony and even a hint of a hedge on the eyewitness identification, his client stood at least a chance of a hung jury, then maybe a plea on a lesser charge. This was very, very big news.

If it were in fact true.

If he could get it in front of a judge or a jury.

And, most importantly, if it wasn't merely hearsay. "Steven," Hardy said, "I've got to ask you this question, and I think I already know the answer, but in the eyes of the law there's a big difference between someone *hearing about* a fact and someone *experiencing* that fact with their own senses. Did you and Mr. Mooney have a relationship?"

Steven needed to take a while with his

answer and Hardy was content to let him. "Yes," he finally said.

With that one word, Hardy's entire view of Mike Mooney underwent a complete transformation. If he was in fact having sex with one of his students — male or female, Hardy didn't care — then he was not the caring and sensitive soul most people took him for. He was a predator. "Would you be willing to testify to that in court?" he asked.

But Hardy couldn't let his reaction slow him down. This was critical information, and though the bare fact of it filled him with outrage toward Mooney, he had no choice but to find a way to use it.

Hardy couldn't imagine why, but the question actually seemed to both surprise and frighten him. He thought another moment, then shook his head. "No."

"Why not?"

"I mean, not unless it's your very last chance to save Andrew by itself, and I don't see how it could get to be that. That's why I asked you to promise before I told you."

"Okay, but I've still got the same question. Why not?"

Randell met his gaze with a steady one of his own. "Are you bullshitting me?"

"No. What would I be bullshitting you about?"

531

"Why I won't testify." He choked off a bitter laugh. "Because I'm not out, Mr. Hardy, I'm not out."

"Okay."

"And I'm not going to be out while I'm still at Sutro. There's no way."

Hardy was leaning forward, his elbows on his knees. "Would it be that bad? I always thought if you were gay, this was the town to be in."

"Maybe for older guys, but don't be a gay teenager. You'll get slaughtered. You want to hear a story?"

"Sure."

"I had this friend, Tony Hollis, you can look him up. He came out last year and got beaten up by cruisers in Noe Valley four times in six months, whenever any prowling group of teenage straights got bored. Then I guess Tony got bored with that and took a bottle of pills." He took a minute collecting himself. "So, no, I'm not saying anything in public. And you promised you wouldn't, either. If you do, I'll deny it. And that goes for Mooney, too."

"What do you mean, it goes for Mooney, too?"

"You promised you wouldn't tell about him."

"Yes, but that was . . ." Hardy paused. "I'm not sure I understand why that is so important now, after he's dead."

"For the same reason it was while he was alive. He didn't want his father to know. It was, like, the most important thing to him. He lived this whole secret life to keep the truth from his old man. If he didn't want to cause him that pain, how am I supposed to let it happen? I can't do it. When you were talking to me today, you said if I knew anything, I should come forward and do the right thing. Well, I've come forward, but letting you tell his father about Mike wouldn't be right at all."

"So then maybe you can tell me how am I supposed to use this information? If I can't let it come out."

"I don't know. That's not my problem." He stood up, a good kid awkward with playing the heavy, and now suddenly anxious to get away from what he'd already done. "Look, I'm sorry, I really am, but I just thought it was important that I tell you, so you'd know what you were really dealing with."

"Don't get me wrong, Steven. I really do appreciate that, but . . ."

The young man cut him off. "But what you do with it is up to you."

Hardy sat in his reading chair for a couple of minutes, pondering. Then he rose and walked back up through the dining room into the kitchen. In the dark and empty family room, he stopped to gaze at his tropical fish for a moment of centering and peaceful reflection. He turned on the room's lights, then knocked on his children's bedroom doors at the same time — perpendicular to each other.

"Just a second!"

"I'm doing homework!"

He knocked again. "I need to see both of you right this minute please."

The familiar grumblings ensued, but he heard movement from inside both rooms. By the time the first door opened and the Beck appeared, he was standing out in the middle of the family room, hands in his pockets, relaxed and casual. Vincent opened his own door, saw his sister pouting, looked to his dad. Having a hunch what might be coming, he wiped all traces of his own bad attitude from his face. He asked helpfully, "What's up?"

Hardy gave them a full ten seconds of low-grade glare, then finally spoke in the calmest voice he could muster. "I don't know if it's escaped your attention or not, but your mother is upstairs in bed, pretty beat up. And while I realize that the critical schoolwork you're both working on so diligently is far more important than the job I work at to keep us fed and clothed, I don't think it's asking too much for both of you to contribute toward the smooth running of the household when I'm, for example, busy on the telephone. And let me say I'm just a tad disappointed that I have to mention this to people of your ages, to whom it should already be, and I thought was, second nature. But clearly I was wrong."

He paused for a moment, made eye contact with both of them. "So here's the deal. Whenever the doorbell or the telephone rings and either your mother or I, or both of us, ask if one or even both of you could please get up and answer it, I don't want to hear about your homework, and I don't want to be told to wait even for a second. I want you both to jump and even race to see who can get to it the fastest.

"And whoever does get there first, I expect you to extend to whoever it is the kind of hospitality that you would expect to receive in the home of a civilized person. For example, Vincent, you don't leave a guest who asks for someone in this house by name standing out on the porch in the cold. And beyond that, if it's an adult you don't know, you look him in the eye, shake his hand and introduce yourself. Then you invite whoever it is in and even — I know this can be grueling — engage that person in small talk and make him or her feel comfortable until the member of this household that he requested makes an appearance. Does any of this sound remotely familiar to you? Have we ever talked about this before?"

Rebecca tossed her hair. "If this is just Vincent, Dad, I've got homework I need —"

Hardy wheeled on her and cut her off. "As a matter of fact, my dear, it's not just about Vincent. Your homework is not an automatic pass on the normal duties of citizenship around here. Vincent has homework, too. Believe it or not, even your father has homework from time to time, like tonight. Relatively important homework. Your mother never stops having homework. So homework is not an excuse to opt out of your duties as a citizen in this house. Is that clear?"

She drew a pained, audible breath. It hit Hardy very wrong. "And while we're on these special moments of politeness, I'd really prefer not to see your theatrical sighs or, Vin, your looks of obvious displeasure. We all live here together. We've all got things we need to do. So we respect each other, we cooperate, we use nice manners to each other and to our guests." He looked from his son to his daughter and back again. "Is there anything about what I've just said that either of you don't understand? Vincent?"

His son was leaning against the door-jamb, downcast. He shook his head no.

"Vincent," Hardy repeated. "Look at

me. In the eyes. Good. Is there something about what I just said that you don't understand?"

"No."

"No what?"

"No, sir."

"That's the right answer. Rebecca?"

"No, sir. I'm sorry."

"Even better." Hardy turned as the phone started to ring in the kitchen. "Don't either of you trouble yourselves," he said. "I'll get that."

"I usually wouldn't call this late," Glitsky said, "but your phone was busy last time I called so I figured you might still be up. How's Frannie?"

"Sleeping, I hope, if she's not lacing up her track shoes. But that's not why you called."

"No."

"Are you waiting for me to beg?"

"No. You'll never believe what we think we found out about the Executioner."

"Don't tell me he's a redheaded dwarf."

"He might be," Glitsky said. "But he may also be using a silencer."

"Still on silencers."

"We didn't have anything else, so I sent out half of homicide to ask around in Twin Peaks. Between the two killings, we talked to twenty-one citizens who were nearby —

just like with Boscacci — and nobody heard a thing. Elizabeth Cary's neighborhood, too. Remember her? Nobody on the whole cul-de-sac, and all of them were home. Nothing."

"So what are you saying. These were all this Executioner?"

"That's the working theory. In any event, you get four shots in high-density areas and nobody hears anything, something's a little funny."

Hardy didn't really agree. It was a noisy city, and people were so inured to near-constant aural assault that he thought a gunshot could easily go unremarked. Nevertheless, though he wasn't ready to mention it to Abe yet, when the time came he might be tempted to call his friend to the stand as a witness in the Andrew Bartlett matter, where the actual sound of the gunshots was the proverbial dog that barked in the nighttime.

Another alternative theory presenting itself, another ball in the air.

But something entirely different struck him. "Wait a minute," he said. "Did you say Boscacci? What's this got to do with him? You think this guy shot him, too?"

"I don't know," Glitsky said. "But it is tantalizing, don't you think?"

"That they all might be connected? Sure. But you've got to admit, it's not much to go on — something people *didn't* hear, especially a shot, which most people think is a backfire if it registers at all. I'll bet most of 'em didn't hear tinkling sounds either, and that doesn't mean Tinker Bell did it."

"You sound like Treya."

"There are worse people to sound like."

"Granted. But it's not all fairy dust. I called down to the lab again, and asked them to physically check Allan's slug. The tech couldn't get a ballistics match with the Twin Peaks slugs — they were too deformed — but he did get to eyeball identical scuff marks on rounds of identical caliber. He couldn't swear to it in court, maybe, but his bet is it's the same gun, silenced."

"Maybe," Hardy said, "though if he couldn't swear to it in court, which last time I checked was where we had to do these things . . ." But he didn't mean to bust Abe's chops. "Anyway, it does sound like you're getting somewhere," he said, "but if you'd told me you'd found something with the other victims about that jury the Cary woman sat on, maybe Allan was the prosecutor on the same case, then I'm thinking you might —"

"That's it!" Glitsky's voice crackled with a rare enthusiasm. "What I forgot. Thanks."

"Don't mention it," Hardy said, but he was talking to a dial tone.

28

Though it had suddenly taken on a much higher profile, Hardy's professional life wasn't all, or even mostly, Andrew Bartlett. First thing Tuesday morning, he had another appointment with Clarence Jackman, so he didn't even check in at the office, but drove directly to the Hall of Justice, parked in the All-Day where Boscacci had been shot, and was talking to the DA at 8:30 sharp.

The issue they were discussing was a theory called "provocative act murder," where the person charged with the crime had not killed the victim. Instead, the theory went, the person charged had done something so "inherently likely to cause a violent response" that they were legally responsible for the murder.

There were two classic examples. The first was when somebody goes in to rob a liquor store, pulls a gun on the proprietor, and the proprietor pulls his own weapon out from behind the counter and shoots, missing the robber but accidentally killing a bystander. The proprietor in this case is completely blameless, where the robber might be charged with provocative act murder. The second example is a scenario where two drug dealers get in a shoot-out, and one of them grabs an innocent person, using that person as a human shield, who is then killed by a shot from the other drug dealer's gun. In this case, while the second drug dealer might be guilty of murder, too, the person who grabbed the human shield in the first place, though he didn't fire the lethal shot, could be charged in the death.

In the case Hardy was arguing, his client was Leila Madison, the mother of a fourteen-year-old boy named Jamahl Madison, who'd gone with a gang of four of his homies to rob the apartment of one of their neighbors. Hardy had gotten connected to Leila because she was the cleaning lady of another of his clients. Besides Jamahl, she had three other children under the age of ten, all of whom lived with her own mother in Bayside. It was a horrible, all-too-common situation, now aggravated by Jackman's initial decision to charge Jamahl as an adult with the provocative act murder of his friend Damon. Jamahl had not shot Damon. In fact, the apartment owner, while the gang was fleeing from the robbery, had taken some shots at all of them, and had wounded Jamahl and killed Damon.

And again, as had been his habit lately, Hardy wasn't planning to take the case to trial. He was facilitating. Though his heart didn't go out to poor Jamahl, it did to the boy's mother, and he'd taken five hundred dollars, donated by Leila's boss, to see if he could persuade Jackman that in this case, provocative act murder wasn't the right call.

". . . if he were even, say, seventeen, Clarence. But the boy's only fourteen. He's gotten his own stupid ass shot already and lost his best friend. I've got to believe that's going to make an impression that maybe it's not a good idea to rob people."

Jackman, behind his desk, seemed to be enjoying the exchange. "So would thirty or forty in the can, Diz. Time he gets out, I'll bet he's lost his taste for it entirely." He spread his hands on his desk. "My question to you is do you honestly think he's going to change, ever?"

Hardy shook his head. "You ever meet a kid that didn't, Clarence? Age fourteen to forever. He might. He gets the right counselors at YGC, somebody catches a spark with him, he comes out in a few years and he's a stand-up human being. But the real question, the legal question, is the provocative act."

Jackman ran a finger under his shirt collar. Now, his deep voice an almost inaudible rumble, he chuckled. "If you break into somebody's home, you forfeit quite a few of your inalienable rights."

"Granted. But Mr. Parensich" — the robbery victim who'd actually shot Damon and Jamahl — "was never really in danger. The boys didn't even have guns. They didn't even know he was home."

"That's what they say, so it's just more bad luck for them. And let's remember, there were five of them." He held up his hand. "*Cinco.* This is a substantial amount of gang throw-weight, and you know it. Even if this guy was only fourteen. I believe Mr. Parensich felt legitimately threatened."

"I don't doubt it, but these kids didn't act up that much. They were already fleeing when Parensich fired at them. Self-defense or not, they're the ones that took the shots. Let's call it square."

"If you're suggesting it, let me just say that no way am I going to charge Parensich," Jackman said. "Somebody's got to stand up for the victims in these situations."

Hardy actually broke a grin. "That's a lovely campaign moment, Clarence, but you can't say that running away is inherently likely to cause a violent response, and that's what the boys were doing, hightailing it." Hardy paused, considered, concluded.

"Parensich's response was legal, but unnecessary, so the murder can't go under provocative act. That's all there is to it."

Jackman had been listening carefully, rolling a pencil under a finger on his desk. "So how do I get the message out to these people, Diz? You break into some guy's house, you don't understand somebody's likely to get hurt? The tragedy here isn't your boy and his mother, but Damon, who was also fourteen and who won't be getting any older. If these dumb fuck kids, pardon me, wouldn't have decided to knock over Parensich, Damon's still walking around. It's such a goddamn waste."

"I hear you, Clarence. I really do. But you're punishing Jamahl in any event. He's going to YA on the robbery. That's appropriate. But you won't win hearts or minds by a reach of a charge like this. You'll just seem unfair and vindictive. Jamahl's only fourteen, Clarence. As you say, he's still walking around, so he's still got a chance. Slim, but real. You don't want to take that away from him on this. And," Hardy was getting to the bottom line, "you and I both know there's no way you'll get any jury in this town to convict him, so why waste the time? You're just pissed off."

"I am pissed off."

"That's fine. But take it out on somebody who's earned it. This one just ain't right, and you know it." Hardy found himself surprised that he'd used these words. He hadn't thought that way in quite some time.

Jackman rolled the pencil some more. By all indications, he was making his decision on Jamahl, but when he finally spoke, it wasn't about that. "I hear through the grapevine that you're working with your associate on Bartlett. That the hearing is this morning, if I'm not mistaken."

"That's right. It should start in about an hour."

"I'm taking your presence on the team to mean that some kind of reason is going to prevail up there."

"Well, we're playing the cards we got dealt, Clarence, if that's what you mean. Amy should never have tried to make the deal with Allan, that goes without question. But not because she didn't deliver."

"No, then why not?"

"Because I'm more than halfway to convinced he's not guilty."

The quiet voice took on an ominous tone. "You think there was a rush to judgment out of this office? Do you think we weren't fair? That we don't have a case? Your own associate was going to plead him guilty less than a week ago. What's changed? Do you have new evidence?"

"No, sir. Not really. Maybe a new approach. That's all."

"Well." Jackman, frowning now, picked up the pencil and tapped the table with its eraser. "I'll let you know my decision on Jamahl, then. When I make it." He looked at his watch. "You don't want to be late for court."

It was a dismissal.

When the meeting ended, Hardy came out into the reception room by Treya Glitsky's desk. "So how'd it go?" she asked.

"The reviews aren't all in yet." But Hardy's face indicated that when they came, they wouldn't be all good, and Treya knew better than to push. His pager had vibrated three times while he'd been speaking with Jackman, and all the calls had come from his office, and now he asked, "Could I borrow your phone for one minute? Local."

"One? One," she said. Then, after she'd made sure the door to Jackman's office was closed, she added, "Abe called. He asks if you get a chance, stop up."

Hardy was punching numbers, nodded abstractedly. "He called me? How'd he know I was here?"

"He didn't. He didn't call you. He called me since I'm his devoted wife and I work here. I told him you were in with his nibs.

546

He's going to want to talk about . . ."

"Excuse me, one sec." Hardy was holding a finger up, stopping her. He spoke into the phone. "Phyllis, Diz. You don't have to call me three times. You leave the number once, I'll call back, promise." He listened. "Who? Okay. Yes, I know her. I got it. All right, then. I'll be going straight out there. Right. Right. That means I won't stop at the office first. After that I'm up at YGC with Amy. Right, okay. That's it. Thanks." Hanging up, he turned to Treya. "I love that woman," he said. "She makes the rest of humanity look so good by comparison. Was Abe important?"

"Always," she said, then lowered her voice. "But I think he just wants to pick your brain on this silencer thing with Allan and the others."

"The others." Hardy leaned over her desk. "You know I think he's a brilliant and fascinating guy, but this is just spinning his wheels until he gets something real."

"That's what I told him," she said. "He just wants to be back in homicide, and this gives him an excuse. He sent out a couple of inspectors this morning to ask relatives of the Twin Peaks people — if there are any — if either of them had ever served on a murder jury. They weren't too enthusiastic, the inspectors."

"Wait'll he sends them downstairs to Records to look up all of Allan's cases over the past twenty years. That'll really juice 'em up."

At this moment, Anna Salarco was, by any of Hardy's standards, more important than Glitsky. So, for that matter, was the hearing, which would start now before he arrived. But he couldn't ignore the summons from Anna, who had called his office. Wu and he had discussed strategy late yesterday afternoon, and he had no reason to believe she couldn't handle it well herself. But he did ask Treya to call Abe back and send his regrets.

Twenty-five minutes later he was back in the Salarcos' bright yellow kitchen. Carla was in her playpen watching Barney on television. Clearly nervous, her head darting this way and that, her hands pushing her hair around, Anna offered him a seat at the kitchen table. He took out his tape recorder, held it up and got a nod from her, and put it on the table between them. She sat where she could keep an eye both on her baby and on the front door. Reading the signs, Hardy asked her if her husband knew that she'd called him.

"No, but I had to. I think about it all the night. The boy. Andrew. The one Juan pick out of the lineup." She threw a look at the door, took a breath, came back to him. "I was there, too. At the lineup. With Juan. But afterward, they only talk to him."

"Because he'd seen Andrew and he'd told them that he could identify him?"

"*Sí*. But they did not . . ." She snapped her fingers, cast her eyes about the room, searching for the right word. *"No sais."* Then: "They did not make it different, the times Juan saw him, like you did."

"Differentiate," Hardy said.

"*Sí*. Differentiate. Between when he went down first and when he came back later, after. Or the other one."

"The one you saw? Outside in front?"

"*Sí*. I don't know what . . . how . . . if Juan saw something that time." She'd gripped her hands, intertwining her fingers in her lap, and now she turned them over on themselves. "But I went over it last night a hundred times, what I remembered, and it was as you say, as Juan said when he . . . described how we went to the window. Me in front of him."

"You're doing fine," Hardy said. "I'm listening. It's all right."

She gave him a darting, empty smile, turned her head toward the door again.

"You were at the window . . ."

"*Sí*. I look out, and I am angry, too, at waking up the baby. I am slapping, you know, at the window. This is why the boy turn around. He look up at me and then he's gone, running."

"And that man, that time, was it Andrew?"

"No." She shook her head. "I don't say Juan is not telling the truth. Maybe he saw different. Maybe I . . . It was too far and I don't see everything just perfect."

"All right. Maybe all that. Listen, Anna. No one's going to accuse Juan of anything because of what you tell me now. It could have been an honest mistake. He'd already seen Andrew twice that night, so who else could it have been? Right? And when was the lineup? A month later? Six weeks?"

"*Sí*. Something like that much. But they bring out the boys, and Juan and I are both there, you know, watching from back in the dark. They keep us apart and we're not supposed to talk, you know. They give us a card and we make an 'X' if we know somebody. But I see nobody I know, and later I find out Juan said it was number two. He knows. I tell him I don't think this is who I saw from the window."

"It was not Andrew?"

Shaking her head from side to side, she said, "No. Not if he was in that lineup." Then, with the confession out, she stopped all the frenetic movement. Her shoulders settled almost imperceptibly. "Juan, he takes my arm and asks me do I know what am I saying. He tells me that there is no doubt. This is who he saw."

"He did," Hardy said. "That's who he did see. Just not that one time."

"*Sí.* But he is . . . angry at me. Very angry. Do I think he does not know who he saw? Don't I know the police will help us with *la migra* if we help them?"

"They can't," Hardy said. "They won't."

"I think that, too. But Juan still hopes, you know. If we go to the trial and he says it was Andrew . . ." She trailed off. "Anyway, I don't fight him anymore." Her head was down, but she raised her eyes to him. "Not until yesterday. When I understand."

29

By the time Hardy arrived at the YGC at 10:15 and got himself admitted to the courtroom and then the defense table in the bullpen, all under the disapproving eyes of Judge Johnson, they appeared to have cleared all the motions, including the continuance request, and now were apparently in the middle of what Hardy supposed was their first witness.

But before they could get back to that, Johnson took off his glasses and spoke up. "For the record, the court notes the arrival of . . . ?"

Hardy stood. "I'm sorry I'm late, your honor. Dismas Hardy, second chair for the minor."

Johnson's lips went tight, his eyes narrowed. "All right, Mr. Hardy. Would you care to approach the bench, please? Ms. Wu? You, too."

This was unusual, but when the judge called you up, you went.

"Yes, your honor?"

Johnson held his glasses in one hand,

and it was shaking. His eyes were cold pools of glacier water. He spoke with a crisp clarity, brooking no misunderstanding. "I gathered from your various motions and witness list yesterday that you intended to make this hearing more of a protracted proceeding than I had intended to countenance in this particular case. Now I see a second lawyer at Mr. Bartlett's table. I don't often see two attorneys for one juvenile defendant in the seven-oh-seven. I wanted to give you both fair warning that I'm not going to tolerate any delaying tactics or tag-team mumbo jumbo from either of you. I'll hear from one lawyer per witness — either one of you, but only one. If your witnesses don't speak to particular criteria, I will dismiss them. If you waste this court's time, I will cut you off. Is that clear?"

"Yes, your honor." Hardy was stunned at not only the force of the warning, but also the severity of the dressing-down. Wu had really ruffled feathers up here, maybe more so even than she had with Boscacci, and Hardy would be well advised to keep it in mind. Still, he wasn't about to roll over. "But as you've no doubt noticed from our motions, your honor, this case has grown in complexity. The —"

Johnson pointed a finger. "That's exactly my point, Mr. Hardy. Don't get me started. This hearing is not about the complexity of this criminal case. It's about whether Mr. Bartlett should be tried as a minor or not. That's all it's about. I've read your motions about calling witnesses for the gravity criterion and it doesn't take a genius to see what you have in mind on that score, but your witnesses had better be about facts and evidence. I won't tolerate any alternative theory nonsense — you can bring all that up in adult court if some judge will let you." He caught himself. "Assuming, of course, that this case goes to adult court."

He leaned down over the bench, shot a look at Hardy, over to Wu. He lowered his voice, which in no way diminished its intensity. "I believe we all know that we shouldn't even be here this morning, and wouldn't be, Mr. Hardy, if your firm had played straight with the DA. But now that we are here, I won't let you make a mockery of this proceeding. That's all."

Summarily dismissed, Hardy returned to the defense table while Wu prepared to continue with her witness. Seated next to Andrew, for several minutes Hardy found that he couldn't get his mind to focus. Johnson's warnings rang in his ears; Anna Salarco's tape burned in his pocket.

Next to him Andrew sat not in one of the courtroom chairs, but propped and

554

shackled to a wheelchair, his wrists cuffed and resting in his lap. A thick, cotton-wrapped white brace of some kind encircled his neck, bringing visions of Frannie back to him — it was neck brace week on the hacienda. Andrew sat straight up, a ramrod, eyes closed, occasionally emitting tiny moans that Hardy did not believe were faked. Behind them both, in the front row, Hardy felt the hostile eyes of the Norths — they'd watched him enter the courtroom, followed him up the aisle and to their son's table, with ill-disguised displeasure.

Gradually, he forced himself to put the distractions aside. He reminded himself that this hearing was merely Act I of what looked more and more like it would become a three-act play — with the preliminary hearing in adult court next and then the trial to follow. On the stand next to the judge was an ex-cop private investigator friend of Wes Farrell's named Jane Huron, whom they were paying $350 and who was to have read Andrew's "Perfect Killer" story and picked it apart for criminal veracity. On the surface, Hardy thought, this was a simple and fairly straightforward task, especially since they'd supplied her with many of the objections Andrew himself had voiced for them.

She'd obviously been on the stand for a good while, and now Wu was apparently in the process of wrapping it all up. "So, Ms. Huron, based on your training and experience, eleven years as a police officer and seven as a private investigator, how would you characterize the criminal sophistication of the author of this story?"

Huron looked the part: short-cropped, dark hair, a dark blue pants suit. She was a hefty, solid woman with a no-nonsense face. Answering, she turned directly to the judge, as Hardy and Wu had suggested. They'd also told her not to mince her words. "Not at all sophisticated, in terms of the real world," she said.

"What specifically do you mean by that?"

"He showed no knowledge of how a real police investigation would treat such a crime."

"Could you give us one example, please?"

"Yes. His alibi was extremely naive."

"In what way?"

"Well, primarily because it wouldn't in any way have eliminated him from suspicion. The times of the deaths would have been consistent with his presence at the scene when they occurred, regardless of what he did afterward. It would have just been stupid. And then going back to the scene, and pretending to discover the bodies. Not even the most remotely sophisticated criminal would consider doing something like that."

"Anything else?"

Again, Huron looked up at the judge, as though for approval, and he nodded down at her. "Almost everything else, I would say. The author demonstrated little understanding of forensics, ballistics testing, gunshot residue, hair and fiber samples, any of the normal details that crime scene investigators routinely analyze as a matter of course. The kind of precautions outlined in the story — the surgical gloves and fingerprint worries and so on — are what you'd expect to get from watching television and movies. Not from any real-life crime experience."

This was all Hardy and Wu could have hoped for, and Huron had pulled it off perfectly. Wu inclined her head, thanked her, and said she had no further questions.

"Mr. Brandt?" Johnson intoned from the bench.

And Brandt was immediately on his feet, approaching the witness with a light in his eye and a spring in his step. Hardy thought this wasn't a good sign, but didn't see where he could go. He was about to find out, and it wasn't a long journey. "Ms. Huron, you've worked in law enforcement for nearly twenty years, isn't that true?"

"Yes it is."

"And you've had a great deal of experience with firearms and forensics, have you not?"

"Yes."

"Ballistics studies, matching samples of bullet slugs and so on?"

"Yes."

"I see. Let me ask you this, then. Prior to reading this story, did you know that guns made in Israel were fingerprinted ballistically before they were sold, and that this information was embedded with the registration number of the weapon, so that any bullet fired from that gun anywhere in the world could be matched to its owner?"

Huron smiled as though in appreciation of a bit of fascinating trivia. "No," she said, "to tell you the truth, I didn't know that. That's an interesting fact."

"Yes, it is," Brandt said, "and you, a sophisticated criminologist, didn't know it." He half-turned back to Wu and Hardy, came back to the judge, nodded genially. "I have no further questions."

The suddenness of it clearly surprised Wu, but Hardy thought it was a very effective jab, trumping Huron's own undeniable sophistication with an even better example of Andrew's. But he didn't want to risk causing damage to Wu's rhythm or confidence, so he just leaned back, crossed his arms, nodded as though he were enjoying himself.

Wu stood and called her next witness, this one someone she had known from college — Padraig Harrington, Ph.D., a teacher at San Francisco State University. But just as Bailiff Cottrell got to the back door and opened it to call the witness, Brandt stood again. "Your honor, sidebar?"

Judge Johnson adjusted his glasses, raised his voice to the back of the room, saying, "One minute, please, Dr. Harrington" and motioned counsel up to the bench. When they were all in front of him, Johnson said, "Yes, Mr. Brandt?"

"Your honor, before we begin with this witness, I'd like to ask Ms. Wu what it is that Dr. Harrington is a professor of?"

"I don't see the relevance . . . ," Wu began.

Johnson cut her off. "I do. Answer the question."

"English Literature."

"English Literature?" Brandt raised his eyebrows, clearly a rehearsed gesture. "Your honor, with the court's permission, I'd like to ask Ms. Wu for the general import and relevance of Dr. Harrington's expected testimony."

"You'll see when I ask him," Wu retorted.

"Not good enough," Johnson said. "It's a legitimate question. Answer it." Johnson was being just nails on the bench and Hardy longed to raise some objection to protect Wu, but knew that anything he said now would only alienate the judge further, and hurt their client's chances. He'd have to stand and take it.

Wu swallowed, blinked, looked quickly to Hardy, then threw a glance at Brandt. "He'll be talking about the nature of fiction and the degrees of similarity between an author and a character that the author has created. In other words, is a person capable of making up things that he's incapable of actually doing?"

Brandt fairly dripped derision. "Your honor, is there some science here that I'm missing? The petitioner is willing to stipulate that fiction authors make things up. If that's the gist of Dr. Harrington's testimony . . ."

Wu interrupted. "He's going to address specific elements in Mr. Bartlett's story, your honor, as compared to elements in the actual crime."

"And this will demonstrate what, exactly?" the judge asked.

"That even the degree of sophistication exhibited by the character in the story, minimal though it is, as my last witness demonstrated . . ."

Brandt corrected her. ". . . tried to demonstrate."

". . . as my last witness demonstrated," Wu repeated, "even that small degree of sophistication is less than that possessed by Mr. Bartlett."

"Or more," Brandt said.

Her stage whisper getting out of hand, Wu shot the question at Brandt. "What do you mean, more?"

He turned directly to her. "I'm willing to accept it's different. The author's either more sophisticated or less. There's no way to tell from what he wrote."

"Both of you, listen to me." Johnson was a few inches out of his chair, leaning over the front of his bench. "You'll both address your remarks to the court and the court only. I don't want anything personal marring these proceedings. As to the point at issue, I agree with Mr. Brandt. Ms. Wu, given petitioner's stipulation that fiction authors make things up, it's this court's ruling that we don't need to hear from this witness."

"Thank you, your honor." Brandt immediately bowed and turned back toward his seat.

Wu stood in shock. "But . . ."

Johnson snapped at her. "Put your offer on the record if you wish."

She returned to counsel table and then

repeated for the court reporter what she had told the judge. When she finished, Johnson wrote something, then looked up. "Dr. Harrington," he said, raising his voice to be heard in the gallery, "you're dismissed. The court thanks you for your time."

Johnson had announced a twenty-minute morning recess before Wu would call her next witness. This one was testifying on Andrew's potential for rehabilitation. Most of the rest of the courtroom had emptied out. Bailiff Nelson — Brandt's "pussycat" — had wheeled Andrew off to go to the bathroom, while Bailiff Cottrell and the court recorder had disappeared through the door that led back toward the judge's chambers. Brandt was just suddenly gone, as were the Norths, probably out into the main hallway. This left Wu and Hardy, at the defense table, alone.

"His honor seems a little bit biased," Hardy said.

"Yeah, like Bill Gates is a little bit rich."

Hardy managed a small smile. "I wouldn't worry too much about it, though. It's going to come down to five, anyway."

"If that's the case, we're in trouble."

Hardy shrugged. "Maybe not." He brought her up to date on the two major elements he'd unearthed since he'd last talked to her with the Norths last night at the hospital — Michael Mooney's gayness and Anna Salarco's failure to identify Andrew as the person who'd run from Mooney's place just before Juan had discovered the bodies.

Wu's eyes lit up. "Will she testify?"

"Maybe. She's got some issues with her husband." He explained the INS problem they faced. "So it's not a slam dunk, but she called me on her own, which is a positive sign. The husband's a good guy, but he's afraid of getting deported. I can't say I blame him."

"Can we do something to help them?"

"Like what?"

"I don't know. Turn them on to some good immigration attorneys? Something?"

Hardy shook his head. "Maybe, but not until she testifies. I don't want to get into the whole question of whether we're suborning or buying her testimony by offering her some kind of immunity. In fact, I was going to attack her husband's ID of Andrew on pretty much those grounds myself, except say it was the police promising to help him if he gave 'em Andrew. So I wouldn't feel right about it. Afterwards, if she comes through, different story."

"But if she'll say it actually wasn't him . . ."

"I know. But it's more than that. Her

husband's on the record saying it was. He'll have to admit he was wrong, and as of yesterday, that wasn't happening. He'll look like a fool and, maybe worse, he'll look like he can't control his woman. And as long as they've got his ID, they've got a case."

They both settled into their thoughts. Finally, Wu asked, "What about the gay thing?"

"The one I'm not allowed to mention?"

"Yeah, that one."

Hardy blew out in frustration. "I've been wrestling with that all day. What am I supposed to do? I promised the kid."

"Against Andrew's life?"

"I know, I know. But the question I have is really, so what? If Andrew didn't know Mooney was gay, then nothing changes. He'd still be just as jealous. Maybe I could run it up for a jury in the trial, but it's weak. It's not going to do it on its own. And without the kid's testimony, it's only hearsay anyway."

"Could you get it somewhere else?"

Hardy considered, drummed his fingers on the desk. "Even if I did," he said slowly, "what does it get us? So Mooney was gay? Maybe Andrew's homophobic and killed him for that?" He shook his head. "And meanwhile we've outed the boy and screwed up his dad. No, it just doesn't work."

"Except it opens up another world about Mooney."

"What do you mean?"

"I mean that everybody loved him, right? He was the world's best teacher, and so on. But the truth is, nobody knew him. He had a secret life. It seems to me anything we could bring up that points that out has got to help Andrew. At the barest minimum, it might give us somewhere else to look for who killed him."

Hardy's fingers stopped drumming. He suddenly sat up, put out his hand over hers. "The wives," he said.

"Whose wives?"

"Mooney's."

"He had wives?"

Hardy nodded. "Two of them." His ridiculous memory had somehow retained the names. "Terri and Catherine."

"Well. What about them?"

"They would have had a hunch, wouldn't you think?"

The regular Tuesday lunch meeting at Lou the Greek's was both a somber and an ill-attended affair. Jackman, of course, was there, but not presiding, since there wasn't much of an assembly. Glitsky, having missed the last few of these luncheons because of scheduling conflicts, had decided on the heels of his involvement in these latest murder investigations that he was going to take a more proactive stance in defining the parameters of his job, and basically do what he wanted to do, pleading out of as many meetings as possible. He sat next to his wife. Gina Roake, like Glitsky a frequent absentee of late, was also at the table.

But missing were Hardy, the "CityTalk" columnist Jeff Elliot, both city supervisors — Harlan Fisk and Kathy West — and, of course, Allan Boscacci. So instead of the big round table in the back that they usually filled, they had a booth for four under one of the alley-level windows.

Instead of the usual — convivial gossip, personalities and politics — they talked about the Executioner, who had apparently claimed another victim last night, although the shooting hadn't taken place in the city, and nobody investigating down in San Bruno had put together a possible connection until early this morning, when the police chief in that town had put in a call to Lanier and wondered if somebody from the city would like to come down and have a look.

Lanier had driven down himself, accompanied by Sarah Evans, and they'd learned that Morris Tollman, an engineer with Amtrak, divorced, living alone in a small house by the Tanforan Park Shopping Center, had taken one shot to the head, point-blank, on his driveway as he was getting out of his car last night sometime between six and eight-thirty. Near sunset, a woman walking her dog had seen the body and called police. The local crime scene people had found a .9mm casing in the weeds beside the driveway, but no slug so far.

On Glitsky's prevailing theory, wild shot though it might be, Lanier, Evans and two of the local cops had gone door to door. The neighbors on both sides of Tollman had been home all evening, and nobody in either house — four adults and five children — had heard anything resembling a gunshot.

That had been good enough to juice up Lanier, and he'd called Glitsky, who, grasping at straws, asked Lanier and Evans to try and talk to Tollman's next of kin, if any, and see if he had a murder trial in his past. After that, he had called the ATF to try to light a fire under them. Then he had come back downtown, where, in response to the request he'd fired off after talking last night with Hardy, he'd already received by fax a long list of names from the California Department of Corrections, convicts who'd been released from California's various jails and prisons in the three weeks or so since just before Elizabeth Cary's murder.

Since these people were in the computer, Glitsky assigned his General Work officers to look up the original case numbers that had been assigned to them, and then begin checking them against the hard files downstairs in the basement to see which of them, if any, Boscacci might have prosecuted. By the time Glitsky left for lunch at Lou's, the two inspectors had identified thirty-one of the four hundred plus case numbers.

"Which is why I'd like to get my hands on more bodies," he was saying to Jackman.

"He doesn't mean dead bodies, either," Treya said. "He means people to check the files."

Glitsky nodded. "I can't ask homicide inspectors to do that, even my event number people. They'd mutiny, and I wouldn't blame them. Even the GW guys are grumbling."

"I'd imagine so," Jackman said.

"I've got a call in to the mayor now," Glitsky said. "If he sees 'serial killer' here, which I'm starting to, he'll give me some more staff, but even so, it's a monster of a job. I don't think the FBI could do it in a month. But maybe hizzoner can also persuade the ATF to get off their duffs. Although that's just one more list to check out."

Jackman lifted a peanut with his chopsticks and looked at it skeptically. The special today was Kung Pao Moussaka — not one of Chui's all-time triumphs — and everyone at the table was picking at their food. "Are you sure it's even worth the time, Abe?"

Glitsky knew what Jackman meant. He sagged a bit. "No. I don't."

"On the other hand," Roake said, "if it's the only thing you have to go on, what do you have to lose?"

"That's my feeling." Glitsky sipped some tea. "Whatever else he is, this guy knows what he's doing. I don't believe somebody's paying him to hit these people, and he's not picking them at random."

"Are you even sure of that?" Jackman asked.

Glitsky had to shake his head. "At this point, Clarence, I'm not sure it's Tuesday."

"And no hint about Allan, either, I assume."

Treya answered for her husband. "Abe sent out Inspector Belou this morning to talk again to Edie." Boscacci's widow.

"Meaning no leads on anything in his professional life?" Jackman asked. "Any of his active cases?"

"He didn't really have any, Clarence, as you know better than anybody. There might be something on the home front Edie couldn't remember with the initial shock. But I'm not holding out much hope there, either."

"So you really think Allan might have been shot by this Executioner, too?" Roake asked.

"No. I can't say I'm all the way to thinking it, Gina. I'm really just back where we were," Glitsky said. "It's the only place I've got to look. What I'm really hoping is that this guy last night has got a huge extended family, who'll tell us that a long time ago he invested in Wong's produce and dated Edith Montrose and bought a used car from Elizabeth Cary, and they all had the same banker."

"Who is a gun collector," Treya added.

"Right," Glitsky said. "That'd be even better."

"But you doubt it?" Roake said.

Glitsky nodded. "Seriously."

Everyone stopped and looked up as Marcel Lanier suddenly appeared at Glitsky's elbow. "Excuse me, I don't mean to interrupt. Abe. I was just up at your office."

Lanier's face was mottled with emotion. His breath came as though he'd been running. "I'm just back up from San Bruno," he said. "I begged crime scene down there to come back and look again and they found the slug."

"Tollman's?"

"Yeah. In the roof of a garage a couple of houses down. Given the circumstances, they let us run it up to our lab . . . ," the San Francisco Crime Lab was halfway down to San Bruno anyway, "where they rushed it. You'll never guess."

Glitsky was already up. "I already did."

"Right. Same gun, no question. And Abe? All silenced. Four of the five slugs have a scuff mark. Same place on the bullet. Microscopically identical. A silencer, and the same one. And guess what else? Tollman? His daughter said he was on a murder jury one time."

"Where? San Bruno?"

"She didn't know. But they lived in the city until she was five."

"So it might have been here. What about the ex-wife? She'd know."

"She might. Except she's on a mission in India."

"How the gods favor the good." Glitsky put his hands to his face and pulled them down over it. He looked back at the table. "This is it," he said to no one and everyone. Then, to Jackman. "I need more people, Clarence. Yesterday."

Jackman nodded. "I'll give you some

clerks and every deputy I can spare."

"Guys." The men looked back at Treya. "Forgive me for speaking up, but I'd be careful about that." She spoke to her husband. "I know you need people, Abe, but you don't need this to make the news, do you?"

"What?" he said. "You're saying the media isn't my friend?"

"She's right," Lanier said. "It gets out, it tells him we know."

"Good," Jackman said. "Then maybe he stops."

"Or maybe he hurries up to finish," Glitsky said.

"Call me slow," Roake said, "but what is it that we know, exactly? What's he going to hurry to finish?"

By now they were all out of the booth, standing in a knot. Glitsky leaned in to Roake. "He's recently gotten out of prison and he's killing the people that put him away. He's already killed the prosecutor and I'm guessing four of the jurors. That leaves eight more, and maybe the judge, whoever that was."

"The good news," Jackman said, "is if you're right, it's a finite list of suspects. Big, but finite. Maybe among your four hundred, Abe."

"That's where I'm starting, for sure," Glitsky said.

"If it's not on that list, though," Roake said, "what are you looking at?"

Glitsky thought of the cavernous basement to the Hall of Justice, nearly a city block square, packed to the fifteen-foot ceiling with file boxes of ancient transcripts. "A lot more victims," he said.

Jackman and Roake walked together across Bryant Street. They were about to say good-bye when the DA put his hand on Roake's arm and said, "I'm glad to see you back down here, Gina. I was worried about you. Although, of course, I understood. We all miss David, though never as much as you do, I'm sure."

"Thank you, Clarence. That's nice of you to say."

"I mean it. May I ask you, though, did anything specific bring you back today?"

She offered a slinky grin. "If credit is due, I'd have to give it to my oh-so-subtle partner."

"No offense to Mr. Farrell, but that would be Mr. Hardy?"

She nodded. "You've got to love the guy, except when you hate him."

Jackman gave his own imitation of a smile. "Yes, I had a little of both experiences just this morning. I wonder if you could give him a message for me?"

"Certainly."

"Just tell him that it's not about scratching backs. It's about justice and that's why Jamahl isn't being charged with murder."

"Jamahl isn't being charged with murder. Got it."

"It's about justice, too. That's important. That's why he's supporting my campaign."

"Jamahl and justice."

A wide grin. "And Jackman."

"Hand in glove," Roake said. She gave the DA a chaste buss on the cheek. "I'm all over it," she said. "See you next week."

30

Outside the YGC courtroom after lunch, Hardy said hello to Ken Brolin, Andrew's anger management psychologist, while he was in the hallway catching up with the Norths. Hal and Linda maintained their chilly demeanor, not saying a word to him as he introduced Brolin to Wu, explaining that she would be conducting Brolin's interrogation on the second criterion when court was back in session.

When the younger bailiff — Cottrell — called everyone in from the hallway, Hardy went out to his car, drove to the 280 freeway and headed south. He'd called Mike Mooney's father during the lunch break. The sad old man had been home, but had no idea how to get in touch either with Terri or Catherine, Mooney's ex-wives. He hadn't heard from either of them in years and years. So Hardy had asked him if he was still in possession of his son's effects. If the dissolution papers were among them, Hardy might be able to track the women down.

As it happened, the reverend had his son's papers and files stored in an empty room of the rectory until he could decide what to do with them. Until now, he hadn't even had the heart to glance at all the stuff, but he said Hardy was welcome to go through it if he'd like, if it would help him identify Mike's killer.

Mooney stood and raised a hand in feeble greeting as Hardy came up the walk. He wore his black coat and collar today, and had obviously been in his chair on the small front porch waiting.

If anything, the house was sadder during the day, in the sunshine. Five painful minutes after he'd arrived, after he had assured Reverend Mooney that he would be welcome to join him if he'd like to take this opportunity to start going through Mike's possessions, Hardy was alone in one of the unused back bedrooms of the sprawling house. Even with the blinds open and the overhead light on, it was a dim room, with a threadbare light-orange carpet. There was a dresser with a mirror over it, a made-up single bed, an empty pocket-door closet, a small bathroom. Three rows of four packing boxes were tucked into the corner under the windows.

Hardy went to the nearest one, cut through the tape and lifted the cover. Clothes. Being thorough, he pulled out each item — folded shirts and pants — until he got to the bottom. He then repacked in reverse order. The entire effort look him less than two minutes. The second and third boxes also contained clothing items, although in the bottom of the third box, he found an envelope filled with snapshots — all students, some with Mooney and some alone — none even slightly objectionable or incriminating by themselves. Although Hardy, with his secret knowledge, found himself fighting a rising tide of anger.

In the fourth box, he ran across his first paperwork, mostly scripts and what appeared to be students' papers. He went through these with a little more care, hoping to find perhaps some correspondence that he'd be able to use. But Mooney had evidently been a careful and very private man, and there was no indication that he had any private life at all, much less, as Wu had called it, a "secret" one.

By the time he'd found the marriage dissolution papers filed among some old tax filings and ancient bank statements in the seventh box, Hardy was tempted to keep looking through the rest, just to see if anything of import to his investigation would come to light. But he'd already thumbed through a thousand or more sheets of paper, including many, many letters (mostly to and from current and former students), and again, there had been no overt signs of impropriety. He decided that he'd gotten what he had come for. If it turned into a dead end and he needed more, he could always come back.

For now, he had to keep moving forward. The way the 707 was going, they could be crucial to the fifth criterion — circumstances and gravity of the offense, the one he'd been planning to argue — by tomorrow. Judge Johnson had made it abundantly clear that neither alternative theories nor hearsay evidence were going to make the cut. Hardy would need demonstrable facts, both from Anna Salarco and from what, if anything, he might discover from talking with Mooney's wives, and even then Johnson might not admit them.

Reverend Mooney lent Hardy the telephone in his office — another room of sepia tones — and he called information to get the number of the law firm Blalock, Hewitt and Chance, and/or the attorney, Michelle Ossley, who had evidently handled both sides of Mike's uncontested divorce from his first wife, Terri. Neither were listed in San Mateo, Santa Clara or San Francisco counties, so Hardy placed another call to his office and asked Phyllis to please check Martindale-Hubbard — a directory of attorneys — and have either Blalock, Hewitt, Chance or Ossley call him on his cellphone, if she could find them.

He had better luck with Catherine's attorney, from the second divorce — the spouses had used different lawyers this time. His name was Everett Washburn, a sole practitioner who practiced out of Redwood City, another fifteen miles south. His secretary informed Hardy that Mr. Washburn was expected to be in court until four or four-thirty, after which he would probably go out to the Broadway Tobacconists for drinks and a cigar, his invariable ritual after a court date, if he wasn't going out with the client. Could she take his name and have Mr. Washburn get back to him tomorrow?

"I'm in a bit more of a hurry than that, I'm afraid. I'm trying to find a witness for a murder hearing that's in progress right now and I think she may have once been one of Mr. Washburn's clients. Does he have a pager number?"

"Yes, but he turns it off in court, and then leaves it off if it's after five or if he's out with clients. He thinks it's rude to let cellphones interrupt important conversations. Also, he had a heart attack a year ago and won't work anymore except during business hours."

Hardy was happy for him, but this

wasn't any help. "Maybe I could try it anyway?"

"Certainly." She also took his name and all of his phone numbers and would tell Mr. Washburn if he called, which was doubtful, that it was rather urgent. Hardy thanked her and sat at Reverend Mooney's desk, staring at the motes flickering in the thin shafts of sunlight that penetrated the window slats. After a moment, and before he forgot to do it, he punched in the numbers for Washburn's pager, left his own cell number as a callback.

His watch said 3:40 as he swung onto 101 South, heading for the courthouse in Redwood City. Traffic was heavy, but the time passed quickly enough as he took phone calls from both Messrs. Blalock and Chance. Ten years ago, their firm had broken up after Hewitt had died, and though both remembered Michelle Ossley, neither of them had kept up with her. Chance thought he'd heard she left the law biz and moved to Florida to work with her new husband in a travel agency, but he wasn't sure. Neither of them had ever heard of Ossley's divorce clients, Mike and Terri Mooney.

Hardy paid five dollars to park in the Redwood City Courthouse lot, only to discover that here at four-thirty, all the courtrooms were deserted and locked up. On the front steps, he saw two middle-aged black men in business suits talking together. Both of them had thick briefcases at their feet; both projected an air of solidity.

Hardy strolled over and excused then introduced himself. "Would either of you gentlemen know where I would find an Everett Washburn?" he said.

Washburn was a different suit of clothes than Hardy's friend and mentor David Freeman, but he was cut from the same cloth. No doubt pushing seventy, Washburn wore suspenders and seersucker rather than Freeman's rack brown suit, but neither believed in shining their shoes, neither shaved with particular care (and Washburn sported an impressive gray walrus mustache), and both seemed to believe that the smoking of daily cigars with some kind of strong alcohol was the key to longevity, to say nothing of sex appeal.

When Hardy found Washburn in the backroom of the Broadway Tobacconists — private humidified cigar vaults, bottles of single malts and rare cognacs on the low tables — he was holding court with a few well-dressed younger people of either sex. Next to him, an elegant and statuesque middle-aged black woman in a bright red dress smoked a cheroot and kept her free hand protectively on Washburn's forearm.

Reluctant to interrupt, Hardy watched and listened to him for a while through the thick, blue, fragrant smoke. Finally, and again Freeman-like, Washburn called the shot himself. Smiling around at the gathered group, whispering something to his attractive companion, he rose and walked directly up to Hardy. "If you're looking for Everett Washburn, son, and by the way you're standing here I gather you are, then you've found him." He had a large watch on a fob chain that he consulted. "There's barely five minutes left in the business day, and even if I didn't have a beautiful woman waiting for me when I get free, I don't work after that, so you'd better talk fast."

"I'm trying to locate Catherine Mooney. You represented her sixteen years ago in a divorce proceeding against her husband, Mike, who was killed a few months ago in San Francisco. I'm representing the suspect in that homicide, and Catherine may have some crucial information that could free my client." This was a stretch, but Hardy didn't care. "I have to talk to her as soon as I can."

Washburn's expression showed nothing. He brought his cigar to his lips, squinted his eyes against the smoke. "You got a card with your cell number? You got your phone on you?"

"Yes, sir."

"Let's have 'em both."

Hardy dug out his wallet, extracted his business card, gave the man his cellphone.

"Let's go find ourselves a little more light." He led the way out of the room, out of the store, stopped on the sidewalk outside and turned around to face Hardy. "You wait here." He walked off ten or fifteen steps and Hardy watched as he first punched some numbers, then talked into the phone, then read from Hardy's card, and finally closed the phone up. When he came back, he handed the phone back to him, pocketed the card in his shirt. "I like the dart on the card," he said. "Nice touch."

"Thank you."

"If she wants to talk to you, she'll call you. That's how I left it."

Hardy knew that that was all he was going to get, and damned lucky at that. If Catherine Mooney had remarried and changed her name, which was not unlikely, Washburn wasn't about to give it to him. Without the call, Hardy might never find her. "I appreciate it," he said.

Washburn waved the thanks away with his cigar. "Professional courtesy, Mr. Hardy. I'm sure you'd do the same for me."

"Could I ask you one more question?"

A quick smile washed away the merest

flash of impatience. "Certainly."

"In case I need to see her in person, would you recommend that I stay in the area, or go back up to the city?"

"And which city would that be? *Pace,*" he said. "A joke. I'd stay nearby."

"Good. Thank you."

Washburn checked his pocket watch again, nodded with satisfaction. "And with twenty seconds to spare, too. If I would have gone over, it would have cost you."

Now it was after six o'clock and Hardy brought his cup of espresso to the pay phone by the kitchen at Vino Santo Restaurant on Broadway, across the street from the tobacconists, about five blocks from the courthouse. He had his cellphone with him, of course, but he didn't want to use it and risk missing Catherine if she called.

"Hello," Frannie said.

"I'm assuming the kids must have put the phone in your bed, right? Which is how you're able to answer it."

"Dismas, I'm fine."

"In other words, not in bed as the doctor — no, scratch that, two doctors have ordered."

He heard her sigh. "Did you call to yell at me? Because if you did, you can just call back in a minute and leave it on the machine."

"I'm not going to yell at you. I'm calling to say I'm probably not getting home any-time soon. I'm down in Redwood City, hoping to talk to a witness for Andrew Bartlett. Are you making dinner?"

"No. As a matter of fact, our two dar-lings are cooking up something even as we speak. It smells delicious. What's gotten into them, do you think? They're being an-gels."

"They love their mother and want to take care of her, that's all. Since, appar-ently, she won't take care of herself."

"You didn't talk to them?"

"I talk to them all the time. It's what a father ought to do."

"That and not nag the mother."

"Unless she asks for it."

"Well, whatever you said, thank you. It's really made a difference."

"That's good to hear. Really," he said. Then added, "But you, don't push it, okay? I don't want to come home and have you on your back in bed."

She lowered her voice. "That's the sad-dest thing. You always used to."

"Here's a little secret," he said. "I still do."

Hardy next reached Wu at the office, where she was getting ready for tomorrow. She told him that the Brolin testimony had gone all right. Judge Johnson had given her considerable leeway with the psychologist, who'd painted Andrew in the best possible light — a young man who didn't need rehabilitation because he was essentially a good citizen already. As Hardy knew, they had also pulled Mr. Wagner from Sutro in, and he'd testified to Andrew's basic goodness, his extracurricular activities, talent for writing and the arts in general. Again, there was nothing to rehabilitate. Brandt had not even bothered to cross-examine, and Wu had thought it was because he was prepared to give her these criteria. After all, he only had to win one of them. "But Mr. Brandt fights everything, I'm learning. He called his own witness. Glen Taylor, the inspector who'd arrested him?"

"And what'd he say?"

"Well, Brandt leads him up from the beginning of the investigation, his first suspicions about Andrew, the mounting evidence, right up to the arrest, then asks him if in all that time, did Andrew show the slightest amount of remorse for what he'd done."

"You objected, of course."

"Of course, and even got sustained, but he just rephrased. 'Did Andrew at any time show any remorse about what had happened?' And of course Taylor said no."

Hardy, at his table at Vino Santo, drew

circles on his legal pad. There weren't any notes to take or comments to make. This was pretty much pro forma police testimony in proceedings of this kind, and wasn't particularly sophisticated or damning stuff. It sounded as though Wu had won her point.

He wasn't so sure, though, about the third criteria — the minor's previous delinquent history. This both he and Wu had considered a slam dunk, since Andrew had no real record. They hadn't even planned to call any witnesses, but would let that fact speak for itself. But again, the short lead time Andrew had demanded — aggravated by his suicide attempt — had left them unprepared and vulnerable to attack, and Brandt was ready for it. He called as witnesses two YGC counselors and another San Francisco police officer who had had occasion to meet with Andrew before this case. For while it was true that Andrew had never been "arrested or convicted," it turned out that, as Brandt phrased it, he had had "previous dealings with the police and youth authority." The joyride.

Wu had fought back with the standard argument that it hadn't been a serious offense — he'd never been arrested or even formally charged — but Hardy thought it was bad luck to get surprised in court, and at the very least doubted if they had helped

587

themselves on criteria number three.

And worse, he knew that the problem with number three would impact criteria number four. Obviously, given Andrew's presence in the courtroom and the fact that he was being charged with special circumstances murder argued more eloquently than mere words could against "the success of the juvenile court's previous attempts to rehabilitate" him. Like all criminal lawyers, Hardy and Wu both knew that once a defendant began showing up in courtrooms, the cycle was more likely than not to go on repeating itself. From the court's perspective, and although not legally accurate, this was really Andrew's second offense. Johnson would be aware of the statistics — people who appeared before him twice most often managed a third; then, as adults, they would start accumulating the strikes that would eventually get to three and put them in jail for life.

"I know we had no witnesses, but did you make any argument at all?" Hardy asked her.

"I just reiterated that he's got no record. There wasn't any previous effort at rehab to be successful or not. I know it sounds bad, but we've got to win these last two on the merits."

Hardy hoped she was right. In a completely fair world, she would be, but

Johnson had thus far shown himself to be so antagonistic that Hardy wasn't sure how it would come out. It wasn't impossible that he'd find against every one of the criteria as an object lesson for Wu to contemplate. And because no one could reasonably dispute his acceptance of the gravity criteria, Johnson would be immune from appeal on the other four. Rejection of any one of the criteria got Andrew into Superior Court as an adult, so the remaining four would be judicial largesse, a personal thumb to the nose.

But if it was to be, it was already done. "So where are we now?" Hardy asked.

"I've served the Salarcos," she said, meaning with subpoenas to appear in court. They'd be there tomorrow. "How are you doing with the wives?"

"Still hoping."

Silence. Wu asked, "You'll be in court tomorrow, though, right?"

"That's my plan."

"Because we're opening with your show."

"I'll be there," Hardy said. "Don't worry."

The cellphone rang an hour later. He'd had another cup of coffee, his first apple pie à la mode in probably ten years. Forgotten tastes, childhood memories. Delicious beyond imagining.

"Mr. Hardy?"

"Yes."

"This is Catherine Bass. I'm sorry I'm a little late getting back to you. We've got three kids under fifth grade and we just finished supper. But Everett Washburn said this was about Mike Mooney."

"Yes, ma'am."

Hardy thought her brittle laugh sounded nervous, or embarrassed. "Don't tell me he left me all his money."

"No. It's not that."

"I'm kidding, of course. Mike wouldn't have had any money." Then: "I was so sad when I heard about that. It's just so unbelievably sad."

Hardy gave her a second, then said, "I realize that this is an imposition, but would you mind if we talked in person? I won't take much of your time. I know about small children. I promise I won't keep you." Hardy's intention all along had been to get some face time with either of the wives. He didn't just want to verify the fact of Mooney's sexual orientation — after Steven Randell, he didn't have any real doubts about that. What he wanted was some sense of where it might have played in his married life, in the hope that some of the habits might have continued. Did he have secret liaisons? Long-term but hidden relationships? Was he consumed with smoldering anger or paralyzed by fear of exposure? Were there enemies? Lovers? Blackmailers?

Too much for a phone call with someone he'd never met.

She came back after talking to her husband. "Where are you?" she asked.

Catherine Bass, like his own wife, was a petite redhead. She didn't have Frannie's world-class cheekbones; her skin was a bit more freckled and her hair cropped short, but with her striking green eyes and dimples as she smiled, she was very attractive nonetheless. Hardy had the impression that she was still dressed from a day of work at some professional job — she wore low black heels, a gray knee-length skirt, a black turtleneck sweater. She exuded a confident warmth as Hardy stood and they shook hands.

He thanked her for coming to meet him. She waved that off as they both sat and the waitress came to the table — by now Hardy was a resident. Catherine ordered herself a dessert called a chocolate heart attack. "I've got CDD," she said by way of explanation, breaking that dimpled smile again.

"No, let me guess." Hardy was immediately taken with her. After a second, he said, "Chocolate something something."

"You're not from around here, are you? Or it would be obvious. Chocolate Deficit Disorder. It's pretty serious."

"Why would I have known that if I lived around here?"

"Because here in the lovely south Peninsula, you have kids and you hear 'D' attached to anything, you know it means disorder. You may not realize it, but right now we're sitting in the Ritalin capital of the world. Every second or third child here has ADD. Or maybe ADHD. At least something."

"Why is that? I mean, why's it so big down here?"

She leaned in toward him and lowered her voice. "This is heresy," she said. "I could be shot if anyone heard me, but it's because they test for it."

"Who does?"

"Any parents with a difficult kid. Your children are failing or acting up in school, take them to a shrink, have them tested for ADD. And see if you can guess — you're a shrink looking for a condition where, if it's present, you've got a lifelong patient and endless billings."

"They tend to find it?"

"Surprising, is it not? Kind of like asking a car mechanic if you really need the brake job." She shook her head. "Because it's not that kids crave attention from their both too busy and can't be bothered parents, it's that they're born with a disorder. Not the parents' fault, not the kid's, either, which is the way we like things down here. Don't get me started."

Hardy was grinning at her. "I thought you already had."

"It's my job," she said. "Forgive me."

"Nothing to forgive."

"I know I get tedious. I'm trying to stop." The dimples. "Chocolate will help."

Hardy wanted to keep her talking until she was comfortable, and it didn't seem like that was going to be much of a chore. "What do you do?"

"I'm a city attorney, believe it or not. I do code enforcement on foster homes and shrinks, mostly, but my real mission is this over-prescribing of Ritalin. It really is an epidemic down here. Maybe it's everywhere parents can afford to get their kids tested, I don't know. Maybe kids have fundamentally changed since I was growing up and everybody needs to be medicated. But if you want my opinion, and it looks like you're going to get it anyway, it's that most of the time — not always, I admit — kids have this attention deficit because they don't get attention from their parents. Is it that complicated? Oh God." She brought her hand to her forehead. "I'm sorry. Especially if your kids have it, and they probably do, don't they?"

"No. Sometimes they get COUD, but we don't medicate for that. We just bust them pretty good."

It took her a second. "Center of universe disorder?"

"You're good," he said, smiling. "You must do this all the time."

The waitress arrived. "This will shut me up." She stuck a spoon into the dessert, brought it to her mouth, savored. "Okay," she said, "Mike. You know, I never asked you what about Mike you wanted to talk about."

"But you still came down here?"

"I still cared about him, although I hadn't seen him in years. He was a good guy."

Hardy kept his opinion on that to himself. "That's what everybody says. But somebody killed him and I'm trying to find out why."

"Somebody? I understood they had a pretty solid suspect." An awareness gathered in her eyes. She killed a few seconds licking her spoon. "You're defending the killer?"

Hardy had gone through this so often that he was tempted to wave it off. But it was the first time that Catherine Bass would have heard it, and he had to give the objection its weight. "The alleged killer, yes. Andrew Bartlett. But I expect he'll be released maybe as soon as tomorrow. I'm all but certain he didn't do it. I want to find out who did."

"And you think I might know? I haven't laid eyes on Mike in years."

"I realize that." He paused, then came out with it. "Mrs. Bass, I know he was gay."

She closed her eyes for a second, drew a deep breath and let it out. "All right."

"I'm wondering if that might have played some role in his death."

"If what did? Being gay? How would it do that?"

"I don't know. If he had some secret life . . . ?"

She poked the chocolate with her spoon. "Wasn't someone else killed with him? A girl? One of his students?"

"Yes."

"That doesn't really point to a sinister gay secret life to me."

"It doesn't to me, either. She might not have been part of the original plan, but as a witness she had to be eliminated."

"Do you really think that?"

"I really don't know. I'm hoping my client is innocent. Beyond that, I'm fishing. But it would be helpful to get the simple fact of Mike's gayness out in front of the judge."

"And how would that help?"

"It might punch some holes in the prosecution's motive theory."

"What about his father?"

Hardy's own expression had grown somber. "I know. I've been trying to figure that one out. Bring it out in chambers, seal the record, something. I see you've dealt with it, too."

Her mouth was a hard line. "God, those years. When I compare them to how I live now . . ."

"How long were you together?"

Her eyes came back to him. "Not so long in real time, I guess. Thirty months, something like that, beginning to end." Her mouth tried to signal a kind of apology for getting so personal. "It was an eternity, though, in psychic time. We really were best friends, even back when he was with Terri. I was the other woman, you know, in their marriage. Broke them up. It was really pretty funny, actually, if you had a taste for irony."

"Did you know?"

"About his being gay? Not at first. At the time . . . hell, you know . . . we were young and living the theater life, all of us. It was assumed that we all led active sexual lives and that some of us experimented with . . . various combinations. We didn't see it as a big deal. And Mike was pretty . . ." She laughed again with the brittle embarrassment Hardy had first heard on the phone with her. "Actually, he *was* pretty, period. Gorgeous. And promiscuous as all hell, trying to prove what he wasn't, you know? God! Was it exciting! Drama every day, especially when he, when we, were cheating on Terri. Sometimes she'd be out on stage doing a scene — I mean in plain sight, thirty feet from us. Jesus."

He gave her a minute to come back to him. "So how did you find out?"

Hanging her head, she drew her dessert near and picked at it. "After we got married, we had a couple of good months. But pretty soon the . . . the physical side . . . I guess what turned him on was the forbidden fruit aspect. When I stopped being that . . ." Her shoulders rose, then fell. "But as I said, we were friends. We liked to do the same things. So at first we pretended everything was the same, fooling ourselves, you know. I'm not sure if Mike really admitted to himself that he was strictly gay, even then. We were always together and busy and . . . shit, I may as well tell you . . . we never had sex in our bed. It was always someplace we might get caught. For me, that got a little old, but as long as we had our busy routine and found time to sneak away, I told myself that we were intimate enough. The lies we tell ourselves, huh? And then, as it turned out — nobody's fault — but the routine changed on us anyway."

"What happened?"

"Mike got called to jury duty."

31

"Lucas Welding. Write it down." Hardy was in his car, speeding north, talking to Glitsky. It was 10:30 and he'd left Catherine Bass fifteen minutes before. His right hand was sore from taking notes, but he remembered everything he'd written. "In 1984, he strangled and murdered his wife, Ginny. Got tried and convicted in San Francisco in '86, sentenced to LWOP."

"But he's out now?"

"Looks like."

"How'd that happen?"

"I don't know. But Mrs. Bass, Mooney's ex-wife, is a lawyer herself now and remembered Boscacci distinctly as the prosecutor. She's followed his career ever since. I'll bet you a million dollars that your Elizabeth Cary was on the same jury."

"You said you're in your car. Where are you?"

"Just passing the airport."

"Meet you at the Hall," Glitsky said. "Twenty minutes."

Since the ground floor of the Hall of Justice was the location of SFPD's Southern Station, the building was open. Hardy and Glitsky opened the front door together and passed through the metal detectors and security cops in the lobby. Lanier was already waiting for them in the hallway outside Glitsky's office, and the three of them filed into the small conference room behind the reception area.

By earlier that afternoon, they'd finally managed to set up a total of six borrowed computers for the use of the two General Work officers and the twenty-two others that both Jackman had provided and Glitsky had recruited out of their respective clerical staffs. All overtime expenses paid.

It had taken a good part of the afternoon to get the computers up and connected, but when Glitsky had left work that night, all of them had been in use. Six volunteers at a time worked the list of four hundred recently released convicts, while six others — armed with case numbers from the computer searches — went downstairs and under the building to Records, where they searched for the physical files on the Boscacci "hits."

By the time of Glitsky's departure earlier that night, out of the first 154 they'd identified seven cases where Boscacci had been the actual trial prosecutor. At 8:00 p.m., the second "shift" of twelve was scheduled to come in and continue through the night and then the next morning, until they got something.

But now the room was empty.

"Where is everybody?" Glitsky asked.

"They're all downstairs," Lanier said. "They got the case number on Welding five minutes after you called. Finding the physical records isn't so easy. It may be a while. He wasn't in your original four hundred, you know."

"So he didn't get out in the last two months," Glitsky said.

"Where'd they keep him?" Hardy asked.

"Corcoran, according to the computer."

Hardy threw a glance at Glitsky, came back to Lanier. "And he's out now?"

"Pretty much got to be if he's killing people, don't you think?"

Glitsky took Hardy's silent cue. "We call, tie it up. If it turns out this guy is the Executioner, we want to know everything about him. The warden gets a wake-up."

Hardy and Lanier followed him around the corner to his office, where he flipped through his Rolodex and picked up the telephone. After a short wait, he identified himself by name and rank and said he needed a record on one of the prison's inmates immediately. It was urgent.

Glitsky listened for a while, then said, "Yes, I realize that. But if he's the only one with that access at this time of night, then I need to talk to him." Another pause while the scar in Glitsky's lips went white. Then: "Could I get your name and rank, please? Thank you, Sergeant Gray. Listen, I could have the mayor of San Francisco call again in five minutes, and possibly even the governor after that, but that seems like a lot of unnecessary trouble. I'll take full responsibility."

Glitsky spelled his name, left his badge and telephone number, hung up. "I guess the warden likes his beauty rest," he said.

They heard the elevator and the scuffle of feet, and in a minute the small army of twelve volunteers had gathered again in the computer room. They'd brought up two large gray rolling trolleys, each about four by six feet wide and three feet high, and on them were piled what looked to be about twenty cardboard boxes. The lead guy, who was in uniform, saluted Glitsky. "This is the case, sir, or as much of it as we could find. Lucas Welding. Eighty-six. There's no room and worse light down there, so we thought we'd bring it up. What are we looking for?"

"The jurors," Glitsky said. "Also, just to be thorough, let's make sure Allan Boscacci tried the case."

Everyone, including Hardy, took a box and started going through the paper — endless, endless reams of paper, the complete record of a California murder trial. The boxes contained everything from the initial police reports to the autopsy and forensics information, to witness interviews, as well as all discovery, prosecution notes, expert witness testimony and background, the transcript of the trial itself. After fifteen minutes, one of the workers said, "I've got Boscacci. Here's the what-do-you-call-it, the front page."

"The caption page," Hardy said, although nobody looked up or seemed to care.

Glitsky jumped, though, and was looking at it. "Okay. So far so good." He flipped through a few of the following pages in that document, then closed it and handed the whole thing back. "Let's keep going," he said.

A long twenty-five minutes after that, Lanier's easy delivery broke the silence. "Here we go." He was sitting across the table from Glitsky, and slid the document across, while everyone else — some from out in the reception area — stopped what they were doing to look.

Glitsky read for a moment, then put a hand to his scar and pulled at it. "He's the one," he said in a hoarse and strangled tone. Then, clearing his throat, he read aloud. "Philip Wong, Michael Mooney, Edith Montrose, Morris Tollman."

"What about Elizabeth Cary?" Hardy asked.

Glitsky looked down, nodded. "Elizabeth Reed. That was her maiden name."

"Jesus Christ," someone whispered.

"I doubt it," Lanier said. "He wouldn't have come back for a murder trial." To a titter of nervous laughter.

But Glitsky was already punching numbers into the phone on the desk, a muscle working in his jaw. While he was waiting, another phone rang in his office. "Diz. That's the warden. Get it," he ordered. "Tell him I'll be right there." Hardy jumped.

"Marcel." Glitsky handed Lanier the conference room phone he'd been using. "That's Batiste. When he picks up, tell him what we've got and that I'll be right back. Now or sooner we're going to need eight teams at least, *at least,* to protect the people who are left." He was moving back to his office. "And when you're done, put out an all points on Welding ASAP."

In his own office, Glitsky strode in and grabbed the phone from Hardy. "Warden Fischer," he said. "This is Glitsky. Thanks for getting back to me. I don't know if you're familiar with these Executioner killings we've been having . . . Okay, great. In the last hour or so, we've developed a tentative ID on the suspect and believe he was staying at your place until recently. We're going to need all the information you have on him immediately — last known address, next of kin, the works. He went up in '86, LWOP. I know. I wondered about that, too. Welding. W-E-L-D-I-N-G. Lucas. Yeah, I'm sure. Why?"

Hardy watched Glitsky's face, already hard, turn to stone. The eyes narrowed, the lips went tight, the jaw muscle by his ear quivered. His hand went to his side and he pushed in as though trying to reposition his intestines. Then, for a long frozen moment, he ceased to move entirely. Finally, he asked, "You're sure?" Then, "Yes, of course, I see. Thank you."

He hung up, raised his head, saw Hardy standing there. "Lucas Welding is dead," he said.

For the next half hour, Glitsky was a dervish. Other people might still be at risk. Knowing that there had to be a connection between the Executioner and Lucas Welding, he sent people to find the names of all of Welding's visitors at Corcoran; correspondents, cell mates, people who put money on his book; everyone who had ever met the guy. He assigned the other half of his volunteers in pairs to track down the other jurors from Welding's trial. Check phone books and reverse listings. Get unlisted numbers from the phone company. Go online — somebody had to know how to locate individuals by name and get their address. Be aware of the maiden name issue. Leave messages with DMV and any federal agency they could think of. Wake up anybody they needed to, the jury records people. He didn't know precisely how the connection fit yet, but he knew that it did.

He ran down the hall to homicide and stopped Lanier from issuing the APB.

Back in his office, he briefed Batiste on the general situation and told him he wanted to assign protection officers to the jury people — to have teams of two standing by to deploy as soon as he could locate the jurors. Then they had to reschedule other officers to fill the affected shifts. Everyone's time would be on the Boscacci event number, if that met with the Chief's approval, which it did.

Hardy listened in, picking up the information secondhand. "He died two months ago in the infirmary in Corcoran," Glitsky told the Chief. "Fischer remembered specifically because it was a bit of a deal — he'd just been cleared on appeal. DNA. It looks like he really didn't do it. But then the cancer got him first."

"If that's true, it's ugly," Hardy said as he hung up. "They put away an innocent man?"

"Looks like." From the expression on his face, Glitsky wasn't happy about it either. "The Executioner seems pretty upset about it, too."

"I can't say I blame him."

Glitsky's look went black. "You don't?"

Hardy held up a palm. "Easy. For what he feels. Not for what he's doing."

"He does what he's doing, I don't care how he feels."

This certainly wasn't the time to discuss it, and Hardy wasn't sure he disagreed so much anyway. Injustice happened, he knew, and sometimes — perhaps with Welding — even innocently. Revenge and violence wasn't going to make anything better. At least, that was the theory. "So who is it?" Hardy asked. "Did he have a kid maybe? Some other relative?"

Glitsky, still in "do something" mode, snapped his fingers and picked up his desk telephone again. "Fischer" — the warden — "will know that. Where are you going?"

"Home." Hardy looked at his watch. "It's twelve-thirty and I've got a hearing this morning."

"You don't want to know how this comes out?"

"I know how this comes out, Abe. For my client."

Glitsky had certainly already known this on some level — Hardy had given him the first inkling of it the night before on the telephone, and tonight the Mooney connection through Catherine Bass had all but cinched it — but suddenly it hit him fresh. He put the phone down on the desk. "And the girl, too."

Hardy nodded. "Laura Wright. She just happened to be there."

32

At 9:40 on Wednesday morning, Dismas Hardy stood up at his place at the defense table and addressed the juvenile court for the first time *In the Matter of Minor: Andrew Bartlett.*

"Your honor," he said. "Before we begin argument and witnesses today, I think it will save the court considerable time and trouble if counsel meet in camera for a few minutes."

Johnson, perhaps sensing shenanigans, considered for a long moment. "We just got out here, Mr. Hardy. I'd like to get a little work done before we take a break."

"We may not need to do the work, your honor. There is new and pertinent information about this case, critical evidence that will, I believe, be persuasive to the court and perhaps even lead to dismissal of all charges against Mr. Bartlett."

The courtroom, as always, was nearly empty, but his words still created an audible buzz from the Norths, who sat behind Hardy, and even from the bailiffs, the clerk and the recorder. Brandt, who sat to Hardy's right, at the prosecution table, pushed his chair back and stared with frank amazement.

Johnson pulled himself up to his full height in his chair behind the bench. "As I mentioned to you at the outset, Mr. Hardy, we're not here to consider the criminal charges against Mr. Bartlett. The purpose of this hearing, and it's *only* purpose, is to determine *where* Mr. Bartlett gets tried — here or in adult court. Not *whether*."

"Of course, your honor, I understand that. Nevertheless, the import of this new information is rather extraordinary and I believe the court will want to have heard it."

"To save the time that is obviously so important to you?"

"To prevent a grave injustice, your honor. I'm talking perhaps ten minutes, maybe less."

Johnson wore his reluctance like a shroud, but finally, shaking his head in disgust, he turned to Brandt. "Does the petitioner have any objection?"

"Nothing substantive, your honor."

"All right. I'll see counsel in my chambers." Johnson stood. "Ten minutes." And he left the courtroom by the back door.

★ ★ ★

Johnson, his arms crossed over his chest, stood in his robes in the middle of his room, so that when the three lawyers trooped in behind him, there really wasn't anyplace for them to go. After Brandt closed the door behind them, they stood with their backs to the wall, their faces to the intractable judge. "All right, Mr. Hardy, we're in chambers. As you can probably tell, I'm not in much of a trifling mood, so let's hear what's so important."

Hardy nodded. "Thank you, your honor. I'll cut to the chase. Andrew Bartlett didn't kill Mike Mooney and I have information which I believe rises to the level of proof, and I think you'll agree."

But Johnson was already shaking his head no. "I won't agree because I won't hear it."

"Pardon?"

"I can't imagine, Mr. Hardy, how I could have made it more clear to you that this seven-oh-seven is not about Mr. Bartlett's guilt or innocence."

Hardy, striving for equanimity, inclined his head an inch in deference. "Yes, your honor, I understand, but this —"

"You say you understand, and follow it with a 'but.' That sounds like an argument coming up. Do you hear yourself?"

"Your honor, forgive me. I'm not trying

to be argumentative. I'm trying to present information that you will, I'm sure, find compelling."

"About your client's guilt or innocence?"

Hardy knew the wrong answer, and tried to avoid it. "About the circumstances of the crime. Which would make it fall under criteria five."

"All right, but be careful." Johnson cocked his head. "We're getting a little obscure here, Counselor."

"I'm talking about the person they're calling the Executioner."

"What about him?"

Brandt got on the boards. "Excuse me, but wait a minute. This sounds to me like we're getting back to who committed these murders."

"It does to me, too," Johnson said. "Mr. Hardy, you're not going to imply, I hope, that some unknown serial killer *might* be guilty of the crimes for which your client is charged."

"Your honor, with respect, it's not a question of *might*. I was in the Hall of Justice last night with Deputy Chief Glitsky. He identified a defendant in a seventeen-year-old case with connections to Allan Boscacci as well as to all the so-called Executioner victims . . ."

"And you're saying the victims in this case . . ."

"I'm saying Mike Mooney and Laura Wright were killed by the Executioner, yes."

"Excuse me," Brandt said again. "Did I miss something? Have they caught him?"

"No."

"Has someone confessed?"

Hardy came back to Johnson. "That's not the point, your honor. Glitsky knows who he is, but hasn't been able to identify him yet by name."

Johnson barked a note of derision. "So he's known but unidentified, whatever that means. It seems we've gotten to quite a long throw from whether or not Mr. Bartlett is an adult."

"I'm getting there, your honor."

"You are? You know, Mr. Hardy, I don't believe you are. Is Mr. Bartlett somehow related to this known but unidentified Executioner?"

"No."

"May I ask how you can know that one way or the other if you don't know who the man is?" The judge gathered himself for a moment, then pointed an accusatory finger at Hardy. "This is *exactly* the type of alternative theory hocus-pocus that I warned you against at the outset, and warned you again before we came back here to chambers."

"But this isn't hocus-pocus, your honor.

You can call Deputy Chief Glitsky and —"

Johnson finally raised his voice. *"I don't have to call anyone!* If there is strong enough evidence to warrant revisiting the charges against Mr. Bartlett, I'm sure Mr. Brandt will hear about it from the district attorney. Mr. Brandt, have you gotten any calls today on this topic?"

"No, your honor."

He turned to Hardy. "Then this court is going to assume, Mr. Hardy, that the current charges are still in effect. If Mr. Bartlett is demonstrably innocent of them, I'm sure that Mr. Jackman will drop them and let Mr. Brandt know as soon as he can. But in the meanwhile, until I hear otherwise, Mr. Bartlett is in the middle of an administrative process to determine where he gets tried. That's all that's happening here. Enough of this!"

Hardy, in a bit of a fury of his own, took a step forward, moving into the judge's personal space. "To the contrary, your honor, with all respect. There has not been enough of this. If it's your decision to refuse to hear what I've got to say, then when we get outside I'm going to open up by making a representation to the court and getting it on the record."

Johnson glared at him. "Talk all you want, Mr. Hardy. Sooner or later you'll have to stop and we'll get on with it."

"If it please the court." They were all back in the courtroom. Hardy didn't even sit down, but got back to his table, turned and spoke. "Last night, acting on information received from a classmate of Andrew Bartlett, I spoke to a woman named Catherine Bass, who was at one time the wife of Michael Mooney." Because proceedings in juvenile court were kept confidential, Hardy could bring up the bare fact of Mooney's sexuality here if he needed to and still keep it out of the public record. But now he realized with some relief that there was no reason even for that. "She informed me, and subsequently I have verified it as true, that in 1984, Michael Mooney served on a jury here in San Francisco in the case of *People v. Lucas Welding*, a murder case. The prosecutor in that case was Allan Boscacci. Other members of that jury included" — Hardy looked down and checked his notes — "Elizabeth Cary, born Elizabeth Reed, Edith Montrose, Philip Wong, and Morris Tollman. All of these people, the jurors I've mentioned and Allan Boscacci, have been murder victims in the past three weeks."

Next to him, he heard Andrew — his neck brace gone now — whisper to Wu, "Is that true?" Even within the bullpen, he saw the bailiffs exchange glances with each other and then the court recorder. Johnson picked up his gavel, then put it back down. It was the first time that he was hearing all of this in detail, and Hardy hoped that the recitation would make an impression.

"Upon receiving this information, I immediately called San Francisco's deputy chief of inspectors, Abe Glitsky, and subsequently met him at the Hall of Justice, where he discovered that Lucas Welding, who had been convicted and sentenced to life in prison for the murder of his wife, had recently won a reversal of his conviction based upon DNA evidence that had not been presented at the original trial. He had been ordered released from prison, but during the course of his appeal, he had developed cancer and ultimately died at the infirmary at the Corcoran Penitentiary before he could be released."

Hardy stopped, wondering if that was enough. It certainly had been plenty for him and Glitsky. He threw a look over to Brandt, but the prosecutor was sitting slumped in his chair, his head down, his hands clasped on his lap. Johnson himself appeared to be waiting for more, and if that door was open, Hardy thought he should walk through it.

"Deputy Chief Glitsky has assigned several inspectors first to find and protect the other jurors from the Welding case, and second to identify and locate anyone who might have had a relationship with Welding, and whose rage over Welding's seventeen years of incarceration for a crime he did not commit might have become a motive for the murders of Allan Boscacci and several members of the convicting jury." He paused to let his words reverberate for a moment, then added, "Including," he said, "the murder of Michael Mooney."

Brandt was sitting up straight now. Johnson was taking some notes at the podium. When he was finished, he looked up. His eyes went first to Brandt, then to the gallery, where Hal and Linda were whispering, then finally back to the defense table. "Thank you, Mr. Hardy. Your representation is noted for the record. Is that the substance of it?"

"Yes, your honor."

"All right, then, let's move on. Do you have another witness for this seven-oh-seven proceeding?"

"Wait a minute." Andrew's voice was still fairly hoarse, but carried in the courtroom. "If you know that somebody else killed Mooney . . ."

Behind him, Hardy heard the Norths and he turned. Hal was on his feet. "That ought to be the end of this," he was saying. Both bailiffs — Nelson and Cottrell —

stood quickly and moved out from their positions on either wall.

"But this is nuts," Andrew was saying to Wu. "It proves what I've been saying from the beginning." He got to his feet and spoke up to the court in general, back to his mother. "It's what I've been telling you guys all along . . ."

Johnson gaveled him quiet. A sharp, loud *crack*. "I'll have order in this courtroom. Mr. North, sit down. Mr. Hardy, Ms. Wu, I'm warning you, get your client under control." Both bailiffs stopped in their tracks for a moment, then Cottrell, with a warning glare at Wu and Hardy, walked out through the bullpen gate and into the gallery.

Hardy turned and watched Cottrell as he continued back past the Norths and positioned himself by the back door.

Wu stood up. "But, your honor, surely the import of Mr. Hardy's —"

Johnson brought down his gavel again. "Ms. Wu. I said that's enough."

Shaking her head in frustration and anger, Wu shared a look with Hardy, put her hand on Andrew's arm to calm him, and sat back down. Hardy was still on his feet. "Your honor," he said, "it's obvious to everyone in this courtroom that Andrew Bartlett did not kill Mike Mooney."

Brandt was up across the room. "Your

618

honor, if it please the court. It's not obvious to me. I've got an eyewitness and a great deal of evidence that says he did. And what about the other victim in this case, Laura Wright? Andrew Bartlett's girlfriend? Does defense counsel contend that she was on this Mr. Welding's bad luck jury, too?"

Hardy spoke to the judge. "Your honor, she was killed because she happened to be there and Mooney's killer did not want to leave a witness."

Johnson used his gavel again, then waited while the courtroom went to complete silence. Finally, he drew a long breath. "Mr. Hardy, I reject your conclusion that your representation rises to the level of proof in the matter before this court. I'll admit that it does rise to the level of coincidence, and the court does not find that compelling. Also, it doesn't change the essential fact of the gravity of the offense — Mr. Mooney and Ms. Wright were murdered. The district attorney has not withdrawn the charges against Mr. Bartlett, nor has he conveyed the gravemen of your most recent information to the court or to Mr. Brandt. As I've already mentioned several times, this seven-oh-seven is about whether Mr. Bartlett is a juvenile or an adult and that's all it's about."

"But, your honor —"

Crack! "Mr. Hardy, your representation is noted for the record. What do you expect me to do, drop the charges?"

"I don't think that would be unreasonable, your honor, given the enormity of what you're calling the coincidence. Mr. Mooney and Ms. Wright were both killed by someone connected to Lucas Welding, and there's no such connection with Andrew Bartlett."

"I understand that that's your theory, Mr. Hardy. Now do you have another witness, or is it time that I make a ruling?"

Hardy bit the inside of his mouth hard. Looking down to his right at Andrew, he whispered, "Hang in there," then came back to the judge and said, "We'd like to call Anna Salarco, your honor."

"All right." Johnson looked to his left — Cottrell's standard position in the courtroom — and frowned. He turned in the other direction. "Officer Nelson, would you please go out to the hallway and call the witness? Anna Salarco. And while you're out there, if you see Officer Cottrell, would you ask him if he'd care to join us again in the courtroom?"

There followed some minutes of confusion. Hardy had told Anna Salarco that they'd call her as a witness as soon as the court was called to session, but then they'd all had the meeting in chambers and Hardy's representation to the court. In the interim, evidently, both of the Salarcos had left the hallway to go to the bathroom. Maybe Bailiff Cottrell had gone looking for them. In any event, Cottrell was still missing from the courtroom when Anna Salarco finally, and nervously, took the witness stand.

Hardy walked her through the by-now familiar recital, making sure to memorialize for the record the understanding that the Salarcos thought they had with the police regarding their immigration status, which Hardy believed served as a strong incentive for Juan to refuse to change his story. When they'd finished, Anna's testimony was all Hardy could have wished for. Just before her husband had gone downstairs and discovered the bodies, she had clearly seen the man leaving the house after the door had slammed, and could not identify him as Andrew. Hardy thanked her and turned her over to Brandt for cross-examination.

Much to Hardy's displeasure, Brandt and Anna weren't complete strangers anymore. Wu told him that when the prosecutor had seen her name on the list, he, too, had called the Salarcos, then gone out to visit with them last night himself. This was why Juan was out in the hallway now, waiting for his chance to talk to the court and possibly refute whatever his wife had said first.

So Brandt advanced to the witness box with a relaxed demeanor. "Mrs. Salarco," he began, "how far is it from your window to the sidewalk in front of your house?"

"I don't know exactly."

"Approximately, then."

She shot a glance at Hardy and he nodded with some confidence. This question was not unexpected. "Thirty feet, maybe forty."

"Thirty or forty feet, thank you. That's about the distance from where you're sitting to the back of this courtroom, is that right?"

Hardy turned around to check and saw that Brandt wasn't far off.

"Something like," Mrs. Salarco said. "Yes."

"And you and your husband live on the second floor of your building, do you not?"

"Yes."

"So you were looking down at the person you saw?"

"Yes."

"And he was wearing a cowl?" At her confused expression, he mimicked with his hands, and added, "A sweatshirt with a hood over his head?"

"*Sí*. Yes."

"Did it cover his whole head?"

Again, she looked at Hardy, and again he nodded. What else could he do? He had to let her tell her story and hope it came out as credible.

She nodded back at Brandt. "Yes. But not his whole face."

"Did it cover part of his face, then?"

She paused. "Yes." Then added, "He looked up."

God bless her, Hardy thought.

But Brandt came right back at her. "What do you mean by that, Mrs. Salarco? That he looked up? Do you mean —"

Hardy stalled to let the witness get composed. "Objection."

"Sustained."

Brandt was ready, though. "At any time, did the hood come off the man's head?"

"No."

"It covered the top of his head and part of his face?"

Hardy stood again, objecting.

"Sustained."

"All right. Let me ask you this, Mrs. Salarco? Was it dark outside at this time? Nighttime?"

"Yes, but —"

"Yes is sufficient, thank you," Brandt said, cutting her off. He must have decided that he'd made enough of his point, and switched gears. "Mrs. Salarco, were you present at the police lineup where your husband identified the person who'd been downstairs at Mr. Mooney's apartment that night?"

"Yes."

"Did you take part in that lineup, too?"

"Yes."

"And you failed to identify anyone in the lineup as the person you saw that night, is that right?"

"Yes."

"You were given a form, and then signed the form, saying you didn't recognize anyone in the lineup, is that right?"

"Yes."

"And Mr. Bartlett, sitting at that table over there" — he turned and pointed — "you did not recognize him?"

"Your honor." Hardy was up again.

"I'm getting to something here, your honor," Brandt said.

"All right." Johnson nodded. "Objection overruled, but get to it."

"Mrs. Salarco, when you did not positively identify anyone in the lineup as the man below your window, did you mean that you didn't know *whether* it was one of the people in the lineup or not? It might have been or it might not have been. Or did you mean to say that none of those people in the lineup was the man you saw?

That is, you could not definitely say that it was Andrew?"

Her eyes by now filled with fear, Anna Salarco looked to Hardy for support, but there was nothing he could do. She came back to Brandt. "I'm sorry. I don't understand."

"Your honor," Brandt said. "May I rephrase?"

"Go ahead."

Brandt gave her a warm smile and stepped a bit closer to her. "Mrs. Salarco," he said, "we are trying to understand exactly what it is that you want to tell the court. At the lineup, you said you could not identify anyone, is that correct?"

"Yes."

"All right. Did you mean that it *could not have been* Andrew? That it was *impossible* that it was Andrew down below you thirty or forty feet away, with a hood over his head on a dark night?"

"No. Maybe not impossible, but —"

Brandt rushed her with the follow-up. "So your testimony now is that what you meant to say was that you couldn't positively identify the person as Andrew? Is that right? That you weren't sure enough to swear to it."

"*Sí,*" she said. "I could not swear to it that it was him."

"Ah." Brandt rewarded her with a

beaming smile. "Thank you, Mrs. Salarco." He whirled to Hardy. "Redirect."

He wanted to take a short recess, perhaps confer with Wu and give Anna a few minutes to collect herself and perhaps realize what she'd said. But he didn't think he could afford to wait. "Mrs. Salarco," he began. "Is there a streetlight in front of your house?"

"Yes."

"Was it on — that is, lit up — when you saw the man come from the downstairs apartment, turn, and look up at you?"

"Yes."

"And could you see the man's face?"

"Yes."

"And was it Andrew's face?"

She stopped, looked for a long time at the defense table, then finally shook her head. "No," she said. "Was not that boy."

During the lunch recess, Hardy stood out in the back lobby making phone calls, to Glitsky, to his wife, to the office. As he was finishing up the last one, he noticed Wu and Brandt sitting on a bench next to the walkway that led up to the cabins. From his vantage, they appeared to be arguing, but there was something about their body language that set Hardy's alarms jangling. Since there wasn't a jury that might be influenced by seeing the opposing attorneys schmoozing during lunch, their tête-à-tête wasn't the breach in trial decorum it might otherwise have been. But still, especially given the Norths' presence just up the hill in the cabins having lunch with their son, Hardy did not think it presented a picture that would be particularly comforting to the clients.

He put away his cellphone, walked out the back door, and started to approach them. When he got close, he noticed the silent signal pass from Brandt to Wu, and they both shut up and put on different faces. Hardy gave them both a polite hello.

"Any word from Glitsky?" Wu asked him.

"He's not answering, so I'm assuming he's too busy. I left a message that we want to know the second he's got anything firm. Meanwhile, I'm going up to have a word with Andrew and his folks. If I'm not interrupting anything here, you want to come along?"

Coming from her boss, this wasn't really a request. Wu hesitated, then stood up and fell in next to him as he continued walking. "He's not going to call Juan Salarco," she said.

Hardy nodded, believing that the decision was the proper one. Though Juan's testimony might have undercut his wife's credibility somewhat, in the end his identification of Andrew in the lineup was already on the record, and the differences in the stories and interpretations of the husband and wife were what juries were for. Further, once he got on the stand, Hardy or Wu would have a chance to cross-examine him and perhaps expose other weaknesses that they could later exploit at the trial. "So that's it for witnesses then?"

"It looks like."

"Then it's over. We get the ruling when we go back in." Hardy took a few more steps, then asked, "What were you two arguing about? It wasn't that he isn't calling Salarco."

"No, it's that he won't call Jackman."

"Why should he? As his honor was kind enough to point out, if they get anything, Jackman will call him. Mr. Brandt is just playing it out."

"A game, right."

"Well, in some ways it is a game, Wu. You know that."

"Not for Andrew," she said.

"No, though it was when you started with him, wasn't it?"

Her shoulders fell with the truth of that. "It's just that keeping track of when it's a game and when it's not" — she broke a weary smile — "it can wear a girl out." They hadn't yet reached the gate that enclosed the cabins, and Wu stopped walking. "But this is just so clearly wrong, don't you think? Andrew didn't kill anybody."

"No. I don't believe he did either."

"That's what I asked Jason, whether or not he believed it. He said that wasn't the point. He didn't want to go there."

"He's right. His job right now is to present the petitioner's argument."

"Even if he knows it's wrong?"

"Even then. And in this case, he doesn't *know* he's wrong. He's just a lot more likely to be wrong than he used to be."

"And so Andrew winds up screwed again?"

"You don't want to be screwed, don't get in the system. But for the time being, that's what it looks like. But it won't last much longer, I don't think."

Wu bit her lip, shook her head. "This is all my fault, you know that? Every bit of it. If I hadn't been so arrogant and stupid, Johnson might be listening to all this new information with an open mind, instead of being so blind . . . I mean, what if Andrew had succeeding in killing himself? That would have been completely my fault. And now, every extra minute that he spends in jail . . ."

Hardy stopped her. "You thought you were doing what was best for your client. That's the job."

"But he wasn't guilty."

"You didn't know that. You thought he was."

"I *always* thought they were. They always have been before."

"Okay, so maybe you won't think that anymore. It's not all about strategy and leverage. Sometimes — not often, I grant you, but sometimes — it's about the truth."

The small visitors' room was too small for all of them, so Bailiff Nelson had accompanied Andrew, Hardy, Wu and the Norths back down the hill to the courtroom, where they now sat. "But this makes no sense at all," Linda North said. "We know that Mr. Mooney and Laura were both killed by this Executioner, don't we?" She looked around at them all, wide-eyed. "Don't we all know that? Is it just me?"

Hardy nodded. "No, it's not just you, and yes, we know it. But we don't have proof."

"What more proof would we need?" Hal asked.

"Physical evidence," Hardy said. "We know that they've matched the slugs that killed at least three of the Executioner's victims. I'm asking the police to take another pass at Mooney's place, try to find the slugs. Either they'll do it or I'll find some investigators and pay them to."

"But what if nobody finds them?" Linda asked.

"Then maybe they'll find this Executioner and he'll confess to killing Mooney. Or maybe Juan Salarco could withdraw his ID. Any of those would be good."

"But what if," Linda went on, "what if we don't get any of them? Are you saying they won't let Andrew go?"

"They still might, yes," Hardy said. "But they might not."

"And in the meanwhile," Andrew said in his damaged voice, "what happens to me?"

"I'll be here," his mother said to him. "I'll be here every day."

"We'll both be here," Hal added.

Hardy put a hand on the young man's arm, gave what he hoped was a reassuring squeeze. "I've got to ask you to sit tight awhile longer. You think you can do that? This is going to work out. I promise you. We're almost done."

Hal couldn't let it go. "But the judge must *know* now, doesn't he? I mean, the coincidence is so great it really couldn't be anything else."

"In fact," Hardy said, "it could be something else. Somebody else besides the Executioner could have had a motive to kill Mooney, or Laura, though I wouldn't bet on it. But Andrew's guilt or innocence isn't what this hearing is about anyway."

"And meanwhile he sits in jail," his mother said.

"Really, though," Hardy said, "not for too much longer."

"This is just a fucking travesty," Hal said.

Hardy met his angry gaze with one of his own. "I couldn't agree with you more."

Nelson's bulk appeared at the table beside them. "Mr. Hardy, Ms. Wu, his honor would like to see both of you in chambers."

They exchanged a worried glance, excused themselves and walked back out through the bullpen. Nelson knocked on the judge's door, got a "Yes?" and pushed it open.

This time, they had room to enter and even to sit on two of the three chairs that had been placed in front of Johnson's desk, where the judge sat without his robes, in shirt and tie. Much to Hardy's surprise, he looked up from the document he was perusing and greeted them more or less genially. "I've asked Mr. Brandt to join us as well, and I'd prefer to say nothing until he arrives." He went back to his document, occasionally taking a note or striking a phrase.

Brandt didn't keep them waiting long,

and as soon as he'd come in and sat, Johnson adjusted his glasses and began to speak. "I want to thank you all for coming by. You'll notice that I have not asked the court recorder to join us. This is because I'd like this meeting to be off the record. Does anyone have an objection to that?"

No one did.

"As all of you I'm sure realize, this has been an acrimonious case from the outset. I've spent the last hour and a half here at my desk thinking about what we've seen and heard about this minor Andrew Bartlett, his attempted suicide, and so on. It's led me to wonder if perhaps some of the earlier defense motions and strategies presented in this case might have antagonized the court to a degree that is incompatible with the interests of justice. The fact of the matter is that I've been very angry and remain very angry at what I've taken to be deliberate manipulation of the court."

"Your honor . . . !"

"That's all right, Ms. Wu. I'm not accusing you of anything now. I'm pretty well over it." He took off his glasses and laid them on the desk in front of him. "Mr. Hardy, your representation in the courtroom this morning was, as you pointed out, compelling and highly relevant. However, as I tried to make clear about half a dozen times, I wasn't going to allow this hearing and the reason for it to become bogged down in the question of Mr. Bartlett's innocence or guilt. But now we've heard from all the defense witnesses, and Mr. Brandt, I understand you won't be calling anyone?"

"That's correct, your honor."

"All right, then, for all practical purposes, we're finished with the seven-oh-seven. All that remains is for me to render my decision, which I've prepared and plan to deliver at the proper time. For my own peace of mind and, frankly, to preserve the integrity of the court, I wanted to share that tentative decision with all of you now, before we go out on the record."

He replaced his glasses then and opened the document that was on the desk in front of him. "The court finds that the minor was seventeen years old at the time of the alleged offense and that the offense falls within Welfare and Institutions Code 707(b). The court finds as follows: the minor is not a fit and proper subject to be dealt with under the juvenile court law."

He looked up, noted Hardy's and Wu's looks of frustration and defeat, went back to his text. "The court finds that the minor is not amenable to the care, treatment and training programs available through the juvenile court based on the degree of criminal sophistication exhibited by the minor for the following reasons: the minor eluded a vigorous anti-weapons campaign at his school for several months before the alleged incident, and carried a loaded gun concealed on his person . . ."

For the next several minutes, Johnson didn't look up as he read from the notes in his folder, finding that Andrew "is amenable to the care, treatment and training programs available through the juvenile court" for the second, third, and fourth criteria, and giving his reasons. So Wu had won three out of four, Hardy was thinking, not that it mattered one whit for their client.

"As to the fifth criterion," Johnson finally intoned, "the court finds that the minor is not amenable . . . the minor is an unfit subject to be treated in the juvenile justice system. The matter is referred to the district attorney for prosecution under the general law. The matter shall be set for arraignment in the adult court."

When he finished, he took a breath and removed his eyeglasses. "That's where we are," he said. "I wanted all of you to understand my position on the law, my reasoning and my ruling. That will be the ruling of the court."

Now he looked to each of the three lawyers in turn. "However, in view of Mr. Hardy's representation, and in the interest of justice and simple fairness, I'm not going to issue this ruling today. I'm going to take the matter under submission for one week, during which time you, Mr. Brandt, will discuss the matter with the district attorney and determine if he chooses to pursue the matter further, and to what degree. In the meanwhile, since Mr. Bartlett remains a minor until I formally declare him to be an adult, I intend to release him from his detention into the care of his parents until next week when I deliver my ruling."

Brandt, having won the hearing on its merits only to have the victory snatched from him, raised a hand and spoke. "Your honor, with respect, you can still issue your ruling today. The DA will be reviewing the case as a matter of course and will —"

But Johnson stopped him. "You're forgetting the special circumstances, Counselor. The minute I declare Mr. Bartlett an adult, he remains in confinement, and that doesn't seem right to me. There's no bail by statute in a special circumstances case. If I say he's an adult today, he goes downtown today. And it's my feeling that he's already been locked up too long. If he's innocent, one day is too long."

"Thank you, your honor," Wu said.

But he turned on her, too. "There's nothing to thank me for, Counselor." He tapped the document on his desk. "This will be my ruling. It goes into effect when I deliver it, one week from today. Meanwhile, your client doesn't leave the jurisdiction. He's under his parents' care and guidance the entire time. There will be a number of strict conditions. Is that clear?"

"Yes, your honor. Of course."

"Of course." Johnson was clearly sick of the whole thing. He looked at his watch and stood up. "If there are any more comments, I'd prefer not to hear them. My decision is my decision and it's final. Now I'd like to go out and put it on the record."

33

Jason Brandt wasn't as disappointed as he'd let on with Johnson's decision on Andrew Bartlett. In fact, as he listened to Dismas Hardy's representation to the court that morning, he'd realized that if even most of what his opposite number in the courtroom was saying proved to be true, he could be prosecuting an innocent man. And since it was all verifiable, why would Hardy lie? Then when the judge had ordered him to confer with the DA on the further disposition of the case, it removed any onus from him. He'd won the 707 hearing on its merits and that was the task he'd been assigned.

Now that was over.

Johnson had made his decision and anything he and Amy Wu might do outside of the courtroom would be irrelevant to the case. Technically, he should possibly wait to see her until the ruling next Wednesday, but there was just no way he was going to do that, not now. He'd take the risk, and if one of his bosses didn't like his timing, he

had an answer that he knew would fly —
they hadn't started until after the ruling.
They would not be adversaries in the
courtroom again.

But after they'd adjourned at the YGC,
he'd had no opportunity to talk with her in
the courtroom, set up a time they could get
together. She, Hardy, Andrew and the
Norths had been celebrating quietly around
the defense table, and he had caught her
eye for an instant — a message or a
promise — then left by the back way. He'd
called Jackman's office and Treya told him
she could squeeze him in at a little after
four o'clock, which meant he couldn't
waste a moment, so he didn't.

When Brandt came in, Jackman stood,
came around his desk and shook his hand,
which Brandt took as a sign of enhanced
recognition and even of approval. They sat
on either end of the low settee in front of
the coffee table. Jackman asked him what
was so important and Brandt gave it to
him in under five minutes.

"We can check this out pretty quick,"
the DA said in his quiet tone. He stood
again and went over to the door. "Treya,"
he said, "is there a chance you could get
me in touch with your husband right
away?"

"I'll give it a try."

"Just transfer him to my line." Jackman

came back into the office, went back to his desk, and the telephone rang once before he picked it up. "Abe. We've had a question come up here. There's a young man in my office, Jason Brandt, who's been prosecuting the Andrew Bartlett case up at the YGC. Mike Mooney and . . . Right. That's right, it's Hardy's case, too . . . You are? Well, the judge has postponed his ruling until he knows more. I'm thinking you might be able to tell Mr. Brandt what you've got and he can report back to me . . . Right, on Mooney, too, but all of it. Thanks."

Jackman hung up. "You know where you're going?"

"Yes, sir."

"Then go."

In the improvised computer room next to his office, a harried and exhausted Glitsky was bringing Brandt up to date between taking the reports of his people in the field and answering the questions of his workers. The clock on the wall read 4:40.

"I know. Hardy has already left me three messages about the slugs at Mooney's, but I've got other priorities at the moment. We don't have any of those slugs. We didn't find any the first time. I don't think it's likely we'll find them next time we look either."

"But do you think, personally, that Mooney was one of the Executioner's victims?"

Glitsky's lips pursed. "You don't?"

"I don't know."

"Well, start knowing. I'm not saying we can prove it yet, but it's a dead lock as far as I'm concerned."

"And Bartlett?"

"I don't know from Bartlett," Glitsky said. "Wrong guy, wrong place, wrong time."

Phones were ringing all over the office, and somebody from outside in the reception area called in, "Chief, your line."

Glitsky picked up the receiver, then pulled a pad over and wrote, furiously taking notes. "How many times?" he said. "What's the name? Anybody see him? Enough for a composite? Do they video the visitors down there?" Glitsky's mouth went tight. "Yeah, that sounds right. Okay. Keep checking."

He hung up, raised his voice. "Everybody listen up," and the other noises in the room stopped. "That was Darrel Bracco down at Corcoran. Lucas has got a son, Ray Welding, visited him in prison forty times in the last three years. No address, no listing. Bracco's requested the phone calls from the pay phone at his father's block and they're going to fax it up direct.

Sarah," he turned to Evans, "you pick three people. I want every four one five, four oh eight, five one one, six five oh" — all the telephone area codes for the Bay Area — "every one reversed for names and addresses. This might be the guy."

"This guy, Welding, the dad." Brandt, wanting to contribute, couldn't stop himself and spoke to Glitsky. "If he won an appeal, he must have had a lawyer. The lawyer would know the son, wouldn't he? Where he lives?"

"He might," Glitsky said. "But he won't talk to us. We're the cops, remember, the bad guys."

"But if the son's the Executioner?"

Glitsky didn't answer because someone else told him to pick up the phone. This time he listened without writing or saying much, and by the time he put the phone down, the room had hushed. His head hung, chin to chest. He slowly fisted the table in a black fury.

Everyone waited until he raised his head. "The last local juror," he said. "Wendy Takahashi, maiden name Shui. The one that just moved last month." Which was why they hadn't been able to locate her sooner.

"She's already dead?" someone asked.

"Before we got there," Glitsky said. "Maybe just before. Belou's been standing

642

outside her place since about two, protecting a dead woman." Glitsky's eyes, opaque with fatigue and anger, were glazed over.

Brandt wandered out to the reception room, stopped next to a uniformed officer. "What did he mean, the last local juror?"

The man, studying a computer printout, answered like a zombie. "There were six locals. Mooney, Reed — that's Cary — Montrose, Wong, Tollman, and now Shui/Takahashi. She was the last one."

The mention of Mooney as the first Executioner victim did not escape Brandt's notice. "What about the other six?" he asked.

"Four moved away, two died. We're trying to find the four. We figure the other two — the dead ones — are out of immediate danger."

Wu got back to the Sutter Street office and, after accepting congratulations from the small group gathered in Hardy's office, excused herself to go and call Brandt back at the YGC. He wasn't in and she left a message that she wanted to see him, with her work and home phone numbers. Maybe, she said, they could even have dinner later tonight. Start over and take things more slowly. In the flush of confidence she was feeling after Johnson's decision on Andrew, she allowed herself to believe that sometimes the right thing could happen in this world.

But Brandt wasn't at his office. She'd have to wait a bit longer.

Her in basket was filled to overflowing with work — mail that she'd neglected, returned materials from word processing and her secretary. On the top was the most recent draft of the notice rule memo she was writing for Farrell — billable work — and she lifted it up from the pile, kicked back from her desk, put her feet up and began to read it over.

Ten minutes later she was back in her working hunch, red pen in hand, scratching out and rewriting, when somebody knocked at her door. "Come in."

"You're working," Hardy said.

"That's what you pay me for. What's up?"

"I'm going down to the Hall, see if I can find Glitsky and get a word with him. Maybe get a commitment on some action with the Mooney scene."

"You want me to come with you?"

"Actually, I was going to suggest that you give yourself a break. As managing partner, I wanted you to know that I've declared today a clear win for the good guys. And they're not so common you want to ignore them, ever. David Freeman, lesson six. So it's your sacred duty to take the evening off and savor the victory."

"David Freeman never took time off."

"Not true. Every time he won, he burned the city down."

Wu glanced down at the draft on her desk, let out a sigh. "I don't consider this over yet, sir. Not till next Wednesday. If then."

"It's over," Hardy said. "Jackman hears that the Salarcos never heard a shot, my guess is that even without scuffed slugs from Mooney's, he'll never go forward. Andrew's home tonight, Wu. You've got to call that a win."

"All right, but it wasn't a win for me."

"How do you figure that?"

"You're the one who found everything that made the difference. I just made problems we shouldn't have had at the outset. Then made them worse as we went along."

Hardy stood a minute in the doorway, then took a step in and closed the door behind him. "Look, Wu," he said, "this was your first major case. So you weren't perfect. Nobody is. The point is, do you think you learned anything?"

Gradually, she softened. Nodded her head in acknowledgment.

"Okay, then. Your client's free, your team just took the flag, your boss is telling you to take the rest of the day off, and you're splitting hairs about how we didn't really win and it wasn't really you and how it could have been better? Don't do that. It could always be better, but you ought to recognize when it's good enough, don't you think?"

She sighed again, glanced at her in box, finally looked up and gave him a chagrined smile. "All right."

"You can go back to punishing yourself tomorrow. I won't stop you. But tonight, give yourself a break and get out of here."

Hardy was right, she thought. You had to take these moments when you could.

It was a bit after five, suddenly warm and still now after all the spring wind, with an almost buttery softness to the air and the light. She parked just off Chestnut and decided to stroll along the avenue, letting her senses dictate where she'd stop, what she'd buy for a private celebration dinner at home. She'd open all the windows to let in some of the outside, then sit alone at her table with her view of the bridge and some great bread and selections of the awesome take-out Marina food and fresh flowers. After, she'd curl up in her chair and read or put on some music or both, and Jason would call or he wouldn't, but either way there would be tomorrow and if it was meant to be, it would be.

It took her most of an hour, dawdling

along, stopping in at half a dozen shops, chatting with the merchants and even some of the other customers. She bought daffodils and some fresh Asiago cheese bread, marinated artichoke hearts, a spinach salad, some pot-stickers, an early pear.

The staircase up to her apartment was suffused with still-bright sunlight as she walked up. When she got to the fourth-floor landing outside her door, she stopped and took another moment to look down over the neighborhood, then the view beyond — the dark green cypresses in the Presidio, a hundred pleasure boats on the bay.

What a gorgeous place!

Suddenly, for perhaps the first time in her adult life, she realized that she felt blessed and even lucky.

She put down the bag of food and flowers. Taking her keys from her purse, she inserted the house key into the door, picked up her groceries again and walked inside. Closing the door behind her, she threw the deadbolt and set the chain lock.

Behind her, a male voice said, "Turn around slowly and move away from the door."

The after-work crowd at the Balboa Cafe wasn't quite as thick as the after-dinner mob, but Jason Brandt still felt fortunate to get a seat at the bar. He laid a twenty-dollar bill down and ordered a beer.

"A beer?" Cecil held up a bottle of Jack Daniel's. "I see you walk in the door, my hand automatically goes to the JD. Double, rocks."

"Not today," Brandt said. "Beer."

"What kind of beer?"

"Wet and cold. I'm looking for Amy Wu. She been in?"

"Not yet." He started pulling a Sierra Nevada from the tap on the bar. "Come to think of it, I haven't seen her in a while. Since she went out of here with you, if I remember. You think she's all right?"

"Yeah. I was with her in court today. She's fine."

"She *is* fine. You seeing her?"

"No. We've been in trial together. Opposite sides. It's against the rules."

"Shame," Cecil said.

"Yeah." Brandt brought the beer to his lips, drank off an inch.

Cecil moved down the bar, served some customers, changed the channel on the television set. When he came back, Brandt was staring into his beer, turning it around and around on the bar in front of him. "You all right?" Cecil asked.

"Yeah, great."

"You don't look great. You look unhappy."

"It's Wu," Brandt said. "I think I'm kind of in love with her."

"You say that like it just occurred to you."

"It did."

"Are you still in trial?"

"I don't think so. Not after today."

"Well, if you're in love, bro, you better make a move or somebody else will snag that babe first for sure. I wouldn't be sitting my poor ass on a stool waiting for her to come in here. I'd go find her where she is, stake my claim."

His glass halfway to his mouth, Brandt stopped and lowered it back down to the bar. Then he was up off the stool and moving.

"Hey, your change!"

"Keep it."

He was sitting in her reading chair, having moved out from behind the changing screen where he'd been waiting when she came in. He held a gun on her — a gun with a long and very heavy-looking tube attached to the barrel. She sat at her table, hands in her lap. The grocery bag remained on the floor by the door she'd locked. "How did you know where I live? How'd you get in here?"

His laugh was guttural, humorless. "I've gotten real good at finding people. And getting in is the same as it was when I was a kid. The point is that I'm here."

"What do you want?"

"I want to finish my work."

"And what's that? Your work?"

"I believe you legal types would call it redress of grievances."

"Then it can't have anything to do with me. I haven't done anything to you."

"No, that's true. Not to me personally. In your case, maybe it's more that I want to keep you from doing more harm."

"Than what? I haven't done anybody any harm."

"Amy, Amy, Amy, please. I hope you don't really feel that. What about Andrew Bartlett?"

"What about him? He got out of detention today. Did you know that? How is that harming him?"

"Are you forgetting his attempted suicide already? Did it really make that little of an impression on you? You don't call that harm?"

"But I didn't —"

He slapped his free hand down on the arm of the chair, bared his teeth in a snarl. "The fuck you didn't! Don't you think he did that because you made him believe he'd never get out? But no, you don't think that way, do you? Nothing's really your fault, is it?"

"No. That's not true. Some things are completely my fault. Please don't point that thing. I'm sorry," she said. "Whatever it is, I didn't mean . . ."

"You don't understand what I'm saying. I don't care what you mean, what you meant. You play the same game they all played with my father, don't you see that? You're just like Allan Boscacci was twenty years ago — arrogant, self-righteous, pig-headed and wrong." He lifted the gun again. "Don't you move!"

"I wasn't. I was just . . ."

He kept his arm extended, the gun with its silencer pointed directly at her chest. "I don't care. I say something, you don't deny it. If I say 'Don't move,' you don't move."

"I'm sorry. I won't anymore. I promise. But I'm nervous. I've got to pee."

"So pee."

She started to stand, but he barked again, came halfway out of the chair with the gun trained on her. "Sit down!"

"But you just said . . ."

"I said you can pee. I didn't say anything about going anywhere."

She stared across at him, squeezed her legs together. "What do I have to do with Allan Boscacci?" Anything to keep him talking, to buy time, even a few precious seconds more.

"You're just like him."

"You said that. But how?"

"You really ask how? As if you don't know. All right, I'll tell you how." He sat back in the chair, rested the gun on his knee. "I saw you that first day with Bartlett, so sure he was guilty, ready to send him away for half his life, no concern at all for the truth, for what might be right. Just like Boscacci did with my father. Sent him up for life when he didn't do it."

"Your father?"

"That's right. My father."

"Didn't do what?"

"Rape and kill my mother, that's what."

She clutched her hands together against her stomach. "I'm sorry, but I really don't know what you're talking about."

"*I'm talking about my father, goddamn it! My father!*" Again he'd come forward, lifted the gun. He held it on her for five seconds, ten. Again he collapsed back. "My father," he said, his voice now going to dead calm.

"What about him? I don't know about your father."

"Lucas Welding. His name was Lucas Welding."

"All right," she said. "Please. Tell me about him."

Jason Brandt got to the landing and

thought he heard voices upstairs. He stopped and listened, almost turned around and went back down, but then decided since he'd come this far, he'd just say he was in the neighborhood and thought he'd stop by and see if she wanted to go out for a drink, or maybe meet him later at the Balboa. Surely, that was harmless enough. Or if whoever was with her turned out to be just a friend or a neighbor, she'd invite him in, they'd finish their conversation, then she'd tell the friend good-bye. After that, the two of them could let the night take them where it would.

When he got to the door, he paused a moment and listened. Yes, two voices, one male and one female. When he knocked — three quick raps — the voices stopped abruptly within. He waited through a lengthening silence, perplexity growing on this face. Then all at once the truth of what he must have been hearing dawned on him.

He blinked a few times, nodded, bit at his lower lip. He wasn't aware of it, but his shoulders fell.

What a fool he was.

He turned back toward the steps.

Then heard her voice through the door behind him. "Who is it?"

For a second, he considered not answering, getting to the stairs and out of sight before he brought any more embarrassment to himself. But she had asked him to believe her, believe in the kind of person she was. At least, he thought, he owed her that. To give her a chance to be straight with him. "Amy. It's me, Jason."

"Jason." He thought he heard a kind of relief in her voice, but it disappeared with her next words. "This isn't a good time. I'm sorry."

"Are you all right?"

"Fine. I'm fine. But really, it's not a good time."

"Okay, but if I could just —"

"*Jason, go away! Leave me the fuck alone, all right! Get out of here! Now! Or you're in trouble! I mean it!*"

"Good," he said. "That was all right. Nobody stays around after that."

"No. He's a jerk," she said, turning around. "Well, you know that. But please, could I go to the bathroom?"

Brandt stood below, in the gathering dusk, looking up at her window. Her outburst against him had punched him in the gut. Even now, frozen in his spot, leaning against the wall of a building across the street, he held his hand there.

He couldn't seem to make himself move. He stared up at the window, saw no shadows, no sign of movement.

Maybe they were lying together in her bed?

That thought came like another kick to his stomach, but suddenly, all at once, he couldn't accept it. That wasn't what was happening up there. And his certainty wasn't a matter of rational thought. It was on another level, a bone-deep conviction. She was up there with somebody, yes, but even if she was being romantic with another man, there was no way she would have gone off on him that way. Beyond the connection he felt that they'd established, that wasn't who she was. She wouldn't have treated him like that, not now.

It made no sense.

And then, suddenly, her words came back at him. *"You're in trouble."* That private, powerful, ambiguous code word between them, and now Amy had screamed it at him through her locked door. *"You're in trouble."* A little out of place, even in that context. Off-key.

A warning? Or a cry for help?

Christ, he thought. What an idiot. She's just dumping me. Let it go.

But he was already crossing the street, going back up.

"Boscacci was so sure," he said. "All the jurors were so sure. They polled them one by one afterward, you know. Every one of them."

He'd followed her into the bathroom, stood in the doorway while she'd gone, walked her back to her chair and now was finishing his story.

"I'm so sorry," she said. "I didn't know that."

"Yeah? Well, here's something else you don't know. You don't know what it's like having your home taken away from you when you're seven years old. You don't know what it's like when your mom's murdered and they blame your father for it and then try him and take him away and put you in foster care. Do you know what that's like?"

"No, I don't," Wu said. "I'm so sorry." And she was, but mostly she was afraid that she was going to die, and thought maybe she could get him to spare her. "It must have been terrible for you."

"Terrible doesn't begin to cover it. And taking away my own name, talking me into taking my mom's maiden name. I didn't want to have people knowing I'm the son of that *murderer*, did I? Wouldn't I be happier with a different name? Don't you understand — they took away my life!"

"I'm sure they didn't mean to do that. I mean, Boscacci and the jury . . ."

"I hope they all rot in hell." He suddenly

jerked and was back to the present. "Thirteen of them, every one of them so certain, and every one of them so completely dead wrong." He found something to laugh at. "And now more than half of them just completely dead."

She felt a wave of chill break over her. "What do you mean?"

"What do I mean? I mean I killed them. You haven't figured that out yet? All of them still living around here, anyway, in beautiful San Francisco and vicinity."

When it came to her, the blood ran from her face. "You're the Executioner."

"Good," he said. "Why do you think I got onto you in the first place?"

"I don't know."

"You don't, really? All right, then, I'll tell you. Because there you were, Miss Professional Lawyer who doesn't believe in *seeing* people you work with. There you were, Andrew's *defense* lawyer, the only person in the lousy system who's supposed to be working for him, and you're talking about pleading him *guilty* and sending him away for *eight years*. And I'm watching you in court, and listening to what you're telling him, and I see it's going on and on, and will always go on with you, since you're just like them all, like all of them have always been."

He raised the gun and she thought he

might shoot her now, but he lowered the weapon then, swallowed, went on. "And it was so funny to me, you see? Because *I knew he didn't do it.* And you know why I knew that? *Because I did.*"

"You killed Mooney?"

He nodded. "And his whining little girlfriend. And while we're at it, I should maybe call your partner after I've gone and thank him for letting me know how close they were to finding me this morning. I wasn't planning to do more of my work today until I heard what he said in court and realized I really had to hurry. Though I would have been gone anyway soon enough."

"Where to?" she asked.

He gave her a ghastly, empty smile. "On the road. But first," he said, "there's you."

"Please," she said, "please don't. Put the gun down."

"Don't make me use it then. I don't like sitting with a corpse. They stink. So you stay sitting there and shut up."

"All right, I will," she said. "I won't move. What do you want me to do?"

"Nothing," he said. "I want it to get dark." Again, that empty-eyed smile. "It's so much easier to walk away when it's dark."

Brandt crept away from Amy's door and

descended from the fourth down to the second landing, which he figured was the closest spot where he couldn't be heard from above. He took out his cellphone and turned it on and couldn't get a signal in the stairwell.

His breath coming in ragged gasps, he broke out of the building onto the sidewalk, got his signal and punched in the number for police dispatch, which, like all assistant DAs, he knew by heart. He didn't want nine one one, somebody getting it wrong and showing up with lights and sirens. "This is Jason Brandt. Patch me through to Deputy Chief Glitsky, please, at the Hall of Justice. Yes, it's an emergency. Tell him I've found the Executioner."

34

The sun kissed the tops of the cypresses, next the roofs of some of the low buildings, and then suddenly full dusk had fallen. There were no shadows anymore, no reflection of the setting sun in the windows of Amy's place across the street. The sky in the east had gone from turquoise to a deep indigo. Behind Brandt, at the western horizon, a garish orange sunset was fading to a purplish yellow bruise.

But no Glitsky.

Four patrol cars had arrived, silently, then three more. Then Brandt had lost count. All of the police cars had parked invisibly somewhere in the surrounding streets and dispatched their occupants out to encircle Amy's place and evacuate anyone inside who lived on the floors below her, and even people in the surrounding buildings. Brandt showed his badge to Sergeant Ariola, the initial ranking officer at the scene, and identified himself as the person who'd called the police. But that cut him no slack with Ariola, who shunted Brandt with an escort back behind the police line.

He could still see Wu's windows, but now he was around the corner on Cervantes Boulevard. Looking behind him and down the other streets, he realized that the entire block had been cordoned off — squad cars parked perpendicular to the curbs in the middle of the streets, stopping any automobile traffic. Teams of cops were keeping pedestrians out of the area, although now small crowds of the curious had begun to gather at the perimeter.

Next, bad to worse, the TV news vans were arriving — the very scenario Brandt had tried to avoid by calling Glitsky direct. If the TV happened to be turned on in Amy's apartment and they broke the story as late-breaking news, there was no telling what would happen inside, but it could not be good. Next, Brandt watched with some admixture of dread and disbelief as the motor home command post of the tactical unit pulled up. He saw Ariola moving toward it and again tried his DA's badge trick with one of the uniformed cops, who this time let him through with barely a glance. He stood right behind Ariola as he reported the situation to the TAC unit commander, and neither of those men paid him the slightest heed either.

The whole TAC unit wasn't here yet —

it usually took forty minutes to an hour for all the members to check in — but the sharpshooter had been one of the first to arrive, and the commander sent him up to the roof of the building directly across the street from Amy's to see what, if anything, he could do. Brandt heard the order, "If you get a clear shot, and he's got a gun on her, take it." Then, motioning to the TV vans, he turned to Ariola. "Inform those jackals that if anyone runs a live feed, I'll hunt them down and kill them and their children."

In the crush of events, Brandt's presence continued to go unnoticed. Ariola went to talk to the newspeople, while the commander ran across the street and disappeared into Amy's building. Every minute or so, another policeman in a black TAC unit jacket would show up and report to the deputy commander at the door to the motor home. At some point — any normal measure of time had long since become meaningless — Ariola reappeared next to Brandt, and they both watched as the commander came out of the lobby, looked up into the sky and jogged back over to where they stood. He spoke to his deputy. "I don't see how we can wait much longer."

"I don't either."

"The Chief ordered me to wait for him. If we bust in, we could lose her. Although

I don't know what else he's got in mind." Again, the commander glanced at the rapidly darkening sky. Shaking his head, he sighed with exasperation, looked up again. "Five minutes," he said, "and it's dark. We've got to go in."

He'd been sitting the whole time, holding the gun with its awkward attachment, the silencer, resting on the arm of the chair. His finger continually, unconsciously, teased the trigger as he flipped one by one — casually, relaxed — through the pages of the various magazines Wu kept next to her reading chair. She became nearly hypnotized with fear, watching it. Once she shifted her weight in her chair at the table and it was as though she'd prodded him with electricity, so quickly did he have the gun raised, all focus and menace. "Don't move!"

Then, satisfied that she wouldn't, he sat back, crossed one leg comfortably over the other and began turning pages again.

Wu didn't know what she could do to save herself, and so sat in a numbed state of panic and resignation. She'd already considered what she thought were her only options. In his chair, he was probably close to ten feet away from her, farther than she could leap in a quick rush. The front door was still deadlocked and chained. The bathroom — the only place she might conceivably escape to — was all the way at the back corner of the large, otherwise open room.

She thought that when the time came, if indeed he gave her any warning at all, she would bolt and try to throw something — the saltshaker, the chair she sat on. But she realized from his demeanor throughout this excruciating wait that he was just as likely to lick his finger, turn a page, check the window (as he'd done a dozen times), decide it was sufficiently dark, lift the gun without a word or warning and shoot her. Then unlock the door and walk downstairs and out into the sheltering night.

Unable to bear watching his twitching finger any longer, she closed her eyes, trying to find some place of inner peace, but found there was nowhere she could go. This was the end of her life, and all she could feel was the coming void. Opening her eyes again, she watched him flip a page, glance at her as though she were a piece of furniture, look back down at his magazine, turn his head to the window, flip another page.

The small hole in the barrel of the silencer, the finger dancing over the trigger guard, had so dominated her consciousness that she hadn't looked at the window herself in what must have been minutes. But now she did and realized that the night had truly come on — she was looking at her own reflection now in the glass, as though in a mirror. There was no more light from outside to dissipate the image.

He would not wait much longer.

Knock! Knock! Knock!

The sound startled them both. Wu gave a little involuntary yelp and he jumped where he sat, the chair legs giving a little screech on the hardwood floor. At the same time, the magazine slipped and fell out of his lap. After all the silence in the room, the two sounds — the knock and the dropped magazine — seemed to Amy to echo like thunder.

She shot a startled glance at him. He lifted the gun, his arm outstretched, centered on her heart. The gun never left her. His eyes went to the door, back to her. The initial moment of panic passed. She felt she could see him plotting what he would do. With the inadvertent noises from inside, there was no way to pretend that no one was home.

Quickly, he pointed the gun at the door, then back to her, and nodded.

"Who is it?"

"Amy. It's me. Diz. We had a meeting?"

She turned to him. Mouthed, "My boss."

Something like a smile curled the corner

of his mouth. *All the better.* He nodded. The message was *Let him in.* He got to his feet.

"Just a second," she said.

In a few steps, agile as a cat, suddenly he'd come around the table and pressed himself against the wall by the door. He moved the gun up and now held it on her head. One foot from her head.

Wu read his intentions with crystal clarity. When she opened the door, it would block him from sight until Hardy was inside. And then he would shoot. And then both of them would die. She couldn't let that happen.

What was he doing here? They hadn't planned any meeting.

She undid the chain, fumbling with it, her hands shaking.

If she threw the door back quickly, could she disable him? She looked down for an instant, saw that he'd planted his foot to prevent that. The door could open only enough to let Hardy in, nothing more. And meanwhile he could fire at will.

If she let him in, Hardy would die, too. She couldn't be responsible for that. If she was going to die anyway, maybe at least she could warn him first.

Her thoughts tumbling over one another, she watched as though from a distance as her hands turned the dead bolt, went to the knob, turned it.

Dropping her hand, resigned now to the gun there at her ear, she heard herself saying, "I don't feel well. You have to go, Diz."

"We need to talk," he said, "face to face. It's urgent."

Hardy knew she'd undone the chain. He'd heard her throw the dead bolt, watched the doorknob turn and heard the little *click*. The door was unlocked. He guessed she was stalling for time, but there was no more time.

He grabbed the knob, turned, lowered his shoulder and exploded into the crack where he'd opened the door, hitting her with a tackle at the waist, taking her down with him.

Before they'd even hit the floor, the four TAC unit specialists who'd crammed into the landing behind Hardy crashed in through the opening with their guns drawn, splintering the door completely off its hinges. There were another four behind them, and then yet another team, rushing unstoppable as a flash flood into the apartment.

The force of the door flying back knocked the gun from his grip and somersaulted him back over the table and onto the floor. Crashing against the counter where Wu kept her dishes and cooking supplies, for an instant he lay stunned on the floor amid the splintered wood and broken glass. But in the half-second before anyone could reach him, emitting an animal cry, he made a last desperate scramble and lunge for his weapon.

But he never made it, as the first pair of TAC unit specialists reached and fell upon him.

Writhing and screaming, a run-over animal whose back had been broken, he grunted and kicked and gouged and spewed his vile rage until they'd gotten his hands behind his back and cuffed him. Now, facedown in his own blood and spread-eagled with a TAC guy on each leg and another kneeling on his back, he couldn't move a muscle.

Glitsky was standing in the doorway, his own gun drawn, but now held down at his side. He could see that his plan — well, his and Hardy's — had worked. And they'd managed to pull it off without anyone having to die. Their backs against the wall, Hardy sat next to Wu on the floor, a protective arm around her. Wu's head was down, her shoulders heaving a little as she cried out some of the tension.

Fine.

Glitsky walked over to where his troops had the suspect in righteous custody, and looked down at the now pathetic and re-strained figure of the Executioner. They'd only discovered his name in the minutes before Brandt had called to say he knew where they could find him.

The Youth Guidance Center bailiff, Ray Cottrell.

The TAC unit police had wasted no time getting Cottrell up and taking him away, and now the room fairly buzzed with the spent energy and the detritus of chaos.

In the destroyed half of the apartment, Wu, Hardy and Glitsky went to almost robotic wordless motion, getting the shattered door to one side and leaning it up against the wall, setting the table back on its legs, righting the chairs, two of them still unbroken, picking up the larger pieces of plates and pottery.

At last, Wu sat heavily in one of the chairs. Hardy took the other.

Glitsky crossed to the dish counter and filled a glass of water from the tap. He went over to the table and handed it to Wu, then went back to the counter, cleared a spot and sat on it. "How did he get here?" he asked.

"I don't know. I had no idea he knew where I lived."

"But what did he want with *you?* You were — what? — twelve years old during his father's trial. You had nothing to do with it, did you?"

Seeming to notice the glass in her hand for the first time, Wu drank off half the water. She dropped her head and appeared to gather herself for another minute. Finally, she began to tell them what Cottrell had said he had wanted with her, as best she could explain it — her connection to the system that had mistakenly and tragically convicted his father.

"No, more than that," she said. "It wasn't just that I was another lawyer. He saw me as exactly like Allan Boscacci had been when he'd prosecuted his innocent dad and sent his dad up. I was doing the same thing to Andrew Bartlett, bartering away years of his life when Ray *knew* Andrew was innocent." She was coming out of her state of shock, and seemed suddenly to realize the import of what he'd told her. "Because he was the one who'd done what Andrew had been arrested for. Don't you see? He killed Mooney and Laura."

"We'd pretty much gotten to that ourselves," Glitsky said.

She raised her voice a notch. "But he *told* me he did it. He actually told me. He called Mooney by name." She turned to Hardy. "That's important," she said, urgency bleeding out of her. "It makes a difference."

"I know." He put a hand over hers at the

670

table. "I don't think Abe's missing it."

Glitsky nodded. "We'll get his statement, then see where we are," he said. "But unofficially, I don't think you need to worry. It'll all come out."

"At least enough to clear Andrew," Hardy said. "Let's hope."

Wu let out a heavy breath. "But how did you know I'd open the door?" she asked. "I almost didn't."

"I didn't know that for sure," Hardy said. "That was Plan A. Plan B was the door comes down anyway about five seconds later. Abe and I both thought it was worth a try to get you out of the way first."

They heard noises from out on the landing, footfalls and voices on the stairs. "I'm going to want a more complete statement from you tomorrow," Glitsky said, "but we can let that go tonight." His eyes went to the shattered door leaning up against the wall, the empty door frame with its hanging hinges. "Are you going to need a place to stay?"

"She can come to my place," Hardy said, turning to her. "If you're good with that? Same spacious quarters and comfortable bed?"

"Same night chef?" she asked.

"It might be arranged."

At that moment, Jason Brandt broke from the ranks of police that were accompanying him up the stairs and stopped in the open door frame. "Jesus," he exclaimed at all the damage. Then, seeing her at the table, he closed his eyes and blew out heavily in relief. Hardy and Glitsky might as well not have been there. "Amy, are you all right?"

Her face lit up. "Jason. What are you doing here?"

"What's he doing here?" Hardy asked. "He's the hero, that's all."

Brandt shook his head in embarrassed denial, spoke to Hardy. "No. From what I hear, you're the hero. I just —"

Hardy cut him off. "You just figured it all out and called Chief Glitsky here and got us moving, that's all. Without which none of this happens."

Wu was staring at Brandt. "But I told you to get away, Jason. To get out of here."

"I know." He shrugged. "I snuck back up and listened at the door."

"But why? How did you know?"

"Because I know *you*, Amy," he said. "You wouldn't have just sent me off. Not that way. No matter what. That's not who you are."

Lanier and Ariola appeared from the steps, on the landing behind Brandt. Hardy turned back to Wu and saw that her eyes had brimmed.

Brandt stepped into the room, out of the

cops' way. He hesitated, then came over behind Amy at the table. He put a hand on her shoulder, and Wu put her hand over his.

In the door frame, Ariola said, "If we're sealing this place up, we're going to want to get to it pretty soon, Chief."

"All right," Glitsky said. He motioned to the civilians. "When they're ready to go down, let's get that done."

Lanier spoke up. "Also, just a heads up, Abe, but there's some people waiting for you downstairs," he said. "Cameras."

Glitsky's face went dark. He took in the scene here one last time, said "Swell" and pushed through to the landing.

Out in the street, at the impromptu press conference, Glitsky stood in a circle of halogen and uniforms and spoke into a hastily assembled cluster of microphones. As usual at this type of event, he found himself on the defensive. "Well," he said. "Assuming that our sharpshooter could not take him out, which was always a viable option, there were really two main objections to simply calling him up on the telephone or using a bullhorn to tell him he was surrounded.

"The first was that we knew that he'd already killed seven people at close range and in cold blood. After some serious discussion downtown, we decided —"

"Who's 'we,' Chief?"

"Myself, homicide Lieutenant Marcel Lanier and Dismas Hardy."

"The lawyer?" A woman's voice. "What's a lawyer doing making police decisions?"

"Mr. Hardy didn't make the decision, Claudia. He had some detailed knowledge of the situation and it proved useful. In any event, getting back to the original question, in view of Mr. Cottrell's behavior in the past few weeks, if we announced our presence, we thought it extremely likely that he would simply kill the hostage and then himself. The second objection was that we thought we had a better plan."

"But one that exposed civilian lives to danger, isn't that true?"

"That's true, but it was only one civilian and Mr. Hardy volunteered, and his involvement was crucial. Ms. Wu is his business associate and friend. And let's not forget, if you don't mind," Glitsky said, forcing himself, "the operation was a success."

Another disembodied voice from out in the darkness: "Yes, but how sure are you that Ray Cottrell is in fact the Executioner?"

"Close to a hundred percent. He confessed as much to Ms. Wu. But now that he's in custody, you'll be hearing lots more about that, I'm sure."

"I understand he was an abused child who grew up in a succession of foster homes."

"Is that a question?" Glitsky asked. "If so, I have no comment."

"Chief? What part of your decision not to use your sniper in this instance comes from the tragic results of the LeShawn Brodie situation?"

"Well, first, that LeShawn Brodie decision wasn't made by me or anybody else in this jurisdiction. Second, as I thought I'd already made clear, Mr. Ralston, we never made the decision *not* to use our sharpshooter in this case, and in fact that option was on the table throughout the course of the operation, if the opportunity presented itself. Which it didn't."

"In other words, you approved the order to have Cottrell shot out of hand, but by the same token you elected not to give him a chance to surrender by letting him know that his options had run out and he was surrounded?"

Glitsky brought one hand to his side and pushed in against the spasm there. He raised his other hand up against the bright lights. Trying not to look too menacing, and to possibly even look cooperative and friendly, and failing abysmally, he glared out into the invisible circle in front of him. "As I believe I've already explained . . ."

35

On the Wednesday of that week, at a little
before one o'clock in the afternoon, Wu
walked up the hall from her office and
turned right toward Hardy's, passing directly
behind Phyllis's workstation. The elderly receptionist obviously had eyes in the back of
her head, because as Wu came abreast of
her, she whirled in her ergonomic chair and
actually held a hand up. "He's busy and
doesn't want to be disturbed. Did you make
an appointment?"

Wu stopped, forced a polite smile. "I
just opened my mail," she said, holding up
a yellowish manila envelope, "and he'll
want to see this. I promise."

"That's what everyone says. All of you
associates believe he'll want to see you,
which of course he does. He and I have
discussed this. He's happy to make time
for the associates, but he'd really prefer
that those times are convenient to him, not
necessarily to them." Phyllis possibly actually thought she was softening the message
with her schoolteacher smile. "I'm sorry,"

she said, as one of the phones in her bank rang behind her and she whirled around again to get it.

Wu didn't hesitate for a moment, but broke right as quietly as she could, got to Hardy's door and knocked.

"Ms. Wu!" — from behind her, as from the other side of the door she heard, "Yo!" and got herself inside.

Her boss, coat off, tie loosened, was rummaging through the drawers of his desk. He greeted her arrival with a smile that seemed more or less welcoming behind the more obvious fluster of his demeanor. "How did you . . . ?" he began, and was interrupted by the sharp buzz of his intercom.

He reached over, pushed the button and said "Yo!" again, this time into the speaker. He knew that of all the things hated by Phyllis, and in his experience this included nearly all forms of human interaction, his cavalier telephone greeting ranked near the top. He winked at Wu during the short, distinctive pause while Phyllis bit back her natural reprimand. "Mr. Hardy! I told Ms. Wu you weren't to be disturbed, and she went ahead."

"I can see that, and I assure you that I'm already disturbed, Phyllis. It's not your fault. I intend to have a word with her right away. Thank you."

He left his speaker on for a second or so while he began in a firm voice. "Ms. Wu, when I tell Phyllis I don't want to be disturbed, I expect you and all the associates to . . ." Then he pushed the button, breaking the connection. "Charging the door isn't very subtle, Wu. I need that woman, believe it or not. She's very good at what she does, none better."

"Maybe, but she's not very nice."

"She's not supposed to be. If she were nice, people would walk all over her. As it is, some of your colleagues are afraid to go to the bathroom if they have to pass her station. So they stay at their desks, working all day. This is good for the firm."

Wu allowed a smile. "You really are becoming more and more like Mr. Freeman."

Hardy inclined his head an inch. "I'll take that as a compliment of the highest order. Have you seen my darts?"

"Your darts? When would I have seen your darts?"

"I don't know. But they were here yesterday or the day before, and now I've mislaid them. Second time in two months. I think I'm losing my mind."

"Maybe you're just saving it for bigger things."

Hardy stopped his rummaging through his drawers, slammed the latest one closed. "Unfortunately, there's not much sign of that either." Scanning the room one last time for obvious places where he might have left them, he finally gave up and sat down in the big leather chair behind his desk. "So what's important enough to risk the wrath of Phyllis?"

She held up the envelope. "This is very cool."

"What is it?"

She handed it to him and he pulled out the pages.

Dear Ms. Wu,

I've been meaning to write to thank you and Mr. Hardy for all that you did for me, but I had so much work to make up at school, I never got the time. As I think you might have heard from my mom, Sutro took me back — some combination of Hal's money and Mr. Wagner making me sign a paper promising that I wouldn't bring a loaded gun to school again.

Oh. Okay. Or what? I get expelled?

Forgetting that we don't *own* a gun anymore, and as if that would stop me if I decided to. But don't worry, I agree that it's a bad idea.

The other reason I haven't had time is that I've been doing some more writing — I started almost the day I got out, totally different stuff than "Perfect

Killer." Working with the narrative voice, wondering if maybe it wouldn't hurt to have it be accessible, even friendly. Anyway, maybe I'm getting somewhere, since just today I heard back from *McSweeney's*. They say they want to publish my latest story. I thought you'd be glad to hear about that, and maybe also to hear that I'm so glad I didn't die when I tried to kill myself. So glad.

You know the famous line from *Anna Karenina*? "Happy families are all alike; every unhappy family is unhappy in its own way." Well, my time in my own unhappy family is getting to the end, and maybe when I get to going out and making one of my own, I can form it a little differently. The story *McSweeney's* is taking imagines a guy from a happier family, way later on. I hope you like it.

Just remember one thing, though, would you? *I made it all up.*

Brandt and Wu were at a table in the restaurant at the back of the Balboa Cafe. The waiter had brought their drinks, but both of them remained untouched. When Brandt finished reading Andrew's letter, he handed it gingerly back to Wu. It was a long minute before he said anything. "I don't like to think that I was trying to send him to prison for the rest of his life." He paused again. "I've never had a defendant be innocent before, you know that? It gives one pause."

"You wonder if you've sent up somebody who shouldn't be there?"

He thought about it for a few seconds. "Not really, no. I don't think so. I mean, Bartlett was unusual. At least I hope he was. But I don't know for sure, to tell you the truth. I'm sure Allan Boscacci thought what's his name, Welding, was guilty. In a funny way," he said, "it almost makes me feel better about the system. I mean, Andrew Bartlett got off, with me and Johnson both trying to bring him down. Sometimes it works."

Hardy and Glitsky hadn't seen much of each other for six weeks.

In the aftermath of the Executioner arrest, and in spite of its successful conclusion, the media couldn't seem to warm to Glitsky's politically incorrect style. The many published and broadcasted comparisons with his role in the LeShawn Brodie debacle, combined with his alleged insensitivity not only to the legal, but to the basic human, rights of suspects, especially those that came from backgrounds riddled with abuse, prompted several public and private calls for his resignation. Other advocacy groups demanded investigations into the police department's decision-making procedures, and called for the formation of various committees to oversee (and second-guess) the command structure.

How had it taken the police so long (nearly twenty hours!) to crib together the clues linking Lucas Welding with his son and his current identity? Why, even working with the luxury of an event number, had no one in the police department been able to discover sooner that the Executioner's victims had all been on the same jury? Surely, the records on these things should be more accessible. How had it taken so long to locate the address of the last victim, Wendy Takahashi? Better police work, quicker and more informed decision-making, would almost certainly have saved her life. How in the world had Glitsky seen fit to allow an unelected civilian to take part in a command decision involving the city's highly skilled and specialized TAC unit?

And on and on and on.

Fortunately, Batiste, Lanier, Jackman and the mayor himself — in a rare and somewhat surprising display of unanimity — had all closed ranks around Glitsky, shouldering their portions of the blame if, in fact, there had been any. Eventually, inevitably, the immediate outcry had died down.

Although Glitsky knew, and hoped, that his days as deputy chief were probably numbered. He couldn't say it broke his heart. He'd even spoken to Lanier and Batiste about the possibility of becoming an inspector at large, where he could float between the investigations of different details without being burdened by an administrative portfolio. He wasn't a politician and everybody knew it, so why not let him work where he could do some good, instead of where, with the best of intentions, a great work ethic and even a record of success, he caused nothing but headaches for the department?

For his part, Hardy had spent most of his time bringing his associates and partners up to speed on the workload surrounding what he called his "influence clients." He'd lost his taste for facilitating. What he liked best and did best was trials. Another of his associates, Graham Russo, had asked him if he'd consider another shot at second chair in a local potential death penalty murder case that would need an incredibly strong psychiatric defense to prevail. Russo was planning to argue some variety of mental illness to save his client's life. And in truth, Hardy had known golden retrievers with more brains than their client, who reminded him of Lenny in *Of Mice and Men* — "Tell me about the rabbits, George." The client had done some terrible things, it was true, but Hardy didn't believe the state should execute him. But whatever the outcome, it was going to be a complex and interesting case. Huge issues. He just wanted to be part of it.

He'd spent the better portion of the rest of his time, at his own expense, boning up on immigration law — there was already an enormous market there, and in California it was only going to grow — and using the Salarcos as his guinea pigs. He'd secured the sponsorship of several of Juan's gardening customers (all of whom lived in comparative splendor), and though it was early in the game, he held out some hope that the Salarcos could avoid some of the bureaucracy and despair of the long-drawn-out citizenship process.

Today, though, Sunday, the first day of June, Hardy and Glitsky sat seven rows behind home plate at PacBell Park. They both wore their Giants caps against the bright sunshine, had removed their jackets. Bonds had dumped one into McCovey Cove and they figured they'd gotten their money's worth already, although in truth the seats had been free, courtesy of one of Hardy's clients with season tickets.

Hardy popped a peanut, chased it with a slug of beer. "Your gallbladder?"

"That's the latest. They want to take it

out." Glitsky sipped his Coke. "I told them no."

"Why not?"

Glitsky shrugged. "I've had enough metal in my guts over the past few years to last me a while. I'm not letting them cut me three more times, which is how they do it nowadays. My doc even said, kind of goofing, 'Yeah, it's like being stabbed in the gut. In fact, it *is* being stabbed in the gut.' Guy's a laugh riot."

"Yeah, but if that's what's causing the pain . . ."

"It's on the other side."

"What is?"

"The pain. It's on the other side from my gallbladder. It's called referred pain. They say it's fairly common. You get a whack on the toe and feel it in your arm."

"Oh yeah," Hardy said. "That happens to me all the time."

Glitsky threw him a look. "Me, neither. It's why I'm a little skeptical about the diagnosis. Plus, what I've got, it's not really pain, I mean like sharp pain. It's more a flutter."

"Maybe it's your heart again."

Glitsky shook his head. "Nope. I know what that feels like, and it's not that."

"So if you don't let them take the gallbladder out, what are you going to do?"

"Live with it. It's been a year already

and it hasn't killed me yet. Treya's convinced it's all stress, and she's not dumb. During all that madness after we got Cottrell, it got pretty unbelievable, a knife in here all the time. Since then, it's seems to be getting better. I've got a theory."

"I hope it's not relativity," Hardy said. "That's already been taken."

"You remember when I got the event number for Boscacci, we were going to do the biggest manhunt in history?"

"Okay."

"So with all that effort and personnel, we pretty much came up with nothing. Not to swell your already large head, but if you hadn't talked to Mooney's wife, we'd never have got him."

"Maybe."

"Maybe, but the point is nobody's ever going to check, go back to it, find anything." He leaned in and lowered his voice. "I'm talking about *us*. Nobody's looking for us. Nobody's *going to be* looking for us. Ever. I don't have to worry every . . . single . . . damn . . . day that somebody's going to find out and my life's going to implode."

Hardy noted the expletive with surprise. Glitsky never swore. He put a hand on his friend's arm for a second. "Nobody's looking, Abe. Really." He squeezed the arm. "Let it go," he said. "Life's too short."

"I guess it's just I know that if I were back running homicide, I'd still be looking."

Hardy had to grin. "That's what makes you such a joy to know. But let me ask you this: are your guts fluttering right now?"

Glitsky sat back into his seat, concentrated a minute, shook his head. "No."

"Let's call that a win, then, and move on."

Acknowledgments

First, my deepest gratitude and love to Lisa Sawyer, my wife, muse, partner and best friend. Her presence in my life is my greatest blessing.

My publisher Carole Baron has overseen my career nearly from its outset. Her guidance, insight, and sense of humor have greatly enriched the whole publishing experience, and I'm greatly indebted to her for her continued encouragement and enthusiasm for my work. I'd also like to tip my hat to my editor Mitch Hoffman, whose keen eye and sense of story are second to none. His suggestions, pithy and on the mark, have contributed greatly to this finished work. A group of highly talented folks at Dutton continually push the envelope on what defines state of the art in publishing. Among this incredible team, I'd especially like to thank Lisa Johnson, Kathleen Matthews-Schmidt and Betsy DeJesu, who have sent me, often kicking and screaming, all around the country, but admittedly to great effect; Robert Kempe for riding the web so expertly; and Richard Hasselberger for his wonderful book jackets.

My pal and true collaborator in this and all the Dismas Hardy/Abe Glitsky books is Al Giannini who, after a distinguished thirty-year career in the San Francisco District Attorney's office, currently works as a Deputy District Attorney in the San Mateo County DA's office. When young would-be writers ask me for advice about becoming an author, I always tell them to befriend someone at fourteen who will someday become a kick-ass DA and correct every mistake in the law that you will ever put in your first drafts. Al does that for me — he's a monster.

I'd also like to acknowledge several people who offered their insights into elements of law, protocol, kids and/or the juvenile justice system: thanks to Kenneth A. Breslin, Ph.D.; Chris, Janet and Jennifer Nedeau; Mary-Patricia Whelan-Miille, President of the Board of Directors of the Yolo County Court Appointed Special Advocate Program (CASA); Andy Clark; Bill Fazio (whom I sincerely hope is by the time of this book's publication now San Francisco's District Attorney); Lieutenant Colleen Turay and Officer Paul Narr of the Davis, CA, police department; and Mark Hicks, Campus Supervisor of Davis High

School. I'd particularly like to thank San Francisco Deputy Chief of Inspectors Dave Robinson for giving me so much of his time while sharing his schedule, duties and worldview.

For their continued support, I would also like to extend thanks to Barbara Peters, Ed Kaufman, Shelly MacArthur, Otto Penzler, Michael Koller, Michael Bufano, Pat Hernandez, Martha Farrington, Eric Lamboley and Debbie Stowell, Susan Honn, Jennifer Held, Ruthie Wittenberg, John Carney, Rachel Ray, Megan Cannon, Bill Lloyd, Pat Boyers, Darby Greek, Cynthia Nye, Antoinette Kuritz, Connie Martinson; and Kat Kinzer.

Several characters in this book owe their names (although no physical or personality traits, which are all fictional) to individuals whose contributions to various charities have been especially generous. These people and their respective charities include Judge W. Arvid Johnson (CASA), Lou and Pat Belou (Davis Rotary), Lanny Ropke (Woodland Christian School) and Dr. and Mrs. James Longoria (Sutter Health Foundation). Additionally, I'd like to thank Chris Stephani's brother Allan Boscacci both for the use of his name and for his great AB& I Foundry cast-iron frying pan.

For important personal reasons, I'd like

to thank Scott, Brenda and Mary Lou at the Cincinnatian Hotel for a memorable celebratory meal; Don Matheson, who belongs in every book on general principle but somehow didn't get in the last one; David Nieves for some key Spanish words; Max Byrd; Peter S. (for Sapphire) Dietrich, MD, MPH; Bill Wood; Richard Herman; Tom Hedtke; Tom Steinstra; my fantastic daughter Justine Rose; Richard Montgomery; Antonio Castillo de la Gala; and Mark and Kathryn Lescroart Detzer.

My assistant Anita Boone is simply an outstanding human being, and the work she does makes my own workdays more a pleasure than they have any right to be. My agent and friend Barney Karpfinger is an unending source of brains, humor and goodwill — he is the absolute best at what he does, bar none, and I remain extremely grateful for our relationship.

About the Author

John Lescroart is the bestselling author of fourteen previous novels, including *The First Law*, *The Oath*, *The Hearing*, *Nothing but the Truth*, and *The Thirteenth Juror*. He lives with his family in northern California.